Dear Reader,

It is hard to believe that a month has passed since I last wrote to you. I do hope that you have been looking forward to reading this new batch of *Scarlet* titles as much as I have enjoyed selecting them for you.

Do keep those questionnaires and letters flooding in, won't you? It is extremely useful for us to receive feedback on how you like the mixture of books we present, whether you are finding them easily in the shops each month and so on. It is only by hearing from *you* that we can be sure *Scarlet* continues to please you.

I know that authors, too, like to have readers' comments on their work, so if you wish to send me a letter for your favourite *Scarlet* author, I'll be happy to pass it on.

Till next month,
Best wishes,

Sally Cooper

SALLY COOPER,
Editor-in-Chief – *Scarlet*

About the Author

Angela Arney has been a published romance author since 1984. She's had a varied career, which has included working as a verbatim shorthand writer, cabaret singer, a teacher, hospital administrator, caterer and finally a full-time writer.

Angela is interested in the theatre – she writes for and directs local amateur companies. And she and her husband love travelling – time allowing. Last year she went to France, Greece, the Czech Republic and New England, USA.

Her other main interest is the farmhouse in Brittany which she and her husband have almost finished restoring. As the author says, 'We love France, the French language and French food.'

*Other **Scarlet** titles available this month:*

THE JEWELLED WEB – Maxine Barry
THE SINS OF SARAH – Anne Styles
THIS TIME FOREVER – Vickie Moore

ANGELA ARNEY

SECRETS

Enquiries to:
Robinson Publishing Ltd
7 Kensington Church Court
London W8 4SP

First published in the UK by Scarlet, 1996

A copy of the British Library Cataloguing in
Publication data is available from the British Library

ISBN 1-85487-702-X

Printed and bound in the EC

10 9 8 7 6 5 4 3 2 1

PROLOGUE

Robert was surprised to receive the invitation written in Veronique's expansive, loopy handwriting.

'Darling, darling brother. Come to the Cathedral Hotel, The Wessex Suite, this afternoon. Michael and I have something exciting to tell you. Love Veronique.'

He wondered what on earth they could have to tell him in the Cathedral Hotel that couldn't possibly have been said in their home at Offerton Manor? He shook his head. Veronique might be his sister but she'd always been a bit of a mystery to him, and lately even more so. There was something simmering away inside her which he didn't understand. Something wild and reckless, despite the very proper face she presented to the world at large.

What was she up to this time? What plans had she hatched for Michael and herself? Stuffing the letter into his pocket he walked from his office into the next one. 'I'll be out this afternoon for an hour or so, Megan. If there's anything very urgent you can get me on my mobile phone; otherwise leave it until I get back.'

'Yes, Mr Lacroix.' Megan bobbed her head in acknowledgement.

She watched him through her open door as he walked away down the long corridor. What a nice man Robert Lacroix was. She felt lucky to be working for such a kind and understanding person. Thank heavens he was not like

1

that snooty sister of his who'd delivered a letter by hand first thing this morning.

At the Cathedral Hotel the door to his sister's suite was unlocked and, after knocking briefly, Robert entered. He saw his sister and her husband standing by the window long before they realized he was there. They were locked in a passionate embrace, Veronique's long dark hair caught up and entwined in Michael's fingers as he held her close. Embarrassed, Robert coughed discreetly. They broke apart immediately.

Michael looked slightly uncomfortable. 'Sorry, I didn't realize you had arrived,' he said. 'I thought you were coming to see Veronique this evening.'

'Veronique said to come this afternoon, and from her note I assumed it was to see both of you.' To Robert's surprise Michael flushed and looked even more uncomfortable. 'Perhaps I got the message wrong . . .' he began.

'No, you didn't.' Veronique, unlike Michael, was not the slightest bit put out. A mischievous glitter sparkled in her dark eyes, and she came towards Robert to greet him, tossing her mass of dark hair back over her shoulders, something she always did when excited. 'I asked you to come this afternoon because I wanted you to share the celebratory champagne before I left.' She looked like a child with a guilty secret, thought Robert.

'Before you leave?' he queried. 'Where are you off to?'

'I'm moving to France. Michael, darling, do pop open the champagne.' Michael moved obediently towards the table.

'Moving to France?' Robert frowned. This was something new. He looked towards Michael for an explanation. 'What do you mean? Have you sold Offerton Manor, Michael?'

'No.'

Michael didn't raise his eyes to meet Robert's enquiring gaze, concentrating instead on his task of opening the champagne. Concentrating just a little too much, thought Robert.

'No,' Veronique repeated, echoing Michael. 'Michael is staying at Offerton. It's just me going to France. I've chosen a wonderful chateau in Brittany. I can't wait to get started on the renovations. It will be wonderful to be living in France again.'

'None of this makes any sense,' Robert said. 'What about you and Michael? What sort of married life will you have if one is in France and the other in England? How can you even think of living apart? You've always done everything together.'

'Not any more. We're getting divorced,' said Michael. His voice held a note of deadly finality.

'Divorced!' Robert heard his own voice as if it were coming from the other side of the room. 'You two! Getting divorced? I don't believe it.'

Veronique tugged at his arm excitedly. 'It's true, Robert.'

'And you've asked me here to drink a toast to the end of your marriage? Have you both gone mad? How can you celebrate a marriage breaking up? How can you celebrate the finish of something?'

'That's just it, Robert,' said Veronique. 'We're not celebrating the finish, we're celebrating the beginning of something new for both of us.'

Robert shook his head, wanting to dislodge the very notion of the two people he'd thought so in love even contemplating splitting up. 'Just now I saw you kissing,' he said slowly. 'It didn't look to me as if you were finished.'

'We're still friends, Robert. There's no bitterness between us.'

Michael sounded weary and suddenly Robert knew that Veronique was behind the idea. She was usually behind every idea, and Michael worshipped her. He'd always done whatever she'd wanted. He put out a cautious feeler. 'Is this what you really want, Michael?'

3

'No,' he said, in the same flat voice he'd used before. 'I don't really want it. But Veronique and I have discussed this at length and decided that this is the best way forward for both of us.'

'But surely there is some other way? I don't know what has gone wrong between you, but surely something can be done to help you. You must talk to someone,' Robert said urgently. 'Someone who can help you to go forward with your marriage. Nothing is irretrievable.'

Suddenly Veronique looked serious. 'Robert,' she said, 'don't think this has been easy for us, because it hasn't. But we have discussed our options at length and have come to the conclusion that this is the best way we can both have what we want. So please don't try to change our minds.'

Robert shrugged his shoulders in a gesture of help-lessness. 'I don't understand.'

Michael handed him a glass of champagne and smiled sadly. 'Perhaps you will,' he said slowly, 'one day.' He handed another to Veronique.

She took it, and smiled, switching from a serious mood back to a mischievous, happy one with mercurial swift-ness. 'What does it matter whether you understand or not, Robert? The point is we want you to wish us well.'

'You know I wish you well. I always have done. What I find difficult is approving of you splitting up.'

'Oh – ' Veronique raised her glass – 'don't be such an old fuddy-duddy, Robert. People split up all the time. We're no different from anyone else in that respect. So drink up and wish us well, and come and visit me in France as soon as you can.'

Robert raised his glass in a toast. But it was an unhappy gesture. 'To your future happiness, both of you,' he said. Surely, he thought, they must both notice what a hollow ring the words had?

But Veronique was oblivious to everything now. He could see she was caught up in her own day-dreams. 'To the future,' she whispered, and held her own glass high.

4

CHAPTER 1

Louise rang the doorbell of her brother's house.

'Damn! It isn't working again!' Cross that Gordon hadn't fixed it properly and because she was in a hurry as usual, she resorted to thumping the heavy brass knocker as hard as she could against the shabby front door. There was no alternative but to wait shivering in the fierce north-easterly wind whipping around the house. Dry leaves flew past, lodging in an ever-growing mound against the rusty gate which was propped open with a piece of broken gravestone. Gordon's house was a large Victorian ex-rectory, and from where she stood Louise could hear her knock echoing hollowly along the cavernous hall which lay on the other side of the front door. Eventually the sound of brisk footsteps on the wooden floor told her that she had been heard.

The moment the door was open Louise jumped in out of the freezing wind only to find that the hall was not much warmer. 'I know it's two weeks before Christmas,' she said, 'but if I don't deliver the presents now, goodness knows when I'll next have time.'

'Hi, Lou.' Gordon, shabby and comfortable in a shapeless multi-coloured sweater knitted by Eugenia, his wife, slipped his arms around his sister and gave her an affectionate kiss. 'Still living life in the fast lane, I see. Hardly time to breathe, as usual.'

'Yes, and enjoying it,' said Louise, wondering why it was she was feeling slightly defensive, as usual, when faced with Gordon's comfortable, poverty-stricken family. Although for the life of her she could never think why.

Gordon and Eugenia, his wife, could have had a different life-style if they had chosen to, and it certainly wasn't envy which made her feel defensive. There was no way she would have swopped her life for his. A wife and four children, never enough money to go round, Gordon waging a permanent battle to make ends meet.

'God! I couldn't stand your way of life, Lou,' Gordon always said. 'I know you say you enjoy it, but I don't see how.'

But it was true. She *did* enjoy her own way of life, and was amazed that Gordon couldn't see why. After all, who wouldn't? She had her own office temp agency named Gilby Girls after herself, Louise Gilby. The business was small, but extremely profitable. It had enabled her to buy a charming flat in a converted Regency house in Blackheath, London, with views across the heath as it sprawled down towards Greenwich and the City of London. Plus there was enough money to have a second home. An ancient little house in Chesil Street, Winchester.

Louise loved her Chesil Street house with its sloping floors and tiny rooms. It was so cosy, bounded as it was on one side by the towering slope of St Giles' Hill, and on the other, at the bottom of a steeply sloping garden, by the rushing water of the River Itchen as it sped along between the ancient city water-mill and the other, more modern, Victorian mill at the other end of the weirs. Neither mill was working now. The city mill was a youth hostel, busy with foreign visitors in summer but quiet in winter, and the Victorian mill house had been converted into exclusive, and expensive apartments. Once, in medieval times, the area Louise lived in had been a thriving, bustling place for traders and merchants, but now it had a gentle mantle of peace and tranquillity which Louise loved.

6

In fact, she loved Winchester itself, England's ancient capital, determinedly straddling the River Itchen as it had done for centuries. A city grown comfortably mellow with age, a city of weathered, moss-grown brick walls, and ancient flintstone houses which gleamed in the light. A city of towers with the spires of the numerous churches clustering around the centre of their universe, the great cathedral itself. A grey solid building, the supporting flying buttresses either side of the nave gave it a sense of subtle lightness. Louise always thought that its lack of beauty in the conventional sense was far outweighed by its solidness. It was as if the original builders had planted the cathedral, not built it. As a child Louise always imagined that it spoke to her, saying, *I have been here for nearly one thousand years and I shall be here for another thousand years and more.*

Yes, she loved Winchester, and wished that this weekend she could stay longer than one Saturday night before returning to London the next day. This weekend there wasn't even time to pop in and visit her mother.

'Got time for a quick drink?' Gordon walked out with her to the car to help unload the parcels. 'We needn't worry about having to hide these tonight.' He loaded three parcels one on top of each other. 'The kids are all in bed.'

'I'll bring this one.' Louise picked up the remaining parcel and slammed the boot of the car shut. 'And yes, I'd love a drink.'

'Damson and banana,' said Gordon, 'my own brew.' Seeing the slightly doubtful expression on Louise's face he shrugged his shoulders. 'My teacher's salary won't stretch to the bought stuff, so it's got to be home-made. Tastes good though, and has a hell of a kick.'

They reached the kitchen, and as Gordon was the most laden, Louise opened the door. It was like stepping into a warm cave filled with aromatic spices. Eugenia was standing at the enormous scrubbed pine table, a large enamel bowl filled with a sticky brown mixture before her.

7

'Just in time to give the Christmas pudding a stir and make a wish,' she said. 'I know I should have made it weeks ago, but I've only just got around to it.'

Louise dutifully stirred the pudding mix, before handing the spoon back to Eugenia.

'Have you made a wish?' asked Eugenia.

Louise laughed. 'Of course. I've wished that something exciting will happen to me. Something different.' She thought for a moment. Something different, that was it. Perhaps that's why I have this strange feeling of discontentment every now and then. I need something different. 'Yes, that's it,' she said, voicing her thoughts out loud. 'I'd like my life to change direction.'

'The trouble with you, Louise,' said Gordon passing her a glass, 'is that you are never satisfied.'

'Nothing wrong in seeking a change. Don't you?'

'No.' Gordon was firm in his opinion. 'I'm quite happy with what I've got.'

'Anyway you shouldn't tell anyone what you've wished,' Eugenia said, accepting her glass from Gordon. 'If you do, it might not come true.'

Louise smiled at Eugenia, knowing she was stepping in between herself and Gordon as they were inclined to argue on the subject of life-styles. Mustn't quarrel with Gordon just before Christmas, she reminded herself. 'Ah! But I haven't really told you,' she said. 'It's a very vague wish, as I don't know what I want. So it doesn't count.'

Eugenia raised her glass as well. 'Here's to all of us, and a special toast to Louise's unknown wish,' she added mischievously.

CHAPTER 2

'Damn, damn thing!' Beattie raised the chopper over her head and brought it down with an almighty thud.

Louise arrived at her mother's house in Winchester on Christmas Eve, opening the door just in time to see her chopping off the legs of the Christmas turkey. 'What on earth . . .' she began.

'Bloody thing won't go in the oven,' said Beattie.

'I'm not surprised. It's far too big. You'll be eating turkey leftovers long after we've all departed.' Louise peered at the turkey. 'What on earth possessed you to buy such an enormous thing?'

'Only weighs twenty pounds,' said Beattie defensively. 'On special offer. A real bargain.'

Eugenia was there, sitting on the other side of the kitchen table with baby Tara on her lap. Raising her eyebrows at Louise she giggled. 'I think the butcher saw Beattie coming.'

Beattie took one of the severed legs and shoved it inside the bird. 'There,' she said triumphantly, 'that one can cook inside the bird. Gordon likes a bit of leg.'

Louise shut the door, and dumping her bags on the floor shuddered at the sight before her eyes. Her mother's house was muddled at the best of times, but now the kitchen was in absolute chaos. Mince pies and sausage rolls, still warm from the oven, spilled from plates amidst piles of

9

unpacked shopping still in the supermarket bags. Half a dozen empty wine bottles nestled amongst the debris, the sink was full of unwashed coffee cups and wine glasses, and a large, half empty bottle of gin stood by the side of the turkey on the kitchen table.

'Have a gin, dear,' said Beattie to her daughter, slapping rashers of bacon over the turkey's breast.

After scouring the inside of one of several cupboards Louise found a clean glass and poured herself a large gin. Eugenia held out her empty glass and Louise poured her a measure as well.

She glanced across at the baby who, sensing attention, turned and beamed at her, exposing one gleaming white front tooth and a mass of pink gums. Louise found herself beaming back, and then felt unnerved. What was she doing smiling at a baby? They couldn't think! Hastily she looked back to her mother who was now busily ramming handfuls of garlic cloves into the neck and rear end of the turkey.

She took a large sip of neat gin. 'Tina's mother-in-law sews the tail back on to the turkey's body to stop the stuffing coming out,' she said.

'Bugger that!' was Beattie's response. 'I haven't got time for such nonsense. I've been very, very busy lately. Christmas has come at an extremely inconvenient time this year.'

Louise laughed, and took another sip of gin. She could feel herself beginning to unwind. Even the untidy kitchen didn't matter as much as it had five minutes ago. 'It's arrived at exactly the same time it does every year,' she said.

'Beattie has been busy painting,' said Eugenia, waving a hand at the surrounding chaos. 'A commission. It had to be finished in time to be delivered today.'

'A portrait?' asked Louise. Her mother was a good artist, and very good at portraits, although she preferred painting strange abstract designs that were difficult, often

10

impossible, to sell. When a commission came along it was invariably for a portrait.

'Yes, the Mayor of Wheatleigh,' said Beattie. 'The trouble was I couldn't get the damn thing right. Every blob of paint I applied made him look so terribly cross-eyed.'

'That's because he *is* cross-eyed,' said Eugenia, giggling.

'But the Conservative Association, who are paying me, and paying me well, didn't want a cross-eyed man in mayoral robes looking down at them from the wall of their club. So I had to try and make him look normal. In the end I half closed his eyes, and tried to make him look thoughtful.'

'It's *what* he's thinking about that worries me!' said Eugenia. 'He's ended up looking positively lecherous.' She giggled again.

Louise looked at her severely. 'I think, Eugenia, you've had rather too much gin,' she said, moving the bottle further away. 'You're certainly not fit to drive, in fact, I'm not even certain that you're fit to be in charge of a baby.'

'Probably not.' Eugenia stood up. 'Here, you take Tara. I think I'll have a glass of water to clear my head, then I'll start to clear up this kitchen a little. And don't worry about me driving; Gordon is picking me up.'

Louise tried to fend off holding Tara. 'No, I'll do the kitchen,' she said hastily. 'You stay put.' But it was too late, the baby was plonked on her lap.

'The least I can do,' said Eugenia, 'is to put the shopping away. Oh no you *don't*, Mr Poo.' With a swift movement she pounced on a small, fat pug dog who had emerged from beneath the table and was in the process of dragging the remaining turkey leg away to a quiet corner. 'Are you going to cook this?' she asked, brandishing the leg at Beattie.

'No, rinse it under the tap and stick it in the freezer,' said Beattie, 'and for God's sake pour me another gin. Then I'll start on the potatoes.'

11

'I'll do the potatoes. You hold Tara.' Louise held the baby out towards her mother.

'No, dear. Dropping a potato is one thing, dropping a baby is another. You keep her. You're the only sober one in the kitchen.'

So Beattie and Eugenia bustled about the kitchen, as fast as their inebriated state would allow, leaving Louise holding the baby. At first she felt uncomfortable and held Tara almost at arm's length. But Tara wasn't having that. With one swift but determined wriggle, she snuggled closer to Louise, and raising her head, looked up. Louise looked down and found herself staring into a pair of startlingly blue eyes fringed with long blonde lashes tipped at the end with what looked like soot. Tara smiled at Louise, showing off her one pearly tooth, and again in spite of herself Louise found that she was smiling back. She relaxed, pulling the baby in closer. Content, now that she had got what she wanted, Tara stuck her thumb in her mouth, and with a gurgling sigh laid her head against Louise's breast.

On impulse Louise laid her cheek down against the softly rounded shape of Tara's head. How warm the baby was, how sweet she smelled, and how very peculiar she herself felt. It was a totally new and delightful experience, and one to which Louise could not put a name. Yet although it *was* delightful, at the same time it frightened her.

'Why, Lou!' Her brother Gordon burst in through the kitchen door, followed by Natasha, Rupert and Milton. All three children were muffled up to the eyebrows, wearing knitted bobble hats, long wrap-around scarves and brightly coloured mittens. 'I never thought I'd see you holding the baby.' He peered closer. 'And actually looking as if you are enjoying it.'

'I am,' said Louise, surprising herself at the admission. 'Tara is a lovely baby. I'm beginning to realize that perhaps you and Eugenia are not as mad as I thought.'

12

Gently she touched the sooty tips of Tara's long, closed lashes with her fingertip.

'Not too late for you too,' said Gordon, pulling up a chair beside Louise and putting his arm around her shoulder. 'All you've got to do is find the right man.'

'But you'd best hurry.' Beattie threw the last peeled potato into a bowl of water with a plop. 'Time and tide wait for no man, or woman, and you, my dear child, are no longer in the first flush of youth.'

'I can't imagine you with a baby,' said Eugenia. 'You don't *really* want one, do you?'

'Of course not.' Louise stood up and handed the still sleeping Tara back to Eugenia. 'I'm not the motherly type. Although I am *not* too old,' she added, scowling at her mother.

Beattie gazed back fondly. 'Of course you're not,' she said. 'I was only joking. As you say, it's just that you are not really the type. I resigned myself to that fact years ago.'

Once Gordon and his tribe had departed, Louise determinedly sobered up her mother with strong coffee, then they both sat down to a simple supper of pasta and ricotta cheese. By the time they had finished laying the table in the front room ready for Christmas lunch the next day, prepared as much of the food as was possible to prepare in advance, and at Louise's insistence finished the washing up – Beattie would have left it – the time had come to leave for the Midnight Mass service at the cathedral.

Louise was staying with her mother over the Christmas, although she would really have preferred to have slept in her own, well ordered house in Chesil Street.

But every year Beattie said the same thing: 'Stay with me. I need a little part of my family with me in the house at Christmas. It keeps me thriving for another year.'

And every year Louise couldn't bring herself to say she'd only come for Christmas lunch. Instead she said as she always had done and probably always would: 'Christmas wouldn't be Christmas without me staying in my small room.'

And Beattie always replied, 'Then that's settled.'

So that was that. Louise was ensconced in the small back bedroom which looked out over the water meadows towards St Catherine's Hill. Now, she looked out across the dark meadows as she hurriedly slipped on a warm top coat and wound a scarf around her neck. They were late for the service.

It was much too late to walk, so Louise drove the short distance down College Street, and parked the car outside the Cathedral Close behind the college. The air was sharp and crisp, and the smooth grass between the lime trees in the Close sparkled with the first crystals of frost. Beattie held on to Louise's arm and together they hurried across the uneven pavements and flint cobbles. The illuminated cathedral rose up before them in awe-inspiring splendour against the dark of the night sky.

'Christmas wouldn't be Christmas without the cathedral,' said Beattie.

'True. And yet we're not religious,' replied Louise. 'We go out of habit I suppose.'

'Speak for yourself,' snorted Beattie. 'When you get to my age you think about things like religion.'

'Only as a form of insurance,' said Louise.

Beattie stopped mid-stride. 'I do hope,' she said sadly, 'that you are not really as cynical as you sound.'

Louise said nothing but, tugging at her mother's arm, urged her along. It was with the last of the stragglers that they entered the vast cathedral just as the service was beginning. Am I cynical? she wondered. Or is it that I hate admitting that some things do touch me, and because I don't understand why, I can't bring myself to acknowledge their existence? She didn't know the answer, but once inside the cathedral it didn't seem to matter, because just as she had as a small child, she found herself caught up in

14

the magic of the timeless service. The ritual chanting, the slow movement of the priests in their gold-encrusted robes, and the flickering candle-light which always gave even familiar objects a different dimension.

When it was over the great cathedral bells rang out loud and clear into the frosty night air, declaring to one and all that Christmas Day had arrived. The small congregation left by the west door, tumbling out, wrapping up against the cold as they came on to the cobbled path of the Close.

'Goodnight.'

'Happy Christmas.'

'Hello, Louise, lovely to see you home again.'

'Christmas wouldn't be Christmas without you and Beattie here.'

Beattie was known to practically everyone in Winchester so the seasonal greetings took some time. By the time they were ready to go the dean came out, his ceremonial robes covered with a great black cloak. He walked back with Louise and Beattie, as the deanery was on the way to their car. 'I hear you've done a wonderful portrait of the Mayor of Wheatleigh,' he said to Beattie.

'Passable,' said Beattie modestly, 'not wonderful.'

'I've been meaning to ask you for some months about the bishop. Do you think you could do a portrait of him from some photographs? He retires next year and I thought a portrait in his robes would be a lovely parting gift.'

'Well, I don't know that I . . .'

'Of course you will.' Louise interrupted swiftly before her mother could turn the commission down. She smiled at the dean. 'I know my mother is hesitating because painting from photographs is so much more difficult than from life.'

'Oh!' said the dean, sounding disappointed. 'I thought it would be easier.'

'No, much more difficult,' emphasized Louise, guessing that the dean was hoping to get the painting done on the cheap, 'and, of course, that will make it more expensive.'

They had reached the deanery. The dean stopped and took Beattie's hands in his. 'If it is more expensive, my dear, then so be it. I dare say there's enough money in the coffers. But photographs it will have to be if we are to keep it a secret.' He pecked Beattie on the cheek. 'Happy Christmas and God's blessing on you both. Send me a note of your fee in the New Year.' The last remark was addressed to Beattie.

'I wouldn't have charged any more,' said Beattie as soon as they were out of earshot. 'And I don't really want to do it. I don't like the bishop. Pompous prig.'

'You won't have to talk to his photo. And as for money, you wouldn't have charged enough. You never do. That's why you've never got any money.'

'Oh, that reminds me,' said Beattie. 'Thank you, darling, for that lovely fat cheque for all the Christmas goodies. We wouldn't be eating nearly so well if it wasn't for you.'

'Providing the money is the easy bit,' said Louise. 'You do all the cooking and organizing.'

By the time they reached the car there was only one other car left in College Street, and apart from the tall man walking towards it there was no other sign of life.

Louise unlocked her car just as the man drew abreast of them. He stopped. 'Why hello, Beattie,' he said. 'I didn't see you in the cathedral.'

They shook hands, rather formally, Louise thought. 'Oh, we were there,' said Beattie. 'But at the back because we were late as usual.' She turned towards Louise. 'This is my daughter, Louise. Louise, this is Robert Lacroix.'

Lacroix, that must account for the faint French accent. 'How do you do,' she said and held out her hand. Apart from the fact that he was very tall and had the broad shoulders of a rugby scrum-half, Louise couldn't see what he looked like. The street lamps in College Street were the same as the original small gas lamps, and although now powered by electricity, the light emitted was dim. They gave a wonderful air of mysterious timelessness, but were not much good for actually seeing anything. She wondered how her mother knew this man.

'How is Milton these days?' he asked.

'He's fine. Four years old now and started school. They say he's way ahead of his age group in class. He reads a lot, and is definitely showing signs of being the clever one of the family.'

'There you are. I told his mother that the knock on his head wouldn't do him any harm. Children are remarkably resilient.'

Robert Lacroix slotted into place in Louise's mind. 'Oh, now I know. You are the neurologist who looked after Milton after he'd fallen out of a tree.'

'The very same.'

He's got a nice voice, thought Louise, wishing she could see him more clearly.

'We must be going,' said Beattie, 'otherwise we'll never get up in the morning. If you're free, do drop in for a drink over the Christmas.'

'I'd love to, but I can't. After tonight, I'm on duty until the New Year. I promised my colleague he could take time off; he's got a family to go to, and as I haven't it seemed only fair.'

'But what about your sister? I thought she . . .'

'She is in Paris with a friend, and let it be known in no uncertain manner that a third party was not wanted. Goodnight.' Without waiting for a reply he strode away into the darkness towards his car.

'Such a nice man,' said Beattle as they drove back towards St Cross, 'and not married either.'

'Don't start match-making, Mother,' said Louise severely.

'Of course not. I wouldn't dream of it,' said Beattie primly. Louise parked the car in the gravel at the side of her mother's house. 'But it does seem such a shame that he's on his own. Now there's a man who needs a family if ever I saw one.'

'Then he'd best look for a wife who will provide him with one,' retorted Louise sharply.

CHAPTER 3

Gordon, Eugenia and the children arrived just as the grandfather clock, which almost filled the tiny hallway, chimed out the half hour at ten thirty.

'We haven't opened the presents you gave us, Louise,' said Natasha, bursting into the kitchen first and letting in a blast of bitterly cold air.

Louise kissed her, realizing with a sudden jolt how much she had grown. Already at nine it was possible to see that she would be a beauty in later years. Now she was tall and gangly, with a brace on her teeth. But in a few years . . . Louise felt a twinge of panic at the thought. How fast time passed. 'My goodness,' she said, 'you look quite grown up.'

'I *am* grown up,' replied Natasha seriously. 'Look at the dress Mummy made me.' Taking off her coat she twirled around, showing off a slim-fitting bottle green dress, cut on the cross so that the skirt flared out at the bottom.

'She insisted on dark green.' Eugenia struggled out of her coat and Louise noticed she was wearing the same needlecord pinafore dress she'd worn ever since she could remember. Suddenly Louise wished she hadn't put on the pale beige cashmere sweater with matching ribbed leggings. The outfit had cost a bomb, and at the time she'd thought it the epitome of understated luxury, especially when teamed with the string of cultured pearls she was wearing. But now, looking at Eugenia, she felt ostentatiously overdressed, and selfish. Any spare money Eugenia had would always go on her children.

'It's a beautiful dress,' said Louise, fingering Natasha's dress. 'I wish I could make things.'

'You can do other things.' Eugenia was cheerfully unenvious as she reached out and smoothed the silky surface of Louise's cashmere trouser suit, 'and this looks absolutely terrific.'

'*And* I got a gift token as well,' said Natasha, impatient to tell Louise everything. 'It's to have my ears pierced. I'm going to have them done as soon as the shops open after Christmas.'

'And silly old Father Christmas brought her a bra,' said Rupert, creeping up behind Natasha and peering over her shoulder, 'and two oranges to put in it because her chest is too flat.'

'I do *not* need oranges for my bra,' Natasha shrieked, and punched Rupert on the nose.

'Darling, I don't think that is very ladylike.' Beattie swept into the kitchen, resplendent in a swirling red velvet skirt, and a peasant blouse with full, puffed sleeves. 'And of course you don't need oranges to fill your bra. Now, kiss your brother and say you are sorry for hitting him.'

'But he was rude.'

'No quarrels on Christmas Day. This is a day of peace and goodwill,' said Beattie, rolling her eyes heavenwards. 'Kiss him and say sorry.'

'Sorry,' said Natasha and turning round kissed Rupert quickly, then smartly nipped him on the ear while nobody was looking.

'Ow!' Rupert aimed a kick at her but then, realizing Louise was watching him, changed the kick into a step and crossed over to her. Giving an angelic smile and looking as if butter wouldn't melt in his mouth, which for Rupert was easy as he was blessed with blond hair and cornflower blue eyes, he held Louise's hand. 'Mum and Dad have given

20

me a steamroller,' he said. 'It's not new, but it works. It's absolutely fantastic.'

Louise glanced at Gordon who grinned, and she remembered a Christmas long ago when he had been given the toy. 'You'll have to show me how it works,' she said.

'I will,' said Rupert. 'I'll even let you light the meths if you promise to be very careful.'

'I had a medical set,' said Milton, the youngest. His voice was somewhat muffled as he was struggling to unwind himself from his long scarf.

'Soppy stuff!' Rupert was dismissive. 'Nurses' sets are for girls.'

'It's not a nurse's set, it's for a doctor.' Finally succeeding in unravelling himself, Milton dropped his scarf and coat on to the floor, and picking up a large box came across to Louise and Beattie. 'I'm going to be a doctor,' he said. 'A head doctor like Dr Lacroix. But for today I shall treat anything. So if you are not feeling well please let me know.'

'I have a pain coming on here,' said Beattie, clutching her stomach dramatically.

'Withdrawal symptoms from lack of gin,' was Gordon's verdict.

Milton was rather small for his age, and had a thatch of dark straight hair which Eugenia could never manage to cut straight so that it stuck out at angles, giving him a permanently surprised look. Now, he not only looked surprised but also very serious. He put the box carefully under his arm. 'If you come this way, Mrs Gilby,' he said, 'and lie down. I shall examine you with my steth . . . steth.'

'Can't even say it,' mocked Rupert.

'Stethoscope,' said Milton triumphantly.

A thin piercing scream of rage filtered through into the kitchen. 'Oh, God!' said Eugenia. 'We've forgotten Tara. She's still strapped into her seat in the car.'

'I'll get her,' Louise heard herself saying. She went

outside to find a puce-faced Tara struggling to get out of her seat. 'Darling,' she said mopping Tara's eyes and wiping her nose, 'what a rotten lot we are forgetting all about you.'

Gordon, who had followed her out, laughed. 'Careful, Lou,' he said. 'Or you may get bitten.'

'Bitten? By Tara?'

'No, by the baby bug,' he said.

'Nonsense. I leave all that sort of thing to you and Eugenia,' said Louise, and having extricated Tara, marched past him back into the house.

The rest of Christmas Day passed as it always did in an orgy of eating and drinking. Gordon's children were spared the morning Matins service because they were always taken to the five thirty Blessing of the Crib at the cathedral.

'So much more civilized,' said Eugenia. 'And because so many children are there nobody notices if yours are the ones making a noise.'

'We went to Midnight Mass,' said Beattie self-right-eously. 'Now, everyone, off you go into the front room, while I do the final preparations here in the kitchen. Gordon, you'd better put another log on the fire and make sure that the fire guard is secure.'

'I can't think why you insist on calling it the front room,' said Gordon. 'It's a terribly naff term.'

'It *is* the front room,' said Beattie, 'it's in the front of the house.'

'Don't take any notice of him,' said Eugenia. 'He's been rearranging our rooms so that he can give piano lessons. We now have a drawing room, a dining room and a kitchen. Not that it makes the slightest bit of difference. We still live in the kitchen, whereas the poor students have to wait in the freezing dining room, then play in the equally freezing drawing room.'

'I won't have any pretentious nonsense in this house,' said Beattie, taking the stance she always took when annoyed, feet apart and hands on hips. 'This house was a bargeman's cottage a hundred and fifty years ago. Apart from the hall, if you can call it that, it only has two rooms, the kitchen, where I live and the front room which I hardly use. Saves housework if you don't use a room.'

'You have the extension,' said Gordon.

'That's my studio,' said Beattie. 'I don't regard that as part of the house. It's my own private place where I work. Now, are you going to see to aperitifs for everyone, and put some wood on the fire? Or are you not?'

'I am,' said Gordon. 'Here.' He handed Tara to Louise. 'You take her, and keep an eye on the kids while Eugenia and I do the drinks.'

'Louise has brought some brandy and champagne for cocktails,' said Beattle, 'but don't make them until I'm ready. Have something else to start with, and I'll make do with this.' She poured herself a large gin, took a sip, then removed the turkey from the oven. 'Everything is nearly ready. I'll be about another half an hour.'

Louise sat next to Tara at lunch who had screamed when her highchair was moved away from Louise.

'She's really taken a fancy to you,' said Eugenia. 'You are very honoured. She has turned out to be the least sociable of all my babies, and usually howls when someone speaks to her.'

The baby had the same food as everyone else. Beattie had tried to mash it up, but Tara had shown her disapproval in no uncertain terms by crashing her spoon on the tray and turning puce with rage.

'She can't eat it whole,' Beattie said, concerned.

'Oh, let her have a go. If she chokes, she chokes.' Eugenia got up and dragged Rupert from his chair where he was banging Natasha on the head with his cracker, and moved Gordon between brother and sister.

'You're very relaxed about everything,' Louise remarked.

23

Eugenia laughed. 'By the time you've had four children, you're either relaxed or a nervous wreck.'

Against her will Louise found herself surreptitiously watching Tara as she determinedly struggled to feed herself, and found it fascinating. Most of the food ended up on the floor where it was quickly eaten by Mr Poo, who had stationed himself beneath the highchair the moment it was put in place. But eventually Tara managed to get a firm grip on a baked potato and happily crunched her one tooth into it.

The rest of Christmas Day passed in a blur of never-ending conversation, which swirled about Louise but did not include her. Everyone laughed at jokes about people she didn't really know, and the children told her that this year they had celebrated Devali, not Christmas.

'Bloody ridiculous,' muttered Beattie loudly. 'We're not Hindus.'

'There are twelve Hindu children in the school now. It is important that they don't feel left out.' Gordon always bent over backwards to be politically correct in his thinking.

'So all the rest of the little buggers were.' Beattie's language always deteriorated with the amount of alcohol she consumed, and she thought PC was some kind of computer.

'Were what?' asked Louise who was finding it difficult to keep up with the conversation as Gordon kept refilling her glass, which made things blurrier than ever.

'Left out, of course.'

'They are doing a full nativity play next year,' said Gordon sternly, 'and I do wish you wouldn't swear in front of the children.'

'I never swear,' said Beattie emphatically. 'And what do you mean, *full* nativity play?'

'Mary's going to come in pregnant,' said Rupert. 'So we'll all see the actual birth.'

'Of course you won't, stupid.' Natasha was scornful. 'She'll just whip a doll out from underneath her skirt.'

By the time Christmas lunch was finished Louise felt quite sloshed. How her mother kept steady on her feet she didn't know. As for herself, the affect of a kir and champagne cocktail before lunch, combined with white wine during lunch and port after lunch, was enough to make her quite happy to sink in a heap on to the settee, and accept Tara being plonked on her lap yet again.

'It's so lovely having someone else look after her,' said Eugenia as she deposited the sleepy baby. 'She's definitely the last. I'm not having any more.'

'Well, we've got two of each,' said Gordon comfortably. 'We don't need any more.'

Two of each, thought Louise, looking down at Tara, who by now was fast asleep. And I haven't even got one. The dull ache she'd been feeling all day began to crystallize into something more tangible. Everyone was so full of life, but their lives were so different from hers. Each person, even Tara, was an indiviual, and yet when together they made a whole. Beattie is part of that wholeness too, but I'm not, because I've chosen to remain outside. For the first time since she'd set out on her path of self-determination Louise began to wonder if she had chosen the right path. What did the future hold? Apart from making money and possessing beautiful things, what else did her life contain? A feeling of dejection settled over her again, a gloomy mantle making her feel more isolated than ever from the festivity around her.

But her presents to the children were a success and that helped in cheering her. Considering she bought them in desperation, not knowing what to get, their rapturous approval surprised her.

'Satin pyjamas.' Natasha held the pale pink pyjamas up against her. 'Oh, they're fab. I shall wear them to Brownie camp this summer.'

'We'll see about that,' muttered Eugenia.

Rupert's wristwatch with built-in computer was equally

ecstatically received. 'I shall programme everyone's birthday in it, and set it to go off every hour,' he announced.

Milton had two presents. A miniature chess set complete with the basic rules for beginners, and a cookery set.

'A cookery set for a boy?' Natasha scoffed and Louise worried that she'd bought the wrong thing.

But Milton was unfazed. 'All the best cooks are men,' he said blithely. 'Who's ever heard of a famous woman cook.' He opened the cookery set and inspected it carefully. 'I shall make some biscuits for tea,' he announced.

'Tomorrow,' said Beattie and Eugenia in unison, 'not today.'

'And there *are* famous women cooks,' added Beattie sternly. Turning to Eugenia she said, 'You mustn't let him grow up into a male chauvinist.'

Tara's present was a humming top, which Milton demonstrated to her, and a gift voucher for some clothes.

'Thanks,' said Eugenia gratefully to Louise. 'I'll save it until spring when the summer clothes come into the shops. By then I shall know what size she will be.'

'You were much more tolerant of the children this year,' Beattie observed. Gordon and his family had finally departed and Beattie and Louise were alone in the kitchen, sitting by the Aga with a nightcap.

'I must be mellowing,' said Louise. It was true. The children used to get on her nerves, but this year had been different. Why, she'd even felt comfortable with Tara. 'Of course they are growing up; that makes a difference. I realized what nice people children can grow into when I met Tina's two boys before Christmas.'

'All children grow up,' said her mother comfortably, giving Mr Poo a gentle prod with her foot to stop him snoring. 'Even you were a child once.'

'What was I like?'

'Difficult,' said her mother. 'Headstrong little thing you were. Still are, come to that.'

'Only not so little now,' said Louise, 'and determined is a better word than headstrong.'

'Headstrong,' said Beattie. 'You would never listen. Once you made up your mind to do something, you went ahead and did it, come what may.'

CHAPTER 4

The gold edging on the invitation card reflected the weak January sunlight. Louise read it then put it on the mantelshelf above the fireplace in her office where it glinted, an enticing beacon in a dull world.

Outside, a bitingly cold breeze lashed at the branches of the small plane tree struggling to survive in the narrow side street leading down into Cambridge Circus. In the gutter a couple of discarded hamburger boxes from a nearby takeaway were bowled along by the same breeze, followed by some ragged scraps of tinsel and a battered silver-foil star. London looked squalid after Christmas, messy and depressing, an empty room after all the party guests had gone. Yes, that's it, Louise decided, watching the debris scuttering before the wind, it's the time of year, that's why I feel the way I do. But even as the thought entered her head she knew it wasn't true. The inexplicable but intense feeling had been with her all over Christmas. A feeling of missing out, of lacking something, which was ridiculous because she lacked for nothing.

'Looks important.' Tina noticed the card the moment she came in.

'It isn't. Just a book launch for that book the agency typed. You remember, the client we had so much trouble with.'

'Oh, God! Yes, I remember. Michael Baruch, that was

28

his name, and so fussy it wasn't true. Lucky for us we had Mrs Melrose on the books. The perfect secretary. She suited him.'

'Mrs Melrose, the perfect doormat,' said Louise dryly. Useful though she'd been, Louise despised women like Mrs Melrose. Always too anxious to please, especially if the person who needed pleasing was a man.

'I wonder if she's been invited.'

'I doubt it. Give her a ring and offer her the invite. It's at the Savoy. She'll enjoy that.'

'OK.' Tina dumped the pile of files she'd been clutching on to the desk. 'By the way, happy New Year; and did you have a good Christmas?'

Louise sat down at her desk and began sifting through the files. 'Thanks. Christmas was OK, and happy New Year to you.'

'Thanks a bunch. I can do without good wishes like that. You sound positively morose.'

'Sorry. I feel morose. I hate January.'

'Well, you can't stop it arriving,' said Tina practically. 'And I forgot. Here's that magazine you wanted. The one with the smoked salmon recipe in it.' She drew out a rolled-up magazine which had been stuffed in her skirt pocket, and smoothed it out on top of the desk.

Louise suddenly smiled. A rosy, round faced, baby girl with brilliant blue eyes beamed out from an advertisement for nappies on the back page. The baby, round and chubby, was clad in nothing but a bright pink nappy. 'Thanks,' she said.

Tina wandered over to the fireplace and looked at the gold-edged card. 'Michael Baruch, head of the Briam Corporation. Even that name makes me shudder. I can't even begin to count the number of times he was rude to me on the telephone, until dear old Mrs Melrose came along.' She peered more closely at the card. 'OUTSIDER IN, that's a funny title. What's his book about?'

'The usual rags to riches story,' said Louise absent-

29

mindedly. She was still looking at the photograph of the baby girl. 'You know this picture reminds me of Tara. She's adorable.'

'Tara?'

'Gordon's youngest.'

'Of course, I'd forgotten Gordon's children. I hope you didn't lavish too many expensive presents on them.'

Louise smiled at Tina's slightly disapproving tone of voice. Tina had very firm ideas on how children should be brought up, and Louise knew she had been very strict with her own two boys.

'Maybe I did spoil them a little. But Gordon and his family live in penury. Well, penury for this day and age. And don't tell me Eugenia could go out to work and swell his meagre teacher's salary, because of course she could. But she doesn't want to, and I don't blame her. If I had kids like theirs I'd want to stay at home and be with them.' She picked up the magazine and looked at it intently, almost feeling Tara's soft downy head nuzzling against her, and the very special fragrance of a warm clean baby. 'Tara is adorable,' she repeated.

'So you've already said.' Tina turned away from the fireplace and stared at Louise. 'I thought you didn't like babies.'

'I don't particularly,' said Louise, hastily replacing the magazine on the desk, and handing Tina a pile of files from her drawer. 'These need filing, and be a dear and fend off everyone for me this morning. I've got a lot of phoning to do. With any luck we'll have a busy start to the new year.'

'Will do.' Tina backed out of the office clutching the files.

Louise caught sight of her expression, and laughed. 'Don't start thinking that I'm wishing I was married with an enormous family of Tara look-alikes. I can read you like a book, Tina Evans. Enjoying Gordon and Eugenia's children doesn't mean that I want that kind of life. I couldn't bear to live in a draughty Victorian house, or trudge around the local supermarket every Friday looking for the cheap offers. There's a lot more to life than that.'

Tina grinned. 'I'll ring Mrs Melrose and tell her about that invitation.'

The door closed and Louise sat staring blankly ahead of her. A lot more to life than that. But what was there apart from money? She was back at the point she'd been on Christmas Day. It was not something she had consciously analyzed before. Now she sat and did some mental arithmetic. Just what does my life amount to? Although not mega-rich, I am never short of money. I've no emcumbrances whatsoever, and that is what I've always wanted. To be as free as air. A wonderful phrase; free as air. But necessary as it was, air was insubstantial, intangible, devoid of reality. As if drawn by a magnet her eyes were attracted back to the magazine. The smiling baby stared up at her, and the answer came. It was quite simple. That was what she needed. A child of her own before she was too old. She'd known it, of course, on Christmas Eve and had been denying it ever since. Baby Tara had been the catalyst, prodding her long dormant maternal instincts, reminding her that time was running out. At thirty-five she didn't have that many more reproductive years left.

'Leaving the desk, Louise walked over to the coffee maker in the corner of the room and poured herself a cup of coffee. The scalding liquid brought her down to earth with a bang. 'Baby indeed,' she muttered crossly. 'I must need my head examined.'

Sitting back down at her desk she got on with the business of securing new clients for the year ahead.

31

CHAPTER 5

On the other side of London a tall, thin woman, with long wind-blown black hair, came out of the courthouse tucking an envelope into the leather handbag slung over her shoulder.

'There,' she said. 'After months of planning now it is almost finished.'

'It *is* finished, Veronique.' Robert, at his sister's side, looked as he always did, as if he ought to be on a rugby field rather than in the expensive suit and overcoat he was wearing. He touched her arm gently, and his brown eyes shone with concern. 'I still don't understand why. But it is finished. The divorce is final now. You've got your decree absolute. It's all over and done with and you need never see Michael again. You can go back to France and get on with your new life.'

'Yes, Robert. I know.'

The tone of her voice made Robert glance down at her but her expression gave nothing away. He sighed. It hadn't made any sense when she had announced that she was leaving Michael, and it made even less sense now. In fact, since their separation he'd had the weirdest sensation that she was surrounded by an aura of strange anticipation; rather, happy anticipation would be a better description. A strange emotion for a woman whose marriage had broken down. He watched her gaze flicker across towards her ex-husband as he stood talking to his lawyer, and worried.

'Veronique? What's going on? Do you still love him?'

Veronique's dark eyes switched back to her brother. For a moment he could have sworn she looked guilty, then she shook her head so that the fine black hair cascaded across her face, hiding her expression. 'Don't be silly, darling,' she said, slipping her arm through his. 'We're divorced and that's that. In fact, I shouldn't be at all surprised if Michael doesn't marry before long.'

'Is there someone?' Robert was surprised.

'Not as far as I know. But I'm sure there will be soon.' Veronique kissed Robert briefly on the cheek. 'Stop looking so worried and get me a taxi for Heathrow, there's a darling. I want to get a plane back to Paris as soon as possible. Then I shall drive down to Chateau les Greves.'

'I wish you wouldn't go straight back to that place all on your own. You'll be lonely. Why on earth you couldn't have moved into something smaller I'll never know.' A taxi pulled to a halt beside them and Robert gave the destination. 'Heathrow, please.' The driver nodded and started the meter.

'Nonsense. I shan't be lonely, and it's not that large. More of a manor than a chateau. And it was such a bargain that I had to have it.' Veronique clambered into the back of the taxi, then shouted through the still open door. 'And don't forget to tell Michael I'll need at least another fifty thousand pounds in French francs to start with. I've still got loads of redecoration to organize. After that, I'll let you know how much more I shall need.'

'Fifty thousand! But that's more than the building cost.' To Robert's logical brain it would have been much more sensible to have paid more and to have bought a house which did not need renovating.

'I know, darling. But Michael said I could spend what I like. And I intend to.'

33

CHAPTER 6

'I think it's absolutely outrageous. In vitro fertilization indeed! Bad enough for farm animals. Poor things. Terribly unfair, I've always thought, depriving them of sex. One of the few pleasures they might have before they get eaten. But as for humans . . . well!'

'Sex isn't that important. For humans *or* animals.'

'Humph!' was Beattie's snorted reply.

It took a lot to drag Beattie away from her easel when she was in the middle of painting. But now she stood, outraged, in the middle of her studio. Her painting smock stuck out in front of her, stiff as a board with years of accumulated blobs of oil paint; Louise thought it made her look pregnant, or maybe, she acknowledged wryly, she simply had babies on the brain. But she couldn't ignore her mother, standing as she was, feet planted aggressively apart, arms akimbo. Her mane of what had been at Christmas iron grey hair, but which at the moment was died the colour of tomato soup and tied back with a pea green scarf, seemed to stand on end of its own accord, in horror at the idea.

'Mother,' said Louise patiently, trying to explain. 'Some women have no alternative.'

To Louise it seemed obvious because she had thought about it very carefully. Once she had made up her mind that having a baby was what she really needed to make her life complete, she'd gone about it in her usual methodical manner. She'd looked coldly and clearly at the possibility of achieving that aim, and the prospect was bleak. There were no permanent men friends on the horizon at the moment. All her ex-boyfriends either had stable relationships with other women or had decided they were gay. Either way they were out of the game plan. Searching for another man was a possibility but would be time consuming, and time was the one thing she didn't have. The more she thought about it, the more the in vitro method seemed the most sensible. 'I visited a clinic,' she told her mother, 'and the doctor told me that it is becoming the method of choice for many women who do not want a man in their lives, but who do want a child.'

Beattie sniffed loudly.

'I needn't have come here. I could have gone straight to my own house, but I wanted to tell you so I popped in here first. Now I wish I hadn't.' Because it all seemed so logical, Louise was totally taken aback by her mother's vehement rejection of the what seemed the ideal solution.

Beattie sniffed again. 'Why can't you get married, or have an affair or something? Then you could produce a child in the ordinary way. Why can't you be normal?'

'How can you expect me to be normal,' snapped Louise irritably, 'when I've got a mother who looks like an advert for some kind of soup? What on earth have you done with your hair?'

'It's called Autumn Gold,' replied Beattie haughtily, 'and don't try changing the subject. My hair may be slightly odd, and I admit it has not turned out quite the way I imagined, but at least I begat you in the normal way.' She glanced up at a large portrait hanging slightly skew on her studio wall showing a darkly handsome man who smiled down at them, and clasped her hands together. 'I was passionately in love with your father. You and Gordon were conceived during nights of bliss.'

'That didn't stop you divorcing him four years after I was born,' Louise reminded her mother.

'How was I to know he'd turn out to be an idle sloth who drank every penny we had?'

'Exactly,' said Louise, pouncing on the words to use as an excuse. 'That's why I don't want to tie myself down with a man.'

'You've had live-in boyfriends.'

'Yes, but I've never kept them for too long because once I began to really know them there were so many things I didn't like that it didn't seem worth the effort of continuing the relationship. Perhaps I'm hard to please.'

'You are,' insisted Beattie.

'But,' continued Louise, ignoring the interruption, 'all I want is a baby. Not a man. I just want to be a mother.'

Beattie Gilby regarded her daughter reflectively. Tall, slim, elegantly dressed in a charcoal grey suit, her dark hair cut short in an expensive bob. Nothing remotely motherly-looking about her. 'You're awfully young to be having a mid-life crisis,' she said thoughtfully.

'Damn it, Mother! I'm not having a mid-life crisis. I just want to have a baby. I want to fulfil my natural function as a woman before it's too late, that's all. I want a baby.'

'A baby is not a banana.'

'Babies, bananas! Have you gone mad?'

Beattie took Louise's hand and led her from the untidy studio towards the equally untidy kitchen. Sitting her daughter down at the table she poured them both a glass of wine from an already opened bottle. 'Darling, what I mean is, bananas come on shelves at the supermarket. When you fancy one, all you have to do is go and pick it up. But babies are not like that. You can't just fancy having a baby and go and collect one.'

'Mother! I know that.'

'What is more,' said Beattie, warming to her theme, 'babies don't stay babies. They grown up and become children, and after that they become adults. But young or old they are with you for the rest of your life.'

'For God's sake! You're making it sound like that RSPCA advert, *a dog is not for Christmas, it's for life.*'

'And a human's life is much longer than a dog's,' replied Beattie seriously. 'Besides, children need a lot more than the occasional walk on a lead. In the beginning they're a full-time commitment. Have you thought of that? How would you cope on your own with a business to run?'

'I worked all that out. I know I couldn't afford a proper nanny. But I can afford an *au pair*-cum-nanny. And I've got room in the flat and at my house here in Winchester to accommodate her. The baby can sleep with me. I'd manage. One-parent families are the accepted norm these days. I shall be just the same as a lot of other women.'

'No excuse for being like them though. Personally I don't approve of one-parent families.'

'*We* were one! You made us one when you threw my father out.' Louise knew it was below the belt, but she couldn't resist saying it.

'I only threw him out because he was a drunken sod,' her mother said defensively. 'And anyway we would have been on our own even if I hadn't. He died less than a year later. Fell down, dead drunk, in front of a bus on New Year's Eve.'

'You have never told me that before.'

'I didn't think it relevant. I told you he was dead. No need to go into the sordid details.' Beattie poured herself another glass of wine and regarded Louise through half closed eyes. 'One-parent families are not the best way to bring up children. Life was always a struggle for me when you were younger.'

'I know that. But it won't be for me. I'm not rich, but I've got more money that you had.'

'I still believe children need a mother *and* a father.'

Louise shook her head. 'That's a matter of opinion. Anyway, I don't intend to have children. Only one.'

Seeing the stubborn look on Louise's face, Beattie heaved a sigh, and the pea green scarf slipped from her hair, making her look more untidy than ever. She got up from the kitchen table. 'Do you want some supper before you go on to your own house?'

'Don't change the subject. I didn't come to eat. I came to tell you of my plans. I thought you'd be pleased at the prospect of another grandchild.'

'Have supper anyway.' Beattie ignored the last remark. 'And take Mr Poo out while I fix it.' She fished him out from his basket under the table, and he snorted irritably at being disturbed while she put on his lead. 'Take him down the lane as far as St Cross and back, and take this torch with you. It's very dark out there.'

'Mother!' Louise paused in the kitchen doorway, and Mr Poo sat down, hopeful that this would be the limit of his walk. 'How old are you?'

'Sixty-five, dear,' said Beattie, searching for a clean saucepan amidst the clutter on the worktops. 'I was thirty when I had you. Elderly, the doctor called me. It still annoys me to this day.'

'Thirty! And I'm thirty-five already.' Louise felt a surge of panic. There was no time to lose. Slipping the catch on the kitchen door she let herself out into the darkness, dragging a reluctant Mr Poo after her. At the far end of the lane she could see the tall chimneys of the alms houses of the Hospital of St Cross. Before her loomed the dark shadow of the Beaufort Tower, and beside that squatted the sturdy, no-nonsense shape of the Norman church of St Cross. All as familiar to her as her own face. And the fact that their shadows had fallen the same way, on to the same place for centuries filled her with reassurance.

Louise breathed in deeply. Here, even in January, the air was sweet with the smell of the river. The silence of the water meadows was broken only by the sound of running water from the many streams feeding through the fields to the swiftly flowing River Itchen. Mr Poo, finding a sudden burst of energy, surged ahead, pulling at his lead, and Louise followed. As she walked she felt the tenseness draining away from her. Her mother's reaction had upset her more than she had expected or shown, but now she began to feel that it would be all right.

Her mother would come round and see that what she proposed was not only sensible, but natural, after a fashion, in the circumstances. The twelfth-century walls enclosing the quadrangle of St Cross dissolved into the darkness, their place being taken by a smiling, pink-faced baby. The baby I'm going to have, thought Louise determinedly.

Her mother's words, spoken to her on Christmas night, suddenly echoed in her head. '*Headstrong. You would never listen. Once you had made up your mind to do something, you went ahead and did it. Come what may.*'

At the end of the lane where one of the many streams funnelled through the remains of a medieval sluice gate, Louise paused. Maybe I ought to compromise, she thought. Perhaps my mother is right. Perhaps it isn't fair to purposely deny a child a proper family. Besides, it might be fun sharing with someone else the pleasures of watching a child grown into adulthood.

Mr Poo, smelling a water vole lurking amidst the spikey rushes at the edge of water, struggled to go on. But Louise turned and pulled him back the way they'd come.

'I promise I won't rush into it,' she told her mother on their return. 'I have listened. Even though you say I never do. I will look for a suitable man, and perhaps even marry him. I suppose there must be someone out there who'd make a reasonable husband.'

'There's Robert Lacroix,' said Beattie quickly. 'I could introduce you to him.'

'I'll find my own man. I know what I want. When I fall in love I'll tell you.'

Beattie banged a saucepan of broccoli about on the top of the stove. 'You'll never fall in love,' she said. 'Not properly.'

'How can you say that?'

'Because you already *are* in love,' said her mother. 'With a stupid idea. You've got it all the wrong way round. A husband should come first, then together you should make plans for a child.'

'I prefer to do it my way,' said Louise.

'So what's new about that!' Beattie strained the broccoli, and slammed two plates on to the table.

CHAPTER 7

It was all very well telling her mother that she would find her own man, but the reality was much more difficult than the theory. Louise was beginning to think that perhaps she'd been wrong to turn down her mother's offer of an introduction to Robert Lacroix. For the first time she realized that, outside of work, her social life was virtually non-existent. She'd been so busy with the business that everything else had ground to a halt and she hadn't even noticed until now.

Sitting on the early morning train from Blackheath into central London, Louise looked around at her fellow passengers. I *have* to do something, she thought. I must start looking. Is my soulmate and the future father of my child to be found here? A Rastafarian in a huge red and yellow knitted hat with a green peak was sitting in the corner, eyes glazed, his head rocking in time to the rhythmic beat echoing along the carriage from the Walkman clipped to his ears. Louise smiled. She could just imagine Beattie's face if she took *him* home. Racial tolerance, as she had demonstrated at Christmas, was not one of her strong points; although Gordon would welcome him and probably get Eugenia to knit him a matching hat to make him feel at home. Louise sighed; nothing doing there. Then she looked at the two men sitting opposite her. City gents, ex-service types judging by the severe cut of their almost identical overcoats and highly polished shoes, both well past their sell-by dates and almost certainly possessing fierce wives and hordes of children and grandchildren. As for the rest of the male occupants of the carriage, they were all much too young, some were scruffy, others spotty, and a few unfortunate individuals were both.

Louise despaired.

The train stopped, the city gents and half the spotty youths got off, and a tall handsome man in casual clothes got in and sat opposite Louise. She perked up. Now, he was a distinct possibility. But how to attract his attention? Even in these emancipated days it was not the done thing to tap a man on the shoulder and say, 'Hi! I'm looking for a soulmate. Interested?' At least, not in London it wasn't. But desperate times called for desperate measures, Louise decided, preparing to drop her newspaper at his feet in the hope that he'd pick it up and speak to her. Then she noticed the earring. Only one. In his left ear. Oh God! Was it left or right that meant gay? Louise couldn't remember and hung on to her newspaper. No point in wasting her energy on a wrong-sided earring.

'The trouble is,' she told Tina when she got to the office, 'I just don't meet any eligible men. When you get to my age they've either all been spoken for, or there is something wrong with them.'

By now Tina knew all about Louise's longing and desires. After Beattie's hostile reception, Louise had told Tina, hoping for a more favourable response. Tina had been more understanding, it was true, but almost equally disapproving of Louise's rush. 'The real trouble,' she said now, 'is that you've left it too late. A great pity your maternal urge didn't surface five years ago.'

'Back to IVF then,' said Louise.

'Not necessarily.' Tina retrieved a copy of the previous day's newspaper from the wastebin. 'There's always a dating agency.'

'Oh, but I couldn't possibly . . .'

'Why not? You've got nothing to lose, and at least the reputable agencies check their clients out before they let them loose. You're less likely to get involved with a pervert or serial killer.'

'Why, oh why can't I meet someone naturally?'

'Because they are either spoken for or there's something wrong with them,' said Tina, echoing Louise's own words. 'Now, look here. This one, the Bureau for Professional People. I know that one is all right.'

'How do you know?' Louise was suspicious.

'Because my widowed friend, Elaine, used them. She was lonely, and through them she met a very nice man with his own business. After six months they married, and she's now living down in Cornwall.'

'No, I think I'd rather leave it to chance. Anyway, I don't want to live in Cornwall.'

'Don't be ridiculous. *You* specify what *you* want. The kind of man, what he should look like, where you want to live, what you want your future to be.' Tina dialled the number and handed the phone to Louise. 'Go on,' she said. 'You want a different kind of life. Use the Bureau to give yourself a kickstart. It's better than touting for men on the train!'

'I was *not* touting.'

A voice at the other end of the line said, 'Good morning.'

Louise stammered nervously, 'Oh! Good morning.'

The voice was female, gentle and sounded sympathetic, and Louise heard herself making an appointment to visit the Bureau for Professional People.

'I look forward to meeting you,' said the voice.

'At least you've done something positive,' said Tina as Louise put down the phone.

The Bureau was organized like a sitting room with a settee, two armchairs and a low coffee table. In the corner of the

43

room was a desk with a computer on it, but apart from that it looked quite homely, and not at all like an office. It was owned and run by a Mrs Marples, a middle-aged blonde with a jolly laugh and a degree in psychology.

'The first thing I always tell my clients,' she said, handing Louise a cup of coffee and coming to sit by her side on the settee, 'is that they are not alone. They are not failures just because they haven't met the right person yet.'

'I've never really looked properly before,' confessed Louise, and before she knew where she was found herself telling Mrs Marples the whole story. How she suddenly realized that life was passing by, and how much she wanted a child of her own. 'So you see,' she finished, 'any man you do introduce to me must want a family too. It's essential.'

'My dear. Most of my male clients are looking for exactly the same thing.' Mrs Marples was most reassuring. 'A normal family life, stability, and happiness. It's what all human beings want and what they need.' She passed a form across to Louise. 'Now, you just fill that in, and put down everything you've told me.'

Louise started filling in the form. When it came to the description of the man, she put fortyish, tall, then thought of Milton with his thatch of dark hair, and put dark haired.

'If everyone wants a normal family life,' she said, passing the completed form back to Mrs Marples, 'how is it we need to come to people like you?'

Mrs Marples's jolly laugh rumbled around the room. 'The opportunities for meeting the right person have never been easy, and nowadays with the busy lives everyone leads, it's even more difficult. In the old days suitable marriages were arranged by the matchmakers, and I would probably have been the village matchmaker.'

'I suppose so.' Louise was still doubtful.

'I believe,' said Mrs Marples firmly, 'that arranged marriages or relationships have a much better chance of succeeding, because the two people have been matched. None of this 'love at first sight' nonsense, which never lasts. One only has to look at the divorce statistics to see that.'

'Yes,' said Louise, feeling only slightly more convinced.

'Now off you go, and don't worry.' Mrs Marples escorted Louise to the door of the Bureau. 'When I have found a man I think is right for you I shall contact you and give you his name and telephone number. At the same time I shall give him your name and phone number. Then it is up to the pair of you to arrange a meeting. I always think a leisurely meal in a good restaurant is a good way to break the ice at a first meeting.'

'Yes,' said Louise, and worried all the way back to the office. Had she done the right thing?

CHAPTER 8

Hurrying through the entrance hall of the Savoy, crowded with powerful people coming and going, as always the hubbub of the 'establishment', Louise made her way to the book launch in the River Room. She was late and hoped Mrs Melrose was not cowering in some corner, overwhelmed by the occasion. Quite a number of people had already arrived and were quaffing champagne and delving into the delicacies being ferried around the room. Taking a glass of champagne from one waiter, Louise dipped a crunchy tiger prawn into the curry sauce proffered by another, and popped it into her mouth, at the same time keeping an eye open for Mrs Melrose.

'Very civilized. Having the function at lunchtime and in such a spacious room. I've never been to the Savoy before, have you?' Turning to look at the speaker Louise found herself gazing into a pair of gentle brown eyes. They belonged to a tall man, with a wide smiling mouth and a slightly crooked, rather large Gallic nose. Louise thought he seemed vaguely familiar. 'I'm Robert Lacroix,' he said. 'Ex-brother-in-law to the distinguished author. And you are Louise Gilby. I met you with your mother after the service on Christmas Eve.'

Now she knew why he seemed familiar, although she would never have been able to recognize him again. 'You must have remarkably good eyesight to remember me. It was very dark that night.'

46

'Aah, I had the advantage. The lamplight shone on you, I was in shadow.'

'Oh, Miss Gilby. Isn't this lovely.' Mrs Melrose zoomed over, champagne glass in one hand, a plateful of goodies in the other. 'Isn't this place wonderful? I'm so glad he asked me.'

'I'm glad you're enjoying it.' Louise smiled at her enthusiasm. 'But it looks to me as if you need another hand.'

'Yes, I do. But never mind, hold this for a moment, will you?' Passing the glass to Louise, Mrs Melrose made a determined assault on her plate of food.

Louise turned to Robert Lacroix. 'This is Mrs Melrose. She actually typed the book.'

Robert raised his eyebrows. 'I understand that Michael can be a bit of a tyrant. I hope he didn't bully you.'

'Oh no, he was always the perfect gentleman.' Having finished the food she retrieved the champagne glass from Louise. 'Oh, look! There's the editor who worked on the book, I must go and say hello. She was so complimentary about my typing.' Her ample rear view disappeared across the room.

Louise laughed. 'I needn't have come,' she said. 'I thought she might need a bit of moral support, but she's doing very nicely on her own.'

'In that case, you can relax and talk to me,' said Robert.

Louise looked at him curiously. 'How come you are here if you are his *ex*-brother-in-law?'

Taking another glass of champagne for himself and Louise, he said, 'I think Michael invited me just to make me envious.' A smile took the sting out of his words. Then he said, 'That's not true, of course. We're good friends, have been for years. He and my sister might be divorced, but all three of us are still good friends.'

'How very sensible,' said Louise. 'It's nice to meet people with no hang-ups. Everyone should be civilized about divorce.'

'Yes,' agreed Robert. He was silent a moment, then said, 'You remind me of someone.'

'Who?' Louise was curious.

'That's the strange thing. I cannot for the life of me think who it is.'

'Can't be anyone important then,' said Louise.

'Can't be,' he joked, then changed the subject. 'You are Beattie's unmarried daughter?'

'Yes. Spinster of the Parish of St Cross. God, what an awful word spinster is.'

'You've not thought of marrying?'

'I might, if I met the right man.' Louise wondered if Mrs Marples had found anyone yet. Robert Lacroix seemed quite nice, but he didn't set her senses on fire. The *right* man would surely cause her to feel something! With a polite smile she began edging away from Robert, intending to circulate, meet new people.

But Robert followed. 'I've never had time to marry,' he said, keeping up with her, 'and since Michael and Veronique split up I've been almost glad I haven't. It has totally shattered my illusions. They always seemed such a devoted couple, then suddenly, without any warning, it was all over. Michael is being incredibly generous concerning Veronique's finances. I know because I deal with all that for her. It might be very civilized, but the whole thing saddens me.' Louise turned and looked at him; he sounded very melancholy. But Robert was not looking at her but across the room to Michael Baruch. 'Yes, such a devoted couple,' he repeated.

'Couples aren't always what they seem to be,' said Louise, also looking across to where Michael Baruch stood. He was easy to spot, not only because there was a large photograph of him at the entrance to the room, but because he was very dark, and taller than most of the men in the group surrounding him. 'You must have been mistaken about their devotion.'

'I suppose so,' said Robert, turning back to Louise. 'Now, tell me. Do you know Michael?'

Louise shook her head. 'Never met him. In fact I was surprised to even receive an invitation.'

'Oh, that's Michael. He's probably hoping to make a sale.'

Louise smiled wryly. 'He won't. I've read the manuscript, so I don't need the book.' She looked at her watch. 'Now, I really must go and catch up with some work.'

'What a pity. Just when I was about to ask you out to dinner.'

Louise laughed. 'You can still ask me.' She thought of Mrs Marples again. It had been over a week. Maybe it wasn't wise to rely on her too much. Dinner with Robert Lacroix would be a way of getting to know him better, and it couldn't do any harm.

Michael Baruch chose this moment to interrupt. 'What am I missing?' he said, looking from Louise to Robert and back to Louise. 'So far I've found this whole affair incredibly dull. How is it you two are smiling?'

'Michael, may I introduce Louise Gilby,' said Robert. 'She's the lady who provided you with your typist.'

'After a few hiccups if I remember correctly,' said Louise, extending her hand.

'Pleased to meet you,' said Michael, and taking her hand, he paused a moment, looked at her long and hard, then raised it to his lips.

Louise, her hand pressed against Michael Baruch's firm, cool lips, knew all about him from the manuscript she'd read. He was forty-two years of age, a Londoner, child of a penniless widow, and now, he was a millionaire. Head of the multi-national Briam Corporation, which he himself had founded a mere ten years ago. In the financial world it was well known that he was always on the look-out for another company to devour; apparently borrowing recklessly to secure whatever he wanted and seeming to lead a charmed financial life. In the City he had the reputation for being ruthlessly tough. If people crossed him, he got rid of them.

Louise wondered if that was what had happened to his wife, because according to what Robert Lacroix had said, one moment they were happily married, the next they were separated, and then two years later, divorced. His ex-wife, Veronique, was hardly mentioned in the book.

Louise had come to the Savoy expecting to dislike him. But now, standing face to face with the man himself, she found herself unexpectedly drawn to him. Not in the same way that she'd been attracted to Robert Lacroix's friendly smile, but in a different, mysteriously dangerous, more *sexual* way. It wasn't just because he was much better looking than Robert. There was something else, intangible, difficult to define. Almost an undercurrent of predestination, and as his gaze caught and held hers, Louise knew without a shadow of doubt that he was pulling her through the two-way mirror of life into a different world. His world. A world where her longing for a child was no longer irrational, but sensible, and attainable. A world where to produce a baby by some unknown donor was unthinkable, because the father would be Michael Baruch. Mrs Marples and her Bureau, and Robert Lacroix, suddenly became redundant. Louise knew she had met the man she wanted.

For a few seconds the rest of the room disolved into a turbulent mist of faces, and Louise felt that she and Michael were standing alone in a cloistered, secluded world of their own. Neither of them spoke because no words were needed.

'He always has that effect on women,' Robert said gloomily as Michael was dragged away by his editor to meet another guest.

'What effect?'

'Of making them go weak at the knees,' said Robert.

'There is nothing weak about me,' replied Louise, cross with herself for letting her feelings show too plainly.

'Could have fooled me. You looked as if you didn't know whether you were coming or going.'

'Nonsense! I know precisely where I'm going. Now if you will excuse me, I really must get back to the office.'

'What about dinner?' asked Robert.

Courtesy forced Louise to say, 'Perhaps later, when I'm not so busy. Give me a ring.' It was Michael Baruch she wanted to meet for dinner, not Robert.

'There's a letter for you in a very elegant envelope. I'm sure it's from the dating bureau. I've put it on your desk.' Tina was excited.

'Thanks.' Louise wasn't interested. Not since she'd met Michael Baruch.

Impervious to Louise's unenthusiastic answer, Tina followed her into the office. 'I can't wait for you to open it. This could be the start of something big, as the song says.'

'Does it?' said Louise absent-mindedly. She was still thinking of the tall, dark man she'd met only a few hours earlier.

'Aren't you going to open it?'

'Of course.' Reaching for the paper knife Louise slit open the long envelope. I'll ring the Bureau, she thought, and say I've changed my mind. Whoever it is, there is no point in meeting this man now. Michael Baruch is the man for me, although how on earth I am going to engineer another introduction to him I don't know. Slowly she withdrew the letter and photograph from the envelope.

'Well?' demanded Tina. 'What's his name, and what's he like?'

There was a long silence. Louise stared, hardly able to believe her eyes. The letter was quite explicit. The man had been separated for two years, and now his divorce was final he was looking for someone to become his wife. His requirements were that his future wife should be intelligent, preferably someone with experience of running a business as the commercial world was his main interest, she should like the fine things in life and be at ease in any type of company. She should be in her mid-thirties and dark haired, and most importantly, she should want a child. His main interest in remarrying was to have a child, as his previous marriage had been childless. Louise looked at the letter, then at the photograph, then back to the letter again. Her gut instinct had been right all along. It was meant to be. Suddenly she felt elated. Why had she ever doubted? Whatever she'd wanted from life she'd always managed to get, one way or another. And now she had the man she wanted. Or to be more precise, soon would.

'His name,' she said at last to the waiting Tina, 'is Michael Baruch.'

Michael Baruch rang Louise the following day, and they had dinner that evening.

Sitting opposite him in the small, secluded restaurant he had chosen, Louise fidgeted nervously with her bread roll. She sensed that Michael was nervous as well.

'Tell me about yourself,' he said abruptly. Then he smiled suddenly, taking the sting out of the abruptness.

'There's not a lot to tell,' said Louise, 'that Mrs Marples hasn't already told you.'

'I'd still like to hear it from you.'

'I'm thirty-five years old, have my own business as you already know, and well . . .' She hesitated, then said, 'And I feel as if life, I mean real life, and by that I mean family life, has passed me by. I'd like to marry and have a child. Maybe even more than one. But I'd be very happy with one to start with.'

Michael laughed. 'It's always best to start with one,' he said.

The remark put Louise at her ease. 'What about you?'

Michael raised his dark brows and smiled. 'You know about me,' he said. 'It's all in the book, as well as Mrs Marples's files.'

'Not why you got divorced,' said Louise, and then immediately knew she had said the wrong thing.

'That's something I prefer not to talk about,' he said sharply, and turned to the menu. 'What do you want to eat?'

Louise cursed her thoughtlessness. His divorce was recent and obviously still hurt. 'I'm sorry,' she said, ignoring his invitation to choose from the menu. 'I shouldn't have asked, because it's none of my business.'

Michael looked up, the expression in his dark eyes was impenetrable. 'No, I was wrong to snap your head off,' he said slowly. 'I can't pretend the divorce has never happened, because it has. But as for the reason, all I can tell you is that Veronique and I could not go on the way we were. So we separated and eventually divorced. We both agreed that that was the way it had to be, there was no alternative that we could think of.'

'Sounds sad,' said Louise.

Michael looked away for a moment, and said almost as if to himself, 'Yes, it was sad.' Then, smiling, he turned back to Louise. 'Now, I want to make another start, and hopefully have a family. Tell me, why have you never married?'

Louise's spirits soared. Now things were moving along on the right track. 'Because I've never met the right man,' she said, looking straight at him and praying that Michael could read the message in her eyes. From his slow, enigmatic smile, which sent a tingle of anticipation down her spine, Louise was certain that he had, although he made no further comment. From then on their conversation was wide and varied and covered a variety of subjects.

This is just like a romance novel, thought Louise, feeling slightly tipsy as she drank a second cognac with her coffee. I wonder if he will kiss me tonight.

Michael drove her all the way back to Blackheath. He stopped the car outside the large Victorian house where Louise had her apartment.

'You have a lovely view here,' he said, looking down

across the heath towards the lights of Greenwich and the City of London.

Louise fished in her handbag for her front door key. Shall I ask him in for coffee, she wondered. Do I want to rush into bed with him tonight? The answer in fact was yes, she did. But instinct told her no, not yet, it was too soon.

In the event, Michael solved the dilemma for her. 'I'll say goodnight now,' he said, and with one swift movement reached over and unlocked her door. Then before she could move he caught her face between his hands and turned it towards him. Slowly but firmly he placed a long, exploratory and pleasantly sensual kiss on her mouth. 'Until tomorrow,' he said.

'Until tomorrow,' echoed Louise breathlessly, and scrambled out of the large car. She watched it purr away out of sight, and humming tunelessly she skipped up the steps towards her white-painted front door. The brass knocker gleamed cheerfully in the light of the street lamp. 'Everything is going exactly according to plan,' she told the knocker before entering the house. 'Exactly.'

CHAPTER 9

Alone in his office, Michael gazed out of the window at the jagged grey sky and the rain slashing down on the steps at the western end of St Paul's Cathedral. His office, high in a building in Ave Maria Lane, gave him a pigeon eye's view of the great cathedral in the centre of the City of London; but it was not normally a view he bothered to look at. Today, however, he watched as a group of Japanese tourists swarmed, like black ants, up and across the steps and into the south-west door of the cathedral. They must be Japanese, he decided, because they were all so small, all dressed in black plastic raincoats and all had small, neat, black umbrellas, and even when viewed from a distance they emanated a resolute tourist-like determination: St Paul's was on their itinerary for today, and regardless of the weather they were going to see it.

Michael's hand hovered over the telephone. He picked it up, then put it down again. Was it raining in Brittany? Was Veronique feeling depressed? She was a sunshine person. Like a rare and beautiful plant she needed sunshine in order to thrive. Perhaps he ought to have bought her a villa in the south of France, not a chateau in Brittany. But Brittany was so much nearer to England. Only a few hours away. So much more convenient.

He picked up the phone once more, his private line, and swiftly, before he had time to change his mind yet again, punched out the number for Chateau les Greves.

Andrea Louedec, the housekeeper, answered. Michael spoke to her in fluent French and asked if Veronique was there.

'Yes, Madame is here. She is in the garden picking some snowdrops. I will get her for you.' If she thought it strange that her employer's former husband should be telephoning, Madame Louedec gave no indication.

So it wasn't raining. Michael was glad. At the same time he was already wishing he hadn't given in to the impulse to ring Veronique. They had agreed no contact unless there was something important to say.

Veronique picked up the phone. She was breathless. 'I ran all the way up to the house from the walled kitchen garden,' she said in English. 'The best snowdrops grow down there on the other side of the wall where they are sheltered by the hazel copse.'

'I hope you are not overdoing it. Should you really be out in the garden in the cold? You know you must be careful. Avoid cold, the doctor said, it places too great a strain on your heart.'

'My heart is fine,' said Veronique, 'and it's not cold outside. It's a wonderful day. The sun is shining, the sea and the sky are the colour of lapis lazuli. It could easily be summer if only there were leaves on the trees.'

'Sounds wonderful.' Outside in London the rain increased in ferocity and was now blowing almost horizontally, smashing against the double glazing of the office window. 'Bloody awful here. Bucketing down with rain.'

'You didn't ring me just to talk about the weather, did you?'

'No, I . . .'

'You've found someone already.'

'I think I have.'

'Oh, Michael.' Veronique's disappointment was almost tangible to Michael, sitting in London. 'Thinking it isn't enough. It's got to be positive. You promised you

56

wouldn't ring unless it was something important, and you know what that means.'

'Yes,' said Michael. 'I'm sorry. It was wrong of me to ring, but I was worried about you.'

'Darling, please don't be. I am perfectly happy here. Andrea and Paul Louedec are looking after me very well. Almost too well. Every afternoon Andrea makes the most delicious crêpes, and I usually eat two smothered with her home-made butter and apricot preserve. I shall be putting on weight if I'm not careful. So do stop worrying and get on with life, and more importantly enjoy what you have to do. It's what we agreed, isn't it?'

'Yes,' said Michael.

'And you haven't changed your mind?'

'No.'

'Then do it, and enjoy it; you know it's what I want. Only contact me again when you have something *really* important to tell me. We both agreed that this was the best way, didn't we?'

'Yes,' said Michael again, 'we did. I shouldn't have phoned, I was worrying about nothing. Goodbye, Veronique, take care, my darling.'

'Goodbye,' said Veronique softly. 'And don't forget I look forward to hearing from you some time in the future, when everything is settled, and the news is good.'

The phone clicked, and she was gone. Michael waited a moment, in his mind visualizing Veronique making her way back outside into the sunlit garden. She was probably walking through the spacious *salle à manger* with its lofty ceiling and mirrored walls, through the French windows at the side of the room on to the terrace and down past the formal boxed hedge garden towards the walled kitchen garden where the vegetables grew. He sighed, it was all right. She was happy there, and the Louedecs were good to her. There was nothing to worry about, for soon, if he played his cards right, he would be telling her the news she was waiting to hear. With a smile he picked up the phone again, this time confirming the arrangements for that evening with Louise.

A whole week passed. Michael and Louise had dinner together every night. But although Michael was charming and made romantic gestures, having exquisite bouquets sent round to her apartment, once giving Louise a frighteningly expensive bottle of perfume, and always rounding off the evenings with increasingly passionate kisses, he made no other moves. At every meeting Louise was sure that she was falling a little bit more in love with him. He was handsome, intelligent, sexy, everything she wanted in a man, but she became very impatient at their lack of progress.

'The trouble with men,' she confided to Tina, 'is that they are so damned slow.'

'Good heavens, give him time. You've only known each other just over a week. This isn't the swinging sixties, you know. Sensible people don't leap into bed with each other the moment they meet. Nowadays you have to be a little more careful, and think of Aids.'

'He hasn't slept around. I probed Robert Lacroix on that subject.' Robert had popped into the agency after a neurology conference in London the previous week, and Louise had plied him with coffee and questions.

'Maybe he's doing a little investigation of his own into your background before he makes a move,' suggested Tina.

'But if all he ever does is kiss me,' grumbled Louise, 'I'm never going to get that baby.'

Tina sat down on the chair opposite Louise's desk. 'I hate to throw cold water over this sudden, and rather alarming, obsession of yours to activate your womb.'

'Activate my womb! You make it sound like a time bomb. Tina, you've been talking to my bloody mother. That's her turn of phrase.'

'What if I have?' responded Tina. 'She's absolutely

58

right. It *is* an obsession, and it *is* alarming; and what's more, there is something you seem to have completely overlooked.'

'Oh? And what is that?'

'You may not even be able to have a child. Has that occurred to you? Having a baby isn't a question of *wham, bam, here I am.*'

Louise snorted. 'Shades of my mother again! Don't be crude, Tina.'

'But it's a fact. Women don't conceive after one night's sex. Some women *never* conceive, because they can't.'

'I will,' said Louise obstinately. 'I just know it. But not, of course, unless I can get Michael into bed. I'll *have* to do something about that.'

Tina flounced out of the office. 'I shall tell Beattie that I tried,' she said over her shoulder, 'but that you are absolutely crazy, and nothing will dissuade you.'

The brilliant sunshine outside in the street mysteriously seemed to darken, and Louise felt a flicker of disquiet. Was she mad? But immediately the answer came back loud and clear, *of course not*, and sunshine flooded the room again. There was nothing abnormal about falling in love and wanting a family. The problem lay in other people's perception of her. Family and friends had all grown so used to her being a single career woman that they just could not imagine her as anything else.

Elbows on the desk, Louise cupped her chin in her hands and made plans for the coming evening when as usual she was seeing Michael again. Tonight, she decided, she would lay her cards on the table, and tell him that she was convinced that he was the right man for her. No point in waiting for ever.

Accordingly, that evening, having fortified herself with two enormous dry martinis before dinner, she broached the subject before she had time to lose her nerve.

'Michael,' she began, and her mind went blank. All the

words, which had seemed so sensible when carefully rehearsed during the day, flew out of her head. But she persevered. I have to say *something*, she reminded herself, just having dinner is futile. 'Michael, do you remember telling me that one of the things you desired most from life was an heir, a child who could inherit your fortune?'

'Of course.' Michael looked up from the menu he was studying. If he was surprised the dark green eyes regarding Louise gave no hint of it.

'And you know that I too want a child. I want a husband and a family before I'm too old.'

'Yes.'

He wasn't making it easy.

'What I'm trying to say is, I think that you are the right man for me. I know we've only known each other for a very short while, but already I think I am a little in love with you. I'd like to marry you and have your children.' Still there was silence. 'I'm sorry,' said Louise, 'perhaps I've shocked you by being so honest.'

Michael smiled. 'Far from it. You've made things easier for me.'

'Easier?'

'I was wondering how to raise the subject myself without appearing to rush you. I am very attracted to you physically and we get on well.' Louise nodded her head, so far so good. 'But,' Michael paused, 'I must be quite honest with you too, and tell you that I am not in love with you, and – ' he hesitated, then said – 'and perhaps because of my divorce, never will be in the accepted sense of the word. However, I am realistic and must face up to the fact that I am not getting any younger.'

'Men can father children until they are a hundred,' interrupted Louise, unable to keep the note of envy from her voice. 'There's not such a hurry for you.'

A faint smile turned up the corners of Michael's mouth. 'True,' he said, 'but from what I've read, the older one gets the greater the chances of having a less than perfect child.'

60

Panic struck at Louise. Perhaps he would reject her because of her age. 'Do you think I'm too old?'

'You're a young, fit, thirty-five-year-old, and anyway, you can always have a test to make sure any baby you conceive is perfect. And as I told you, ever since my divorce was finalized I have been looking for a suitable woman who might provide me with an heir.'

'And you think I could be that woman?'

'Yes, I do.'

This is bizarre! This is unreal! Ordinary people don't talk like this. Every atom of common sense she possessed told Louise so, but was ignored.

'I can accept that you don't feel as affectionate towards me as I do to you,' said Louise. 'But perhaps in time you will change.'

'Perhaps,' replied Michael. Reaching across the table he laid his hand over hers. 'And you really do want to get married?' he asked.

Louise laid down her menu; food had long ago been forgotten. 'You don't have to marry me. You can have your heir without tying yourself down.'

'I want to be tied down, it's important to me. I would want us to be legally married for the sake of the child. It must be official that any child we have is partly mine. Say you'll agree.'

Surprised, Louise felt the hand on hers tremble, and looking into his eyes she saw that it *was* important. As important to him as it was to her. The knowledge touched an optimistic chord deep within her. Her *idée fixe* was not as ridiculous as Beattie and Tina thought. Not only would she have marriage, and a family, there was also the distinct possibility of love. Although Michael had just said that he was only attracted to her, and had emphasized that it was nothing else, the trembling of his hand, and the look in his eyes said otherwise. Louise felt a bubble of happiness beginning to grow inside her; nothing was impossible, and it was conceivable that affection was already beginning to

61

blossom but that Michael was unwilling to acknowledge it because it was too soon. The few misgivings still smouldering at the back of her mind abruptly dispersed, gone like bonfire smoke before a puff of wind. No matter what anyone else might say or think, she *would* have her child, and she *would* be happy. It wasn't true, that silly old adage, that you couldn't have your cake and eat it.

'I agree,' said Louise.

'There is just one more thing,' said Michael seriously. 'Before we married you would need to be tested to make certain the baby is perfect. I've made enquiries and think chorionic villus sampling would be the best method. Apparently this can be done through the cervix into the placenta at ten weeks, and it takes about a week to get the result.'

'Oh.' A faint ripple of unease disturbed Louise's euphoric musings. Michael had been thinking and planning just as she had, only apparently more thoroughly. 'You mean that I must get pregnant before we marry.'

'Of course. It's the only sensible way. For two reasons. One, you might not conceive, and two, the baby might be imperfect. Either would put a stop to our plans.' He paused and looked hard at Louise. 'You don't mind, do you?'

'Well, no. I suppose not.' Louise wasn't sure. It was beginning to sound more cold blooded than she'd thought, and she wasn't at all sure what her own feelings would be if the baby wasn't perfect. Could she get rid of it, without a second thought? The possibility hadn't even occurred to her before.

As if sensing her indecision, Michael said, 'Surely you agree that the last thing we would want is a handicapped child? Anything less than perfect is unacceptable. It would have to be discarded.'

'Like a banana that's gone brown at the edges.' Louise suddenly thought of her mother.

'A banana is not a baby,' said Michael, looking puzzled.

'That's what my mother says.'

Michael raised his eyebrows, unable to follow her train of thought, then snapped his fingers at the hovering waiter. 'We'll order now.'

For a fleeting second Louise had a sudden, and unwanted, vision of Robert Lacroix. He'd been into the office again that day trying to persuade her to go out to lunch with him while he was up in London. Louise had refused because she'd had too much work, and had sent an overjoyed Tina instead. But now, remembering his friendly brown eyes, Louise wondered if he would say *anything less than perfect is unacceptable*. Somehow she couldn't visualize it.

'To us.' Michael's glass clinked against hers.

'To us,' echoed Louise.

The decision had been made. They would try for a baby and, if successful, marry. It was what she had wanted from the moment she had met Michael. Only now, contrary to all her expectations, instead of feeling triumphant she felt slightly scared, and realized that wanting and getting are two completely different things.

As soon as they left the restaurant and were in the darkness of the car park, Michael turned and, pulling her roughly into his arms, began to kiss her with a feverish passion. A passion that momentarily surprised and slightly frightened Louise. His kisses, although sensual, had always been so controlled before. But the fear was only momentary, the power of his ardour was infectious, and soon she found herself kissing him back with equal intensity.

'My apartment is nearer than yours,' said Michael when he finally released her. He unlocked the car. 'We'll go there.'

As eager as he to consummate their newly-found fervour, Louise agreed.

Michael's apartment was in a tower block overlooking Hyde Park. Louise hardly had time to register the sumptuous elegance of her surroundings however, as the moment the door closed and they were alone, she found herself swept along in a flood tide of sexuality which stunned and overwhelmed her, and at times was almost alarming.

Afterwards she couldn't even remember how they had got to the bedroom. All she could remember was the sense of devastating need, a fiery red hot river of passion which engulfed them both, tearing them apart and yet binding them together at the same time. When he entered her the first time Louise cried out from the sheer fierceness of the pleasure which shot through her body and numbed her mind.

They made love two, three times – Louise lost count – in quick succession. Michael's need seemed insatiable. He thrust deeper and deeper each time, locking her mouth to his, his hands guiding her buttocks ever upwards as if he wanted to pierce the very core of her being.

Then the pace slowed. Michael was still intent on making love, but now he took more time. His mouth roamed her body. His tongue and lips exploring every secret crevice, giving her a pleasure so exquisite that it was almost unbearable. No man had ever succeeded in making her feel the way Michael was doing now.

This must be right, thought Louise hazily. He is the man for me. No one could make love in this way and not mean it. He must love me, even though he can't say so in words. That will come.

Finally he moved on top of her again, and this time slid gently into her body. Satiated and happy, Louise opened her eyes properly for the first time since they started lovemaking, and was suddenly afraid. His face was an expression of total concentration, not happiness. A disturbing concept suddenly occurred to her. He was making love to her because he'd been programmed to do so. At their first meeting, when she had imagined Michael pulling her through the two-way mirror into his world, she had gone eagerly, but now she began to wonder what sort of world it was that he inhabited. To her heightened senses it seemed that dark currents swirled about him, currents of desperation and inexplicable sadness. He had said that he wanted her to have his child, but was that the real truth?

Unable to contain her doubts Louise whispered, 'Michael, you do want *me*, don't you? Not someone else?'

She thought there was a moment's hesitation before he answered. 'What makes you ask?' His voice was soft in her ear.

'Just a feeling.'

'I must be doing something wrong.' Michael cupped her breasts in his hands and kissed her gently. 'What do you think I'm doing, if not worshipping *your* body, no one else's? Don't you like it?'

'Oh, yes,' whispered Louise. His words were reassuring. 'I don't know what I was afraid of.'

'You were afraid?'

'Yes. For a moment you looked like a stranger.'

Michael lay his head in the hollow of her shoulder. 'I suppose I am,' he said. 'Just as you are to me. But every day we'll learn a little more about each other, and I promise I'll try not to hurt you.'

'You haven't.'

'It wasn't a physical hurt that I meant.'

'Why should you hurt me in any way? We both want the same thing from this relationship; a child. And if in getting that child we can have fantastic sex surely that's a bonus?'

Michael lowered his head and kissed the faint curve of her stomach. 'You might find when you have a baby that you get tired of it,' he said. 'You've always been a career woman, perhaps you'll find that motherhood is boring.'

'Oh no.' All the new-found longing for a child showed in her voice. 'I shall never, never be bored.'

Michael was silent for a moment while he continued to caress her stomach, then he said, 'I see.' Just for a moment

Louise thought his voice sounded strained and sad. Then he trailed his mouth down to where the silky hairs of her bush grew. 'Let's start again, shall we, and maybe you'll get pregnant tonight.' This time his voice wasn't sad, but rough with desire.

Louise joyfully complied. Finally sated and exhausted, they lay side by side. Louise would have liked them to have been lying curled together, but now that they had finished Michael seemed to want to be alone.

'If having an orgasm is necessary to conception,' said Louise, 'then I am most certainly pregnant.' She laid the palm of her hand flat against Michael's chest, wanting to be closer to him.

Michael covered her hand with his own and squeezed. 'If everything goes to plan,' he said, 'and we do get married, we shall we live in my house in Hampshire, not here. I want my son to breathe in fresh unpolluted air, not the filthy stuff that passes as air here in London.'

He patted her stomach, as if feeling for the baby they might have already created between them. Louise smiled and turned in towards him sleepily. Everything was right with her world. She *would* get pregnant, she was certain, and although he might not love her, she and Michael were marvellous together in bed. And anyway, the happy thought occurred to her before drifting from the twilight world that precedes sleep, I do love Michael, that's the important thing. Eventually he will love me too. It is inevitable.

Three and a half weeks later Louise knew for certain that she was pregnant.

CHAPTER 10

Robert fidgeted restlessly, he felt uncomfortable, and wished that he'd worn a lighter weight suit. Although it was only the second week in April the weather was behaving as if it were midsummer. The temperature, however, was not the only reason for his discomfort. I wish, he thought for the umpteenth time, that I hadn't been so weak-willed. Why didn't I say no when Michael asked me to be a witness to this damned wedding? Although, he reflected with ever increasing gloom, it's a waste of time worrying about that now, I said yes, and so here I am.

'I hope Louise is not going to be late. That damned mother of hers is so unpunctual. Probably still trying to decide which damned hat to wear. I gather from Louise that she's bought two, although God knows why. She hasn't bought anything else new and all her clothes are revolting. She'll probably turn up in the ghastly caftan she wears most of the time.'

Robert glanced at Michael standing, equally restlessly, beside him. For a man about to be married he didn't look very happy.

'Don't you like Beattie Gilby?'

'Apart from being too flamboyant for my liking, the wretched woman is so disorganized. Anyway, I didn't think it necessary for her to come today.'

'It's natural for her to come. She's Louise's mother. Mothers always go to weddings; usually it's the highlight of their lives. If your mother were alive she'd want to come.'

'I wouldn't have encouraged it.'

Robert was about to ask why, then thought better of it. He remembered Veronique saying once that Michael had told her his mother had been an uneducated woman, and he'd not been close to her. Safer, he decided, to leave Michael's mother out of the conversation and concentrate instead on Louise and try to persuade Michael into a better mood than his present one.

'I'm sure Louise will get her mother organized; she's a very efficient young lady.'

'Yes, she's efficient,' said Michael. To Robert's surprise there was a note of disapproval in his voice. 'She's efficient almost to the point of masculinity in the way she runs that business of hers, and in the way she goes after what she wants.'

Robert glanced sideways at Michael, a discreet, dispassionate inspection. Male chauvinism was not something he had ever suspected in Michael. 'Since when has efficiency been a masculine prerogative?' he asked mildly.

'You know what I mean. Men and women are different. I've always thought that women should be like . . .' Michael paused, and for a moment Robert could have sworn he was going to say Veronique. But he did not. He said instead, 'vulnerable, gentle, reliant on the male of the species to make the running. I've always liked fragile, flower-type women.'

He might just as well have said Veronique, mused Robert. Why the hell had Michael divorced her if he thought like that? She was all the things he'd listed, and what was more important she had really needed Michael. Probably still did. The thought was disquieting, and Robert felt increasingly uneasy. First his sister's divorce, which happened for reasons he'd never fully understood, and now this marriage. None of it made any damned sense. Why had Louise, a sensible career woman, been captivated by Michael to the ultimate point of folly, getting herself pregnant? He probed a little, cautiously feeling his way. What did Michael really feel? Did he love her? He wasn't acting like a man in love at the moment.

'Louise certainly doesn't come into the fragile flower category,' he said, 'so I take it you must be head over heels in love with her.'

'She's nearly three months pregnant.'

A frisson of alarm sent warning bells jangling in Robert's head. Michael's reply had a harsh bleakness about it which was abhorrent. It was a mere bald statement of fact concerning the pregnancy, intimating that affection did not come into the equation at all. Now all Robert's misgivings surfaced in full force once again. Ever since Louise had so joyfully announced to the world at large that she was pregnant, he had felt a faint sense of unease that all was not well. This, in spite of the fact that she was so obviously over the moon about the pregnancy and Michael. At first he'd put it down to plain old-fashioned jealousy on his part. He'd seen Louise first and had felt an immediate attraction, but then Michael had appeared and that was that. Louise hadn't given him a second glance, apart from being friendly as a sister might be to a brother.

But as the weeks passed Robert had determinedly put such thoughts to the back of his mind. He liked Louise, and her mother, and had put the romantic notions he'd so briefly harboured out of his mind, and the three of them were now good friends. No, it was not jealousy which made him uneasy because he would never allow himself to covet Michael's good luck. But why wasn't Michael happier? And why should the feeling that something was wrong persist? What was the problem? There was nothing positive, nothing tangible, nothing at all that he could pin down; but still the feeling persisted. And another thing, why had they not married before? Why had they waited for three months? So many questions, and no answers. At the risk of offending Michael, Robert now decided to ask.

'You've waited three months before marrying, was there a reason?'

Michael turned towards Robert. 'Of course there was a reason,' he said. 'We had to wait to find out if the child was healthy. Louise got the results last week. It's a perfect boy.'

'A child is a child, perfect or imperfect.'

Michael smiled, but his eyes remained remote, inward looking, as if his mind were elsewhere. 'Only a perfect child will do for our purpose.'

'Purpose? What purpose? You make it sound as if you have special plans for this child. Planning his life before the poor little thing is even born.'

The words were half joking, but there was no disguising the guilt which flickered across Michael's face. As soon as it appeared it was gone, but Robert knew he had not been mistaken. Yet again, it didn't make sense. Nothing seemed to make sense. Michael turned away and looked at his watch. 'Where the hell are they?' he said.

'For God's sake, Michael, it's another five minutes before they are even due.' Robert's anxiety began to show and he snapped irritably at Michael. 'You can't accuse them of being late.'

Robert tried telling himself that he was over-reacting, imagining emotions that didn't exist, and resolutely tried to put his unease out of mind. It was none of his business anyway. His only concern now was for Veronique. She was his responsibility, not Louise. Louise was a capable woman, she could take care of herself. But Veronique was a different matter. How would she take the news of Michael's remarriage so soon after the divorce? Even though she had told him she was prepared for it, Robert worried that, in fact, she would be devastated by the knowledge that Michael had already taken another wife. He voiced part of his thoughts out loud. 'I suppose I'd better tell Veronique you have remarried.'

'*No!*' The vehemence of Michael's reply shocked Robert, and he knew the shock must have shown on his face for Michael repeated, 'no,' in a gentler tone. Then said, 'I'll tell her myself.'

'Is that wise? You've only recently been divorced. Surely it will be better if I tell her?'

'No!' The same vehemence. 'I'll do it. I may have divorced your sister, but I still have feelings of responsibility for her. I don't want her hurt or upset in any way. Please trust me. I promise I'll tell her.'

After the wedding there was a brief reception at Claridges. Apart from Robert Lacroix who came with Michael, all the other guests were Louise's family and friends. Her mother, Gordon her brother, and Eugenia his wife, and Tina from the office accompanied by her husband Alistair.

Having mutually decided that a honeymoon was unnecessary, the newly married couple drove straight from the reception in London to Michael's country home, Offerton Manor, in the village of Offerton, near Winchester in Hampshire.

'I hope you'll be happy at the manor house.'

'I'm sure I shall be.' Louise fingered the sparkling diamonds swinging from her ears. Michael's wedding present to her. They were beautiful brilliants set in old gold and must have cost a king's ransom. She smiled, remembering the message on the card which had come with them. '*To the mother of my child for whom I would lay down my life.*'

'There you are, he *does* love me,' she'd said to her mother, who'd always professed doubts on that score.

'Words can mean anything you want them to. And he doesn't actually say he loves you.'

Louise thought Beattle surprisingly stubborn. How could she doubt? Louise did not. Not now. Because every day during the past few weeks since she'd known she was expecting Michael's child, she had interpreted every little kindness, every touch, every kiss as proof that he was beginning to fall in love with her. In spite of his declaration at the beginning of their relationship that he could not love her, she was sure he was changing, just as she too had changed. And it was no use her mother telling her that all women fell in love with the men they slept with. That it was the female Achilles' heel. A fatal weakness which had clouded more than one woman's judgement. Louise simply didn't believe it. She was happy and fulfilled, with a baby boy developing in her womb and the father of that child beside her. She felt a rush of affection every time she saw Michael, and that was something she was sure would not diminish with time.

'I should have brought you down before the wedding –' Michael's voice interrupted her thoughts – 'but somehow there never seemed to be the time.'

'It doesn't matter, I know I'll love living there.'

The early April countryside slid past the speeding car. The fields forming a vivid patchwork of colours. Winter wheat, now standing tall and straight, was a dark emerald green, contrasting with the acrid yellow of oil seed rape. Each field was neatly divided by the soft fuzz of the pale green leaves of the hazel hedgerows, and down along the roots nestled dark green patches splashed with brilliant yellow flashes, which Louise knew to be the burnished gold stars of damp-loving celandines. Every now and then a dense clump of trees showed where once all this land had been an impenetrable ancient forest. Beeches, tall and proud, uplifted arms rosy pink from the yet unopened red buds, and horse chestnuts shimmered in the slight breeze, their graceful sweeping boughs already unfurling young, luscious leaves and displaying the white and pink candle flowers announcing that summer was near. Viewed

72

from the motorway Louise thought the countryside looked as if it had been sewn together by some heavenly seamstress. Not a stitch out of place.

'I know Offerton Manor slightly,' she told Michael. 'We used to go to the summer fête held there every year by the previous owners.' She smiled at the memory. What perfect summers they had been. In memory it never seemed to rain. 'I got my first bottle of perfume at one of those fêtes. A bottle of Devon Violets from the lucky dip barrel.'

'It's not open to the public now,' said Michael abruptly, his sudden, acerbic tone of voice shattering Louise's rosy dreams of times past. 'I like my privacy.'

He turned off the motorway, the Mercedes hurtling down narrow country lanes overhung with enormous beeches, their roots exposed like skeletons, protruding through the chalky soil of the banks either side of the lanes.

It will be all the nicer being utterly private, Louise told herself firmly, although at the back of her mind lurked the idea of how much fun it would be organizing an annual summer fête. Then she put the idea away and watched every turn in the road. They were near; soon they'd be arriving at her new home.

The enormous wrought-iron gates of Offerton Manor appeared quite suddenly after Michael had negotiated a narrow humpbacked bridge and a bend. After a second's wait they swung silently open, and the car shot into the long carriage drive which led through Offerton Park.

'Magic,' said Louise, looking back at the gates.

'Electronic,' replied Michael, indicating a tiny button on the car key ring.

Parkland stretched, smooth and green, either side of the drive. On one side a group of cattle stood cropping the grass, all facing west towards the now fading sun. Enormous lime trees, now just sprouting translucent green leaves, were dotted about at regular intervals throughout the park. Louise remembered the trees from her childhood visits, recalling their distinctive sweet smell mixed with the scent of freshly mown grass.

She looked at the cattle. 'You farm as well?'

'Not me. I rent the land to a nearby farmer on the understanding that the cattle are no trouble and he does not make too much mess. It's a cheap way of keeping the grass down.'

On the left-hand side of the park the land sloped gently upwards, forming a softly rounded field. A tractor was ploughing, chugging up and down, followed by the inevitable mêlée of noisy rooks, crows and ever voracious seagulls. 'I love that sight,' said Louise. 'Birds following the plough, all dive-bombing for the tasty morsels of worms and beetles turned over with the earth.'

'Do you?' Michael turned his head briefly, looking surprised. 'I've always thought of you as a city person. Not someone attuned to the country at all.' Then he added under his breath, 'Veronique loves the country.'

An alarming, bone chilling fear suddenly lodged in Louise's chest like a heavy stone. She had not been meant to hear that. What was Michael doing thinking of his ex-wife when he was bringing her, his new wife, to the home they were to share together? The temptation to challenge him was great, but she bit her lip and remained silent. Some things were best left unsaid.

'You forget,' she said lightly, 'that I was born near here, in Winchester. I only moved to London ten years ago. Basically I am still a country girl at heart.'

'Well, one lives and learns,' was Michael's only comment.

'One certainly does.' Louise was still thinking about the *sotto voce* remark referring to Veronique. Then she told herself that it didn't matter. Veronique was gone. Now, she, Louise, was Michael's wife and mistress of Offerton Manor.

The car purred to a halt before the magnificent portico of the house upheld by five Doric pillars. 'Welcome to

Offerton Manor,' said Michael, assisting Louise from the car.

A short woman, in a brown skirt and red blouse, came out and waited on the top step of the entrance to the house. 'Who is that?' Louise asked.

'The housekeeper, Mrs Carey,' said Michael brusquely. 'She lives here with her husband who is the gardener and handyman.'

Louise stood momentarily rooted to the spot. She had forgotten how large the manor house actually was. Much too large for just two people, and although beautiful, it looked cold and unfriendly. Most of the shutters on the windows were closed, making it look as if the house were asleep and did not want to be disturbed.

'Well,' she said finally, collecting her wits and desperately trying to lighten Michael's mood which seemed to have plummeted the moment they'd driven through the gates. 'I'm glad there will be someone to help me with housework. It *is* an enormous house.'

'You won't have anything to do.' Putting a hand under her elbow to assist her, Michael started to climb the steps. 'Mrs Carey takes care of everything, including the cooking.'

'But I shall want to do something.'

'There is no need.'

'Oh, but I . . .'

'Louise, I'd prefer it if the arrangements are left the way they are. Mrs Carey knows my tastes.'

Louise seethed, but bit her tongue and remained silent. What the hell did he expect her to do? And wasn't this supposed to be her home too? Suddenly she wished they had talked more about what they would do after they were married, and not just talked exclusively about the baby.

On the top step she met Mrs Carey. A woman in her mid-fifties, discreetly made up and with rigidly permed grey hair. Louise was glad to note that she had a kind face, although she was obviously rather in awe of Michael.

'Welcome to Offerton Manor, Mrs Baruch,' she said.

Her tone was so deferential that Louise almost expected her to curtsey. 'I'm very pleased to meet you, Mrs Carey,' she said, extending her hand. It seemed to her that Mrs Carey hesitated before taking it, as if she thought Michael might not approve. 'And I'm sure we shall become good friends,' added Louise, trying to put the housekeeper at her ease. 'I shall need all the help I can get to find my way around this place.'

'I shall be glad to help you.' Mrs Carey sounded slightly doubtful. Doubtful about helping, or doubtful about being allowed to? wondered Louise.

'Is there something to eat?' asked Michael.

'Yes, sir. I've laid a light meal ready for you in the orangery. You said nothing too heavy, and I thought it would be less formal in there than the dining room, and more restful at the end of a long day.' She turned briefly and called, 'Dick!' A middle-aged man in a grey shirt and trousers emerged from a door at the far side of the portico. 'Please take all the luggage up to the St Swithun suite.' She turned back to Michael. 'I've had all your things moved from your old rooms into the new suite, just as you asked.'

'Good,' said Michael. He turned to Louise. 'Let's go,' he said, 'I could do with a drink.'

Louise accompanied him, trying to brush away the aura of disquiet surrounding her. The house was not only enormous and unfriendly looking from the outside, it felt very unwelcoming inside. The oval entrance hall was huge and empty, apart from statues standing in alcoves in the walls, and they didn't look too happy, thought Louise, glancing quickly at their rigidly muscled forms and blank stone eyes. The ceiling arched upwards to form a cupola, and the marble flooring echoed to the clack, clack of Mrs Carey's high heels as she led the way.

'Whatever made you buy such a big house?' she asked Michael.

76

'We . . . I mean, I, like big houses. There is no point in having money if you don't spend it.'

'I suppose not.'

Michael turned and suddenly smiled. 'I'm sure you'll soon get to love it,' he said.

She tried to smile back but found it difficult. 'I'm sure I shall.'

Louise had not missed the slip of his tongue. *We*, he had said. *We*. There was only one we he could have meant, and that did not include Louise. He'd meant Veronique and himself. Veronique had obviously liked large houses, maybe had even chosen this one. But I don't like it, thought Louise, glaring resentfully at the paintings adorning the walls, and the exquisite antique furniture filling every nook and cranny, and I never will. The whole place is like some enormous museum which is closed to the public. These rooms need people, not inanimate objects. This place is dead; it has no soul.

'I love the quietness here,' said Michael. 'I've always liked places devoid of people.'

His words gave Louise an unpleasant jolt, reminding her of how little they really knew about one another. It seemed that their tastes were poles apart if this place was anything to go by. Perhaps her mother had been right. Maybe it had been a mistake to rush into marriage.

'Would you like a drink, Madame?'

'I'd love an orange juice.'

Louise made a mental note to tell Mrs Carey to call her by her first name. Having a housekeeper was one thing, but treating her like a servant was another. Louise had always had a young woman to do the housework in her Chesil Street house, but she and Jane were friends as much as employer and employee and always called each other by their first names. She glanced at Michael. Now was not the time to speak. But there *would* be some changes at Offerton Manor, and making friends with Mrs Carey was a top priority. I'll have to feel my way slowly, thought Louise; Michael is different here, he's not the man I thought I knew in London.

Mrs Carey poured Louise a glass of fresh orange juice from a crystal jug into an exquisite crystal glass. 'Do you wish me to serve you tonight, sir?'

'Certainly not.'

'I thought perhaps that tonight, as Mrs Baruch must be tired . . .'

'She's not that tired. Everything *is* cold, isn't it?'

'Yes, sir. Just as you ordered.'

'Then you can leave. We shall serve ourselves. You know I prefer to be left alone.'

'Yes, sir.' Mrs Carey departed.

Well, one thing is certain, thought Louise, feeling increasingly unhappy, Michael has no intention of being friendly with his staff. He is a loner. That is another facet of his character which I didn't know about before. With a sinking heart she wondered how many more things she would find out before her wedding night was over.

Michael was drinking whisky, but because of her pregnancy Louise had cut out alcohol. Now she longed for something stronger than orange juice. They started to eat in silence. Michael seemed disinclined to talk. Mrs Carey had made Gazpacho soup, and all the bits and pieces to go with it, chopped hardboiled eggs and parsley, diced cucumber, and croutons, which any other time Louise would have found delicious. But tonight it seemed to lodge in her throat, and she had difficulty swallowing. The humidity of the orangery combined with the dark shiny leaves of the huge citrus bushes was overpoweringly claustrophobic. She felt sick, and yearned to be in Beattie's untidy, comfortable, *comforting* kitchen. Suddenly the huge mausoleum of a house and Michael's distant manner overwhelmed her. If Beattie had been there, Louise knew that she would have thrown herself into her mother's arms and wept uncontrollably.

'I think perhaps I'd better lie down. I don't feel well.'
For one hysterical moment she visualized Michael's expression if she threw up on to the pristine black and white tiled floor.

Michael was at her side in a moment. 'I should have been more thoughtful. Today has been very tiring for you.'

Almost before she had time to draw a breath Louise found herself upstairs and lying in the middle of a king-sized bed.

'Is this our bedroom?' she asked, struggling to raise herself on her elbows to see. The room was enormous. Eau de nil walls, a white ceiling with an elaborate centre rose and a carved cornice running round the room. The heavy drapes at the huge windows matched the walls, and on the floor was a thick pile carpet in a dusky rose pink. The walls towering up to the high ceiling were bare apart from three paintings. All French Impressionist. From her position on the bed Louise guessed them to be prints of a Cezanne, a Monet and a Pissarro, although none of the painted scenes were familiar to her.

'Lie down,' said Michael. 'Yes, this is our bedroom. On either side there are dressing rooms and bathrooms. Our own suite so that we are completely private.' As they were the only two people in the house apart from the Careys, Louise thought his emphasis on privacy was unnecessary, but said nothing. He felt her brow and placed a glass of iced water in her hand. 'Drink a little. Perhaps I should send for a doctor. We don't want anything to happen to the baby.'

'Nonsense, you don't need to send for any doctor,' said Louise, who was feeling better now. 'The orangery was rather stuffy. I'm all right now.'

'But the baby . . .'

'The baby is fine.' He is much more concerned about the baby than he is me, she thought. The hope she'd been nurturing that Michael was falling in love with her for herself alone had already begun to fade since they arrived at Offerton, and now it began to wither even faster. It was the baby he was in love with, and she was foolish to deceive herself into believing anything else. She took a sip of the water, and placing the glass on the bedside cabinet lay back against the pillows. The earrings Michael had given her pricked uncomfortably so Louise took them off. Then her spirits surged again. He had given her these priceless earrings and sent them with that wonderfully romantic message. Of course he felt something. She was being silly. 'I'm sorry. I feel better now. Let's go back down.'

'Definitely not. I'm not letting you take any chances. Especially not at this stage of your pregnancy.'

His concern was comforting. He did care. Louise relaxed and looked again at the paintings. 'They are beautiful prints. I love them all.'

'Not prints,' said Michael in a scandalized tone. 'They are the genuine article. Worth a lot more now than when I bought them at auction. In fact they were my first investments when I started out in the business world.'

'Investments? But surely you wouldn't sell them?'

'If necessary, of course,' said Michael. 'That is what investments are for.' Louise glanced at the earrings still lying in the palm of her hand, and wondered if they too had been an investment. Artificial light enhanced their brilliance, giving them a life of their own. Michael saw her looking. 'They were not an investment,' he said, coming to sit on the side of the bed. 'I bought them especially for you. A wedding gift. All brides should have one.'

Veronique loves the country. We . . . Veronique loves big houses. 'What did you give Veronique when you married her?' The question was out before she could stop it, and Michael's reaction was violent and unexpected.

'I do not want to talk about Veronique or that part of my life,' he shouted. The veins on his forehead stood out as he nearly exploded with anger, and Louise shrank back away from him. 'That subject is taboo. Do you hear me? *Taboo!* I never want to hear you mention her name. Not ever again.' Then he walked out of the bedroom, slamming the door behind him.

Louise gasped, letting her pent-up breath out in a sigh of relief. Thank God he'd gone. Then she cursed herself, and her thoughtlessness. Damn! What a fool I am. Why did I bring up her name? But she knew the reason why. It was because she could feel Veronique's presence in the house, and because Michael had inadvertently referred to her twice himself, which reinforced the feeling that she had not really left. Veronique! Veronique! That was who he was thinking of from the moment they had driven through the gates of the manor house. Louise suddenly realized that she did not even know what Michael's ex-wife looked like. She'd not been particularly curious before. Jealousy was not something she had bargained for when she'd married Michael. She'd thought then that the past was past and would remain that way. But now . . . now it was different. Now, she was not so sure.

Putting the diamonds aside, Louise got up and wandered over to the window. Outside, the park was in total darkness. Pushing up the old-fashioned sash window a little and leaning out, she breathed in the cool night air. All was silent save for a sudden harsh screech, screech. An owl out hunting; then she saw it, a dark shape drifting smoothly through the air before disappearing behind one of the lime trees. Now all was silent again, the owl might never have been.

Just like Veronique; she might never have been, because now she has gone, and I am here, Louise told herself firmly. I am the new mistress of Offerton, the new Mrs Baruch. But an uncomfortable image remained. Although out of sight, she knew the owl was still there, terrorizing the mice and other small animals hiding in the grass, and in much the same way so was Veronique. But Louise was resolute. Her memory is not going to worry me. I won't let it. All second wives must have doubts about their predecessors, but I will make my own mark on this house, and our life will be good. Michael is mine now, not hers; he is the father of my child and my husband. If our marriage is to work and be harmonious, she lectured herself sternly, I must guard my tongue, and remember that Michael married me because he wanted to. I did not force him into the liaison.

Michael eventually came back and came straight to the point. 'I'm sorry I lost my temper and shouted, darling. But you do understand, don't you? The question surprised and unnerved me.'

'Of course I do.' Louise was contrite. He did truly look sorry. 'I was very tactless, Michael, and I'm sorry too.'

Michael slid his hands down and fondled her breasts. 'Beautiful,' he murmured; tracing the delicate feathering of veins leading into the darkening blush of the nipple. 'You are changing already because of the baby. Come to bed.'

Once Michael starting making love to her all the doubts about the house and Veronique seemed ridiculous. It's my hormones, Louise told herself. They're all in a turmoil because of the baby. That is why I'm so irrational. Then she wrapped her long legs around Michael and gave herself up to the pleasure of feeling him move inside her. He really is a marvellous lover, she thought dreamily, he knows exactly how to make me feel . . .

'Aah!' she gasped as she began to climax, then burying her chin in his shoulder she shuddered in ecstasy.

Michael said nothing. He moved rhythmically, in perfect control, prolonging her climax as long as possible before finally letting himself come.

Later, Michael was sound asleep beside her. Louise was warm and happy and contented. Stretching languorously she turned in towards Michael. What had she been worrying about. Veronique – poof! Smiling, she whispered the word under her breath. 'Poof.' Veronique was about as substantial as the dandelion clocks whose seeds she used to blow away with one breath when she was a child.

CHAPTER 11

Chateau les Greves lay bathed in moonlight. From her bedroom window Veronique could see straight across the vast expanse of the bay of Michel en Greve. The tide had just turned and now the sea was racing in, a rush of curling, coruscating foam, the dark water greedy in its haste to cover the miles of smooth, glittering sand. Far away in the distance the winking lights of Loquirec sparkled, intermittent flashes of light leaping the spumes to die a silent death in the glistening darkness of the sea. On her right the towering dark cliffs which formed the headland leading to Pointe de Sehar were in total darkness. No lights there, everyone in the few isolated farmhouses, clinging precariously to the windblown headland, must be asleep. But Veronique could not sleep. Impossible, absolutely impossible. She paced the room, restless, excited, her emotions racing like the sea outside on the sands of Michel en Greve. The news from England had been good.

Morning found Veronique in the small breakfast room at the side of the large *salle à manger* with a vast array of wallpaper books and colour charts spread out all over the breakfast table. 'Ah, thank you, Andrea,' she said, making room for the breakfast tray as Andrea walked in.

Andrea Louedec poured the coffee, at the same time

trying to see what sort of wall covering it was that Veronique was studying so intently. 'Jean-Paul came up especially from the village with a dozen of the first batch of croissants from the *boulangerie*,' she said. She twisted her head sideways to get a better view; surely that couldn't be nursery wallpaper? 'I know you like them when they're really fresh.'

'Delicious.' Veronique took one and dunked it in her coffee. 'You spoil me.'

'Will there be anything else?' Andrea could see clearly now. It *was* nursery paper. Blue, scattered with pictures of teddy bears, rabbits and other assorted animals.

'No thank you. I'll bring the tray down to the kitchen myself when I've finished. Then I shall be busy with this,' she indicated the books and charts, 'for the rest of the day.'

'You're decorating again?'

'Yes, the small room next to my bedroom.'

Veronique smiled vaguely, and Andrea noticed that the pupils of her eyes had narrowed down to the smallest pinpricks. Her eyes, usually so dark, were a diffused grey, and the housekeeper had the uneasy feeling of seeing right into Veronique's head, only to find there was nothing there to see, because all her thoughts were somewhere else. For a moment she toyed with the idea of mentioning that she knew Veronique had been out walking during the night, but then decided against it. However, she could not resist asking about the proposed new decorations. 'Is the new room to be a nursery?'

'Of course,' said Veronique, turning to another page decorated with Micky Mouse characters. 'I'll need one soon. I'm not going to live here on my own for ever, you know.'

'But she's only just divorced.' Andrea told Paul all about the new decorations when he came in at twelve noon promptly for his *dejeuner*. 'And I've not seen any sign of another man about. So how can she need a nursery?'

'It's none of our business,' said Paul, refusing to show an interest, much to his wife's fury.

'But there is something strange about it, and something strange about *her*. You should have seen her expression. It wasn't normal.'

Her husband let his soup spoon fall with an angry clink back into the soup bowl. 'Keep your thoughts to yourself, Andrea. I want to stay here until I retire. If Madame Veronique hears you saying she's crazy we'll both get the sack.'

'Don't worry, I won't say anything.'

'To anyone,' said Paul sternly, 'and that means your friend Marie-Therese in the Bar Tabac in the village.'

'My lips are sealed,' said Andrea, pouring herself some soup. She sat down opposite her husband. 'All the same though, you must admit that it is odd.'

Paul said nothing; merely helped himself to another bowlful of steaming *haricot au lard*.

At Offerton Manor life slipped into a pleasant routine which was much better than Louise had anticipated. It hadn't taken her long to establish a firm friendship with Lizzie Carey and her husband, Dick. Helped by the fact that as soon as Lizzie and Beattie met, in spite of the disparity in their life-styles, they had immediately liked one another. Now they swopped recipes and gossip as if they'd known each other all their lives.

Both Lizzie and Dick doted on Eugenia and Gordon's children, although Louise took care only to invite them when she knew Michael would be away. Between them they all helped breathe life into the once dead hulk of Offerton Manor, the house often ringing with laughter and the sound of running children's feet. And to everyone's surprise, Rupert had attached himself to Dick and shown a keen interest in gardening.

'The first thing he's ever really concentrated on,' said Gordon. Rupert was proudly showing him a bunch of radishes which he'd grown himself.

'It's because he can see the results,' said Dick.

'From tiny seeds I could hardly see, to this, in four weeks,' said Rupert triumphantly, crunching into a juicy red radish.

Michael was never mentioned. The Careys were much too discreet. But Louise was sure they thought him cold and aloof, which he was, particularly towards them. Veronique was not mentioned either, and because of that Louise felt unable to broach the subject herself.

Michael quite often stayed in London, and Louise herself went up to her office at least twice a week, although she always returned to Offerton at night. The rest of the time she contacted Tina and the agency from the office which she'd set up in the house. When Michael was at home he was loving and attentive most of the time. But he was unpredictable, and Louise felt an increasing sense of disappointment and confusion. Sometimes she thought she loved him, especially when he was gentle and tender, and at other times she almost hated him; he could be so aloof and remote. Apart from his mood changes, she knew nothing more about him after three months of marriage than she had when they had first married.

He never talked about his childhood. Louise had even read his book again looking for clues, but apart from the fact that it said he was brought up in Battersea after the war, there was nothing.

Beattie had said when she read the book, 'Perhaps he's got a hang-up because he lived on the wrong side of the river?'

'What difference does that make?'

'To some people, a lot. Why don't you ask him?'

'Mother, I can't,' said Louise.

'Why not? You're married to him.' Beattie couldn't see what the problem was, and Louise couldn't explain.

She couldn't tell her mother that it was as if there was an invisible wall beyond which he did not allow her to step.

Veronique, of course, was never mentioned, and Louise noticed that there was not one photograph, not one personal item of hers left in the house. All trace of Veronique had disappeared completely from Offerton Manor.

In the greenhouse one July morning, picking a fat lettuce for lunch – Louise now ate with the Carey's when Michael was away – she watched a snail crawling slowly across one of the panes of glass. Picking it up she threw it to the relative safety of the dense spinach patch outside. Dick exterminated snails and slugs ruthlessly and Louise hated finding their corpses. Back in the greenhouse she looked at the faint silvery trail where the snail had crawled. 'A creature as small as that has left his mark in this world,' she said out loud, 'but of Veronique there is nothing, not even the faintest whiff of perfume.'

'Madame always used her own special perfume. It was especially made for her in Grasse.' Lizzie Carey stood in the doorway of the greenhouse. Because of her generous bosom, small hips and very thin legs, and her habit of favouring red blouses and tight brown skirts, Beattie had dubbed her 'Mrs Robin'. She took the lettuce from Louise. 'Sometimes when I go in to clean the rooms they used to use, I think I can still smell that perfume.'

'I didn't realize our rooms were different.'

'Other side of the house, dear,' said Lizzie, 'and a good thing too. The rooms are sunnier. Your side is much more cheerful.'

'Did you like her?' As Lizzie had volunteered the information about Veronique, Louise now dared to ask.

Mrs Carey stopped, and putting the lettuce down on the path, pulled some radishes and spring onions from the neat rows radiating out in geometric precision from the pathways. 'I didn't dislike her,' she said. 'But I didn't know her. She always kept herself to herself.' She stood up, perspiring slightly from the effort of pulling the vegetables.

Louise felt a sense of relief. How good it was to hear someone talking naturally about Veronique.

'Lizzie,' she said carefully, 'Michael and I never talk about Veronique. It's as if that part of his life never happened. That is the way he wants it. But I . . .' she faltered, unsure of what to say next.

Lizzie Carey looked at her kindly. 'It can't be easy being the second wife,' she said. 'Not that I've had any experience, having been married to my Dick for nearly forty years, but I can imagine it. There's bound to be a degree of jealousy.'

'Oh no, I'm not jealous. Not really.' But I am, thought Louise as the words were leaving her lips. I'm jealous because Michael only married me for the child I'm bearing, and because once he must have loved Veronique enough to marry her, even if that love did eventually die. 'It's just that I know absolutely nothing about her,' she continued. 'There are no photographs so I don't know what she looked like, no one speaks of her so I don't know what sort of person she was. And yet I sense that she is still here. Maybe if I could get to the reality I could get rid of my demons.'

'Demons?' Lizzie raised her eyebrows. 'More than one?'

'Twin demons. Jealousy and doubt,' replied Louise, pulling a rueful face. 'You were right. I am jealous. I know perhaps you will never believe it, Mrs Carey, but before I married and became pregnant I was such a sensible woman. I always knew what I wanted and where I was going. Now I'm not sure at all.'

Ah, but who wanted a baby, and was determined to get one? asked her conscience. The answer, as Louise knew, was that she had what she wanted, but there was a price.

Mrs Carey began to walk slowly along the kitchen garden path back towards the house. 'The first Mrs Baruch was very beautiful.' She stopped and looked at Louise, and then continued walking. 'In fact, now I come to think of it she was very like you. Tall, slim, with pale skin, dark eyes, dark hair. But your hair is short and beautifully styled, and hers was very long, almost waist length. Sometimes she let it fly free, and other times it was piled on top of her head. As for her personality, she was distant. Quite unlike you. In that respect she was similar to Mr Baruch. There was a wall around her, and she lived behind it. The only time she really came alive was when she was with Mr Baruch. They adored each other. Oh dear.' Mrs Carey stopped again, her face becoming almost as red as the blouse she was wearing. 'I'm sorry. That was a tactless thing to say.'

Louise shook her head. 'I know that. Robert Lacroix told me. He also said that he was very surprised when they split up.'

Lizzie looked relieved. 'Well, to tell you the truth, dear,' she said confidentially, 'so was I. But there you are. You never can tell what people are really feeling.'

'Yes,' said Louise, wondering if Michael would ever adore her. 'Did you know, Lizzie,' she said slowly, 'that statistically, second marriages have a greater chance of not lasting?'

'Is that what is worrying you, dear?'

'No. Once I've delivered this baby safely, *nothing* will worry me,' said Louise. 'I shall have a child at last.'

'Now that I *can* understand.' Louise was startled, and Lizzie noticed. 'Dick and I are not childless through choice,' she said a trifle sharply.

Louise suddenly realized how lucky she was that her own longing had been fulfilled.

They reached the house. 'I'd better go and work in my office,' she said. 'There is probably a pile of faxes to be answered.' She paused. 'Thank you for talking to me, Lizzie. I feel better about Veronique now. She's not quite so mysterious.' Not true, nagged a small inner voice. She's even more mysterious. Why *did* Michael divorce her? And if she adored him why did she give him up so easily?

90

CHAPTER 12

'I think it's Mrs Baruch on the telephone for you, sir.'

'What do you mean, you think it's Mrs Baruch?' Michael looked at his watch. 'Nonsense! My wife is on the London train at this moment on her way up to her office, and we are meeting for lunch. At least I hope we are. I did ask you to book it, Yvonne.'

'I mean,' Yvonne hesitated, and Michael could tell his secretary was embarrassed, 'I think it's the first Mrs Baruch.'

'You'd better put her through then.'

'Hello. Michael?'

'Veronique! Is there a problem?'

'Yes and no. I am very well, but I'm lonely. The waiting seems so long. Besides I need your advice, and you didn't ring two weeks ago as you said you would.'

Michael was silent as a wave of guilt broke over him. It was true he had broken his promise. The first time ever as far as Veronique was concerned; and he knew why. He'd broken that promise because he was a coward, unable to face the conflict of emotions beginning to erupt inside him. How could he tell her that he was becoming more and more confused. That their original agreement made less and less sense with every week that went by, and that he was beginning to think that their plans were wrong. What would she say if he told her that now he was not sure that he could go through with it?

91

'I'm sorry,' he said at last.

'Come to France this weekend,' said Veronique. 'Let me show you the changes I've made to the chateau. Let me show you how I've spent your money.'

'I'm not sure that's a good idea.' Michael had a momentary vision of a dark vortex from which there was no escape, a vortex of his own making.

In France, it seemed that Veronique could sense his unease, for she said firmly, 'Michael, if you are having doubts then it is all the more important that we should meet. We need to talk.'

Michael made up his mind. She was right. They *did* need to talk. 'I'll fly myself to St Brieuc this afternoon, and drive down to Chateau les Greves in a hire car. Expect me in time for dinner.'

Louise waited for Michael in Soho Square. The Italian restaurant where they planned to lunch was in nearby Frith Street. Not far to walk. The large flat leaves of the encircling plane trees provided welcome shade against the hot August sun. By now Louise needed to wear maternity dresses, and was wearing a pale lemon cotton one, the coolest thing she could find for such a hot day. She leaned back on one of the wooden benches and slipped off her shoes. Nearly seven months pregnant now, she thought, resting her hand on her swollen belly. The baby kicked as if in protest at being disturbed by her hand, and Louise smiled. Maybe her motives for procuring a child had been less than perfect, but nothing could detract from the joy she felt every time the baby moved. The thought of the small baby boy growing inside her womb was the most exciting and wonderful thing that had ever happened to her. Of that there was no doubt.

'Darling.' Michael came up behind her, and bending over, placed a kiss in the nape of her neck. 'Not too hot I hope.'

'No, it's perfect here in the shade.'

Michael has changed these last few weeks, she thought contentedly. He still hasn't said that he loves me, but these days he's not so distant, and most of the time he does seem happier. Perhaps he is beginning to care. Although she had to admit also that there were still the worrying times when he seemed to slip away into a world of his own, which Louise sensed was an unhappy world. She longed to ask what was troubling him, but never dared. Time had taught her to accept that Michael would only tell her what he wanted her to know. Probing would do no good at all, and might even harm the rapport they had managed to establish. I'm learning patience, Louise thought now, the hard way.

'Come on, we don't want to lose our table.' Michael took her arm and together they walked from the shady square towards Frith Street. Suddenly he shivered.

Louise, feeling the shiver, looked up at him. 'Someone walked over your grave,' she said lightly.

'You could say that.' Michael's voice was sombre. He touched her cheek gently. 'Darling, I know you are going to kill me, but I'm afraid that I won't be home this weekend. Unexpected business problems have cropped up in France, and I shall have to go there.'

'Never mind. I shall be quite happy spending the weekend quietly at Offerton. I've had a very hectic morning at the agency, and look like having an even more hectic afternoon. I shall be pleased to put my feet up and do nothing but snooze and read.'

'Perhaps you should give up the agency. You don't need the money. I have plenty of that.'

The temptation to do nothing was great, but something always held Louise in check. The thought of being totally dependent on someone else was frightening. She never had been, not since the day she left school. Marriage hadn't changed anything, and her own money in the bank gave her an added sense of security. Too often she'd seen it in other women, the vulnerability of having nothing. What if Michael grew tired of her as he had done Veronique, and they divorced? Louise couldn't bear the thought of being bought off; it would be too humiliating. But none of these thoughts could be voiced to Michael; it would be hurtful. Besides, she doubted that he could even begin to understand her reasoning. So she said, 'I'd go mad with boredom. I need something to occupy my mind.'

'Do some voluntary work. Then you could do it when you felt like it.'

'No, I need the agency. It's a part of my life, and I like knowing that I have something of my own.' There, she'd voiced part of it.

'You mean I don't give you enough.'

'Michael!' Louise turned and stared. His expression was dark and brooding. 'I don't want to quarrel. You know perfectly well that I don't mean that.'

'Then give it up and take care of my child.'

Surprise and annoyance at his sudden attack on her independence had the effect of making Louise even more determined. 'No, Michael,' she said quietly. 'I will not give up the agency. But you can be sure of one thing, neither will I neglect *our* child. Ours, mark you, not just yours.'

It seemed her words struck a chord somewhere within him, for there was a long silence, then he said, 'I know,' and his black mood evaporated as suddenly as it had appeared. He smiled, and said, 'Of course I know you won't neglect our baby, because you are sensible, loving and very well organized. All the things a man could wish for in a wife.'

Louise laughed. 'Good grief, Michael. Now you're making me sound like a saint!'

They reached the restaurant, and, after effusive enquiries as to their well-being, the head waiter showed them through to the garden area and sat them at a table shaded by a huge and ancient mulberry tree.

Michael took the proffered menu from the waiter and

smiled at her across the table. Pleased, Louise smiled back, glad that the dark look had faded now. Suddenly he reached across the table and took her hand. 'I wish I didn't have to go to France this weekend,' he said.

Louise twined her fingers in his. 'I told you I understand. One weekend is neither here nor there.'

'But,' Michael hesitated, gently rubbing the palm of her hand with the ball of his thumb, seeming to fumble for the right words, 'I still wish I didn't have to go. I wish I didn't have to leave you.'

There was something in his voice. A longing, almost a wistfulness. Something Louise had never heard before. It gave her hope, and courage. The courage to ask the question she'd been wanting to ask for months.

'Michael, do you love me? Just a little bit?'

There was a long, long silence. Michael continued holding her hand, still gently rubbing the palm with his thumb. Then at last he spoke. 'Yes, I think perhaps I do,' he said.

No matter that it hadn't been an unqualified declaration of affection; it was enough. If someone had handed Louise the crown jewels on a plate she couldn't have been more ecstatic. 'Oh, Michael,' she said.

'I thought I would feel nothing,' said Michael softly, almost as if speaking to himself. An expression of melancholy flickered momentarily across his face, then he smiled. 'But life is full of strange twists. I suppose our emotions are never totally under our own control. No matter how much we might like to think they are.'

The baby kicked violently as if to remind Louise of his presence. She patted the bulge beneath the lemon dress. 'Our baby is a love-child after all,' she said softly. 'He may not have started out that way but he is now.'

'A love-child.' Michael savoured the words. 'I like that.'

Louise slid her hand away. 'Excuse me, but I must. They're clip-ons, and they're killing me.' She removed a pair of yellow button earrings which matched the dress, and rubbed her earlobes. 'That's better.'

'You never wear the diamonds I gave you.'

'Well, I . . .' Louise looked down at the tablecloth, and began nervously pleating the edge. What could she say? Michael might have just declared his love for her, but that didn't mean the subject of Veronique was no longer taboo. The truth was she couldn't bring herself to wear them because every time she looked at them she was reminded of their quarrel about Veronique on their wedding night.

'They remind you of our quarrel about Veronique.' Michael accurately guessed her thoughts. Louise nodded. 'Well, forget it. I've often wanted to apologize again, properly. But there has never been an appropriate moment until now.'

'I'm sorry too for what I said that night,' said Louise. 'It seems stupid now, but at the time I was insecure and feeling hurt.'

'I promise I'll never hurt you, Louise. Not willingly,' said Michael slowly. 'No, never willingly,' he repeated.

Louise looked up. He was no longer smiling. The sadness was there once more. 'What's wrong, Michael? You look so worried. What are you thinking about?'

'My trip to France,' said Michael truthfully. 'But my problems there are business problems. They have nothing to do with you. I'll get it all sorted out this weekend.' He turned to the menu. 'Now what do you want to eat?'

CHAPTER 13

The Cessna turned and banked as Michael positioned the plane ready for the descent into the small airport of St Brieuc. Below him the distinctive mass of rocks which formed the rose granite coast of Brittany glowed pink in the evening sun; the sea was a brilliant blue, each wave tipped with gold from the setting sun. Beyond the coastline Michael could see the dark, undulating shapes of the Black Mountains surrounded by neat patchwork, the fields of the farms. The scene had a timeless tranquillity about it, the land hushed now, ready for the night and sleep.

Michael felt anything but tranquil. He had not seen Veronique since that day in the court in London. Speaking on the telephone was one thing, but actually meeting face to face was quite another. He felt peculiarly vulnerable and defenceless, which he knew was ridiculous because Veronique was the defenceless person, not he.

The formalities after landing were brief. Carrying his one small bag of luggage Michael made his way towards the car park where the hire cars were kept.

'Michael!' He turned. 'I'm here.'

It was Veronique, running towards him, her long dark hair streaming behind in the slight breeze like seaweed. In her green dress she looked like a mermaid who had escaped from the sea. The next moment she was in his

97

arms, and his senses were swamped with the unique perfume she always wore. For a split-second he thought of Louise, blooming like a tulip in her yellow dress, but the image was pushed out of the way, out of focus by Veronique's pale face, her dark eyes and her dazzling smile. Her physical presence hypnotized him with a powerful intensity, and once her mouth was on his Michael knew he was lost. He couldn't break their agreement, he couldn't desert her, because he loved her with a passion which swept away all barriers. A love beyond reason. Nothing else mattered, only his love for her. It was a weakness, but Michael knew there was nothing he could do. All was forgotten in the erotic movement of her mouth beneath his. Clasping her tightly in his arms, Michael wondered how he had ever had the courage to let her go.

Veronique drove to the chateau. 'I know the way, darling. All the little back lanes. You sit and relax.'

Michael sat back and watched the countryside slide past. The fields of artichokes, silvery green spiky leaves with the occasional burst of violent purple where a plant had gone to seed. Field after field of maize, taller than a man, the dark green spears tipped with brown now in August; in another few weeks it would be harvested and stored away as winter feed for the creamy coloured Charolais cattle grazing in adjoining fields. 'Do the Louedecs know I'm coming?'

'Yes, but don't worry, they are not given to gossip. No one in the village of Michel en Greve will know that I have a visitor. We certainly don't want your new wife knowing that her husband is visiting his old wife.'

'No,' said Michael, 'we don't, and I'd rather we didn't talk about her.' Now that he was here with Veronique his life with Louise seemed unreal, although he was unable to stop the sick feeling of guilt churning his stomach. What had he done? What had they done, all of them? How was it to be resolved without anyone getting hurt?

'Fine by me,' said Veronique happily. 'I don't want to talk about her, I don't even want to think about her.' They came to a crossroads, Michel en Greve was signposted left, but Veronique turned to the right, driving up a steep winding lane that led steadily upwards.

'Where are we going?' Michael peered out into the now semi-darkness. There was nothing to be seen as high banks rose precipitously either side of the lane.

'To renew our love in the pure free air. Where the wind will blow away all memories of the last year.' The car emerged from the deep cutting and was suddenly exposed to the bleakness of the headland. Here the land was devoid of vegetation except for the fronds of hardy tamarisk interspersed with bracken and sloe bushes, all bent and stunted by the wind.

Veronique parked the car and led Michael down a dangerous, sloping path that wound its way ever downwards between the sloes and bracken. 'Is it safe?' Not knowing the way, Michael continually stumbled over the enormous lumps of granite protruding into the path at awkward intervals.

'Of course it's safe.' Veronique had to shout now above the pounding of the sea on the jagged rocks below. They scrambled down the steep path for about ten minutes before Veronique stopped by the side of an enormous menhir, one of the huge perpendicular lumps of granite for which Brittany is famous. 'Here,' she said, drawing Michael down with her behind the stone, 'where we are sheltered by the menhir and tamarisk, and the ground is covered with sea pinks, and wild pansies. This is my special place.' She slid her arms around his neck and kissed him on the mouth. As she drew back Michael could see that her eyes were bright with tears. 'It's been such a long time,' she said. 'Such a long, long time.'

As his body covered hers Michael had the strange feeling that he was slipping back in time. Not the time they'd had together before, but a different time, one which held the seeds of danger and destruction. For a moment he was afraid, and the sea thundering on the rocks below seemed like a hungry monster waiting to swallow them up. But then his brain ceased to function. The firmness of Veronique's small breasts, the narrowness of her upward thrusting hips, was a potent magic, scouring his mind of all thoughts save her. Undressing each other between kisses, their naked bodies cleaved together as if drawn by some gigantic magnetic force. Sea, sky and wind all merged together into one pounding rhythm, matching the frenzied reunion of their bodies. Every last vestige of self-control was blown away and Michael heard himself crying out as the world turned inside out and he succumbed to the all enveloping softness of Veronique's body. Hers, and yet not hers, for she was part of him. They were one, and had been made for each other since the beginning of time.

Afterwards they lay, still clamped together, her lips in the hollow of his shoulders, his mouth in her tangled hair.

'I love you, Veronique,' said Michael.

'I know.' She smiled in the darkness. 'You always will.'

CHAPTER 14

Gordon's children spilled out of his battered estate car the moment it pulled to a halt in front of the portico of the house. Like the tribe of Israel, thought Louise, watching them from the top of the steps with amusement. Clad only in faded shorts, tee-shirts and sandals, their skins tanned a healthy brown, they looked the picture of youthful exuberance.

Tara, the baby, now eighteen months old, made a bee-line for Louise the moment she saw her. Her progress up the long line of steps was uncertain, but determined, her fat legs hindered somewhat by the bulky padding of her nappy. Louise remembered Tara at Christmas, when she couldn't walk and had been dumped in her arms. Baby Tara, little did she know that she had been the catalyst in her life. Without her perhaps she would never have realized her need for a child, the need which had propelled her into Michael's arms, and the charmed life she now saw opening up before her.

Robert Lacroix's car pulled up almost immediately after Gordon's, and Beattie got out after Mr Poo who, sensing freedom the moment the car door opened, bounded out with an unusual show of energy.

'That child really ought to be potty trained by now,' said Beattie disapprovingly, watching Tara's unsteady progress towards Louise.

'She will when she's ready,' Eugenia replied.

'I sat Gordon and Louise on pots almost as soon as they were born.'

'Now you know why we're both a little peculiar.' Gordon grinned at his mother's exaggeration.

Eugenia laughed. 'You poor little things.' As usual she was completely unfazed by her mother-in-law's criticism. She let her children grow up naturally, without undue guidance on her part. As a result they were happy and uninhibited, and possessed a self-confidence well in advance of their years.

I wonder what sort of mother I'll be, thought Louise. Possessive? Strict? A worrier? Or just loving? She hoped she would be loving. Surely love was enough.

'I've told Robert he can stay. He's off duty and has nothing special to do today,' said Beattie as soon as she reached Louise. 'He gave me a lift here.'

So it was agreed and Robert helped Dick Carey carry the blankets and picnic baskets down to the small river which meandered along the edge of the park. A slight hollow in the land made it a perfect suntrap, and two ancient horse-chestnut trees grew conveniently near the edge of the water, giving plenty of shade if needed.

'I've put netting across the river at two points, between the shallowest part. So it will be quite safe for the young ones to splash about,' said Dick.

The children couldn't get their clothes off quickly enough, and were soon screaming with laughter as they plunged about, splashing wildly in the cool river water.

Louise sat in the shade and Robert sat with her. Beattie, Gordon and Eugenia paddled in the river, keeping an eye on the children. Even Mr Poo, who Louise always said was the laziest dog on earth, took to the water before eventually retiring to the bank with a sneezing fit.

'Don't you find this boring? A rather noisy family picnic?' Louise looked curiously at Robert. He was lounging back beside her, chewing a piece of grass. Since their first meeting she'd learned more more about him. He was extremely famous in his field of neurology. Not only did he look after patients at the hospital in Winchester, he did research and regularly travelled to London and other countries to speak on his research papers. He was a very busy man, yet very modest, and, Louise thought, probably rather lonely.

Now he was relaxed, and his brown eyes sparkled as he smiled, and Louise found herself thinking what a lovely colour they were. Clear, golden and uncomplicated. The colour of a forest pool. It seems that every time I meet him I discover something new, she reflected. Almost without her realizing it he'd become her best friend and a necessity in her life.

'I like the noise of children,' he said. 'It makes me realize that I should have put down some permanent roots years ago and had a family of my own.'

'Why didn't you?'

'Looking back I can see now that I had a tramline mentality. All I could think about was medicine. Perhaps if my parents had lived I might have been different. But apart from Veronique I had no family, and my whole life was medicine. Still is, come to that.'

'What happened to them? Your parents, I mean.'

'They were killed in a road accident in France. Veronique and I were both at school in England at the time, so we stayed. I bought a house with the money we inherited, hired a housekeeper, and the rest you know. I went to medical school and Veronique married Michael.'

'She must have done something before she married.'

'Of course she did. She did a Fine Art course and then worked for Sotheby's specializing in French Impressionist painters. That was how she met Michael. She advised him on some purchases.'

So she probably chose those paintings hanging in the bedroom, thought Louise. A few months ago that fact would have upset her, but not now, not now when she felt secure. Veronique was no longer a threat, and never had been, except in her imagination.

She turned to Robert. 'I can understand how medicine has become your whole life, because the work you do is so important.'

'Not important enough to shut myself off from the mainstream of ordinary life,' said Robert. 'But I didn't realize that I'd done it until it was too late.'

'Too late!' Louise rounded on him indignantly. 'What rubbish you do talk. Of course it's not too late. You must go out more often, find yourself a nice girl, and then marry her.'

'Easier said than done,' replied Robert. Then turning towards her he said, 'Do you believe in love at first sight?'

'Love at first sight,' Louise repeated the words thoughtfully. She thought of her immediate attraction to Michael, but wasn't sure whether it was love or need which had forged the initial attraction. 'I'm not sure,' she said slowly.

'You surprise me. I was expecting you to say yes immediately. You and Michael seemed drawn together from the moment you set eyes on each other. If that wasn't love at first sight, what was it?'

'I suppose it must have been,' she said. It was easier to say that than try to explain.

Robert lay back, positioning his head comfortably amongst the knotted roots of the old tree. 'That's what I thought,' he said. 'Michael is a very lucky man.'

Louise leaned on one elbow and looked down at him. 'Oh, I do wish you could find someone nice and fall in love,' she said impulsively. 'I'd like you to be happy.'

Robert opened his eyes and smiled up at her. 'Thank you, Louise,' he said.

'I shall look out for someone.'

'No, don't.' Robert reached up and softly traced the line of her jawbone. 'The falling in love part is easy,' he said. 'It's the being happy ever after which is difficult.'

'Everyone deserves some happiness.' Louise heard her voice waver. The touch of Robert's fingers on her cheek was strangely unnerving, and with a shock she realized that she wanted him to caress her again. Disconcerted, she moved slightly, putting herself out of range.

Robert folded his hands across his body and closed his eyes. 'Yes, everyone deserves it, but not all are destined to get it.'

Louise leaned back again against the trunk of the tree. 'I suppose you're right,' she said. 'Life isn't always fair.'

'No,' said Robert. 'It most certainly isn't. I see a lot of unhappiness in my work.'

He's sad, thought Louise, and I wish I could help him. Unable to think of anything to say she reached out a hand and squeezed his shoulder, and Robert, still with his eyes closed, smiled.

'Time for the picnic,' Eugenia called. The blanket set down near the edge of the river was now piled with food.

Lizzie Carey arrived with flasks of ice-cold lemonade for the children, and hot tea for the adults. She brought her knitting as well and settled herself down between Eugenia and Beattie, who had Tara firmly wedged between her knees.

'Aren't the children good,' said Lizzie.

'You can have them any time.' Gordon joined them, and sat cross-legged beside them.

'Like a family of gypsies,' grumbled Beattie good-naturedly as the children, barely stopping to dry themselves, excitedly tore open packets of sandwiches as if they'd not eaten for a week.

'And you the gypsy queen,' teased Louise.

Beattie, wearing a flowing dress of paper-thin Indian cotton dyed a violent purple, and with her hair, now a dark henna red, tied up with a gold coloured scarf, did indeed look like a gypsy queen.

'I can't imagine you any other way,' said Robert.

'Neither can I,' said Louise. 'I may have hated having a hippy mother when I was at school, but now I'm glad you are. It makes you less of a mother, more of a friend.'

'I shall take that as a compliment,' said Beattie.

'That's how Louise means it, don't you,' said Gordon. 'We're both glad you're not normal.'

'Normality can be terribly boring,' said Beattie, lapping up the attention and feeding Tara with small squares of salmon sandwiches.

'Like me,' said Lizzie. 'I'm normal, and boring.' She sighed. 'But it's the way I'm made.'

Louise smiled at her affectionately. 'Not boring, but sensible,' she said. 'Some of us need to be. Can you imagine a whole world full of people like Beattie?'

Robert suddenly laughed. 'Yes,' he said. 'There'd be chaos.'

'I thought you liked me.' Beattie was slightly indignant.

'I do, but I can only take chaos in small doses.'

'So you see,' Louise told Lizzie, 'sensible people like us are needed.'

'If you're so sensible, my girl,' said Beattie, suddenly serious, 'you wouldn't have made some of the mistakes you have.'

Louise flushed. She knew her mother was referring to her marriage. Beattie still didn't approve of Michael, and never let Louise forget it.

'Everyone is entitled to make some mistakes.' Robert smiled, diffusing Beattie's unexpected flare of ill-humour. 'Come on, admit it. You must have made some.'

'All the mistakes I've made,' said Beattie, 'have been on purpose. So they don't count.'

'Oh, do shut up, Mum, and have a piece of fudge cake.' Gordon waved the plate under her nose.

'I can't. I'm on a diet.'

'Since when?'

'Since tomorrow,' said Beattie, taking the largest piece of cake.

106

Everyone laughed and Lizzie's knitting needles started busily clicking again.

But for Louise her mother's remarks had caused another ripple in the previously smooth surface of the day. The first one had been her reaction to the touch of Robert's hand. She glanced across at him. He was laughing and talking to Eugenia, while Milton, his shock of dark hair even more untidy because it was wet, held his hand and gazed up at him with rapt adoration. With alarm Louise suddenly realized that she was looking at Robert for the first time as a man, and not as an extension of her brother. Even more alarming was the fact that she found him very attractive. A woman who is seven months pregnant, she told herself sternly, has no business looking at any man!

The baby suddenly kicked in Louise's womb, and everything swung back to normal, much to her relief.

Eugenia started collecting the picnic things together. 'We should do this more often. If the weather holds, perhaps we'll manage another picnic before the end of summer.'

'Not long now before the autumn term starts.' Gordon, with Lizzie Carey helping, started changing the children into dry clothes, while Beattie sorted out Tara.

'I won't be able to come and help Dick with the garden when school starts,' moaned Rupert crossly.

'You can come at the weekends,' said Lizzie, then suddenly looked embarrassed. 'Oh no, I forgot. Mr Baruch will be at home then.'

Louise felt cross. Why couldn't Michael be more sociable?

'This is a weekend, and we're here now.' Milton as usual had been following the conversation very closely.

'And Michael's in France.' Louise tried to cheer up Rupert. 'Perhaps he'll go more often. Then you can come.'

'I sincerely hope not.' Robert's voice was surprisingly curt. 'Michael needs to be here with you. Not in France.'

Louise looked at him. Was it her imagination or were his

eyes clouded with worry? What is he thinking about? she wondered. And what does he think of me?

Only three weeks after the picnic the weather changed. Instead of balmy end of summer days, usually the case in September, autumn chose to arrive early. Deciding she needed some warmer maternity clothes Louise went into Winchester. Having completed her shopping she took a shortcut to the car through the cathedral close, and instead of passing the great west doors of the cathedral, on impulse, she went in.

Stopping to drop some money in the boxes pleading for donations for the cathedral's upkeep, she wandered up the nave. Strange how the ancient stones gave out such a feeling of peace. For the first time since she weekend of the picnic Louise began to feel calmness seep into her mind and body.

Since Michael's return from France on the Sunday evening of the picnic, life had been difficult. Not that he was unkind, he wasn't. But he was edgy, irritable, and then suddenly contrite, almost overwhelming her with affection. Something had happened that weekend and Louise wished she knew what it was.

Turning from the nave as she reached the altar, Louise passed by the small chapels set aside for private prayer. There was a man in one of them, his head slumped in his hands. Louise particularly noticed him because the slope of his shoulders emanated a kind of desperate hopelessness. Poor thing, she thought. Then he raised his head and Louise drew her breath in so suddenly it caused a pain in her chest. The man was Michael, and there was no mistaking the despair etched on every line of his face.

Michael never knew what drew him to the cathedral. He'd come back from London early and driven into Winchester intending to buy some flowers for Louise. A peace offering for his bad temper of the previous few days. Thinking of

Louise and Veronique, he'd parked in the multi-storey car park and wandered up the High Street, so engrossed in his thoughts that he passed two florists without noticing. If only I had someone to confide in, he thought, envying Louise's closeness with her mother. Briefly he thought of his own mother. Not that she could have helped. His problems would have been beyond her comprehension. Poor, hardworking and a devout Catholic, she'd seen things in black and white. Michael had been dragged to mass every Sunday until he'd rebelled. A scholarship to grammar school had opened his eyes to another world, and given him the ambition to be rich. Church was a waste of time; he preferred to spend time in Petticoat Lane, where his quick wits and glib tongue were soon earning him more money in a morning than his mother made for a whole day's cleaning.

'Lovely flowers, sir. Three bunches for the price of two.'

With a jolt Michael realized that he'd walked up Winchester High Street as far as the Butter Cross. A woman was sitting on the steps of the ancient stone market cross, where once the local farmers came to sell their butter and milk. She was surrounded by metal pails full of carnations, and he remembered his original mission. 'I'll take three bunches,' he said.

'Bless you, sir.' The woman started to wrap the pink carnations, then said, 'Tell you what, I'll put in another bunch for luck. It won't cost you no extra.'

'I could do with some luck.' Michael paid for the flowers and still without thinking clearly wandered on through the passageway which led into the cathedral close. The next thing he knew he was standing before the great west door.

The last time he'd been inside a church was at his mother's funeral, and he had no intention of entering one again. Staring up at the stone statues in the niches above the door, he envied them. Cold stone had no emotion, their faces remained as serene as the day they'd been carved. As he stood and stared, the stone faces were replaced by other, more familiar faces. Veronique's wild beauty, her eyes pleading, haunting him, then superimposed was Louise. They were there all the time, both of them, and he couldn't untangle either himself or them.

Later he knew he was a fool to think an answer might lie inside. He'd spent a long time on his knees, but ended up feeling more alone than ever. He left knowing one thing for certain; he alone would have to make a decision. Behind him, their petals already falling on to the cold stone floor, he left a crumpled bunch of pink carnations.

CHAPTER 15

Robert did his Thursday morning ward round, dictating notes concerning his patients' progress, or lack of it, as he went from bed to bed. He felt disheartened. Why had he chosen neurology? Such a depressing speciality; almost without exception the prognosis of each patient was pessimistic. The pessimism seemed to spill over into his own personal life. Something was wrong, and it was all bound up with Louise, Michael, Veronique and himself. The four of them seemed tied together with invisible cords, and he sensed the cords were hopelessly tangled.

'Sir, Mrs Watson's blood pressure is very high again, and she only has partial use of her right arm today.'

Even the most well trained minds are guilty of occasional lapses, and cursing his lack of vigilance, Robert hastily dragged his thoughts back to the ward round. 'Well, Mrs Watson. Now what are we to do about you?' He sat down and concentrated on his patient.

Tomorrow, he would visit Veronique.

Veronique was not pleased to see Robert. He hadn't asked. He'd told her he was coming across on the Thursday night car ferry crossing from Portsmouth to St Malo. 'But Robert,' she had protested, 'I am perfectly all right. You needn't worry.'

'I'm not worried,' Robert said firmly. 'But I need a few

days break and who better to spend it with than my sister. You don't begrudge the time to see me, do you? I need a holiday.' Put like that he knew she couldn't say no.

'No, of course I don't mind.' But she did. He knew she did.

Robert drove his car from St Malo to Chateau les Greves. In the early morning, the sea shone with a pearly light, iridescent and beautiful, spreading a tender blush upon the landscape. Robert felt his anxiety falling away. Unrequited love, that's my problem. Loving Louise has blighted my judgement. As for Veronique and Michael; probably financial ties, that's all. He thought of the large bank draft Michael had given him to put into Veronique's French bank account, and doubted that many men were so generous to their ex-wives.

'How are you?' On arrival at the chateau Robert kissed his sister and looked at her with a critical eye. She looked well, more beautiful than ever, her pale skin faintly tanned by a summer spent by the sea. She looked strong too, the heart condition that Michael had always made such a fuss about was a trivial matter, a chance in a thousand that her heart would fail her. In spite of her frail frame, she was physically strong, and Robert had no doubt that she would probably outlive all of them.

'I am very well, as you can see.' Veronique kissed him back. 'You are in good time for lunch. Dump your bags and we will go to a lovely fish restaurant I know overlooking the bay. You've never been there, I know you'll love it.'

It was true, Robert had never explored this part of Brittany at all. His only visit being a very brief one to look over the chateau after Veronique had first moved in.

The food in the restaurant, all fish, was out of this world, a gourmet's delight. The panoramic view of the bay was spectacular, and seemed oddly familiar. Halfway through the meal Robert realized why. He had dreamed about a bay like this. In the dream, he and Louise walked on the sand, at first apart, and then close so that their footsteps had merged into one single line. A vivid dream, activated, he ruefully acknowledged, by wishful thinking.

'I feel as if I've been here before,' he said.

Veronique laughed. 'That's exactly the way I felt when I first came to this place. I love it here. Strange, isn't it? We're both city people, and yet we like this wild place. Michael loves it too.'

'Michael!' Robert looked up sharply. 'Has Michael been here recently?'

Veronique's laughing face suddenly became shuttered. She remained smiling, but the light was gone, a veil drawn, effectively shutting Robert out on the other side. She looked down, concentrating on shelling a langoustine. 'He came of course when he purchased the chateau, but not since. Why should he?'

'Exactly. Why should he? Silly of me to ask.' Robert reached across and held his sister's hand. 'But tell me, Veronique. Tell me the truth. Are you happy?'

'Yes, of course I am. And I'm always telling you, I say it in my letters and on the telephone.' Veronique looked up, straight into Robert's eyes and smiled. But although he searched, he could find no real answer in her beautiful dark eyes, for the smile did not reach that far. It remained fixed on the curves of her mouth.

'I wish you weren't so lonely.'

'Robert! I am *not* lonely.'

'Is there a new man in your life?' Robert probed gently.

Veronique laughed again and shook her head. 'I don't want a new man. I am happy as I am. But you, do you have a new woman?'

Robert thought about Louise. How he longed to say yes. But she was not in his life, she was in Michael's. He too shook his head and gave a wry smile. 'No, you know me, Veronique. You are the only permanent woman in my life.'

'And Michael?' Veronique said casually. 'I know he is married and they are having a child. He told me, although goodness knows why he felt he had to. But he did. What he didn't say, and of course I couldn't possibly ask, was, what she is like.'

'Louise is very nice. Tall and dark,' Robert looked at his sister, then continued slowly, 'and I suppose in a way she looks rather like you. Except that her hair is cut very short in a bob, and her bone structure is slightly larger.'

'And they get on well? She and Michael?'

'They are in love,' said Robert sharply, far sharper than he had intended. His anxieties returned in full flood. Why had Michael chosen a woman who looked like his first wife? For the same reason you were attracted to Louise, common sense told him. People always tended to be attracted to certain types, often similar to people they were already familiar with. It was a known fact. Veronique's voice cut across his musing.

'I rather thought he was fond of her,' she was saying softly.

'Of course he's fond of Louise,' said Robert. 'He married her, didn't he? So he must be.'

Veronique pulled the head from a langoustine with a deftly vicious twist. 'But I wonder,' she said, slowly pulling the orange legs off one by one, 'if it will last.' Holding the remains of the shellfish by its tail she crunched her way through the juicy flesh, then said, 'Only time will tell,' and flicked the mangled remains of the tail on to her plate.

She doesn't want Michael to love anyone else. Robert was sure of that now. He felt a rush of pity for his sister. Poor Veronique, discarded by Michael, and unless she moved from this lonely place surely destined to remain alone for the rest of her life.

'You must show me all the alterations you've made to the chateau,' he said quickly, changing the subject. 'But before that, perhaps we should go into Lannion and put

114

this into your bank account.' He waved the bankers' draft beneath her nose.

Veronique seized it with glee. 'Just what I needed,' she said, and gave a sudden mischievous smile. 'I bet Louise doesn't know the luxury in which Michael is keeping me.'

'No,' said Robert sadly. 'She probably doesn't.' He wondered what Louise might say if she did know.

'The nursery remained locked again.' Andrea Louedec relayed the information to her husband once Robert had departed for St Malo.

'I'm beginning to think the woman is mad,' said Paul.

'I said something similar not long ago and you jumped down my throat.' Andrea was indignant. 'If I remember correctly, you said you can't go around saying things like that about your employer.'

'Quite right too. I can say it to you, but to no one else.'

'And another thing,' Andrea continued, 'why was she so insistent that we were on no account to mention Monsieur Baruch's visit here?'

'I don't know.' Paul sighed heavily. 'I hate mysteries.'

'Well, what do you think?'

'I'm not thinking anything. I shall concentrate on working the land like always. I know what's going on there. I plant seeds, and after a while things grow. And what's more, the things that grow turn out to be the things I'm expecting. No surprises, thank God. That's what I like, a quiet predictable life.'

'Oh, Paul!' Andrea Louedec was exasperated. Something was going on, something very strange indeed, and she'd give her eye-teeth to find out what it was.

'I'm ready for a nightcap,' said Paul. Still cross, Andrea slammed a bottle of cognac on the table and Paul poured himself a more than generous measure. He saw her looking at the amount in the glass. 'I need a good night's sleep,' he said defensively. 'There's an important *petanque* match tomorrow between Michel en Greve and St Efflam.'

115

So he *was* worried, although he wouldn't talk about it. Andrea had never known her husband need cognac to ensure a good night's sleep before.

'Really, dear. I'm not sure that this is a good idea. Not sure at all.'

'But Mother, I want to look around the part of the house Michael and Veronique shared. Maybe that will give me the answer.'

'If you want to know why your husband was on his knees in a chapel of the cathedral the simplest way is to ask him. I doubt that you will find the answer here.' Beattie tripped over Mr Poo. 'Damned dog. I'm going to take him back down to the kitchen and leave him with Lizzie for half an hour. I'll be back in a few minutes.' She handed Louise a bunch of keys. 'You open up the doors while you're waiting.'

Louise hesitated, and looked at the heavy keys in her hand. Perhaps she was being stupid. Instead of looking here, maybe she should ask Michael what was troubling him. But the streak of determined obstinacy which had been with her since childhood won. She *wanted* to see, and she would. Hand trembling slightly she slid the key into the door of what turned out to be a large lounge. The first thing that assailed her senses was a faint scent of perfume, a familiar perfume. Was this the perfume Lizzie Carey had spoken of? The one especially made for Veronique? No, that was not possible, because Louise knew she had smelled that very same perfume somewhere before.

Beattie returned. 'Well,' she said briskly, 'what revelations have you found?'

'Nothing, except,' Louise sniffed, 'can you smell that perfume?'

Beattie sniffed as well. 'No,' she said, 'I can't. Although I must say the rooms smell fresh and clean. Although they are kept locked Lizzie must come in a regular basis to dust and polish. Come on, let's hurry up and look through. I

116

can't hang about here all day. I've got a dealer coming to visit my studio; with luck he might buy some of my paintings.'

Together they went through the rooms. They were much the same as the suite Louise now shared with Michael, except that they were decorated in a more flamboyant baroque style. All the covings and centre roses were picked out in gold leaf, and the walls hung with a multitude of mirrors. In the bedroom Louise idly pulled open the drawers of the dressing table and cupboards. All empty.

'Nothing here,' she said.

'Well, dear, what exactly did you expect?' Beattie put her hands on her hips and looked at her daughter through narrowed eyes. 'Louise,' she said carefully. 'Answer me this. Why should the fact that you saw your husband praying worry you so much?'

'It wasn't the praying, it was . . .' Louise hesitated, then blurted out, 'It was his face. He looked tormented. But why should he look that way? Everything was turning out fine, and now suddenly he's changed. I thought I was beginning to know him, but . . .'

'But . . .' Beattie prompted, then when Louise remained silent she finished the sentence for her. 'But now you know you don't. And why? Because you rushed into marriage so that you could have what you wanted.' Louise flushed and hung her head. Her mother sighed. 'What a way for a child to be brought into the world.'

'But I love the baby,' protested Louise, 'and Michael does too. I know it.'

'Hum!' Her mother sounded unimpressed. 'I warned you right from the beginning that life has a nasty habit of catching up with one. Dishing out unpleasantness when one least expects it.'

'But . . .'

'But nothing, don't interrupt me! Whatever is wrong between you and Michael can only be sorted out by yourselves. Not me, nor anyone else. If you want to know what is troubling Michael, then there is only one way to find out. You must ask him.' Beattie started towards the door which led outside into the passageway. 'Come on, there's no point in hanging about here.'

Louise followed. Everything her mother had said was right. What had happened to that wonderful feeling she'd had only a few weeks ago? Where had it gone?

On the way out she noticed one of the sideboard drawers was not shut properly. With an irritable movement she pushed the drawer in sharply, and as she did so something inside slammed hard against the back of the drawer. In all these empty rooms it seemed that one drawer did have something left in it after all. Curious, she reopened the drawer and reaching to the back drew out a small framed photograph. It was of Michael and a woman with long, flowing dark hair.

'This must be Veronique.' The words were spoken as much to herself as to her mother.

Beattie came back and took the photo from Louise. 'She's very beautiful,' she said, 'and a little bit like you.'

'Yes,' said Louise dully. The beauty was the first thing she'd noticed. 'Lizzie Carey told me she was beautiful. I wonder why Michael divorced her.'

Her mother was no help. 'Only Michael can tell you that,' she said.

'Yes,' said Louise again, and putting the photograph back in the drawer led the way out and locked the outside door. Only Michael can tell me, the words rang through her head. Futile words, because he never would. He'd made it quite clear right at the beginning of their marriage that the subject of Veronique was off-limits, and Louise had no reason to suppose that he had changed his mind.

The two women made their way back to the kitchen where Beattie was to pick up Mr Poo before leaving, each of them worrying about Veronique.

Louise, shriven through with the cold, tearing claws of

118

jealousy again, was tensely aware of a chilly isolation. Veronique was *very* beautiful. Words were one thing. They'd not prepared her for the actual reality. Even though she had only looked at the photograph for a few seconds she seen the wild sensuality in Veronique's beauty. She was the kind of woman men flew to, like moths attracted to a flame. She herself was not like that. Louise had no false pride; she was attractive, she knew it, but Veronique had something special and it showed. Again the question, why had Michael divorced her? But they had parted by mutual agreement, that was what he'd said. In which case Michael couldn't still love Veronique. Besides, Veronique had not given him a child. Perhaps she was one of those women who didn't want children for fear of ruining her figure. But she, Louise, would soon present Michael with the child she knew he wanted. The baby moved about inside the security of her womb as if to reassure her, and Louise resolved to be sensible and not to think about Veronique again.

CHAPTER 16

Louise felt fabulous. And more than that, she felt happy and able to tackle anything life might throw at her. Smiling, she made her way towards the library, but once within a few feet of the door she halted in her tracks. From the library came the sound of Michael's voice. He was on the phone. Then he said, 'Veronique.'

Louise took a step backwards. Suddenly she felt cold and shivery, yet at the same time beads of perspiration started breaking out on her brow and body. Her clothes stuck to the dampness.

'I *had* to marry Louise. It was necessary. Nothing else would do.'

Had! Necessary! Not want? Louise suddenly felt sick. What was he talking about? Who was he talking to? To Veronique? Was that who it was?

Then he said something else she couldn't hear properly. His voice was too soft. He said it again; it was the name Veronique. She was certain, absolutely certain. *Veronique, Veronique*. The name echoed in her ears.

Louise had heard enough. She fled upstairs towards the haven of the bedroom. The happiness of the day evaporated leaving a sour, evil taste in her mouth. She was suddenly sure now that she knew the reason Michael had divorced Veronique. It was because she could not have children, and not because he had stopped loving her. She,

Louise, was his baby machine, nothing more nor less. Flinging herself on the bed she burst into tears.

'Darling, Louise, what is it?' Deafened by her hiccuping sobs Louise hadn't heard Michael enter the bedroom. Now, he knelt beside her on the bed, his arms around her.

'I heard, I heard . . .' She could hardly speak for sobbing. 'I heard you talking on the telephone. You still love Veronique, not me. Why did you let me think you loved me? You didn't have to. You could have left things as they were.' Louise struggled free of Michael's arms and tried to gather together the tattered shreds of her dignity. 'That at least would have been honourable,' she managed to say between sobs.

Michael's face was white, his eyes a dark green slate colour. He watched her, anxious, intent. 'I'm not deceiving you,' he said quietly.

'Then who were you talking to? Why did you say you *had* to marry me? That it was necessary.'

'How long did you listen, Louise?'

'Only a few seconds. That was enough.'

'If you had listened for longer you would have realized that I was talking to my accountant. He was querying various financial settlements I've made. That was why your name was mentioned. He thinks I'm being over-generous. But I want you and my son to be financially secure. And I do want you for my wife.'

'You said Veronique too.' This time Louise was determined. She was not going to be fobbed off. 'Why did you mention her? She's your past. I'm your future.'

'Even the past has to be dealt with,' said Michael, his face grim. 'Especially when money is involved.' Then with one swift movement he pulled Louise into his arms and kissed her.

'You do want me?' whispered Louise. 'You really do?'

'I really do, my darling. I really do. I don't deserve you, I know that. I don't deserve you or the baby. But I'm going to cherish you both.' Michael pressed his mouth against Louise's smooth dark hair. 'I want you both,' he whispered, 'very, very much.'

Now is the time, thought Louise. Now I can ask him what he was praying for in the cathedral chapel. But the memory of his tormented expression stilled her tongue. It wasn't right to pry. 'I love you,' she whispered back, and tried to convince herself that what she'd overheard was what Michael had said. A conversation with his accountant, nothing more. But a stubborn doubt remained. She would never know for certain.

CHAPTER 17

The pain seemed to go on for ever, a great surging wave, rising, rising, rising. Louise tried to breathe deeply the way she'd been taught at the antenatal classes, and to empty her mind of all thoughts except the thought of breathing – light short breaths, breathe, breathe, steady, steady.

The contraction gradually died away and Louise let her breath out in a long steady hiss. She moved her head restlessly; the pillow soaked in perspiration was uncomfortable. 'I've changed my mind,' she groaned. 'I don't think I want a a a baby after all.'

'Too late now, dear,' said the midwife briskly, exchanging the damp pillow for a plump clean one. 'The cervix is almost fully dilated. You'll be wanting to push soon.'

'Oh, how I wish I'd said yes to an epidural.'

'Shush.' Beattie, looking unfamiliar and strangely efficient in a cap and gown, gently sponged Louise's forehead. 'Not long to go now.'

A doctor popped his head in through the door. 'How's she doing?'

'Fine,' said the midwife. 'No problems at all.'

'Awful,' moaned Louise. 'The bloody thing has got stuck.'

'Don't worry. It'll pop out like a champagne cork in a moment.' The doctor grinned at the midwife and Beattie and left.

'You wanted natural childbirth, and that's what you've got.' The midwife sounded unsympathetic. Then her tone softened. 'But you are doing splendidly, my dear. This baby is in a hurry. He will be born before your husband arrives.'

'But he'll be here in about an hour.' Louise wanted Michael to arrive before their son. She had telephoned him immediately the contractions started, just before Dick Carey had driven her to the hospital at Winchester. 'He said he was starting out straight away.'

'An hour is too long. Your son will be here in half an hour or less. Right, my dear!' The midwife stood up and patted Louise on the shoulder. 'Now you can push just as soon as you want to.'

Twenty minutes later it was all over, and a lustily bawling infant was placed in Louise's arms.

All the efforts of her scheming now lay safe within the circle of her enclosing arms. The baby she had wanted so much had finally arrived. But nothing, nothing in the world had prepared Louise for the fierce rush of emotion she felt as she gazed down at the red, crumpled face of her son, topped with a mop of dark hair which looked as if some unearthly hairdresser had cropped it into a fashionable flat-top style. His mouth was a perfectly formed 'O' as he howled, long and loud, and his eyes, when he opened them briefly, were almost black.

'Daniel,' she whispered softly. 'Oh, Daniel.' Then she looked at her mother, eyes shining bright with pride. 'That's what we've agreed to call him. Isn't he wonderful? I never thought a baby could be so beautiful.'

'Beautiful!' exclaimed Beattie. 'Good heavens, he looks like Mr Poo on a bad day.' Then she kissed Louise. 'Only teasing, darling. Of course he's beautiful, and healthy too by the sound of him.'

'And mine, all mine,' said Louise putting him to her breast. Oh he was strong. He clamped on to the nipple with his hard little gums as if he'd been doing it for months. Louise winced, her nipple was tender, and his gums were tough. But the pain was exquisite, only adding to her already overflowing love.

'Well, my girl,' said Beattie with a wry yet tender smile, 'you've finally caught up, just as you wanted. You've joined the club which ensures the human race survives in spite of its continual efforts to self-destruct.'

'Caught up,' repeated Louise, savouring the phrase. 'Yes, I have haven't I, and what's more everything is all right. It really is, Mother.'

They couldn't talk about Michael in front of the midwife, but Beattie knew what she meant. 'I'm glad,' she said quietly.

A new phase had entered their marriage during the last couple of weeks. Ever since Louise had overheard the phone call in the library, Michael had been trying his hardest to show her that he truly meant what he had said. That he wanted them both, her and the baby, and that together they would forge a new life, be a proper family. Gradually Louise lost her distrust; she could see that Michael was more relaxed and at ease with himself, and with her. As a result she relaxed too and they were able to laugh together, something they'd never really done before, and the last two weeks of her pregnancy were very happy. All was well.

Michael arrived a quarter of an hour later. Louise was glad of the extra time she'd had to herself, for she was back in her own room and had washed and changed into a pretty nightdress. Daniel too had been cleaned up and dressed. He now lay in a cot by the side of Louise's bed, wrapped like a little mummy in the snow white shawl she had brought in with her especially for him.

Michael entered the room hesitantly and Beattie immediately got up to go. 'Go on,' she said. 'Look at your son, he's not going to bite.'

As if he knew his father had arrived Daniel shot one

125

small fist free of the shawl, his tiny hand grasping and groping, exploring the new-found space around him.

'He's perfect. Beautiful. And his hands, look at the length of those fingers, and those perfect miniature nails.' Michael put his finger against Daniel's hand, and immediately the tiny fingers curled round, grasping hard. 'He's so strong,' he said in awe.

'We did well, didn't we? First we were alone, you and I, then we were two, and now we are three, joined together like a clover leaf.' Radiant, and suffused with a mixture of emotions she could never, not in a million years have explained to anyone, Louise reached across and stroked Michael's cheek. 'Never in my wildest imaginings did I dream that I could be so happy. We never will be separated, will we.' It was not a question, it was a statement. Louise felt secure enough in her new happiness not to doubt.

Michael reached up and taking Louise's hand pressed it to his lips. Then leaning over the bed he kissed her long and passionately. Smiling, he looked down. 'I don't know who I love the most, you or baby Daniel.'

It was the first time he had actually said that he loved her. 'You must love us equally,' said Louise happily. 'We are one and the same. A mother and child are part of each other, and belong together.'

'Yes,' said Michael slowly, still smiling. 'You *do* belong together.' Then it seemed to Louise that the smile in his eyes faded, and his eyes took on a darker hue as if reflecting some great pain. But before she could properly register and catalogue the change, his mouth was on hers, and all was forgotten in the tender passion of his kiss.

It took Louise a fortnight to settle down into a routine once she'd got back to Offerton Manor. At first it seemed that her whole life, every twenty-four hours of it, was spent attending to Daniel. Frantically she wondered how on earth other women, like Eugenia, coped with other children as well as a baby, with a husband, with housework and sometimes a job as well. She suddenly developed a healthy respect for women who managed to juggle all the conflicting demands made upon them. Being a career woman seemed an easy option in comparison.

'I don't think I can keep this up,' she told Beattie, picking Daniel up to feed him yet again. 'This is the third time this afternoon. His appetite is insatiable.'

'Personally I don't agree with this modern idea of "on demand" feeding,' said Beattie.

'Neither do I,' said Lizzie, bringing in a tray of tea and a plate of home-made scones. Since the birth of Daniel, afternoon tea had become something of a ritual between the three of them. Lizzie poured Louise a cup of tea and placed it with a scone on a small table beside her chair. 'I know I've never had any children of my own, but I was the eldest of a large family. My poor mother would never have managed to do anything if she'd fed "on demand".'

'But if I don't feed him he screams.' Louise was beginning to realize that there was a lot more to rearing a baby than she had thought. She'd read all the books, but Daniel hadn't, and obviously had no intention of behaving as the books predicted. 'And the health visitor says . . .'

'Damn the health visitor. She's not feeding him, *you* are,' said Beattie.

'Make him wait for a little while, then the next time he'll suck harder and take more.' Lizzie sipped her tea. 'He reminds me of my youngest brother, Arthur. He was just like that. I remember my mother saying he was a lazy baby. Just sucked enough to satisfy himself for a short while, then promptly fell asleep.'

'There you are.' Beattie nodded towards Daniel who had dropped off the nipple and was now snaring content-edly. 'Wake him up, Louise. Make him suck for a little longer.'

Louise changed breasts, and after some vigorous jig-gling Daniel did wake sufficiently to suck some more. But he did it reluctantly, with a lot of snuffling and grunting. 'He is just like Mr Poo,' she said laughing. 'He's certainly letting me know that he doesn't think this is a great idea.'

'And you must let him know who's boss,' said her mother.

'Yes, I must,' agreed Louise. 'Especially if we're to have this celebration dinner Michael wants to hold. If I don't get Daniel into some sort of routine, I won't be able to enjoy it.'

'I can't understand Mr Baruch's sudden urge to entertain.' Lizzie Carey got up and began collecting the cups and plates together. 'We've never had a dinner party here at Offerton Manor. Now he wants one in two weeks time, on November the fourth.'

'Oh dear.' Louise suddenly worried. 'It will be an awful lot of work. I hadn't really thought of that. Do you mind?'

'Mind!' Lizzie looked scandalized. 'Of course I don't mind. I love cooking on a grand scale. I'm going to start washing all the best china tomorrow. There's a wonderful Royal Doulton dinner service in the cupboard which has never been used.' She tottered over to the door, holding the tray beneath her ample bosom, and looking more birdlike than ever, because in the afternoons she always wore shoes with very high heels which made her legs seem even thinner.

'We'll help.' Louise and Beattie spoke together.

'No you won't. Dick and I will do it, and if necessary get in some outside help. There's nothing I like better than a challenge. It will do me good to be rushed off my feet for a change.' She beamed back happily at Beattie and Louise from the doorway.

Beattie looked at Louise when she'd gone. 'Fancy *liking* hard work,' she said.

'And fancy Michael suddenly wanting to be sociable,' said Louise happily. 'You know, I think the arrival of Daniel has really affected him very deeply. He's changed. No longer do I wonder what kind of mood he'll be in, because I know. It's always the same, a good one. And the first thing he does as soon as he gets here at night, is to rush in to see Daniel.'

'I'm glad.' Beattie's tone was slightly wary. 'So things have settled down at last. Let's hope it stays that way.'

Louise laughed, supremely confident. 'Don't be so sceptical, Mother, of course it will. Now my life is absolutely perfect, and I know it's going to stay that way.'

'There's no such thing as perfection,' said Beattie, 'and don't tempt the fates by even saying it.'

'Tempt the fates! Mother, I've never thought of you as being superstitious.'

'I'm not superstitious. But by the time you get to my age you know from experience that perfection doesn't exist. There's always a fly in the ointment somewhere.'

'Rubbish!' said Louise.

'I don't want anything at midday. I'm going out.'

'But you must eat something.' Andrea Louedec was worried. Veronique had visibly lost weight over the past few weeks, and had become increasingly restless and obviously unhappy. Andrea wished she could help, but it was not her place to ask, let alone offer advice.

'I'll eat out at a restaurant. Don't fuss, Andrea.'

'As you wish, Madame.' Andrea cleared away the untouched brioche and croissant. Veronique had drunk the coffee, but that was all. 'Well, it's a wonderful day to go out,' she said, trying to inject a cheerful note into the conversation.

'Yes, it is,' replied Veronique. But her voice was dull and disinterested.

It could be pouring with rain as far as she is concerned, thought Andrea as she left the room. What had brought on this black mood of depression that seemed to be gnawing away at the very life of the young Madame Baruch?

Veronique left the breakfast room and went back upstairs to her bedroom. Taking a key from her jewel box she went across and unlocked the door to the nursery. The pale blue room sparkled cheerfully in the early morning sunlight. The cover in the cot billowed like a foaming pale blue wave, and the mobiles of exotic birds and animals which Veronique had so carefully pinned to the ceiling eddied in the draught from the open door, their colours reflecting in a kaleidoscopic pattern on the walls.

Veronique shut the door and leaned against it. Here, no one could see the tears pouring unheeded down her cheeks. Bitter, bitter tears for the child she could never conceive herself, and for the child that she longed to sleep, laugh, and cry in this room. It was wrong that this room should be so perfect. It should be untidy; piles of baby clothes everywhere and it should be filled with the warm smell of a living child. As it was, it was merely a sterile parody of what it should be. Like me, she thought wretchedly. A sterile parody of a woman.

But Veronique had courage. She was not a woman to allow herself to weep for long. Depressed she might be – Andrea Louedec had been right in her assumption of the black mood which enveloped her – but rarely did she allow herself the luxury of weeping. Or even the luxury of looking into the nursery. So she left the room, carefully locking the door behind her. It was the last Sunday in October. Michael should be at Offerton Manor. Surely his wife, Louise, must have had her baby by now. She looked at her watch. If she rang now, it was likely that Michael would answer the phone. He often worked in the study on Sunday mornings. She needed to know about the baby, and also she needed to know why Michael had not returned to visit her again as he had promised.

Sitting on the edge of her bed, looking out across the wide bay shimmering in the October sunlight, Veronique carefully tapped out the long number for England and Offerton Manor.

As both Louise and Michael were upstairs with Daniel, Lizzie Carey, who happened to be passing by the study,

130

went in and answered the phone. 'Offerton Manor. Mrs Carey speaking.'

'Oh!' Veronique slammed down the phone. She dare not ask for Michael; Mrs Carey would recognize her voice.

In England a puzzled Lizzie Carey replaced the receiver. After just one brief exclamation the caller had gone, and yet, she thought, tapping her way briskly towards the kitchen, if I didn't know better I could have sworn that was Veronique's husky voice. It couldn't have been, of course. Veronique had no reason to ring the manor. Not now, not after all this time. Back in the kitchen she busied herself scoring the skin on a hand of pork which she was about to put in the oven ready for Sunday lunch, and forgot about the phone call.

In France, Veronique blinked back the threatening tears. She had so longed to speak to Michael. Where was he? And what was he doing? And why hadn't he rung? She decided to ring Robert.

'Robert, is that you?'

'Yes.' Robert stiffened warily. Veronique was speaking in French, a language they very rarely conversed in nowadays, and something she usually did when she was agitated or upset. 'What is wrong?' He answered in French.

'Wrong?' Veronique laughed. 'Nothing is wrong, Robert. Except that I haven't spoken to you since you paid me that surprise visit here at the chateau. So here I am, on a Sunday morning, ringing my brother to find how he is, and checking that he is not working too hard.'

Robert relaxed. He was being stupid. Now she was back living in France it was only natural that she should lapse into French when speaking to him. She spoke it all day every day now. Her mother tongue was once more her first language.

'I'm fine. I'm on call this weekend, and was just about to pop up to the hospital. I swopped my duties with Richard Meacher because I wanted next weekend free for . . .' He

131

stopped; he'd been about to say the dinner party at Offerton Manor. 'For,' he continued hastily, 'a dinner with some friends.'

'Oh, anyone I know?'

'No,' lied Robert, 'people from the hospital.'

'Oh,' said Veronique again. There was a long pause, then she said, 'I suppose Michael's latest wife has had the baby now.'

'What do you mean "latest wife"? I sincerely hope that she will be his last.' Robert spoke sharply; he had that sensation yet again that Veronique did not consider her relationship with Michael to be finished.

'Very well, wife then. If that makes you happy. But – ' Veronique's voice took on an impatient tone – 'what about the baby? Has she had it?'

Robert was acutely aware of a baffling tension emanating from Veronique. It was so strong he could almost fancy that he could hear it crackling down the line. She was desperate to know. But why? Most women, once they were divorced, wanted to kick over the traces, and put away all thoughts of their previous life. In Robert's opinion that was a natural reaction in the beginning; it was only later that people came to terms with the failure of a relationship. But for some obscure reason Veronique was the opposite. She wanted to be kept up to date with Michael's present life, and that was wrong, because it was a life which no longer had anything to do with her.

'Yes,' he replied after a slight pause. 'She had a fine, healthy baby boy on the nineteenth of October. He is called Daniel.'

'Daniel!' Veronique wailed. 'But I wanted him to be called Alexander.'

'*You* wanted him to be called Alexander!' Robert said very slowly, and very, very quietly.

Veronique gasped, realizing that in her distress she had said too much, and was in danger of giving herself away. 'Well . . . I,' she floundered, feverishly trying to collect her thoughts, knowing she needed to compose a sensible explanation. 'I suggested Alexander to Michael because I happen to think it is a lovely name. At the time Michael seemed to agree with me, so naturally I assumed . . .'

'You had no business making suggestions. It is not your child.' There was no answer, and Robert shouted, 'Veronique, the boy is not yours. He belongs to Michael and Louise and has nothing whatsoever to do with you.'

'Goodbye, Robert.'

Veronique put down the phone, and leaving her bedroom in the chateau, set off across the shining wet sand towards the towering cliffs of the headland.

CHAPTER 18

On the evening of the dinner party, once Daniel was tucked up, sound asleep, Louise was free to bath and change. Humming happily, she rushed about getting clothes out of closets and sniffing half a dozen different perfumes before she finally decided on the one to wear. But all the time she felt there was something strange about the room, although for the life of her she couldn't think what it was. She'd almost finished when Michael arrived.

'Sorry I'm late, darling.' Giving Louise a brief kiss he went straight into his dressing room and through into the bathroom. 'I've had a difficult day.' He shouted above the noise of running taps. 'I'm glad to get back here away from those City traders.'

Louise wandered through and stood in the doorway. He sounded harrassed. 'Why? What are they doing?'

Michael climbed into the bath and sank down into the water until it reached his neck. He flexed his shoulders. 'That's better,' he said.

'The City traders, what have they been doing?'

There was a moment's silence, then Michael turned his head and smiled. 'They're bloody-minded, that's all. Querying stock I put up as collateral.'

'Oh.' Louise wondered what Michael needed the collateral for and was about to ask when he interrupted.

'If you don't hurry, you're not going to be downstairs in

time to greet our first guests. We can't both be late.'

'Good heavens!' Realizing he was right, Louise rushed back to the bedroom to put the finishing touches to her make-up. It was as she was leaving the room that she knew what it was that was different. The paintings had gone. Her first thought was theft, and she rushed back to the bathroom. 'Michael, the paintings have gone.'

'I know.' He sounded very matter-of-fact. 'They went yesterday while you were out.'

'But . . .' Louise was puzzled.

'I told you they were only investments. Prices are high. Now is the time to sell them and make a killing.'

'Oh!' Louise was disappointed; she had liked them.

'You can put some prints up if you miss them.'

'I think I will.' Louise left the bedroom and went downstairs. In that respect she would never understand Michael. He only ever looked at things in terms of monetary worth. But it was a minor thing; the important thing was that he loved her and Daniel, even to the point of having the dinner party to celebrate Daniel's birth.

Robert and Michael were alone with their drinks at one end of the room, Eugenia and Gordon were poring over the paintings at the other. Ever since the disturbing telephone conversation with Veronique he'd been wondering whether or not to mention it to Michael. Now, he decided that he had to find out whether or not Veronique had been wildly exaggerating. He prayed that she had.

'I was speaking to Veronique on the telephone last weekend,' he said casually. They were standing near the fireplace and Robert half turned so that his own face was in shadow and Michael's illuminated by the flames.

'Oh, really. How is she?' Michael words were casual, so was the tone of his voice, but the bright glow from the fire cruelly exposed the effort it cost him to speak with such apparent disinterest.

Robert's heart sank. What was going on that he didn't

know about? 'I told her that you and Louise have a baby son named Daniel.'

'Oh, good. That saves me telephoning. I said I would let her know. She was interested.' Aware that his expression was probably giving too much away, Michael turned abruptly away and stepping to the sideboard took another glass of champagne.

'Much *too* interested,' said Robert, following Michael. 'She seemed to be under the impression that you would be calling the baby Alexander. Her choice I understand.'

'Yes. Well . . . perhaps I misled her.' Michael was floundering now, just the way Veronique had floundered on the phone. 'We, I . . .' We stopped and walked back to the fireplace.

'Just what are you up to?' hissed Robert, following. 'You have no right even talking to Veronique. You have a new wife and a lovely son. What do you want? To have your cake *and* eat it?'

'It's none of your business,' snapped Michael, suddenly aware of Robert's hostility and shaken by it.

'It *is* my business. Veronique is my sister, and Louise . . .'

'And you're in love with Louise,' said Michael. It was not something he'd thought about before, but now he saw it in Robert's eyes. The irony of it! Unwittingly Robert had joined the trio, now making it a quartet.

'Yes, I love her.' Anger forced the confession from Robert's lips. 'But you've married her,' he added bitterly, 'and I'm damned if I'm going to stand by and watch you ruin her life the way you've ruined my sister's.'

The two men faced each other across the flickering light of the flames. Both rigid, both tense.

'I have *not* ruined Veronique. Keep out of my life.' Michael's face was ashen. Even the light from the fire failed to give it warmth. Fighting desperately to keep his fear and guilt under control, he managed to maintain a totally impassive expression.

'It's not *your* bloody life that concerns me. It's everybody else's that you're so intent on fucking up. I think you're still seeing Veronique, still sleeping with her. And then you're coming back here, playing the loving husband and father and sleeping with Louise as well. You think you've got everything you want, don't you? A wife in France, and a wife here who has provided you with the son you wanted. All so bloody convenient. A sort of board-room merger, only this time it isn't money you're juggling with, it's people and their emotions.' Robert paused, shaking with rage. 'You make me *sick*.'

'You don't know what the hell you're talking about,' said Michael in a low voice.

'Don't I, Michael? Well then, deny it. Go on, deny it!'

Michael's composure began to fracture. 'As I said before, you know nothing. Nothing, nothing, *nothing*.' The guilt. The monumental guilt. For a brief second Michael was tempted to tell Robert everything and ask his advice. But it was only a brief moment, because he knew he couldn't. That would be a double betrayal of Veronique. But Robert's angry words, and the knowledge that he loved Louise had shaken him. He had to do something, and soon. The problem was, what?

'Keep your bloody voice down,' hissed Robert. 'We don't want everyone knowing what a shit you really are.'

Michael glanced up. Gordon and Eugenia had heard the raised voices and were looking in his direction. With an enormous effort he forced himself to smile and raise his hand in a half-salute, before turning in towards Robert as if they were having a friendly argument.

'Robert, please,' he begged. 'Believe me when I say I won't do anything that could possibly harm Louise or Daniel.' He was desperate to try and reassure Robert, to divert his thoughts from the dangerous path they were pursuing. 'But neither do I want to hurt Veronique any more than I've done already. That's why I talked to her. I can't just pretend she's not there.'

'Don't speak to my sister again,' said Robert coldly. 'If

you do need to say anything, tell me. I will do it.'

'Yes,' said Michael. 'I will.' He turned away to face the fire again, and said in a low voice, 'You won't let Louise know that Veronique and I discussed the baby's name, will you?'

'What the hell do you take me for,' growled Robert.

'Thank you.'

'I'm keeping my mouth shut for Louise, not you,' said Robert.

'Dinner will be served in about five minutes,' said Louise from the doorway.

'I can hang about for ever as long as there is plenty of champagne.' Beattie joined Robert and Michael and helped herself to another glass. 'Cheers!' She glanced at their faces. 'Cheer up, you two. I've never seen you with such long faces before. Have you had a row?'

'Of course not,' said Michael and Robert together.

So they have, thought Beattie, sipping her champagne, and smiling so sweetly that they were forced to smile back. Now I wonder what on earth that can have been about. Or rather *who* it was about. Was it Veronique? Or Louise? With a sudden flash of percipience she realized that both men were bound to the two women. By the past, by blood, and by emotion. So what had they been arguing about? It was so unlike Robert to argue about anything. Worry made her thirsty. She took another glass of champagne.

'Do you think you ought?' said Robert.

Worry also made her tongue sharp. 'Yes,' she snapped back, quick as a flash, 'you are driving. Not me.'

Louise glanced along the dinner table. The evening was turning out to be a great success. Lizzie Carey had pulled out all the stops and presented a menu fit for a state banquet. Now, her good humour restored by numerous glasses of wine, Beattie was on sparkling, *risqué* form, managing to make everyone laugh. Even Robert, who

Louise thought had seemed rather serious at the beginning of the evening, now appeared totally relaxed. Michael too had been on edge, she had sensed it, but now seemed at ease. Amazing what good food and wine could do.

'We should do this more often,' she whispered to Michael between courses.

'I agree,' he said. 'I'm enjoying myself.'

It was when they were on the liqueurs and coffee that Michael's mobile phone rang.

'Curse of mankind,' said Beattie. 'Those things can get at you anywhere.'

'Why did you bring it in?' Louise was not pleased at the interruption.

'I've been waiting for an important call.' Michael answered it. 'Yes, yes, I see.' Then he said, 'Excuse me a moment, I'll go to my study.'

'Nothing serious, I hope,' said Louise when he returned. It was an automatic question, not one to which she was really expecting a reply. So the tone of his voice when he answered both surprised and worried her. She had been married to him long enough to recognize the suppressed fury in his voice. There *was* something, and he was not pleased.

'Not a call from France I hope,' said Robert.

Louise looked across at him, her senses tingling with apprehension. He was worried too. What was going on?

'No, the call was from Hong Kong. Not that it is any of your business.'

Louise thought that surely everyone would recognize the hostility in Michael's voice, but they appeared not to, and the conversation flowed unabated, Beattie at her hilarious best. Although later, catching her mother's eye, Louise saw that she was not fooled. She too knew something was wrong.

When they finally left, to the casual observer it would have seemed a normal, happy, noisy crowd, full of good food and wine, that spilled out of the house on to the top step of the portico to say their goodbyes to Louise and Michael. But, in fact, of all of them, only Eugenia and Gordon were blissfully unaware of the dark undercurrents.

'Goodbye, and thank you for a wonderful evening.' Eugenia kissed Louise, then turned to say goodbye to Michael.

'It was a pleasure,' said Louise, once again envying Eugenia and her brother. They led such uncomplicated lives, always seeming blissfully happy. Why can't my life be like that, she thought resentfully, instead of vacillating wildly? One moment up, the next down. This evening started off so perfectly, but now something is wrong and I don't know why, or what it is.

'Terrific evening.' Gordon hugged her. 'What a lucky girl you are, Louise.'

'Yes, I am, aren't I,' Louise replied automatically, but her mind was niggling away at the worry. She watched Michael speaking to Eugenia. There is something he doesn't want me to know. The moment the thought entered her head so did the stubborn determination to find out what it was. All her life she'd hated uncertainty, so why should she endure it now? She'd find out, then confront Michael with the knowledge. No relationship could succeed unless everything was out in the open.

Turning, she saw Robert kissing Eugenia warmly on the cheek. She was giggling happily at something he'd said. That was how I was at the beginning of this evening, thought Louise. But now, the congenial warmth she'd felt then had vanished, to be replaced by a frozen unhappiness. Why is it, she pondered miserably, that whenever I think that I've found the key to happiness, I open the door, step through, only to find that yet another door is there? And behind that door lies yet another puzzlement, another set of emotions I do not understand, all waiting to be unravelled. No one, she decided, was quite what they seemed. Not even Robert. Why had he been so unfriendly towards Michael at the beginning of the evening? Even now his attitude was distinctly frosty. It seemed everyone had their secrets.

'Goodnight, Louise.' Robert came across to her, and kissed her on both cheeks. 'It was a perfect evening.'

'Do you think so?' Louise looked into his eyes, searching for a clue to the mystery. But tonight his usually open face seemed shuttered. 'Why are you so tense?' The words were out before she could stop herself, spoken lowly so that no one else could hear.

Robert stepped back, looking startled. He'd been congratulating himself on covering his tension very well. Louise's question told him that he wasn't. But, thank God, she didn't know that it was Michael and Veronique he was worrying about. Ignoring the question he took her hands in his, and attempted to sound light-hearted. 'Mmm, they're cold,' he said.

'Cold hands, warm heart,' said Louise, attempting the same lightness. So Robert wasn't going to answer her question.

But he did, in a strange way. 'You have nothing to worry about,' he said.

'I don't need you to tell me that,' Louise replied sharply. Why on earth should Robert even say that unless there was something?

Robert didn't reply, merely squeezed her hands once more. 'Now I must say my farewells to Michael,' he said, and leaving her strode across the top step to where Michael was standing.

'Goodnight, Robert.' Michael was very formal. 'I hope you enjoyed this evening.'

'I did.' Robert looked Michael straight in the eyes. 'I enjoyed seeing you with your new family.' The slight emphasis on the word new told Michael all he needed to know. It meant keep away from Veronique.

'I will,' said Michael in a low voice, in answer to Robert's unspoken command. 'I promise.'

'You damn well better.' Robert abruptly turned away, and ran down the steps towards his car.

Beattle shivered. 'It's a chilly night,' she said, kissing Louise. 'Get back inside in the warm, dear, before you catch cold.'

'What did you think of the evening?' What Louise really wanted to say was did you see Michael's reaction when I asked him about the phone call? But that, of course, was impossible with Michael standing so near.

Beattle looked up at Louise, a worried expression on her face. 'What can I say?' she said, and Louise knew that she had seen, but, that like her, she did not understand.

'Goodnight, Mother,' she said, and standing by the side of Michael watched her mother make her way down the flight of steps towards Robert's car. Louise noticed that he already had the engine running, as if impatient to get away.

Michael waited until Louise was sound asleep, then quietly eased himself from the bed, and going into his dressing room closed the door silently. Once inside he put on a warm dressing gown and slippers. The curtains of the dressing room window were not drawn, and an opaque light filled the room. He paused for a moment to look out of the window. The moon hung low in the sky, flickering like a feeble lantern through serrated misty clouds, illuminating the distinctive outlines of the horse-chestnut and lime trees. The smooth grassland of the surrounding parkland spread as far as his eye could see. He felt the familiar thrill of pride. It was his, all his. Through his diligence and hard work it had been brought up to the standard it was now. No other country estate was in better condition than his; and Michael liked things to be perfect. Money made things perfect, and he was damned if some fool in a bank or investment house on the other side of the world was going to stifle his ambition by sticking rigidly to the rules. Money only made more money if one was bold enough to gamble; and that he intended to do. Money was the key to everything. Although, unwillingly, his thoughts were drawn back to the world that existed at Offerton. To get a son he had needed more than money. He'd needed guile and deceit, and most of all he had needed Louise.

But he wouldn't think about that now, otherwise unease and worry about Veronique and her place in the scheme of things would start submerging him. Now he needed to concentrate on money. The thought spurred him on and out of the room, and along the passageway towards his study. Something had to be done now. The morning might be too late. The last thing he needed were rumours about Briam's stability floating around the London market.

People who eavesdrop never hear good. Louise remembered the old adage after following Michael. She crept back to the bedroom and wished she had never listened. But too late. She had. And because of that she was now anxious and puzzled.

Lying alone in the big bed Louise tried to make some sort of sense of the conversation she'd just overheard. Michael's fortune seemed to be much less secure than the world at large thought. But was he a *real* criminal, or was he just going through a bad patch and trying to tide things over until the situation improved? Robbing Peter to pay Paul. Remember the Lehar stock, he'd said. So he'd done it before. Louise remembered reading about similar manoeuvres concerning other companies in the financial press. But always found it difficult to understand where the line was drawn between dishonesty and financial strategy. What was Michael doing, and why? Louise shivered. She had wanted to find out and confront him, but her eavesdropping had done nothing except worry her more than ever. How could she confront him when her understanding of what was happening was so hazy? It would achieve nothing except drive a rift between them, and that was the last thing she wanted.

All the same, she was afraid. The security which she'd taken for granted suddenly seemed very insubstantial. Taking Daniel from his cot, she cuddled him close. Staying that way for the rest of the night, half dozing, half waking, breaking all the rules by taking the baby into her own bed; but she felt safer that way. With Daniel in her arms, they were safe, both of them.

In the morning she was rewarded with a stiff neck and a very grumpy baby. The bright light of day made her night-time fears seem quite ridiculous. There had to be some logical explanation. Michael's affairs were incredibly complex. Owning hundreds of companies as he did, there were bound to be problems from time to time. It was inevitable that he'd become worried and sometimes angry, and of course he needed to be ruthless and order people about. No one got to Michael's position without having a streak of ruthlessness. It was something for which he was renowned, and more than that, Louise told herself, he needed to be that way in order to survive.

Michael had obviously not returned to the bedroom, he must have slept on the couch in his dressing room so as not to disturb her. When she took Daniel downstairs with her to the breakfast room she found a note. It said that he'd gone up to London for an urgent and unexpectedly early meeting, but would be back that evening. He ended the note with love and kisses which made Louise feel better.

She tucked the note into her skirt pocket, and decided that she had let her imagination run riot. That is what comes from listening to other people's conversations in the middle of the night, she told herself as she buttered a piece of toast. Outside a cold November sun shone on the frosty countryside; everything looked the picture of normality which, of course, was what it was.

CHAPTER 19

Michael stared out of his office window at the familiar view of St Paul's Cathedral. As it was Saturday the office block was empty, and apart from some cleaners in the lower offices he had the place to himself. Was it really only in January of this year that he had gazed out upon the same scene, then lashed by cold January rain, and told Veronique that he thought he had found someone. It seemed a lifetime ago. So many things had happened since then which he had not foreseen, and now the day of reckoning had come where he and Veronique were concerned. He must tell her that it was over. That he would not be coming to France, and that the plans they had laid so carefully had been unrealistic. It was for that reason they had crumbled into dust before the onslaught of emotions and needs he had never foreseen. Abstract plans with unknown people were easy to conceive, but they counted for nothing when brought face to face with the complexities of flesh and blood human beings. She would understand that. Surely she would. The fact that he had promised Robert that he wouldn't speak to his sister again was irrelevant. It was a promise he'd made knowing he would break, in fact, *had* to break, because only one person could say the words that had to be said. Only one other person besides Veronique knew the full extent of their conspiracy, and that was himself.

145

Michael picked up the phone. He would do it now, while he still had the courage.

In Brittany it was cold and frosty, a much heavier frost than the one which was sparkling on the parkland of Offerton Manor. Veronique stood before the window of the small salon, a breakfast cup of coffee held between her hands. She felt restless. It was so difficult being patient. No one but herself knew how difficult. The hoar frost on the trees and grass reminded her that Christmas was near. Christmas! She took an impatient sip of coffee; she had thought everything would be settled by Christmas. When the phone rang she was standing right beside the extension and picked it up immediately.

'Why, Michael,' she cried, spilling coffee in her haste as she set down the cup. 'I was beginning to think that you had forgotten all about me.'

'Never,' said Michael. 'You know that.'

Veronique's face lit up with a smile. Already she felt better. A surge of pleasure swept through her, so intense it was almost sexual. Soon she would be busy, leading the real life of a real woman, not the empty, sterile one she'd been existing in. Soon all their plans would come to fruition because Michael was ringing her to tell her when.

'I was only teasing,' she said. 'I know that you can never forget me, because you love me just as I love you.'

'Yes, it's true. I do love you,' said Michael slowly, his voice very solemn, 'and part of me probably always will, but I . . .'

'Part of you? Probably?' This was not what she wanted to hear. Veronique's bubble of happiness abruptly ruptured. There was an elegant gilt chair by the side of the telephone table and she sat down on it heavily.

'Veronique, are you there?' The long silence worried Michael.

'Yes, I'm here.'

'Veronique, forgive me. I know I'm being a coward not

146

coming to see you myself, not coming to tell you in person, but I . . .' Michael's voice faltered.

In comparison Veronique's voice was strong. 'Tell me what, Michael?' she said carefully.

'I'm staying in England with Louise and baby Daniel. Don't think that this has been an easy decision for me. It hasn't. But I know, without a shadow of doubt, that it is the right decision, and the only one I can make. I can't let them down. Everything has changed since the last time I saw you. I thought I could do it. Now I know I can't, because I cannot walk away with a clear conscience.'

'I see. Out agreement is null and void then.'

Michael thought Veronique's voice miraculously calm. Telling her wasn't turning out to be nearly as bad as he'd thought. But he was in England, and she was in France, and what he couldn't see was that her face was the colour of pale slate, and her features set with the rigidity of stone. Only one movement indicated that she was anything other than a beautiful statue. The tears streaming unchecked down her cheeks.

'You do understand then,' he said. 'I knew you'd see that what we had planned to do was wrong.'

'Wrong for you, Michael,' said Veronique, in the same, cool, clear and totally calm voice, 'but not for me. However, I'm not your wife now, Louise is, and if you want to stay with her then that is what you must do.'

She put down the phone, and remained motionless, staring with unseeing eyes out of the window.

In London Michael put the receiver back in its slot and heaved a sigh of relief. The deed was done. He had told her. But, God, he felt guilty. With a groan he held his head between his hands and slumped across the desk. Would he ever stop feeling guilty?

CHAPTER 20

'I don't know what to call this room.' Eugenia, balancing precariously on the top of a pair of rickety pair of steps, was looping paper chains across an enormous, sparsely furnished room, ready for Christmas. 'Is it a living room, sitting room, or drawing room?'

'This is definitely not for living or sitting in,' said Beattie with a shiver, 'it's too damned cold.' She nodded at the paper chains. 'Can't think why you're bothering to put those in here anyway. You'll all end up staying in the kitchen as usual.'

Louise passed Daniel over to Beattie and went to help Eugenia, who by now had one foot on the steps and the other on the top of the sideboard. 'I agree. Why don't you give up? Let's go back to the kitchen.'

'No.' Eugenia was obstinate. 'After dining at Offerton Manor I've decided I ought to make more of an effort. We've got an enormous house, and we really ought to make more use of it.'

'The problem is, dear –' Beattie bounced Daniel up and down on her knee – 'having an enormous house is one thing, having an enormous amount of money like Louise and Michael, is quite another.'

'We haven't got an *enormous* amount,' said Louise. Reluctantly her mind went back to the midnight telephone call again. Michael had never once mentioned needing a loan, so Louise didn't know whether he'd succeeded in getting one or not; and she couldn't ask, not without giving away the fact that she'd been eavesdropping. Neither had he mentioned the sale of the paintings again. They had just disappeared and that was that. Since that night she'd scoured the *Financial Times* every day, looking for some mention of Michael's company, Briam Corporation. But there was nothing, which must mean that everything was all right. In spite of that Louise couldn't rid herself of the worry that something *was* wrong. Michael was spending more time in London, and often when he came back to Offerton the pressure showed in the haggard lines on his face. But every time, just when she was on the point of asking, he suddenly seemed carefree again. Playing with Daniel, and even joking about the wheeling and dealing which went on in the heart of his financial empire. At those times she could almost persuade herself that all her anxieties, even the conversation she'd overheard, meant nothing. Almost, not quite. The niggling doubts never completely disappeared.

'What exactly would you call an enormous amount?' queried her mother. 'Personally I'd call a couple of hundred that at the moment.'

'I'd settle for fifty pounds,' said Eugenia wistfully.

Louise felt guilty. She lived in the lap of luxury whereas her mother and Eugenia both worried about where the next penny was to come from, and were much too proud to accept more than token help from her. 'I don't know how much money Michael has,' she said truthfully. 'Sometimes when I listen to him talking, I think it's all on paper, and not real at all.'

'Mine is real enough.' Eugenia laughed. 'It's what I've got in my purse at the moment.'

Beattie shuddered. 'Ugh! Money, such a depressing subject. Let's talk about something else. When will the children be home from school?'

'Not for ages. We'll have time for some tea in peace.'

Daniel, who was still being bounced, managed to catch hold of Beattie's necklace. Chuckling with pleasure he tried to ram it into his mouth.

'You know this baby has got a real laugh,' said Beattie. She looked at Louise. 'I may not have approved of the way you set about acquiring him, but I wouldn't let you send him back now. Not for the world.'

Louise smiled at Daniel, feeling the familiar rush of tenderness she always had whenever she looked at him. 'I don't think he'd be willing to go back. He seems to like it here. I take it you withdraw your remark about babies and bananas now?'

Her mother shook her head. 'No, I still don't approve of the way you went shopping.'

'Shopping!' Eugenia nearly fell off the ladder.

Louise felt she owed her some sort of explanation. 'When I decided that I wanted a baby before it was too late for me to reproduce, I have to admit that I did go shopping. I shopped for a baby and a man, in that order.'

'And lucky old you got both, and a millionaire to boot!' Eugenia sighed. 'Oh, I do envy you, Louise. How is it you are always so well organized? Everything I do happens by accident.'

'Organization had nothing to do with it, she was damned lucky,' said Beattie. 'Pure luck. It could so easily have turned into a complete disaster.'

'Nonsense! Nothing can be a complete disaster if you plan it properly,' said Louise, smiling at Daniel's antics. At nearly three months old he was the light of her life. His thatch of dark hair had disappeared, leaving him bald, although a fine fuzz of fairish down was now beginning to appear, but his eyes remained as dark as ever and were now sparkling with glee as he tugged at Beattie's necklace. 'He was worth waiting nearly thirty-six years for,' she continued, 'and I'm glad I married Michael.'

'Sounds almost as if you need to convince yourself,' her mother remarked shrewdly.

Louise wished Beattie was not so perceptive. How did she know that she was continually reassuring herself that everything was all right. The night before, Sunday evening, Michael had been particularly distant. Physically he was with her, but mentally he was far away. Louise had tried to tackle him about it and asked him outright.

'Michael, is there something worrying you?'

'Of course not.' Michael kissed her.

Louise noticed that he always kissed her if she asked awkward questions. But this time she pulled away, freeing her mouth from his. 'I ask, because I sense there is.' She wished she could admit to eavesdropping on his conversation, but dare not. 'You seem distant, and preoccupied.'

'Nonsense, Louise,' he'd replied. With unnecessary vigour Louise had thought. 'You have an over-active imagination. It's all those hormones of yours settling down after the birth of Daniel.'

'It has nothing to do with my hormones. I want to know . . .' Louise was on the verge of blurting out that she had eavesdropped when Michael pulled her roughly into his arms, and began making love to her. The moment for confession and perhaps getting at the truth was lost, and Louise knew later, to her cost, that such moments are not easily found again.

'Louise! Wake up.' Beattie's impatient voice jerked her out of her reverie. 'Eugenia was asking where Michael is this week.'

'He's staying up in London as he has a lot of late meetings. He's using my apartment in Blackheath as a base now that he's sold his own apartment.'

'Why did he sell it?' Eugenia looped up the last paper chain and climbed down the steps. 'There,' she said, stepping back to look at her handiwork, 'that looks festive, and it covers up the fact that the ceiling badly needs painting.' She turned to Louise. 'Yes, why did he sell his and you keep yours?'

Louise shrugged. 'He needed the money and his property was worth much more than mine. He's been trying to raise as much capital as possible to buy the majority shareholding in

151

this new Ceecall mobile phone company.' It was the one piece of concrete information Michael had given her which might account for the loan. 'Personally, I think he's making a mistake; there's stiff competition and Ceecall has so much ground to make up that it will be years before he sees a return on his investment.'

'I thought he was a financial whiz-kid, and knew the markets inside out and backwards,' said Beattie.

'Even whiz-kids can make mistakes.'

From what she'd read Louise had decided that Michael thought he was invincible. But she also knew from her reading that there was the possibility of gambling once too often. It happened to other people. Another reason, she thought now, for keeping on the agency and not selling her own properties. They were real assets, not paper ones.

'Well, I'm glad you kept both your houses,' said Beattie, almost as if she could read her daughter's mind. 'But you ought to let the one in Winchester, rather than leaving it standing empty. You'd get a good income from it.' Still carrying Daniel she followed Eugenia and Louise through into the warmth of the kitchen.

'What on earth does Louise need an income for?' Eugenia busied herself making a pot of tea.

'Every woman needs some money of her own behind her,' said Beattie firmly.

'You've never had any,' Louise pointed out. It always amused her that her mother had such definite ideas, but never practised what she preached when it came to applying any of them to her own life.

'Exactly! That is why I know you need it. One never knows what unpleasant surprises life has in store for you. Money may not buy happiness, but it can provide a damned comfortable cushion.'

Eugenia laughed. 'I don't think Louise is going to have any unpleasant surprises or need of cushions.'

'Neither do I,' said Louise, wishing she felt more convinced than she sounded. Once again her mother had put into words her own vague unease. 'I think I *will* let the house in Chesil Street,' she said slowly. 'It's a good idea. I should try and get more income. I'm having to pay Tina quite a bit at the moment as she's virtually running the agency single-handed.'

'When are you going to start going up to London again?' asked Beattie. 'When you do, Lizzie Carey or I will have Daniel.'

'After Christmas,' said Louise, 'and I'm going to employ Lizzie's niece, Melanie, as a proper nanny. I've already spoken to her; she's fully trained, and will be glad of the job.'

'That's not necessary,' protested Beattie.

'It is. I can't rely on you or Lizzie to always be available. You both have other things to do. With a full time nanny I shall be free whenever I need to be. But don't worry,' she added, noticing both Eugenia and her mother's disapproving faces, 'I have no intention of neglecting Daniel. I love him far too much for that.'

'You will regret it,' warned Beattie. 'Fully trained she might be, but a young girl is never going to fuss over him as much as I or Lizzie Carey would. *We* wouldn't let him out of our sight.'

'That's what I'm afraid of,' said Louise, kissing her mother to soften the blow, and at the same time picking up Daniel. She laid her face against the soft warmth of his cheek. 'He'll enjoy being fussed over all the more if he doesn't get it too often.'

'Huh! It's a mistake,' grumbled Beattie. 'Something bad will happen. I feel it in my bones.'

'Rubbish!' scoffed Louise. 'Since when have you been clairvoyant?'

'Since this minute,' replied Beattie decisively.

'Louise, I'm off on holiday for a few days, and I wanted to see Michael about some financial matters concerning Veronique before I went.'

Louise was surprised. She knew Robert dealt with his sister's financial settlement from Michael, but had thought it was all signed, sealed and settled; and if it wasn't, then in her opinion it certainly should have been. She felt a sudden spurt of anger. Was the shadow of Veronique always going to hang over her? The anger showed in the briskness of her voice. 'I'm sorry, Robert. He isn't here. He's staying up in London this week. I can give you the address and phone number if you'd like it.'

'No, it's not that important. I'll send a fax to his office and catch up with him when I get back.'

'When are you going?'

'Tomorrow, unless the hospital throws some dire emergency at me.'

Feeling guilty for having snapped his head off, Louise tried to make amends. The last person in the world she wanted to be bad friends with was Robert. 'In that case, come round and have dinner with me tonight. You can admire Daniel and see how much he's grown.'

'Thanks, Louise, but I have quite a few things to sort out here at the hospital before I go, quite apart from making my travel arrangements. I'm afraid I always leave things until the last moment.'

'Some other time then.' Louise was disappointed.

'It's a date,' he said.

Robert put down the phone. After speaking to Louise he had telephoned the chateau, but Veronique was not at the chateau. She was in England; the housekeeper had even given him the name of the hotel in St James's Street, London, where she was staying. Now he was feeling distinctly uneasy. Christmas shopping, the housekeeper had said. He tried to reassure himself, of course, that was a perfectly justifiable motive for visiting London at this time of year. Except that Veronique had always hated shopping, especially the crowded shops of Christmas. But quite apart from that, why had she decided to go when she knew he was planning to visit her? Was it possible for her to have forgotten? He found it difficult to believe. But whatever the reason, he didn't need his holiday now. The practical thing to do was to cancel it. He'd take it later, and hope to see Veronique then.

Leaving his office he sought out his colleague Richard Meacher, and told him his plans had changed. 'So if it's not too late to go on that climbing trip you were talking about, I'll do your duties for you.'

Richard needed no second bidding; next to medicine, climbing was his *raison d'être*. 'Great,' he whooped, and charged off down the corridor to make the necessary phone calls. 'I'll do Christmas for you,' he called back over his shoulder. 'All my friends are married and spend time with their kids then, so I'm always at a loose end.'

'Thanks.'

Richard had already disappeared. All *my* friends are married, thought Robert, especially the one I care about most. He tried not to let his mind dwell on Louise, but was not successful. In spite of the fact that she was Michael's wife and had given birth to his son, the initial attraction had never diminished. His love for her had grown slowly but surely ever since the very first day they'd met. Louise had never given him any sign of encouragement, and he knew he was being totally illogical. But love, as Robert had come to realize, was quite independent of logic; it was a powerful, wayward emotion against which there was no defence. He sighed in exasperation at his own foolishness and turned his mind to more practical matters. Should he go up to London and seek out Veronique, or should he leave her alone for the time being? He decided to leave her alone.

Michael stopped dead in the foyer of the office block that housed Briam Corporation. For a split second the familiar scene became unreal, and yet every minute detailed registered in his mind. The girl at the reception desk was wearing a brilliant red suit, two men with bulging briefcases were standing talking by the sunken fountain surrounded by potted palm trees, the lift door was open, the interior light shining on the carpeted beige walls, and in the middle of all this was Veronique. She was dressed in black, her face was pale and her eyes as black as the woollen cloak swirling about her slender figure. Her hair was pulled back in a chignon, and she was wearing the long, heavy, drop silver earrings he'd had made for her; the intricate design combining their two initials, M and V.

Through a blur of conflicting emotions Michael heard his own voice, strained and alien to his ears. 'Veronique! What are you doing here?'

'I'm sorry, but I had to come.'

When he saw her eyes, bright with unshed tears, the emotion he'd tried so hard to suppress leaped and bounded, twisting like a knife in his chest. 'Wait here,' he said, and crossing to reception picked up the internal phone and buzzed through to his office. 'Put everything that I'd planned for this afternoon on hold. Something more important needs my attention.'

'But Mr Baruch – ' he could hear the panic in his secretary's voice – 'you were scheduled to see Mr Bridges and Mr Shelley at three o'clock. They are flying over from the Channel Islands especially.'

'Give them my apologies and tell them I'll see them tomorrow, and fix them in my schedule somewhere in the morning. Oh, and you'd better book them into a good hotel for tonight, courtesy of Briam Corporation, of course.' Replacing the receiver he turned back to the waiting Veronique and held out his hand. 'Come,' he said, and as he said that single word Michael knew he had taken a fatal and irrevocable step in the wrong direction.

'Darling,' whispered Veronique, her eyes blazing with triumph. 'I knew you wouldn't turn me away.'

* * *

'I shouldn't have come here,' said Michael. He looked out of the window of Veronique's hotel bedroom down at the busy street below. All the traffic was streaming one way, red double-decker buses nose to tail, squat black London taxis mixed with private cars, already building up to the gridlock which occurred every afternoon at about five o'clock in London. 'I shouldn't have come,' he repeated.

'Darling, why not?' Standing behind him Veronique slid her arms around his waist and leaned her head against his back. 'I love you,' she said softly.

Michael turned round. 'Oh, Veronique, Veronique.' He held her close, shutting his eyes tightly, afraid that she might see his own eyes were bright with tears. 'I love you too. We made the most terrible mistake getting a divorce.'

'It was necessary at the time.' Veronique unbuttoned his shirt and slid her hands inside, across the smooth muscles of his chest.

'Veronique! Don't! Please.' Michael grabbed her hands. 'I can't make love to you. I can't. I mustn't. What I said on phone was true. Everything *is* different now. I've tied myself to Louise, and I'm finding it impossible to untie the knot.' Veronique rubbed herself against him, and freeing her hands started fumbling with the top of his trousers. 'So don't you see? By making love to you again, I shall be betraying you both. A betrayal twice over.'

'No,' said Veronique, 'I don't see. Any knot can be untied.'

'Oh, Veronique.' Michael hardly recognized his own voice as he spoke. Then lifting her up, he carried her across to the bed. I'm weak, was his last coherent thought as he gave himself up to the ecstasy of her body. I'm weak and there is nothing I can do about it.

On the Friday night Michael was due to return to Offerton Manor. 'Stay tonight, and go back tomorrow morning,' said Veronique, her eyes filling with tears. 'Louise has so much, and you are all I have. You know that, don't you.'

The sight of her fragile face, dark eyes awash with love, lacerated Michael's heart. She'd been so brave, not once had she ever mentioned Louise and the baby, and he knew how much she wanted to know about Daniel, and much she must envy the two of them. Mother and child, a blessed state of being which she had longed for with a fanatical fervour all her life. She had a woman's normal expectation, but life had cruelly denied it to her.

'We should never have got divorced,' he said yet again, knowing that a large part of the present mess was his own fault. 'We could have stayed together and still been happy.' He cursed his own weakness. Why had he just given in and gone along with her plans? Only to find later that he couldn't fulfill his promises.

'Ring Louise, make an excuse.'

Michael picked up the telephone. One more night with Veronique would not harm Louise, as long as she didn't find out, and it would mean so much to Veronique.

'Louise, it's Michael here.'

'Darling. Where are you?'

'Stuck in a hotel with some boring business men, I'm afraid. I'm going to stay up in town tonight and come back to Offerton first thing in the morning.' Standing beside him Veronique could hear a baby crowing and chuckling in the background. She clenched her fists tightly, the knuckles shining bone white through her skin. 'Is that Daniel I can hear?' asked Michael.

'Yes, he's learned how to make a noise. It almost sounds like Dadda.'

'Terrific.' Involuntarily Michael grinned with pleasure, then his voice tailed away. For a moment he had forgotten Veronique, until her tension spread across to him, and he cursed his thoughtlessness. How could he have been so stupid; it must tear her to pieces listening to him talking to Louise about Daniel. 'I'll see you tomorrow then,' he told Louise. 'Goodbye.'

'Louise sounds very happy,' said Veronique when Michael had replaced the receiver.

'Yes,' he said abruptly, desperately attempting to prevent the two halves of his life overlapping.

'I'd like to seen a photograph of Daniel.'

'I don't think that's a good idea.' Michael's voice softened at the stricken expression on Veronique's face. 'There is no point in tormenting yourself, my darling.'

'I'd like to see a photograph,' said Veronique stubbornly. 'You must have one in your wallet. All fathers carry one.'

'Well, I haven't,' Michael lied, 'so you can't . . .' His words ended in a gasp as Veronique moved swiftly, and deftly extracted his wallet from the inside pocket of his jacket.

'Liar,' she cried, flourishing the photograph. 'I knew you'd have one.'

'Darling, don't.' Michael tried to retrieve the snapshot but Veronique eluded him and ran across to the window where the light from a large standard lamp flooded the room.

'He's beautiful,' she said softly, carefully holding the photograph so that all the light fell on it. Daniel's smiling chubby face beamed out from the picture, he was sitting in an armchair, his feet were bare and he was proudly holding one of his toes: 'Look how dark his eyes are. He could easily be my very own child.'

'But he isn't, Veronique,' said Michael gently. 'He belongs to Louise, and she is not going to let him go.'

'He's half yours, so if you love me as you say you do, that makes him half mine as well.' Veronique put the snapshot in her handbag. 'You can't stop me looking and loving your half of him.'

Michael watched her in silence. My God, what have I done, he thought, what have I done? It was then that he knew that Veronique would never take no as the final answer. She would always hope, always scheme, and he would always be torn in two because he lacked the courage to make the break one way or the other. He refused to allow himself to acknowledge that a time might come when a decision would be made whether he liked it or not. No, he couldn't possibly acknowledge that. The trauma of such a scenario was too awful to contemplate.

'Let's go and eat,' he said quickly. 'I'm starving.'

The moment Robert saw them together in the restaurant of Veronique's hotel he knew that they were still lovers. His sister had the same starry-eyed look that had shone throughout the years of her marriage to Michael, and her whole body oozed a prurient possessiveness towards the man beside her. The hairs on Robert's neck prickled. He wished he hadn't come, wished he hadn't witnessed Veronique's unhealthy preoccupation with the man she had divorced. He also wished he didn't feel so angry, but he couldn't help himself.

The anger propelled him across the room. 'You make me sick. The pair of you,' he said, walking up to their table.

Michael rose to his feet, his face ashen. 'It's not what you think.'

The maitre d' came rushing up. 'Sir,' he said to Michael. 'I'm afraid this gentleman came in here unannounced. If he is bothering you I can have him shown out.'

'If I am bothering them, it is nothing to do with you,' said Robert.

'No, it's all right.' Michael indicated that Robert should sit down.

'Just what the hell is going on?'

Robert was consumed by a mass of opposing emotions. Love, pity and anger for his sister, and a boiling, white hot rage where Louise was concerned. The woman he loved was patently being betrayed. Michael had promised him that he would have nothing more to do with Veronique, and I, like a fool, thought Robert, believed him. But mixed in with his anger was a sense of utter incredulity. How

160

could Michael behave like this? He had a son he loved. How could he be so stupid?

'I was in London shopping,' said Veronique, 'and, of course, I looked up Michael. There is nothing wrong in being friends, is there? He is only buying me dinner.'

Her black eyes stared at her brother, but they were shuttered and closed, revealing nothing but a reflection of the lights in the restaurant. Robert knew he would never prise the truth out of her until he managed to get her on her own. Perhaps not even then. He turned to Michael.

'Does Louise know?' he asked harshly. 'As this is all so innocent and above board, I assume she does.'

Michael dropped his eyes, and carefully topped up his wine glass. But for all his studied composure, Robert noticed that the hand pouring the wine was trembling.

'No, she doesn't,' Michael said at last.

'Only because she might not understand,' said Veronique, jumping in quickly. 'We don't want her jumping to conclusions, because then she might leave Michael, and take off with baby Daniel.'

'And she'd have every justification,' said Robert, trying to stifle the longing that Louise *would* leave Michael and turn to him instead. 'Do you love Louise?' Robert's question was directed straight at Michael.

Michael looked up. For a split second Robert fancied he saw through the windows of Michael's eyes into a nightmare of turbulent complexity. He saw a man full of despair, a weak man being annihilated by conflicting emotions.

'Yes, I do love her,' Michael said after a moment's silence. 'She has given me a lot.'

'Of course. She has given him Daniel,' said Veronique. Robert glanced across at his sister quickly. Why did her voice ring with that strange note of triumph? What had she got to be pleased about? 'Michael must never lose Daniel.'

'In that case,' he said coldly, 'I suggest that Michael

161

returns to Winchester now, and you, Veronique, go back to France first thing in the morning.'

'Louise is not expecting me until tomorrow,' said Michael.

'I know. But you can tell her that your meeting ended unexpectedly early, and you couldn't wait to get back to Offerton and your family. I'll book a room here, and stay overnight so that Veronique won't be lonely.'

'I don't need company,' said Veronique.

'But you're going to have it.' Robert's tone was grimly determined.

Michael looked at Veronique. 'You'll be all right?' he said.

Veronique laughed. Robert noted that she looked calm and determined and much less vulnerable than usual. 'Of course,' she said brightly. 'Although it is pity we are not to have dinner. But as my big brother, with his rather Victorian moral attitude, has firmly put a dampener on the evening, we might as well say goodbye now.'

Michael rose to his feet. 'Well,' he hesitated, then said abruptly, 'goodbye. Take care.'

Veronique tilted her face towards him and Michael bent and pecked at her cheek. 'Goodbye,' she said in the same bright voice, 'and just you make sure that you take good care of that son of yours.'

Michael didn't reply. Without a word he turned and strode away out of the restaurant.

Robert watched his departing back, and in that moment hated him. Michael was going back to Louise, the woman he had cheated, while he, Robert, who loved her, had no alternative but to remain silent. And then there was his own sister, Veronique, the cause of all the problems. Robert was forced to the conclusion that not only did she have some very strange ideas about divorce, but that she was unhealthily interested in Louise's son. He turned to her. 'Louise is more than capable of taking care of her son herself,' he said.

162

'I shouldn't be too sure of that,' said Veronique.

Robert opened his mouth to ask her what on earth she meant, but then closed it again. Veronique's bright look had gone, replaced by a cold, closed expression. She was shutting him out. He knew from experience that he would have to wait for explanations until she dropped her guard.

He picked up the menu. 'By the way,' he said firmly. 'Don't go making any arrangements for Christmas, because I'm expecting to spend it with you at Chateau les Greves.'

Veronique suddenly reached out and clasping his hand raised it to her cheek in a gesture of affection. 'I was expecting you,' she said, smiling up at him ingenuously. 'Christmas would be very lonely without you.'

The smile, the gesture, all reminded Robert of Veronique as a little girl. When they'd been young she'd always relied on him, her big brother. Hopefully he began to wonder if his imagination had been working overtime. Perhaps there *was* nothing to worry about. Perhaps there *was* nothing more sinister in her meeting Michael than two people learning to be friends again after splitting up. Robert wanted to believe it. Tried to believe it. But he couldn't. All he could think of was doubt, betrayal and intrigue. It lapped all around him.

CHAPTER 21

'Glad I came back early?'

'Yes.' Louise answered automatically as she watched Michael. He was sitting at the dressing table in his dressing room, his face softened by the shadows cast from the small table lamp which stood to one side. In the dim light he looked almost boyish. Perhaps this is how he appeared as a child, she thought. But he is not a child now, he is a man, my husband, and am I being foolishly old-fashioned to expect him to be faithful to me, his wife? Or is that a bizarre expectation in this day and age? Perhaps it is. She looked again at his softened image. How did he think he was going to fool her? Did he really not know that he reeked of perfume? A woman's perfume.

'Did you have a good week?' she asked carefully.

The question was superfluous; of course he must have had a good week. He'd been with another woman! Louise wanted to be angry, to feel the release of a seething, roaring and totally self-righteous rage, but instead, other, confusing emotions fought for supremacy. The emotions of despair, anger, hate, and strongest of all, a sense of treachery.

'I had a boring week,' said Michael, smiling.

So boring that you felt the need for another woman? That's what I should be saying, she thought, but the words lodged unspoken in her throat, held back by an aching pain. Now she knew what it felt like, the pain of betrayal. She had steadfastly kept her promise. Why couldn't he? Perhaps Veronique had felt like this once. Perhaps that was the real reason they had split up. Unable to think of what to do or say, she turned away and said, 'I'm sorry to hear that,' and left the dressing to return to their bedroom.

After checking on Daniel who was sound asleep, Louise threw her silk robe on a chair and climbed into bed.

Michael called out. 'How was your week?'

'I doubt that it was as exciting as yours.' The aching pain of betrayal was slowly beginning to simmer into a rising anger. Her voice hardened, became acerbic.

Michael came into the bedroom, and Louise stared at his reflection in the mirror opposite the bed. He didn't look guilty. Nothing in his face betrayed his feelings. He appeared quite normal.

'You sound very unfriendly,' he said.

'Do I?'

Their glances met and locked in the mirror, the glass slightly distorting everything so that they appeared farther apart than they actually were. Very appropriate, thought Louise sombrely.

'Louise, are you bored?'

'No, why do you ask?'

'Well, I thought that perhaps you were bound to start feeling bored sooner or later,' Michael said. 'Being just a mother, and stuck down in the country at Offerton is not really your scene.' Louise didn't answer so Michael carried on. 'Once a career woman always a career woman. So they say.'

'Do they,' said Louise. 'I wouldn't know. And I seem to remember we had this conversation once before. I told you then that once I had a child I would never be bored. And I'm not.'

Michael got into bed beside her. 'Louise, I've been thinking. It's perfectly OK with me if you want to start back at the agency before Christmas. I know you wouldn't let Daniel suffer, that he'd be well cared for.' She had her back to him, and he slid his arm across her back, cupping a breast in his hand.

'Thanks for the permission,' said Louise coldly. 'But I've made all the arrangements to go back for two days a week after Christmas, and I intend to stick to that. And don't think that I'm doing it because I'm bored. I'm doing it to retain my independence.'

'Oh!' Michael sounded surprised and slightly worried. 'And why should you want to be independent?'

'Because I do. Just because I married you doesn't mean that we should be glued together.'

'No, I suppose it doesn't.'

Louise couldn't decide whether he sounded sorry or glad. He was still holding her, and unfastening his hand she pushed it away and moved across the bed so that there was a gap between them. 'I have a headache,' she said abruptly. 'Goodnight.'

Gripping the edge of the bed in an effort to stay as far away from Michael as possible, Louise felt the simmer of anger begin to boil into rage. How dare he! How dare he cheat on her, and then want to make love while he still reeked of another woman! True, he had married her originally for convenience, not love, but all the same, she had thought it was based on mutual trust.

Then he had told her that he loved her. But I didn't ask him to love me, she thought angrily now; he didn't *have* to say it. Just three words. That was all it had taken to make her believe everything in the whole wide world was perfect. And I believed him because by then I had persuaded myself that I loved him.

The sudden revelation shook her to the core, and Louise had difficulty in restraining herself from sitting bolt upright in bed. *I had persuaded myself that I loved him.*

Trembling with fear at her own self-deception, she forced herself to face it, confront the unpalatable truth. Nothing has really changed, she thought, and I've been hypocritcal by pretending that it has. I slept with Michael

166

to get a baby, and I married him to give the baby a name and a fortune, just as he married to have a child he could call his own. Louise lay thinking about it. Now the consequences had to be accepted. That thought was painful too. I like Michael, she acknowledged, and I'm fond of him, *but I don't love him*. Then suddenly anger at his betrayal returned in full flood. Like or love, it made no difference. She had never cheated on him and had no intention of ever doing so. So why was he doing it to her?

Daniel began to whimper in the next room. She waited for Michael to get up; he usually attended to Daniel at night now that all he needed was a drink of water and a change of nappy. But Michael did not move. She waited a moment longer and listened. Michael's breathing was deep and slow. He was obviously sound asleep, oblivious to Daniel's cries. Not even damned well troubled by a conscience, thought Louise, feeling even angrier as she silently slid out of bed and went into Daniel.

'Quiet, darling,' she whispered. The anger suddenly evaporated. A familiar surge of love swept through her as she cradled him in her arms. It happened every time she touched him. In the dim glow of the nursery night-light she could see Daniel smiling up at her. 'So you are wide awake and want to play,' she said, tickling him under the chin which made him chuckle. 'But now is the time for sleeping, young man, so you can have a drink, and then you are going back to bed.'

The bottle of boiled water was standing ready at the side of the cot and the moment Daniel saw Louise pick it up he strained towards it, managing to grasp it with both little hands, feverishly trying to ram the teat into his mouth. With a little assistance from Louise he managed, and with a contented sigh began to suck greedily. He was already half asleep while Louise changed his nappy, and he snuggled down contentedly once she tucked him back into the cot.

Louise bent over the cot looking down at her sleeping

son. The silken down on his head was darker now, and shone with a delicate sheen in the soft light, and his long dark lashes fanned out on to his pink cheeks. One plump hand had already escaped from beneath the quilted eiderdown and was spread out like a starfish on the pillow.

Louise gripped the side of the cot. 'Whatever happens, darling,' she whispered, 'I shall never regret having you.'

Daniel hiccuped and smiled in his sleep, and although she knew it was only wind, Louise fancied that he was smiling at her words.

Back in the bedroom she paused by the bed. Michael was still sleeping soundly, and suddenly he rolled over and snored. Louise stopped dead. She felt so angry that it was difficult to restrain herself from beating him on the head as he lay there. How could he sleep so bloody soundly? Untroubled by his conscience? Afterwards, Louise decided that the snore was the catalyst which made her decide to do it. To find out if there was any concrete evidence of the other woman in Michael's life. Silently she walked across to the dressing room. If there was any evidence it was most likely to be found in one of the pockets of his suits. Firmly squashing the unpleasant sensation of feeling like a seedy detective in a second-rate movie, Louise began a methodical search. When her prying fingers finally retrieved a woman's lacy handkerchief from the pocket of Michael's jacket, the triumph of finding the proof was immediately shattered by the illogical wish that she had found nothing. But, as with everything else in life, there was no going back. She had looked, and now she had found. Louise stared at the handkerchief for a moment, then pressing it to her nose breathed in the exotic perfume. Abruptly, a submerged memory clanged like a bell in her head, and she knew what to do next.

Light suddenly flooding the room caused Louise to jump. 'What the hell are you doing here in the middle of the night?'

Michael stood in the doorway of the salon. The salon which led into the suite of rooms in Offerton Manor once occupied by himself and Veronique.

'Looking for the answer to a question,' said Louise.

'What question?'

'The question of who it was you were sleeping with last week.' Louise heard her own voice, cool, calm and seemingly completely detached from herself. It was as if she were two people. One woman was standing to one side, watching another man and woman talking. The two people talking had nothing to do with her at all, and yet at the same time she was horribly aware that they were treading a dangerous path. One false step by either of them would cause her, Louise, to pitch over into a dark abyss.

Michael stared at Louise. 'I was sleeping alone.'

Louise's composure broke. The two separate women suddenly merged into one, and she shuddered with a mixture of anger, contempt and sorrow. Then to her horror lost control completely and burst into tears.

'Liar! Liar! Liar!' Half shouting, half sobbing, she rushed from the room.

'Darling, please, don't be absurd.' Michael followed her.

'You've been sleeping with Veronique!' she screamed.

'No, I . . . you don't understand.'

'Yes, Veronique!' Was that really her voice screaming like that? 'Don't try and deny it. You reek of her perfume. Why do you need another woman? And why her? Why her of all people?'

'Louise, I . . .'

But Louise was not listening, she was running down the corridor towards their room. On reaching it, she slammed the bedroom door shut, and locked it.

Gasping for breath, and wiping the fine sheen of perspiration from her face with the back of her hand, Louise leaned against the door, holding on to the doorknob as if her life depended on it. She could see her reflection in the mirrors opposite the door. A pale, wild-eyed, dark-haired creature. Not like me at all, she thought. Then, in a blinding flash, she knew. I'm like Veronique except that my hair is short.

I'm like Veronique! I'm like Veronique! The revelation was shattering. Is that why Michael chose me for his second wife? Because I am like the first? It was as if her own identity was being sucked away. The mirrors opposite seemed to magnify and multiply her image, until the whole room was full of Veronique look-alikes, all tilting crazily towards her. Louise felt sick.

Beneath her hands the doorknob rattled. Louise held her breath, waiting for Michael to speak. But there was no sound. When after a quarter of an hour there was still no sound, Louise assumed he must have gone away to sleep in another bedroom. Only then, when she was quite certain that he had gone, did she begin to move.

CHAPTER 22

'Good heavens, it's you! You've practically given Mr Poo a heart attack, not to mention me as well. And neither of us, as I need hardly remind you, are in the first flush of youth.'

'Let me in.' Louise brushed past her mother, and put Daniel's carry-cot on top of the kitchen table. 'And for God's sake keep that damned dog quiet,' she added irritably.

'He has every right to bark,' her mother said sharply. 'It's the middle of the night.' It began to register with Louise that her mother sounded displeased. 'What on earth are you doing here? Has Offerton Manor burned down?'

'Michael has been unfaithful to me,' said Louise, and burst into tears.

'Oh My God! Is that all?' Her mother threw up her hands in exasperation. 'That's not a good enough reason for tearing about the countryside with a baby in the middle of the night. I've never heard of anything so stupid. But now that you're here, I suppose you might as well stay.' Beattie turned and filling up the kettle lit the gas ring on top of the stove and put the kettle on to boil. 'I'll make us both a cup of hot cocoa.'

'I don't want cocoa.' Louise slumped into a chair. Perhaps her mother was right, running away in the

171

middle of the night wasn't the most rational thing to do. But she didn't feel rational, far from it. 'I need a brandy,' she said.

'You'll have cocoa,' said her mother calmly. 'And while I'm doing it you can go up to your old room and make yourself up a bed. It's nice and warm in there; I always leave the radiator on. Daniel can sleep in there with you in his cot.' Louise got up, and stood looking slightly bemused and surprised at her mother's matter-of-fact reaction. 'Go on,' said Beattie, shooing her towards the stairs. 'Off you go. I'm not staying up all night.'

'But, Mother,' said Louise. 'There are so many things I want to talk about.'

'We'll talk about it in the morning,' her mother said firmly. 'I need *my* sleep even if you don't.'

There was nothing for it but to do as she was told, and Louise thought she would never sleep a wink. In fact she did. Like a log. It was the sound of raised voices in the kitchen below that awoke her. Michael's voice, and her mother's.

Louise got up and drew back the curtains. She looked out across the water meadows towards the ancient iron-age settlement of St Catherine's Hill. Outside, a magical December day spread its enchantment; the tangle of dried sedge, outlining the criss-crossing paths of the medieval waterways, glittered with hoar frost in the morning sunlight, and in the distance the smooth round hump crowned with a diadem of beech trees that was St Catherine's Hill, stood silhouetted against a clear, pale blue sky. The bell on the church of St Cross began to chime its melodious notes; it was nine o'clock. Louise wished she could be outside in the peaceful, timeless magic of a frosty morning, not inside, having to face the problems she'd run away from the night before.

She didn't want to talk to Michael. What was there to say? Nothing could alter the fact that he'd been sleeping with Veronique. But Daniel was eating some solids in the

172

form of cereal as well as taking milk from the bottle now, so there was no question of staying upstairs on the pretext of feeding him. He too was awake by now and was letting her know in no uncertain terms that he was hungry. One of her old dressing gowns was hanging on the back of the door. Louise put it on and picked up Daniel. There was no alternative but to go downstairs and face Michael and her mother.

'Good morning, dear,' said her mother impassively, as if she was used to Louise arriving in the middle of the night followed by Michael the next morning every day of the week. 'I've already warmed Daniel's bottle, and his cereal is ready in the milk saucepan on the top of the Aga.'

'Thank you.' Louise avoided looking at Michael who was leaning against the cluttered Welsh dresser.

She knew he hated the chaos and muddle of her mother's house, and could see out of the corner of her eye that he had fastidiously cleared a space amongst the jumble so that he could lean back. How out of place he looks, she thought. Immaculately attired as usual, not a hair out of place on his handsome head. Louise began to feel the anger bubble again. God dammit! This is a crisis, and he looks as if he is off to some City luncheon. Do you have any real feelings, Michael? she asked silently. Or are you emotionally bankrupt?

Sitting herself in the old armchair by the side of the battered and ancient Aga, she began to give Daniel his milk.

'There's coffee and toast for you and Michael. I'm going through into my studio to paint,' said Beattie tactfully. 'I'm sure you have a lot to talk about.'

'The understatement of the year,' muttered Louise.

'Life never turns out the way we expect it,' said Beattie, pointedly looking at Louise. 'Haven't I always told you that? But once you're on a certain path there is no turning back. You have to go on and find a new way if necessary.' She turned to Michael. 'And failing to face up to

173

difficulties only makes it worse. You've both got to give and take, or at least attempt to. Always assuming, of course, that either of you intend to make your marriage work.' With those few cryptic remarks she was gone.

Louise would have preferred her to stay, and opening her mouth was about to say so, but her mother was too quick for her. She disappeared before she had the chance to say anything. Once they were alone, rather than look at Michael she looked down at Daniel instead. His brilliant dark eyes looked up at her and he smiled, temporarily losing his grip on the teat so that a dribble of milk ran down his chin. Carefully wiping the milk away she wondered what she could say without losing her temper, and more importantly what was Michael going to say.

'I love you,' he said.

'You've a strange way of showing it. Sleeping with your ex-wife.'

'Look . . .'

'No, *you* look.' Louise raised her head and stared hard at Michael. With an effort she forced her voice to be low and calm. 'This may be the nineties, and it might be fashionable for other people to have non-existent morals. But I'm not other people. I'm me, and I'm old-fashioned.'

'You weren't particularly old-fashioned when it came to getting pregnant. You wanted a baby, and chose me as the means of getting what you wanted. Why else did you go to that dating agency?'

Louise flushed, and lowered her head. Michael wasn't making it easy, but facts were facts, and he had a right to air them. 'That's true,' she said, 'we both went there for similar reasons. To get what we wanted from life. But I was honest about it, and so, I thought, were you. And I don't regret having Daniel.'

'Neither do I,' said Michael.

'But getting back to me being old-fashioned. You've missed the point, Michael. What I mean is this: I married you, and I have no intention of sharing you with another

174

woman. Not your ex-wife nor any other woman. Some women put up with unfaithfulness, but that's not for me.' She looked back up at him. 'I wouldn't tolerate it even if I were madly in love with you, which I'm not.'

'But . . . I thought you did love me.'

Michael was surprised at her statement; it showed in his face. As surprised as I was myself when the truth hit me, thought Louise. Perhaps he was counting on that to bind me to him but if so he will be disappointed.

'I did think that,' she said quietly. 'But I've realized that I was fooling myself. I like you, but liking and loving are two very different things between a man and a woman. However, that wouldn't have changed anything if this hadn't happened. When I married you and promised to be faithful, I meant it. Mistakenly I thought you did too.'

Michael looked down at the floor. 'I don't want to lose you and Daniel,' he said softly.

'You should have thought of that earlier.'

'I promise I won't see Veronique again.'

'I don't believe you. Anyway, if not Veronique it could be someone else. How am I to know?'

'No, it was only ever Veronique.' His voice was ragged, as if the words cost him a great effort.

Louise stared at Michael. She remembered him kneeling alone in the cathedral chapel, the tortured look on his face. Now she knew why. It *had* happened before, and he felt guilty. Suddenly anger and pity fused into one confusing emotion. Nothing was clear-cut, all was a hopeless mixture.

'Last week wasn't the first time with Veronique, was it?'

Michael continued to study the floor. 'No,' he said at last.

He raised his eyes and looked at Louise, and she could see her own confused emotions mirrored in the dark green of his eyes. For a second she fancied that when gazing into his eyes she was looking into the sea. Deeper and deeper she looked, and the greater the depth the more the torment, the more the pain. She knew then that his affair with Veronique was more than just a sexual thing. He was bound to her in some way she couldn't understand.

'Well, Michael,' she said finally. 'You've said that you don't want to lose Daniel and me, and strangely enough I believe you.'

'Then you'll come back with me now to Offerton?' Michael's voice vibrated with a sudden eagerness. 'You'll forgive and forget?'

Louise shook her head. 'Forgive perhaps, when I can fully understand why. Forget, never. The knowledge will always be there. To forget is like trying to unpick part of your life, smooth it over and make something new. It can't be done. What's gone is part of our lives now, it will always be there.'

'But, Louise.' Michael slid down on to his knees so that he was level with her sitting in the chair. He put his arms around her and Daniel. 'We needn't let it become a barrier between us. I love you. I truly do. But I'm weak. I admit it. I met Veronique, and I felt sorry for her and before I knew where I was . . .'

'You were in bed with her.' Louise finished the sentence for him, adding dryly, 'Well, let's hope you don't go to bed with every woman you feel sorry for.'

'Louise, you know I wouldn't. It's just that Veronique is . . .'

'Someone special.' Again Louise finished his sentence. Daniel, on finishing the milk in the bottle, began to suck in air noisily. Removing the empty bottle Louise handed it to Michael. 'You can take his cereal from the saucepan and put it into that dish on the side there.' She was glad when he left her side to fetch the cereal for Daniel. Having him so close with his arms around her made it difficult for what she was about to say. Carefully sitting Daniel upright to burp him, she said slowly, 'I'm not coming back to Offerton with you now, Michael. That doesn't mean that I shall never come back. But I need time on my own, and I think you do too. You must decide, once and for all, whether you want Veronique or me, and I must decide whether or not I *can* live with you again as your wife.'

Michael handed Louise the bowl of cereal. 'Please come back. For Daniel's sake, if not mine. You have a responsibility to *him*, if not me.'

'So do you,' said Louise. 'Or did you forget that?'

'No!' Michael spoke fiercely. 'And I never shall. I would never have believed that I could care so much for another human being as . . .' He stopped and for one dreadful moment Louise could have sworn he was going to say 'as Veronique'. But he didn't. He said, 'as I do for Daniel.'

His vehement declaration touched Louise, and reaching out she placed her hand gently on his arm, filled yet again with a curious emotional mixture of compassion and sorrow. 'I think it might be all right,' she said slowly. 'But please, give me time to think things through. I need to be on my own.'

'Christmas will be lonely without you,' said Michael, 'and it is Daniel's first Christmas.'

'Christmas is two and a half weeks away,' Louise replied. 'A lot can happen in that time.'

CHAPTER 23

Louise was glad she'd not let her house in Chesil Street, because by the Saturday lunchtime following the Friday night she'd fled from Offerton Manor, she was back in her old home and settled in with Daniel. The small flintstone house with tiny lattice windows was warm and cosy, as the central heating had been left on, and apart from re-arranging the tiny boxroom next to her own bedroom as a nursery for Daniel, and getting in some provisions to fill the fridge and deep-freeze, it was as if she had never left.

Her mother always teased her about the house in Chesil Street. 'It shows you have a split personality,' she said. 'In London your apartment is so smart and Spartan that it looks as if it should be on the pages of a modern art magazine, and in Winchester, apart from adding modern amenities, you seem determined not to let the clock move forward an hour from the seventeenth century.'

'There is no way this house could look modern, and you know it.' Louise always vigorously defended the decor of her Chesil Street house which, if truth be told, she really preferred to the London one.

By Saturday evening, she was lounging back, her bare feet stretched towards a roaring open log fire, and feeling strangely contented for a woman who'd just left her husband. It was nine o'clock and Daniel, none the worse for being bumped around Hampshire since the middle of the previous night, was sound asleep upstairs. She looked around at the comfortable, but old, furniture, the bulging uneven walls and the floor that still sloped slightly despite the strenuous efforts of the local carpenter. Jane, the young woman who did the cleaning for her, had thoughtfully left a pot of brilliant yellow chrysanthemums in a copper pot in the one dark corner of the room, so that now the whole room glowed with warmth and life. Louise always fancied she could feel the hundreds of other people who must have lived, loved, and passed on to the other world in this small house since the late seventeeth century. But they were happy ghosts, and she never felt lonely.

'Daniel will be happy here,' she murmured to herself, 'happier than in that great mausoleum of Offerton Manor.' She could see him now, when he was a few years older, running down the steeply sloping garden to fish in the River Itchen which rushed past the bottom of the garden from the ancient watermill by St Swithun's bridge on towards the weirs. 'We will both be happy.' As the muttered words escaped her lips she knew that she did not want to go back to Michael.

'Damn!' She stood up. The front doorbell was ringing. Who on earth could it be at this time of a Saturday night. Surely not Michael?

'Can I come in?' It was Robert.

'Well, yes, but . . .' Louise was surprised. 'How did you know I was here?'

'Michael and your mother told me.' Robert followed her into the tiny sitting room where the fire was burning. Shedding his coat, he slumped down on to the settee in front of the fire.

He looked exhausted. His rugged face was drawn and taut, his usual healthy colour replaced by a greyish pallor. Louise suddenly found herself longing to throw her arms around him, to comfort him back into being the Robert she knew and loved. *Loved*! No, not love, *like*. The mental correction was made swiftly; she couldn't afford to complicate her already complicated life.

'Would you like some coffee?'

Robert looked up. 'Haven't you got anything stronger?'

Louise fished a bottle out of the wooden settle which stood against the longest wall, doubling as a cupboard and a seat. 'I've got quite a reasonable brandy.'

'I don't care if it's only fit for cleaning the cooker, I'll have some.'

In the kitchen Louise loaded up a tray with the brandy, two balloon glasses and a plate of cheese and biscuits. Robert didn't look as if he'd eaten recently by the colour of him. 'I thought you might be hungry,' she said on her return to the sitting room.

'A mind reader,' answered Robert gratefully, proceeding to wolf back about half a pound of cheddar cheese, and the entire contents of a packet of digestive biscuits. After Louise had poured him another brandy, he leaned back and said, So you know about Veronique and Michael.'

'Yes. That's why I'm here.'

'You don't look exactly heartbroken.'

'And how does a heartbroken person look? Do you know?' Louise felt apprehensive. The remark implied she didn't love Michael, which was far too close to the truth for comfort.

'Yes,' said Robert slowly, thinking of his sister's face when she had left him that morning to return to France, 'I do.'

'Michael is still in love with Veronique, isn't he, and she with him?'

Robert's expression was impossible to read. 'What makes you say that? Has Michael said so?'

Louise shook her head. 'No, of course he hasn't. But I'd be a fool if I didn't sense it, and although this may sound strange to you, I feel that it isn't only a sexual thing. Michael sleeping with Veronique is only part of it. There

180

is something much deeper between them. Something I don't understand. In fact, I'm beginning to wonder why he divorced her.'

'So am I,' said Robert with a heavy sigh. 'So am I. And what is more important, to me anyway, is why did he marry you?' He patted the empty space beside him on the settee. 'If I'm to help you, and believe me I want to, I think you'd better tell me your side of this triangle.'

Louise moved across, and sat beside Robert, her hands clasped tightly around her knees. Robert threw another log on the fire, and a rush of sparks flew up the chimney, lighting the thin film of soot at the back so that it glowed in a mass of tiny red dots. 'The people going to church,' said Louise staring into the fire.

'What?'

'There, look. The soot particles burning, they're the people going to church. That's what my mother always said.'

'What else did she say?' Robert sensed that Louise was getting round to telling him something difficult.

'She told me that I'd pay the price for trying to catch up. That it was wrong.'

'Catch up?' asked Robert gently.

'Yes, that's what I wanted to do. Catch up with other women. Have a baby before I was too old. And that's what I did. I thought it was possible to have what I wanted, provided I organized everything. So I did. Everything fell into place so easily. Too easily.' She was silent for a moment, then looked straight at Robert. 'I was totally selfish, and thought only of what I could take for myself. I was so absorbed with my need that I persuaded myself I was in love with Michael.'

Robert leaned forward, and tenderly unlocking the hands still clasped tightly around her knees, took them in his. 'Start at the beginning,' he said quietly, 'and tell me all about it. Take your time. We've got all night.'

Louise told him. All of it, including thinking of IVF,

181

looking for a suitable man and not finding him, and then the visit to the dating agency, and the meeting with Michael. Nothing was left out, even though she knew that it showed her in a less than flattering light.

'So you see,' she finished, unable to keep the tremble from her voice now that she reached the end of the story, 'that's why I don't look heartbroken, because although I like Michael and initially felt very attracted to him, I've always had doubts, which until now I've suppressed. But now, I'm not sure that I can ever bring myself to be a wife to him again.'

'Oh, Louise,' said Robert sadly.

Louise turned, and was suddenly aware of the affection for her blazing from Robert's tawny eyes. It caught and held her, wrapping her in a warm glow. 'Oh, God, I've been such a fool,' she whispered. 'You were here all the time. Why didn't I see?'

As though drawn by a magnet they moved slowly towards each other, faces getting closer and closer, until only a whisper of breath separated them. Then they were fused together, mouths, arms, bodies, all melting into one shining brightness. Louise wished the bone-melting kiss could go on for ever, but at last, reluctantly, they drew apart.

'I love you,' said Robert, cupping her face between his hands. 'I know you belong to someone else and that I shouldn't. But I can't help myself.'

Turning her face into the warmth of the palm of his hand, Louise closed her eyes. The effect of the kiss had momentarily shocked her into silence. Hesitantly she explored her new-found feelings. No man had touched her in quite the same way before. How was it possible to feel raw sexual desire, a clamorous ache, and yet utter peace at the same time? Then she turned back and opening her eyes looked into his eyes, and saw her own feelings mirrored there. The magic had bewitched him too. 'Kiss me again, please,' she whispered.

182

Robert began kissing her eyelids, her cheeks, her neck. But Louise threaded her fingers in his thick brown hair and pulled his face up to hers so that his mouth was on her mouth.

They sank down together on the rug in front of the glowing fire. Neither spoke; words were unnecessary. It was as if they had made love a thousand times before, so attuned were they to each other's needs. The flickering light of the fire washed over them. Undressing between kisses, they began to make love very slowly. The feel of him was an enchantment Louise had never experienced before. Strange and beautiful, and yet familiar, like coming home after a long time away. Hands, lips and bodies, moulding into one another as if they had been fashioned for this purpose since the beginning of time. Instinctive and knowing. Louise knew that he had loved her for a long time, because he came to her with a familiarity which was comforting, and yet was sensual and erotic. Relaxing completely she opened her body and soul to him in a way that she had to no other man, and knew that if she lived to be a thousand years old she would never forget this night. At last they fused together, two bodies into one, thoughts and senses one, lost to everything but the mindless impulse driving each throbbing second known only to lovers. The world began to disappear, drowning in an unbearable sea of pleasure. Louise heard Robert cry out her name, and in that same moment heard her own voice crying for more. Then succumbing to their fate, time and place disappeared completely and they became one.

Later, still sated in the aftermath of love, but almost afraid of the onslaught of affection and passion which had so suddenly engulfed them, they clung together. Not speaking, not kissing, but just being. Close and warm, fitting together like two halves of a puzzle.

Then at last Robert slowly held her away from him so that he could see her better.

Louise gazed at him, wondering why she had not seen

before how strong his mouth was. How it was made for her, and her alone. 'What shall we do?' she whispered.

Robert sighed, and pulled her in close again. 'You must decide. I love you too much to try and persuade you into anything.'

'Are you telling me that I must stay with Michael?' Louise clung tightly to Robert, unwilling to let go of the magic which had just been theirs, but at the same time knowing that it was irrevocably slipping away.

'I'm not telling you anything. But remember love between a man and a woman is one thing. Love between a mother, father and child is another. We can't think only of ourselves.'

'Why not?' cried Louise impulsively. 'I can't bear to lose you. Not now when I've only just found you.'

'There is Daniel. It would be wrong of me to persuade you to take him away from his father.' Robert spoke slowly. 'I know you've run away from Michael. But you must think long and carefully before you finally decide anything, and remember, whatever he might have done, Michael does love his son.'

'I know,' said Louise. She clung to Robert, burying her head in the hollow of his shoulder. 'Oh, Robert,' she cried. 'Doing the right thing is so hard.'

Robert knew then that she would return to Michael. Holding her close he stared into the fire, his eyes bright with unshed tears. Tears for what might have been if only things had been different.

CHAPTER 24

Michael agreed to everything that Louise demanded, and she told herself firmly that she ought to respect him for that. But it was impossible. He was trying very hard, she knew that, but the disconsolate expression on his face whenever he thought she wasn't looking made her feel irrationally irritable. He was like a dog who'd been kicked, but still hung around hoping for a pat on the head. She felt guilty. Though God knows why, she told herself. I didn't start all this; *he* did by going back to Veronique.

The arrangements were that her mother, brother and sister-in-law and children stay at Offerton for Christmas, and that Tina, her husband and sons also be invited down to stay at the manor house. Louise reasoned that if the house was full of people there'd be so much to do she'd never have time to think about the barren existence she'd chosen to embark upon.

She also left nothing to chance about their relationship in the immediate future, saying, 'You know I've come back to you because of Daniel.' Michael nodded silently, and Louise continued. 'But as my mother pointed out, we've hardly given ourselves time to think, and I certainly haven't thought much about us. Only about Daniel's needs, and that's why I'm here. Therefore, I want you to move out of our bedroom into another room. I can't be a wife to you. I can't go back to living as we were, pretending nothing has happened.'

Was it her imagination that a look of relief flickered briefly across Michael's face? Louise couldn't be sure, and at the same time she sensed an undercurrent of a strange emotion. Unable to put a name to it, all she knew was that it was elusive, intangible, and defied logic. They might not love each other, and yet there *was* something. Louise could almost feel a force pulling her towards him. Reluctance to acknowledge it changed nothing. It was there. Dragging her away from her own life and into his. Is it because I look like Veronique? The unwelcome thought sent a cold shiver down her spine. Being Veronique's *doppelganger* was not a role she relished.

'I understand, and I agree.' Michael's voice was low, the expression on his face now blank, all emotion gone. 'Of course it will take time for you to trust me again. It's only to be expected. But I give you my solemn oath that from now on you will be the only woman in my life.'

'You made the same solemn oath not so long ago,' Louise reminded him sharply.

'This time I promise faithfully. I mean it.'

'And what did you promise Veronique?' The words were out before she could stop them.

Michael turned away abruptly. 'Nothing,' he said harshly. But he was lying. Louise was certain.

To Louise's great relief Michael was called away urgently to Colombia. One of his pharmaceutical companies located there was being investigated by the United States Government; it was alleged that the company was a front for drug smuggling.

'And is it?' asked Louise, when he told her.

'How can you ask?' Michael was angry.

Louise looked at him. Surely he understood that since finding out about Veronique she was finding it difficult to trust him about anything? Once again she remembered the

186

midnight telephone conversation. He'd not been worried about sanctioning unlawful share dealing. Why stop at that? Why not make money from drugs? Why not ask him? Why not confront him with it now? But no. Louise pulled herself up with a joit. They were supposed to be making a fresh start for Daniel's sake. What good would it do Daniel if she started accusing Michael now? With an effort she kept her thoughts to herself, merely saying, 'It's possible. Maybe some of your employees are doing the drug smuggling.'

'Maybe.' Michael sounded slightly mollified. 'Whatever the reason I've got to get the US Government off my back; that company is one of my most profitable operations. I could never get factory labour as cheap in any other country. It's a key factor in the Briam Corporation's yearly increase in percentage profits.'

'Why do you need to increase the profits every year? You can't spend all of it.'

Michael looked at her as if she was mad. 'That's what business is all about,' he said. 'Increasing profits, making more money. To have the perfect life one needs money.'

'And we have it, do we? The perfect life, I mean?' asked Louise. 'Do you call living with continual suspicion the perfect life?' She hadn't meant to blurt it out, but the implication that money could buy anything was more than she could stomach.

He flinched, and Louise knew her barb had struck home. 'What do you mean suspicion? I'd thought we'd put all that behind us. I know I have.'

'Then you are very lucky. Personally I'm not finding it quite so easy.'

Michael wheeled around and looked hard at her, but his expression gave nothing away. What was he was thinking? What really lay behind the bland stare of those dark eyes? Was money the only thing that made him tick? Louise thought not. There were hidden depths to him which he'd never let her see. Suddenly, she wondered, if he were given the choice between Veronique and money, which would he choose?

'Louise, I thought you said that you'd try.' His voice interrupted her thoughts. 'I thought that was what you wanted. For us to make a success of our marriage.'

'I *am* trying. Why else do you think I'm living here with you?'

'Well, I . . .' Michael hesitated, seemed about to say something, then stopped abruptly. After a silence he said, 'I'm sorry. I know it can't be easy for you.'

Something in his face made her turn away, a wretchedness that was familiar. She was not the only one to feel the pain of loss. 'And not, I suspect, for you either,' she said softly.

Michael looked down at the floor. 'No,' he said. 'It isn't.'

It was the first time he'd ever admitted it, and Louise felt a surge of hopefulness. Surely, if they could learn to be honest with one another that would be a step in the right direction? But she kept such thoughts to herself: now was not the time nor place to try and analyze their relationship. Instead, she changed the subject on to safer ground.

'By the way. I've arranged to have the library redecorated as we agreed. It will be ready by Christmas. We can hold our festivities in there.'

'Yes,' said Michael heavily, and Louise knew that Christmas was the last thing on his mind.

CHAPTER 25

Some of the stone paving slabs in the pedestrian precinct of Winchester High Street were uneven, and Louise struggled with the pram as the wheels got stuck in the cracks. Winchester High Street, crowned by the remains of the city castle gate at the western end, was long and ran down the length of the hill until it reached the River Itchen and St Swithun's mill. Louise was going the difficult way, up the slope. Weaving in and out of the colonnades which ran for about a third of the High Street, she paused every now and then to look in the windows of one of the many small shops huddled beneath the half timbered buildings above the colonnade. Christmas gifts abounded. Expensive hand-made chocolates, silk ties, scarves, sheepskin slippers. But what to get?

It was the day before Christmas Eve, and she still had two more presents to buy. One for her mother, and one for Michael. Her mother was easy, she needed so many things, but Michael was a problem. At the end of the colonnades was the stone Butter Cross, and beyond that stood a tall Christmas tree blazing with lights. Today the steps of the stone monument were crowded with children, all sitting, muffled up to the eyebrows in hats and scarves against the cold, while singing carols with the Salvation Army Band. Louise stopped to listen. Christmas in Winchester had hardly changed at all since her own childhood. There might be videos and computer games instead of puzzles and books in the toyshops, but the magic was still there.

As soon as he heard the band and carol singing, Daniel struggled to see what was going on. Too young to sit up yet, he had nevertheless found out that by grasping the sides of the pram he could pull his head up high enough to see out.

'That young man will soon be too large for you to take him out in that.' It was Robert. He stood in front of Louise smiling hesitantly, holding a parcel.

'I know.'

The brassy notes of the band, slightly off-key because of the cold, played. 'God Rest Ye Merry Gentlemen'. But Louise and Robert hardly heard it. They stood gazing at one another, oblivious to the josting crowds. Both half smiling, both inexplicably shy. Why, we're like two gauche teenagers, thought Louise.

The smell of roasting coffee beans, and freshly cooked doughnuts pierced the chilly air with voluptuous fingers. 'Do you think Daniel is old enough to have a hot doughnut?' Robert grinned, breaking the spell.

Louise burst out laughing. 'Hardly! He is only two and a half months old.'

'I'm sure he can suck on a piece of doughnut while you and I eat one each and have a coffee. We ought to celebrate Christmas in some small way. Will you come?' He nodded towards the upper half of the High Street, to the crooked, half timbered house which was the coffee and doughnut shop.

Smiling, Louise nodded her agreement. She found a safe place for the pram outside, and followed Robert, who was carrying Daniel, through the low doorway. They were lucky and found a table right at the back, by an open fire and well away from any draughts of the shop doorway. The coffee house was busy, the front half of the shop sold home-made preserves and hand-made chocolates, and there was a steady stream of customers.

'All buying last-minute Christmas presents I suppose,' said Louise nodding towards the queue at the till.

'Talking of Christmas presents,' said Robert, placing his parcel on the table, 'this is for you.'

'Oh, Robert.'

'I know I shouldn't,' said Robert quickly, 'but I wanted to give you something to remember me by. I don't want you to forget me.'

'I'm not likely to do that.' Louise's voice was unsteady with the effort of holding back the threatening tears. 'I'm uncertain about many things, but I do know one thing. And it's something I never believed would happen to me, in fact I didn't really believe such a thing existed. But one night was all it took for me change my mind, to know that you are my once-in-a-lifetime love, and because of that you will always be part of me, even though we won't . . .'

'Ever make love again,' said Robert softly. 'I know, I feel the same way too. But you see,' he said, his voice suddenly urgent, 'sex is only a little part of love, all the rest is composed of much more complex emotions. The emotions of our hearts, or so the novelists would have us believe. But I think it is something much deeper than that. Too complex for us mere mortals to even begin to fathom out. All we can do is to feel it, and be grateful we've had something very special.' He stopped, looking embarrassed, as if he'd opened up his heart too much, then reached over and took Daniel on to his knee. 'Go on, open your present.'

'Can I take your order?' A plump, pink-faced girl in a long flowery Laura Ashley-type dress, complete with frilly apron and equally frilly mop cap perched on top of a mass of untidy hair, rushed up and stood, pencil poised.

'A pot of coffee for two, and two, no, make that three, of the fresh jam doughnuts.'

'Three pots of fresh coffee and two jam doughnuts.' The girl's Hampshire accent was heavily pronouned as she scribbled laboriously, pink tongue wriggling in the corner of her mouth as she concentrated.

'No, a pot of coffee for two . . .' Robert corrected the order.

'Oh yes. Sorry sir. It's the accent. Got me muddled up.' She rushed off, frilly apron tails flying behind her.

'God knows what she'll actually bring,' said Robert, shrugging his shoulders expressively, 'and what on earth did she mean about an accent?'

'Yours, of course,' said Louise, smiling while she struggled with the parcel which was extremely well wrapped. I feel quite ridiculously happy, she thought, just sitting here with Robert and Daniel. The smell of cinnamon, toast, doughnuts and coffee, the sound of carols being played outside in the frosty air of the high street, and the general air of festivity which always abounds just before Christmas, added to her happiness.

'What accent?'

Louise finally succeeded in untying the silver ribbon of the parcel. 'Your French accent,' she said fondly. 'Don't tell me you didn't know you had one?'

Robert grinned. 'I'm so used to it that I forget about I have one. I imagine I am speaking impeccable Queen's English, but obviously I'm not. However, that reminds me. I'm going across to France tomorrow, to spend Christmas with Veronique. I'll be away for a whole fortnight.'

'Oh.' Louise stopped unwrapping the parcel. She'd been so careful not to let anything intrude on their short time together, but now Robert had done it. By mentioning Veronique, he'd caused everything else to come tumbling into her mind, all the disturbing things she'd rather not think about.

'I can't pretend she doesn't exist,' said Robert quietly, seeing the distress on Louise's face. 'She *is* my sister.'

'I know,' said Louise, 'and I can't help wishing she wasn't.'

'I'm glad she is,' said Robert firmly. 'Because it means that I can stop her hurting you again. You needn't worry

192

about Veronique upsetting your life with Michael any more.'

'I'm not worried about that,' said Louise. 'It's . . .' She shook her head. No, she wouldn't tell him. It wasn't fair to burden Robert with her suspicions about Michael's finances, or the strange feeling she had that something beyond her control was binding her and Michael together. None of it had anything to do with Robert. Some things she had to resolve on her own, and her marriage was one of them.

'It's what?' asked Robert quickly.

'Nothing. When I'm with you nothing worries me. Let's enjoy this half-hour together.'

'Then open your present. I've never known anyone take so long.'

'There you are.' Triumphant, the pink-faced waitress plonked a tray between them. 'I think I've got your order right.'

'Yes, thank you. Well done.' Robert smiled at her and the girl fled, apron tails jiggling more excitedly than ever.

'Oh, Robert.' Louise had finally finished unwrapping the present. It was a silver cup. Tall with a wide bowl, and a handle on each side.

'It's for your Chesil Street house. Your mother tells me you will never sell the house and I thought it would fit in well there.'

'It's lovely.' Louise touched the delicate tracery on the silver. 'It's very old, isn't it?'

'Yes, it's a seventeenth-century loving cup. I saw it in an antique shop and fell in love with it. A loving cup.' He paused, then said, 'It seemed appropriate.'

'It's wonderful. I shall think of you every time I look at it.' Impulsively Louise leaned across to Robert, intending to kiss him on the cheek, but he turned his head at the crucial moment and their lips touched briefly. How was it possible for so much emotion to exist in such a brief encounter? One fleeting kiss and she was shaken to the core. Quickly she resumed her seat. A glance at Robert told her that he felt exactly the same. 'I haven't got you a present,' she mumbled in sudden confusion.

'Half an hour with you is present enough for me,' said Robert.

After leaving Robert, Louise finished her shopping, buying a silk tie and scarf for Michael, and sheepskin boots for her mother. But before returning to Offerton Manor she went to her Chesil Street house. It was a struggle hoisting Daniel, who was getting very heavy, out of the carrycot at the back of the car, balancing him on one hip with the present tucked under her other arm, and at the same time fiddling to get the keys into the front-door lock. But she managed, and at last they were inside. Once there, Louise carefully placed the loving cup on the mantelpiece above the fireplace.

'Will I ever sit here again and look at it?' she wondered out loud. She looked down at Daniel happily bobbing up and down on her hip. He gazed back at her, a serene smile on his round pink face. 'What does the future hold for you?' Louise whispered. 'What does it hold for either of us?' She hoped that it would be as serene as Daniel's expression, but had her doubts.

CHAPTER 26

Michael paused at the top of the stairs leading down into the oval entrance hall, and looked out of the window. The manor house was alive with noise, laughter and the smell of food. How Veronique would love this, he thought. He hadn't meant to think about her, but it was impossible not to. The children's voices were the trigger. It had snowed in the night, and now they were outside, Christmas presents momentarily forgotten. He watched them rushing about, busily making tracks in the virgin snow of the parkland. In the distance he could see Tina's two sons pulling a sledge towards the slope on the far side of the park.

'Look, here are some tracks.' That was Milton's shrill voice.

'And some more, but these are bigger.' Rupert was shouting excitedly.

Dick Carey answered. 'The little ones belong to a rabbit, and those bigger ones are a fox.'

'Do you think the fox was after the rabbit?' Michael smiled; Milton's voice sounded very worried.

'Sure to have been,' said Dick. 'If you look around you might see some blood.'

'Oh no.' Rupert was very firm. 'I wouldn't like that. I hope the rabbit got away.'

'So do I,' said Milton.

'Let's go round to the back lawn and start on that snowman you wanted to make.' Michael watched as Dick headed them away from the area where there might well be the gory remains of a rabbit. He was good with children, so was Lizzie Carey. For the first time since he'd employed them Michael wondered why they didn't have children of their own.

The telephone rang in his study, and Michael turned back to answer it. Christmas, the children and even Veronique were forgotten. There were pressing business matters to attend to. He'd spent most of the previous night on the telephone. Christmas Eve made no difference when it came to money matters, especially not when so many of his companies were ailing. Michael had hardly heard the riotous party return from midnight mass at the cathedral. Everyone had gone except Tara and Daniel, who'd been looked after by Melanie. Even the Careys had been persuaded to go, but Michael had made his excuses. Afterwards Louise had come up and asked him to join them in sherry and mincepies before they went to bed, but he'd refused.

'Let me work tonight,' he'd said, 'and then I'll be free to join you tomorrow.'

He'd looked tired, and seeing the piles of papers on his desk, and the screen flashing the changing share prices throughout the world, Louise had left him. 'If you want to spend Christmas making money, that's up to you,' she said.

Michael wanted to tell her that he wasn't making money, merely trying to salvage some. But he couldn't. To confess to anyone that he was in trouble was an admission of defeat. Michael Baruch and the Briam Corporation were synonymous with success, and that was the way he intended it to stay. The world recession would not beat him, no matter what he had to do to prevent it.

Now, with his study flooded with the bright sunshine of a snowy Christmas day, he picked up the telephone.

'Yes.'

It was Mark Lehmann, one of his associates. He was brief and to the point. 'There's no alternative,' he said. 'It's either borrow or bust.'

Michael didn't hesitate. 'We'll borrow.'

'It's one hell of a gamble. What if the market drops even further?'

'I think the market has reached the bottom. It's bound to pick up from now on.'

'I bloody well hope you're right.'

'I am,' said Michael with more conviction than he felt. 'Go ahead and convert £400m of the pension fund into assets we can use. Through the Swiss Bank, of course. Once the traders know my companies have been made secure by a massive injection of capital, they'll start dealing again.'

'We've still got the problem of a static market.'

'It'll pick up. Nothing stays static for long.'

'You do realize that will only leave £20m in the fund?'

'Of course I do. But once world trade picks up, it can all go back in.'

'*If* world trade picks up,' said Mark Lehmann gloomily.

'Don't give me that shit,' shouted Michael, his anger erupting. 'You said yourself it's borrow or bust. Well, I've no intention of going bust. He who dares, wins. Remember that.'

'OK,' said Mark. 'I'll do it. Happy Christmas!'

Michael didn't answer, merely slammed down the phone.

'This is wonderful,' said Beattie, looking around at the assembled company now sitting round an enormous oval dining-room table. 'The first Christmas I've ever had when I've not had to do the cooking.' She sampled the starter. 'The smoked salmon and asparagus is delicious.'

'God! You make me feel guilty,' said Eugenia. 'I ought to have cooked sometimes.'

197

'Don't say God like that,' said Natasha. 'That's what you're always saying to me.'

'It's different for grown-ups,' said Beattie cheerily. Then peering across the table at Natasha she said, 'I must say, dear, you are looking very pretty today. That is a very nice dress, even if it is black.'

'Oh, this old thing.' Natasha blushed, and looked shyly across at James and Alexander, Tina's two teenage sons. But they were busy talking to Gordon about motorbikes and were not interested in a ten-year-old girl, no matter how pretty.

'It's not old,' hissed Eugenia. 'I only made it last week.'

'An muffy maferave ee . . .' Milton, who'd had protruding plastic teeth in his stocking and was wearing them, was unintelligible.

Eugenia leaned over and snatched the teeth out. 'Mummy made her have the white lace on it and the red belt. Otherwise she looked like an undertaker.'

'If that's all you've got to say, you might as well have kept the teeth in,' said Natasha crossly.

'I shall,' said Milton, and putting the teeth back in his mouth picked up a piece of asparagus, and sucked it noisily through the plastic.

'Revolting child,' said Gordon.

'I just dread the day,' Tina was saying to Michael, 'when my boys are old enough to ride motorbikes on the road. I shall never have a minute's peace.' She looked across to where Daniel was sitting, propped up in his highchair, between Louise and Beattie. 'You'll feel the same when Daniel grows up,' she said. 'You wait and see.'

'It's not something I'd thought about,' said Michael. He looked at Daniel and tried to imagine the round-faced baby as a young man. 'I just can't see him grown up,' he said.

'You will,' laughed Tina, 'believe me, you will. And it all happens so fast.'

Lizzie Carey brought in the turkey and set it in front of

198

Michael. 'As master of the house I take it you will be carving,' she said.

'Of course, he must,' said Beattie. She waited a moment while Dick assisted by Melanie set out the serving dishes filled with steaming vegetables. 'But before he does, and before you go back to your own Christmas fare we must have a toast.' She rose to her feet and raised her glass. 'To the cook and her assistants.' Lizzie, Dick and Melanie beamed as the toast echoed around the room. 'And now,' said Beattie, turning towards Michael, 'to Michael, the founder of the feast.'

Michael smiled his thanks as the glasses were raised in his direction. He could see nothing but friendliness, kindness and warmth in their faces, and knew that they all, even Louise, wanted him to be part of their lives, to share in their happiness. But he couldn't. He had the strangest feeling as if someone had drawn an invisible line around them, and he stood alone on the other side of the line where it was cold and cheerless, quite unable to cross over into the warmth of their magic circle.

He looked at Louise and wondered if she could feel how far away he was. And then he looked at Daniel. For a second, a split-second, he saw Daniel as a young man. Tall and dark like himself, but with Louise's ready smile, and Beattie's carefree spirit. Was that all he was destined to see of his son as a man? That split-second? The thought was ridiculous, and he pushed it away.

'Come on, Michael,' said Louise. 'Start carving, we're all starving.'

'I think I'll take my teeth out,' announced Milton as a little spurt of steam arose when Michael plunged the carving knife into the roast turkey.

The train stopped in a deep siding not long after it had left Winchester. Louise sighed; a bad omen. In the three months since Christmas, during which time she had been commuting to London twice a week, the trains were often late. Today was obviously going to be one of those days.

The guard's voice echoed through the loudspeaker system. 'Due to unforeseen technical problems, this Wessex Electric Service to London, Waterloo, will be delayed for approximately thirty minutes.'

'Damn!' said the man sitting next to Louise. 'If they say thirty minutes you can bet your bottom dollar it will be at least forty-five.' Fishing a cellular phone from his brief-case he punched out a number. 'Eric? is that you?'

Louise noticed the phone was a Ceecall, the company in which Michael had borrowed heavily to get a third of the shares.

'John here,' the man continued in a loud voice. 'Look, the bloody train is late again. Move my item on the agenda down to the bottom, will you? I should be there by the end of the meeting, I'll speak to it then.' He turned to Louise. 'Damned useful things these,' he said, waving the phone. 'I'd like to have money invested in this company. Ceecall is proving to be the most reliable mobile phone around at the moment. The shares are rocketing up.'

Louise looked at the phone. So she'd been wrong and Michael had been right. He'd do well and recoup the stock he'd used as collateral. He was more astute than she'd given him credit for, and she'd been worrying needlessly.

'Want to use my phone?' Her travelling companion interrupted her train of thought. 'Do you want to tell anyone you're going to be late?'

'Thanks, I will.' She took the phone and told Tina she'd be late. 'And get me a low-calorie sandwich for lunch,' she added.

'You don't look too fat to me,' said the man when she handed back the phone.

'Well, I *feel* too fat,' said Louise.

Since Daniel's birth she was about seven pounds heavier than before and was determined to lose it. It was for her own sake, not Michael's, that she wanted to be thin. In fact she didn't want to be anything for Michael. Thank God he hadn't suggested moving back into the bedroom with her. Louise had long ago stopped being angry with him for sleeping with Veronique, but instead of the anger being replaced by affection it had been replaced by indifference. There was no doubting that he adored Daniel. But the more they were together, the more she realized how little she really knew him. Sometimes she felt as if they inhabited different planets. What motivated him? What did he feel about anything, herself included? Because of this she had decided to read his autobiography again, hoping that perhaps there was something in it she had missed first time round. A clue to his true personality. She'd brought the book with her to read on the train, and got it out now.

'Oh, I've read that book,' said the man, who obviously felt like talking. 'In my opinion the man's a crook. No one makes that amount of money so quickly in an honest way. When you read it you'll see how he skims over his early years; it's almost as if he made his first million by magic.' The man nodded his head sagely. 'Take my word for it, that Michael Baruch is a crook. It will come out one of these days. They always come a cropper, these get-rich-quick merchants. Wouldn't trust any of them as far as I could throw them.'

Louise smiled politely, and wondered what he would say if she told him she was Mrs Michael Baruch.

CHAPTER 27

Robert drove at speed down the Cherbourg peninsular. It was three months since Christmas when he'd last visited Veronique, and just over three months since he had seen Louise. Three months and two days, to be exact. The morning he'd given her the loving cup, the day before Christmas Eve.

Whenever he was in the city of Winchester he always detoured down Chesil Street and gazed at Louise's house in the hope that he might see lighted windows and know that she had left Michael. But the windows remained depressingly dark, and he knew from Beattie, who he saw regularly, that Louise and Michael were still together. Although, not, according to Beattie, as a man and wife should be. Robert said nothing, but it did give him a slight cause for hope.

At the moment, however, he had other things to worry about. He had caught the overnight ferry from Southampton to Cherbourg and was on his way down to see Veronique in response to an anxious telephone call from Andrea Louedec. Something was worrying her, she'd said, but wouldn't say what.

Early morning mist still hung like swathes of grey crêpe in the valleys between the hills, and the road stretched as far as the eye could see, straight as an arrow, the line only broken by the undulation of the landscape. Robert tried not to think about Louise. Something he found very difficult; she even crept into his thoughts when he was working at the hospital. Once, during the middle of a lecture to students, something had reminded him of her and he had completely lost his place, and had to ask what he'd been saying. His colleagues joked, saying that he was growing into an absent-minded professor. But no matter how much he wanted to see Louise, he had no intention of breaking their agreement. Other men's wives were out of bounds to honourable men, and apart from that one lapse, Robert was an honourable man.

He stopped for coffee at Dinan, deciding to drive down the steep gorge to the old port on the River Rance below the cliffs on which the medieval town of Dinan was perched. Although it was only March it was warm enough in Brittany to sit outside at a pavement café. The water of the river, smooth as glass, reflected the sunlight and Robert began to relax. Several tables were already occupied by laughing groups of holiday-makers, English and German by the conversations, and for a moment, as he sipped his strong dark coffee and ate two freshly baked croissants, Robert felt like a holiday-maker too. But it was only a moment; as soon as he started driving again he began to wonder what on earth was worrying Veronique's housekeeper.

His arrival at noon coincided with Andrea and Paul Louedec's midday meal. Always their largest meal of the day, and always eaten on the dot of twelve.

Andrea Louedec came out to greet him, wiping her hands on her apron. 'Ah, Monsieur Robert. I am pleased to see you. But I'm afraid Madame Veronique is out walking at the moment. She is on the headland, I expect.' She nodded towards the soaring cliffs edging the huge bay of Michel en Greve. 'Paul – ' she turned and called to her husband – 'come and take Monsieur Robert's bags to his room while I prepare some food.'

Paul came ambling out. 'No need,' said Robert. 'I'll do it myself. You go back and finish your meal, both of you. I should have been more thoughtful and not arrived at midday, but I've got into the English way and don't eat my meals at regular times.'

'Oooh la la, what a terrible country that must be. Not to eat at the right time is bad for the stomach.' Andrea was horrified.

'Exactly – ' Robert couldn't help smiling at her horror – 'so that is why you and Paul must go back and finish your meal.'

'You could always join us,' said Andrea shyly. 'Our table is not elegant the way Madame Veronique likes hers, but the food and wine is good.'

'I should like that very much.' The smell of cooking from the Louedecs' kitchen had already made Robert feel hungry.

Paul flung out his arm in a gesture of hospitality, and Robert entered the kitchen. A place was swiftly laid, and he was soon sitting down.

'The pâté is home-made,' said Andrea, cutting him a huge slice. 'My father made it only two days ago. He killed a pig last weekend, so this pâté is fresh. None of that shop-bought rubbish which has been standing around for God knows how long.'

'Andrea's father is renowned in the district for his pâté and sausages,' Paul said.

'Delicious,' Robert pronounced, swallowing a mouthful with a piece of fresh baguette.

'Wine?' Paul held up a bottle.

'From my brother-in-law's vineyard at Beaune,' said Andrea.

'Delicious,' said Robert again, after sipping the dark red wine. 'This meal makes me realize how much I'm missing by living in England. I'm glad I came.'

'Ah, yes, your visit.' Paul looked serious and laid down his knife. 'Don't let's spoil the meal by talking about such things now. Talking about serious matters and eating at the same time ruins the liver.'

'I certainly want my liver to remain healthy, so it's agreed. We'll talk about my sister after the meal.' Robert had difficulty in keeping a straight face. He'd been living away from France so long that he'd forgotten how serious the matter of food was to them; he'd also forgotten all the old superstitions.

It was a good two and a half hours later before Paul left the kitchen to return to his work in the chateau's gardens, and Robert was left alone with Andrea Louedec. There was still no sign of Veronique.

The housekeeper took a bunch of keys from her pocket. 'Follow me,' she said, and led the way from the kitchen.

'Where does Veronique eat?' asked Robert. 'In a restaurant somewhere?'

Andrea shook her head. 'She eats very little. Perhaps it is because she too has lived in England that she never eats regularly. Only *petit dejeuner*; she likes her coffee and croissants. When she returns later this afternoon I will make some crêpes for her. She likes those.' She led the way upstairs and into Veronique's large bedroom which overlooked the bay. Keys in hand she went towards the door in the side wall.

'I thought that room was full of junk,' said Robert.

Andrea shook her head. 'Take a look,' she said, and flung open the door.

Robert stepped inside. 'Mon Dieu!' he said. Then he turned back to Andrea Louedec. 'A nursery,' he said, 'but why? What for?'

Andrea shrugged her shoulders in a typically Gallic fashion. 'Who knows why? Paul and I certainly don't. Only your sister can tell you the real reason.'

Robert wandered around the room. Everything was perfect, and everything was blue. Blue for a boy. He felt an uneasy prickle of an unthinkable premonition. 'How long has this been here?'

'Oh . . .' Andrea thought for a moment. 'Since early April last year,' she said.

'I see.' Robert immediately realized that Veronique must have had this room done at about the time Michael married Louise.

'But apart from us, and the men who did it for her, of course, she has kept this room hidden. It is always locked. She did not tell you, neither did she tell Monsieur Baruch when he was here.'

Robert wheeled around. 'Michael has been here?'

'Last year. But not since.'

'I should bloody well hope not.' Robert lapsed back into English. What the hell was going on between his sister and her ex-husband? It didn't make sense. Not any of it. He looked at Andrea Louedec, who was now worrying about the wisdom of telling Robert Lacroix. He looked so angry. Perhaps Paul had been right, and she was stirring up a hornet's nest. Maybe she should have kept her mouth shut after all. 'What other visitors has my sister had here?' Robert demanded to know.

'None. She sees no one. No one at all. As far as I know she has no friends. La Chatelaine from Chateau St Jean du Doigt along the coast has visited and tried to make friends, but Madame Veronique sent her away. She said she didn't like her, and that anyway she didn't need any friends.'

'You're sure Monsieur Baruch hasn't been here since Christmas?' Robert was worried.

Andrea Louedec shook her head. 'No. No one has been here since you left.'

'Then if this nursery has been established for as long as you say, and she has seen no one, why did you telephone me? What is it that is worrying you at this precise moment in time?'

Andrea wrung the ends of her apron, twisting it like a dishcloth between her hands. 'Paul told me to mind my own business. But I can't help worrying. I'm fond of Madame Veronique, I feel sorry for her. She's like a lost soul.'

'Yes, but what *is* it that is worrying you? It must be more than this room.'

Andrea entered the room and walking across to a chest of drawers pulled open the top drawer. 'Baby clothes,' she said.

'So I see. What of it?' Robert couldn't help thinking they were no more puzzling than the nursery itself.

'She is changing them. Each month she is buying new ones. Always a size larger.' Andrea picked up a blue cardigan and showed Robert the label. 'See this is for a baby aged five to six months. She changes the clothes as if there were a real baby here. A baby that is growing every month into a little boy.' She looked at Robert, then blurted out, 'Paul said I wasn't to say this, but I'm going to. If you really want to know what is worrying me, it is the fact that sometimes when she talks to me I think there is a real baby for whom these clothes are intended. But other times I wonder, and think the baby exists only inside her head.'

Robert took the blue cardigan from Andrea's outstretched hand. The label inside read for babies five to six months. Daniel was now five and a half months old. The prickle of unease he'd felt earlier returned, and multiplied fourfold. He remembered Veronique crying on the telephone, saying that Daniel should have been called Alexander. That Alexander was the name she had chosen for the baby. At the time he'd thought it was interfence on her part, a reluctance to give up Michael to Louise and his new son. And he'd been right, because he now knew she had not given up Michael, not completely. But suddenly he was facing other fears. Was his sister mad? Or were she and Michael engaged in some fearful conspiracy? Was it planned that Daniel would end up here in the chateau? No. Robert dismissed the embryonic idea beginning to form in his mind as too dreadful, too ridiculous for words. No, the answer must be that Veronique was ill. She missed Michael, she was lonely, and the loneliness had unleashed the longing for a child she knew she could never have. Hence the nursery. A nursery for a make-believe child, the same age as Michael's own son.

He turned to Andrea. 'Don't worry. You were right to tell me. I think my sister needs help, and I shall make sure she gets it.' He held out his hand. 'I'll take the key to this room.'

Andrea handed it over. 'What are you going to do?' she asked.

'I don't know yet,' said Robert truthfully, 'but one thing is certain. I cannot let her go on pretending.'

He saw Veronique on the headland long before she saw him. She was scrambling up the steep cliffs, as sure-footed as any mountain gazelle. Robert watched his sister. She must have been right down to the bottom where the sea boiled, for ever angry and threatening, around the lumps of granite which lay scattered, as if thrown by some giant hand, far out into the water. It was terribly dangerous and he remained silent, not wanting to startle her and cause her to slip.

So he watched and noticed that instead of flying loose as it usually did, her hair was tied back, giving the impression that it was short. Suddenly Robert felt a heart-stopping jolt of fear. Stunned, he brushed a hand against his forehead, as if to brush the unwanted thought away. The familiarity he'd sensed when he'd first met Louise now took on a concrete form. The likeness between Louise and Veronique was uncanny, frightening. Was this what Michael had seen? Was this why he had rushed into marriage with Louise? Reluctantly Robert realized that it was more than possible; and given the likeness between the two women, Daniel could easily be mistaken for Veronique's son. The unspeakable beginnings of the idea he'd had before rushed back into his mind, to be rejected. No, it couldn't be. Logic prevailed. He told himself that people were often attracted to people of a familiar type to those they already knew. Probably the reason he himself had fallen in love with Louise. Life had a strange way of twisting things; he had fallen in love with a woman who looked like his sister without ever realizing the reason until now. The same probably applied to Michael.

'Robert.' On reaching the clifftop, Veronique had seen him. Now she was walking along the soft springy turf sprinkled with primroses and wild violets, smiling broad-ly, arms outstretched. 'What a lovely surprise.'

He decided not to tell her that he'd come in answer to Andrea Louedec's summons. He would wait until the right moment presented itself before he tackled her about the nursery. Holding his own arms open wide he laughed and said, 'I'm glad you're pleased to see your brother.'

'Oh, I am,' said Veronique. 'I am. I'm glad to see anybody. Life is very lonely sometimes.'

Tucking her arm through his, Robert led the way along the narrow path to the lane which led down into the village of Michel en Greve. 'This is a lonely place,' he said looking about at the trees, gnarled and stunted by the sea winds, and the vast expanse of grass and last year's dried bracken. 'There is not a living soul to be seen, unless you count the seagulls.' He looked up at the birds wheeling far above them, coasting effortlessly on the warm thermals rising from the sun-drenched headland.

'This place isn't lonely.' Veronique flung out her arms, encompassing the headland. 'I never feel lonely when I am here, only when I am in the house or with other people. That is when I feel lonely.'

'Perhaps you should move. Why don't we look for a house for you in a city? There you'd have shops and markets, meet plenty of people who could be your friends. Who knows, you might even meet another man and fall in love with him and marry.'

Veronique shook her head vigorously. 'I shall never marry again,' she said firmly. 'There is no need.'

Robert said nothing. Did she mean there was no need because she thought she still had Michael? But there was no point in resurrecting the time he'd caught her with Michael in London. The less said about that the better. He'd avoided a terrible quarrel then, and it would do Veronique no good for them to quarrel now. 'Lets go along to Perros Guirec,' he said, 'and have a snack in one of those restaurants by the harbour. You must be famished. I know you haven't eaten because I had my midday meal with the Louedecs.'

'This was a wonderful idea,' said Veronique half an hour later as she finished her spinach and cheese galette, 'and that was delicious.'

'You ought to eat at proper mealtimes,' said Robert. He caught Veronique's thin wrist in his hand. There was the difference between his sister and Louise, and probably the reason he'd initially missed the likeness. Although their features and colouring were similar, Louise looked healthy and robust, whereas Veronique looked fragile, as if a strong puff of wind might carry her away. 'You are not taking care of yourself,' he said.

'We'll eat together tonight,' said Veronique. 'I'll ask Andrea to cook us something special. She's a marvellous cook. And we'll dress up for dinner, and have candles on the table.'

Robert straightened his tie, looked at himself in the mirror of his bedroom at the chateau and took a deep breath. It was now or never. He could never get through dinner without first confronting Veronique about the nursery, and now, while she was in her bedroom changing for dinner, was the ideal time. Fingering the key to the nursery which was in his jacket pocket, he made his way to Veronique's room wondering how he was going to broach the subject of the nursery.

There was no answer to his tap on the door. Robert waited a moment then tapped again, more loudly this time. Still no answer. Puzzled, he tried the handle. The door was unlocked. Opening it wide he walked in, then saw there was no need to worry about how to raise the subject of the nursery because the door to it was open and Veronique was inside.

'Veronique!'

She swung round. Robert registered the confusion which flickered across her face; a mixture of fear, guilt and an odd kind of triumph. Then it was gone, replaced by

210

the shuttered, veiled expression she always used when she wished no one to know her thoughts. 'Robert. What are you doing here? It is a full ten minutes before we are due in the dining salon.'

It was the perfect excuse. Robert looked at his watch. 'Oh, is it? My watch must be very fast,' he lied. 'I thought you were late so I came up to escort you down.' He took a step towards the nursery, now dimly lit by a porcelain toadstool lamp formed in the shape of a little house with tiny figures inside. 'What is this place?' he asked, purposely keeping his voice as casual as possible. 'It looks like a nursery.'

'It is.' Veronique's voice held a definite note of defiance.

'Why? You have no child.'

'Not yet. But I shall. One day I shall have a child. A child of my own to use this room.'

The defiance had gone from her voice now, and Robert, accustomed to detecting his patients' fears, identified a desperation in her voice which he'd never heard before. Was it possible that she had lost her reason, and was now playing out a pathetic charade?

'Veronique,' he said tenderly, but very firmly and quietly, 'you know you can never have children of your own. Why torture yourself by having a room like this?'

'It is not torture.' The pain in her voice was almost palpable. 'I *shall* have a child. This room *will* be used. I know it.'

Robert tried another tack. He had to know whether Veronique was still living in the same world as himself, or whether she had retreated so far into her fantasy world that she needed treatment. 'I didn't know you were even thinking of adopting,' he said. 'It won't be easy. A woman alone.'

'I don't want to adopt. I have no intention of adopting. I want my own child. Do you hear me, *my own child*.'

Robert looked into Veronique's eyes and found himself trembling. No longer shuttered, he could see that she was

211

on the brink of hysteria. He had to be careful, so very careful. One false move and she could tip right over the edge.

He held out his arms and smiled. 'Darling Veronique, let's talk about it over dinner. We'll work something out. Something to make you happy.'

Veronique clung to him. 'You won't take my room away,' she said in a small voice like a child. 'I shall need it soon. You do understand, don't you?'

'Of course I understand,' said Robert.

'How can you?' asked Veronique, her mood suddenly changing. Now she was angry and tearful. 'You are a man. You have no idea what it is like to long for a child. To want one so much that it is a pain. A pain that blots out everything good, leaving you alone in a dark and empty place.'

He held her close, and stroked her hair. 'I know I'm a man. But I do understand, Veronique, truly I do.' Now, he fully understood what Louise had been trying to tell him. Why she had rushed into a liaison with Michael, got pregnant and then married him. She too had felt this longing for a child. For both women it was a tragedy. Louise had got her child but married a man she didn't love, and Veronique had lost the man she loved, and would never have a child. 'We'll have to see what we can do,' he said.

'Will you?' Veronique raised her head, eyes shining fiercely. 'Will you help me?'

'Yes, of course I'll help you' said Robert. He took her hand. 'Let's go down to dinner now, shall we?'

Veronique smiled for the first time that evening, but Robert's heart was heavy. He would help, but knew that what he had in mind was not what Veronique was hoping for. Only professional counselling from a psychiatrist could possibly help his sister. He hoped that, in time, she would be able to reconcile herself to the life fate had dealt her.

CHAPTER 28

Problems with a new client at the agency kept Louise late in the office.

'Damned nuisance,' she grumbled to Tina. 'If that wretched train hadn't been so late this morning, I could have sorted it out by now. As it is, I'll have to stay late.'

'Don't stay. Tomorrow is another day,' said Tina.

'And procrastination is the thief of time,' replied Louise tartly. She was tired, and bad-tempered. Quite apart from the weariness which resulted from commuting, sleep had been very elusive lately. 'If I don't do it now. I'll never do it.' She glanced up find Tina watching her with dismay, and felt guilty. 'Sorry to be so snappy. But you know as well as I do, an unhappy client means lost business.'

'But what about Daniel? I thought you liked to get back for his evening feed.'

Louise sighed. 'I do. But I'm afraid Melanie will have to do it tonight. It's lucky for me that he's really taken to her, and that she's good. I feel safe leaving him with her. In fact – ' she paused – 'I've been thinking that instead of travelling backwards and forwards every day that I come up to London, I'll start staying overnight in my apartment in Blackheath.'

Tina frowned. 'I didn't think that work was *that* important to you. Besides, you told me that Melanie's room was on the other side of the house, near the Careys'

213

rooms, not yours. How can she look after Daniel at night if she's not near him?'

'I'll do a little reorganizing of the sleeping arrangements. And yes, Tina, work *is* important to me. It's important to my future. One never knows what is going to happen. I can't afford to let the agency slide.'

Tina's frown deepened, becoming positively disapproving. She picked up a bundle of files and went towards the door. 'If one thing in this life *is* certain,' she said as she left Louise's office, 'I would have said that it is your future. You are guaranteed a lifetime of luxury. The last thing you need to be is a working mother. I know I haven't got your flair for running the agency, but I could keep it ticking over nicely enough. I could even find the right girl for this picky client you're so uptight about if you gave me time. You'd still make plenty of money. But anyway, what do you need more for? Michael's got loads.' The door slammed behind her.

Left alone Louise sat and stared at the closed door, and worried. Oh, dear, now I've upset Tina. She thinks I come into the office because I don't think she can do the job. Which of course in a way was true. True, Tina could keep the agency ticking over very well, but no more than that. Tina didn't have the clout to procure new accounts the way Louise did. The trouble is, thought Louise, feeling gloomier than ever, she also thinks I don't need the money, and will never need the money because I've got Michael. But the truth is that I might not have Michael for ever, and the *real* truth is that I don't want him at all. I want Robert.

'Oh Robert,' she whispered, and cradling her head in her hands let the bitter tears fall. 'I've got my child, only to discover that the price was to lose the chance of spending my life with the only man I'll ever truly love.' But the weak moment didn't last long. Louise knew only too well weeping did not change a thing; besides, she had been the architect of her own fate. No one else was to blame.

Her thoughts returned to Tina. My colleague and best friend, and now I've upset her. Perhaps I should tell her that all is not perfect bliss between Michael and myself. She sighed; everyone, except Beattie, the Careys and Robert thought her marriage was happy, and Louise had not disillusioned them. Now she seriously began wondering if this had been a wise move. Perhaps Michael and I should have had a proper trial separation for a longer period. After all, what have we really achieved? We're not living together as man and wife, and somehow I don't think we ever will.

With hindsight Louise knew Beattie had been right, and she'd gone back to Michael too soon. Too soon for either of us, she thought, remembering their conversation before Christmas, and the wretched look on Michael's face. He is unhappy too. What is the point of it all? Two people locked together in a loveless marriage. Surely it would be better for both of us to acknowledge that fact, and do something positive about it.

She resolved to talk to Michael about it that night. Other people could, and did, make civilized arrangements without hurting their children, and as they both loved Daniel, surely they could do the same for him? It would be better to make the decision now, she reasoned, before Daniel is old enough to be traumatized by the break-up. Still mulling over the details, she picked up the phone and told Melanie she would probably be late back to Offerton that night. By the time she'd finished speaking she'd made up her mind. Tonight, she decided, I shall definitely tell Michael that I want a proper trial separation, with everything out in the open, no secrets from anyone. It will clear the air, and force both of us to look long and hard at our future.

Once she had made that decision the problems with the new client seemed much easier to solve. Looking down the list of possible temporary secretaries, she picked a suitable girl. Then she phoned her, told her of the problems and made arrangements for her to start at the client's office the following day. Next, she faxed suitably abject apologies to the client's office for any inconvenience they had suffered, and finished by saying that she was sure they would be pleased with the replacement secretary who would arrive in the morning.

Breathing a sigh of relief, Louise leaned back in her chair. Luck had been on her side in that Helen Townsend had been available for work at a moment's notice. Helen was efficient, and self-confident enough not to be intimidated by the bullying M.D. she'd be working for.

The hands of the electric clock in the office moved on to the hour with a loud click, and Louise realized that, if she hurried, she still might catch her train and be home in time before Daniel's bedtime. Slinging the files in the drawer, she collected together her belongings, and scooting from the office disappeared into the subterranean network of the tube, knowing it was pointless having a cab at this time of the evening as they just got stuck in the traffic jams. Squeezing herself on to the already crowded tube she trod on an elderly man's foot.

'Sorry.' Breathless, Louise just managed to stop her shoulderbag getting caught in the sliding doors.

'You could have waited for the next train. There are too many people on this one.' The man was bad-tempered.

'I couldn't,' said Louise, 'I'd have missed my British Rail connection home.'

'Huh!' the man snorted, then fishing a *London Evening Standard* from his pocket, attempted the impossible, reading a newspaper while standing in a packed tube train.

Louise managed to look at his watch as he held up the paper. Good. She'd be able to catch the six forty-five to Winchester and definitely be back at Offerton before Daniel went to sleep.

The train screeched to a stop at the next station, people piled in and out, but mostly in, so that Louise and the bad-tempered man were squeezed even closer together. With her nose only inches from his newspaper Louise began to read it. The main headline was about some IRA terrorists who'd been arrested with enough explosives on them to blow up the entire Houses of Parliament and half of the City of Westminster. But it was the second lead article which made her catch her breath and go cold with shock. '*OUTSIDER IN, MICHAEL BARUCH, MIGHT SOON BE OUT. Questions are being asked about the true ownership of stock the Briam Corporation has been using as collateral.*'

The train rocketed into Waterloo and the man, his newspaper, and practically every other occupant of the train swarmed off in the same direction, leaving Louise standing where she was, trembling from head to toe. Her own suspicions of months ago were now in the headlines. But no, it couldn't possibly be true. Newspapers were notorious for printing anything to sell newsprint.

'Mind the doors.' The voice of the recorded warning echoed tinnily along the platform, jerking Louise back to the present.

Stumbling from the train she very nearly lost her shoe between the platform and the train door as the doors slid shut behind her.

'You should be more careful, miss.' A station guard came up to her and looked into her face. 'Are you all right, miss?'

'Yes, yes thank you. I was half asleep. Nearly forgot to get off.' Louise started running. She ran down the curving dingy corridors, ran up the first set of escalators, and took the stone staircase instead of the second set of escalators because it was quicker. On Waterloo concourse she snatched an *Evening Standard* from the newsagents and threw double the amount of money needed in the vendor's tray, not waiting for the change. She *had* to know what else the paper said.

The six forty-five to Winchester was still standing at the

217

platform and Louise made it by the skin of her teeth. Breathless, she sank into the first available seat just as the automatic doors closed shut.

'Good heavens, you cut it fine.' Louise looked. It was the man she'd sat next to that morning.

'Yes,' said Louise. She didn't want to talk. She wanted to get on and read the rest of the article. She turned to the front page.

'There, see! There's that chap you were reading about this morning. I was right, wasn't I?' The man also had a copy of the paper and stabbed a triumphant finger at the front page. 'I said that Michael Baruch was a crook, and now it turns out I was right.'

'News stories aren't always true,' said Louise, trying to stop her voice shaking.

'No smoke without fire, as the saying goes,' said the man, and laughed, rustling his paper triumphantly.

'Perhaps,' said Louise, and flicked her paper up so that it formed a barrier between herself and the talkative man. She turned back to the paper and started reading.

'*OUTSIDER IN, MICHAEL BARUCH, MIGHT SOON BE OUT. Recent events indicate that Michael Baruch who has always had the reputation for operating at a million miles an hour, may have run out of steam. The rapid expansion of his empire appears to have been founded on the shifting sands of other people's money. The former slum boy mesmerized individuals and some of the biggest companies in the land into pouring money into his corporation, with the promise of big dividends to come in the future. Hollow promises. His empire is crumbling hour by hour, minute by minute. A one-time colleague has said. "He'll be lucky if he avoids prison, and he'll certainly end up with nothing but the suit on his back."* '

Louise lowered the paper for a moment and stared out of the window. It was dark outside, and raining. Rain lashed at the train windows, the wind blowing the rainwater so that it trickled down across the windows in diagonal droplets. The

218

blackness outside was illuminated every now and then by a flash of light from the lighted windows of a house. Other people are sitting in those houses, thought Louise, people whose lives have not suddenly been turned upside-down by unwelcome knowledge.

The train slid to a halt, the automatic doors hissed then opened and Louise jumped up. Winchester already. She'd been so absorbed she'd not even noticed when the train stopped at Basingstoke. Stuffing the newspaper in her briefcase, she alighted and prayed that there would be a taxi free to take her to Offerton. She never drove her own car to the station as parking was impossible, and normally she telephoned so that Dick Carey could come and pick her up, but tonight there hadn't been time.

'Damn!' All the taxis had been taken.

'Louise, over here.' It was her mother waving frantically, her head stuck out of the beaten up old Renault she drove, which was parked at the far end of the car park.

Louise hurried across in the pouring rain and climbed into the car. Immediately all the windows steamed up and Beattie switched on the heater fan and began wiping them. 'Bloody awful weather,' she said.

'You haven't met me to talk about the weather.'

Switching on the interior light Beattie looked at her daughter. 'I can see you've heard the news,' she said, and switched the light off again.

The two women sat silent for a moment in the darkness of the car. 'I didn't hear it,' said Louise. 'I read it in the *London Evening Standard*. But nothing there actually proves Michael has done anything wrong. As far as I can see it is all allegations.' Who am I trying to kid? she thought, even as the words came from her mouth. I know from what I overheard that he's been less than honest in the past. What I don't know is, how big the fraud actually is, whether he can put some of it right with his own money, or whether he might actually end up being imprisoned. 'Newspapers are notorious for putting two

219

and two together and coming up with five,' she said, making a half-hearted attempt to convince herself.

'I'm afraid the television news was much more specific,' said Beattie quietly. 'That's why I came down on the off-chance that you'd be on this train. I wanted you to know the full story before you got back to the house. I understand from Lizzie Carey that Michael is already there. He arrived back from London early this afternoon.'

'Tell me what was said on television.'

'I'll drive back to my house and tell you over a cup of tea.'

'Tell me *now*.' Louise clenched her fists into tight balls, then said quietly, 'I'm sorry, I shouldn't have shouted. But I've got to know now.'

'Well,' her mother took a deep breath and then said, 'I am afraid there is no doubt that Michael is almost certainly going to end up completely penniless. The investigating journalists have traced all kinds of deals, the complexities of which are totally beyond me. But basically it seems to come down to the fact that Michael has been using money that was not his, moving it about to prop up some of his ailing companies. Instead of cutting his losses and selling the companies, he's siphoned off money from other parts of his empire to shore them up.'

'Why did he do it? Why couldn't he have been content with what he had?'

'Why indeed,' said Beattie. 'It still would have been more than most people ever have in a lifetime.'

Louise felt angry and confused. 'I would never have got involved with Michael if I'd known that . . .'

In the darkness Beattie put her hands out and reached for her daughter's. She covered Louise's cold hands with her own warm ones and drew them down on to her lap. 'Don't say anything rash, and don't start making judgements,' she said. 'Remember I am telling the facts as they have been presented; I've no doubt that there is much more to it than that.'

'I've always thought he cared more about money than people,' said Louise. 'That's what his book is about, you know. All it really says is, look at me, I started out with nothing, and now see how much money I've made.'

'He's not the the only self-made man to think like that. Money becomes their *raison d'être*.'

'But they're not all dishonest.'

'Huh!' Beattie snorted. 'Personally, I doubt that much of what goes on in the higher echelons of business could be called honest. Michael's unlucky. He's been caught. The others haven't.'

Louise turned in the darkness and looked at her mother's profile. 'You sound as if you are sticking up for him.'

'Yes,' said Beattie slowly. 'I suppose I am. It's because of his book "Outsider In".'

'What about it?' Louise was puzzled.

'That's it. Don't you see? He never was *in*. He only thought he was. But he didn't go to the right school, belong to the right clubs or lodges, and as a result he was never accepted into the old-boy network of the establishment. But worse than that, they were jealous of him.'

'I hadn't thought of that.' Louise was silent for a moment. 'Do you think that if he'd been part of the City clique this may not have come to light?'

'Probably not,' said Beattie cynically. 'And if it had, they'd have rallied round, and covered up for him, as they've done for so many others. A case of "you scratch my back and I'll scratch yours". But Michael, unfortunately, is, a loner.'

'I had no idea you were such a cynic,' said Louise.

Beattie made a noise somewhere between a snort and a laugh. 'When you get to my age, my dear, you've seen it all before. Just keep reading the papers long enough and you'll find there is nothing new in the news.'

Louise sighed heavily. 'I was planning to tell Michael

tonight that I was going to leave him, and that I wanted an official trial separation.'

'Well, you certainly can't do that now,' said Beattie. 'It would be too cruel. He needs your support.'

'Last week you were telling me that I *ought* to leave him.'

'That was last week. Now it's different. I don't approve of kicking a man when he's down,' retorted her mother.

Louise smiled in the darkness. Beattie was kind to everything on earth, even to the point of ushering bluebottles out from the kitchen rather than killing them. 'Don't worry, Mum. I have no intention of doing that. I'll stick with him, for now. Then later, when all this furore has died down, we'll both have to review our relationship.'

'You haven't called me Mum in years,' said Beattie.

'I need a mum at the moment,' said Louise. 'Beattie or Mother doesn't fit the circumstances.'

It was true. For the first time since she had left home Louise felt totally and utterly vulnerable, and unclear in her mind as to which direction she should go. She was unprepared for the unknown trauma which loomed ahead, and her instinctive reaction was to turn away, to have nothing to do with it. But that was impossible. Whether she liked it or not she was involved because she was Michael's wife and the mother of his child. But she needed guidance and comfort from the one person who had guided and comforted her, albeit unconventionally, throughout her childhood.

Beattie guessed something of what was going through Louise's mind. 'Don't worry,' she said. 'It will all come right in the end, you'll see.'

'I hope so.' But Louise was not convinced.

The first thing to confront was the press.

Beattie and Louise arrived at the wrought-iron gates leading into Offerton Manor to find them tightly shut.

222

'If you think you're going to get in there, luv, you've got another think coming.' A photographer with a sou'wester and oilskins on, a plastic cover over his camera, peered in through Beattie's open window.

'Nonsense, of course we'll get in,' Louise shouted back across her mother.

The photographer lit a cigarette under the shelter of his large sou'wester, and puffed gloomily. 'Like Fort Knox,' he said.

Louise got out of the car and, pushing her way through the crowd of men, reached the gate. A man in oilskins, holding a two-way radio, was standing the other side of the gates. 'Let me in,' said Louise.

'Sorry, miss. I've got my orders. No one is allowed in.'

'Don't be ridiculous, I live here.'

'Hey, she lives here.'

'It's his new wife.'

'Turn round, Mrs Baruch.'

'Look at the birdie.'

'Say cheese.'

'Piss off,' said Louise.

To her relief the security man, who was having a conversation on his two-way radio, started opening the gate. 'Get in quick,' he said, 'before that mob pushes past.'

Louise waved her mother on, and whilst the security man held one gate and she held the other, Beattie put her foot down and roared through the assembled pressmen who scattered like chaff before the wind at the sight of the Renault screeching towards them.

'I enjoyed that,' said Beattie, when the gates had clanged shut behind her.

Louise got back into the car. 'Vultures,' she said. 'Why can't they leave people alone?'

'You're newsworthy,' said Beattie.

'Well, I don't want to be.'

Beattie drove in silence along the curving drive and pulled up in front of the portico of the house. Louise realized that Michael must have been waiting for them in the entrance hall, because the moment the car stopped he was outside on the top step. Heedless of the rain, he came down the steps to meet her.

'You know?'

'Yes,' said Louise.

'Don't take Daniel away, please. I know you must want to leave me, and you'll want to take him. I can understand that. But don't, please.'

How could I have thought I felt vulnerable, wondered Louise. One look at Michael and she knew he was not only vulnerable but shattered. Whatever he had or had not done, she could see that the revelations in the press had demolished his life. The life he'd worked so hard to establish, and of which he'd been so proud. She remembered her mother's words about kicking a man when he was down, and reaching forward took his hands in hers, and felt them tremble. 'I'm not leaving you,' she said. 'We'll face whatever is to come together. The three of us. You, me and Daniel.'

'Well done,' whispered Beattie behind her.

But as she walked back with Michael into Offerton Manor, Louise found herself thinking of the gleaming silver loving cup standing on the mantelshelf in the house in Chesil Street.

CHAPTER 29

BRIAM CORPORATION'S VALUE SLUMPS BY MILLIONS IN THE SPACE OF A FEW HOURS said the headlines, and splashed across all the business and financial papers: '*Will Michael Baruch's Empire Survive?*'

The fickle world of finance was divesting itself of Briam shares. The scandal sent the dealers scurrying to sell.

Louise knew that Michael was furious. The vulnerability of yesterday had disappeared, and now he was angry. He was raging against the press, and the other members of his board who were faxing and telephoning Offerton Manor at, what seemed to Louise, five minute intervals.

She was finding it much more difficult to live with her decision of the evening before. It had been easy then, when she'd been overwhelmed with compassion for what she perceived to be his vulnerability, his genuine need for her. But now she had doubts about everything. Was he really worried about losing her and Daniel? Did he need her support as she'd thought? Or did he merely want her there so that he could present himself to the world as a respectable family man? Last night it hadn't mattered that he didn't love her, nor she him. He was a man who'd needed someone to stand by him when everyone else had deserted him. But in the cold light of day, Louise's doubts multiplied by the hour.

'They want a board meeting,' he told Louise, 'but I've said not yet.'

'Why not?' Louise asked.

They had not talked at all the night before. She had wanted to. But Michael, usually so rigidly self-controlled, and who only drank alcohol with his meals, had been drinking heavily before she'd arrived. As a result he was in no fit state to talk intelligently about anything, but now she had to know what was really going on.

'Why not? Because . . . Oh, God!' Anger suddenly disappeared, and Michael slumped at the desk in his study, his head in his hands. Once again he was the beaten, hopeless man of the night before.

If I am ever to get to the truth, I've got to take this one step at a time, thought Louise. Michael's abrupt change of mood was more than usually unnerving, oscillating as he was between rage and despondency. Over the months of their marriage she'd become accustomed to his mood swings, but they'd never been as violent as this. Determinedly she took a deep breath and steadied her nerves. All the more reason now to make certain that she did not lose a grip of things herself. Someone had to stay calm.

She found herself wishing Robert Lacroix was near. Not for herself, but for Michael. The feelings she and Robert had for each other were unimportant at the moment; whatever happened she knew that Robert would always be a good friend to Michael. More than that, he was a doctor, used to listening to people in trouble. He would know how to deal with Michael's moods, whereas Louise felt inadequate. She looked at Michael still slumped on the desk. He needed someone to talk to. There was no chance of contacting Robert however. She had telephoned his home early that morning, only to get the answering machine, and the hospital office had said he had a few days' holiday. As far as they knew he had gone to visit his sister in France. Louise didn't know Veronique's home number and couldn't ask Michael. There was no alternative; she would have to manage alone.

Louise asked again, 'Why not, Michael? Why don't you want a board meeting?'

'None of your bloody business,' shouted Michael, violently angry again.

Louise persevered. 'If I'm to stand by you, I think I'm entitled to know the truth.'

'Truth! There's no such thing as the truth. It's all a pack of lies. Malicious rumours, innuendoes put about by jealous rivals.'

'In that case, surely you have nothing to worry about.'

Michael turned on her. 'You understand nothing. Truth or falsehood, the share prices are falling. Everything else is unimportant.'

'It's important to me,' said Louise quietly. Then she asked, 'Did you sell stock that was not yours to sell?'

Michael looked at her sharply. 'I thought you said you were going to stand by me,' he said. 'Why rake that up again?'

Louise was about to retort that it was not she who had raked it up in the first place, but the media. But second thoughts kept her silent. Michael needed careful handling. 'I know I said that,' she replied in a calm voice, 'and of course I will. But I need to . . .'

Another fax chugged its way out of the machine. Michael ripped it out and read it. 'Bloody hell!' he exploded. 'The Bloody US Government are reopening the investigation into my Colombian company. They were quite satisfied when I left, but all this damned business has made them curious again. Before I know it, all the rats will have scuttled from the ship, and the whole damned shooting match will be down the drain. Briam Corporation will disappear and in a few years time no one will even remember it.'

'Is it really that bad? Can rumours ruin you?' Louise found it difficult to visualize a huge company like Michael's just folding up and disappearing without trace. 'Surely some parts of the Corporation are secure enough to stand firm and survive, no matter what happens?'

'Of course they can ruin me. Like all big companies my profits are on paper, there is virtually no cash, and I depend on keeping the banks sweet.' Michael paused, then slammed the fax down on the table. He paced restlessly about the room, clenching and unclenching his fists. 'I shall make a statement. Deny everything. Nothing can be proved, and anyone who says otherwise will have to be silenced.'

'I don't think that is wise,' said Louise.

'What the hell do you know about it?'

Now is the time, thought Louise. Now I should tell him what I overheard that night. The night of the dinner party to celebrate Daniel's birth. How long ago that seemed now. A lifetime away. 'You can't silence everyone,' she said slowly, 'especially not if they are telling the truth.' But now was not the time to challenge him about the phone conversation because she could see that her words fell on deaf ears.

Michael was suddenly oozing confidence again, and looking like his old self as he paced the room. Hands relaxed, pace leisured. 'How can anyone prove anything,' he scoffed. 'I can run rings around the lot of them. Always have, always will.'

'I doubt that.' Judging from what she'd read Louise thought he was being too optimistic.

'It will be their word against mine,' said Michael aggressively. 'I've already instructed all members of staff to say nothing.'

Louise decided she had to say something now, before things got completely out of hand. Michael's new confident mood was as nerve-wracking as his defeatist attitude of a few moments before. Was he really in touch with the events going on around him, or was he seeing the world the way he wanted it to be? 'Before you start making statements,' she said, 'I think I ought to tell you something.' She put up her hand to silence his interruption, and told him what she had overheard that November night the previous year.

When she'd finished speaking there was a long silence. Then Michael said, 'People do that all the time; robbing Peter to pay Paul. I've already bought back some of the stock I borrowed.'

'But the whole point is – ' Louise was impatient – 'the reports about your methods of operation are true.' There was another silence. 'Well,' she said, 'you can't deny it, can you?'

Michael sat down heavily in his chair by the desk. The ebullient mood had evaporated and he was despondent again. 'No,' he muttered, 'I can't deny it. Not to you.'

'Nor to anyone else,' said Louise. 'Because if you do then you will rightly be called a liar as well as a thief.'

'I'm not a thief. All I did was to try to keep everything going. There's a slump in world trade, I had to hang on to everything as best I could.' A new note crept into his voice, one of doubt. 'Perhaps I should have sold when I could, but . . .' His voice tailed off. Louise felt sick. Where did they go from here? She didn't know, and looking at Michael she doubted that he did either. 'What shall I do now?' he asked.

'I don't know. Wait, I suppose. But perhaps you had better agree to that board meeting. Arrange it for tomorrow.'

'Yes.' Michael sounded curiously meek, as if he was relinquishing responsibility. 'I'll do that. Thank you, Louise.'

He smiled in a strange detached kind of fashion, and with his elbows on his desk sat gazing out of the window. Outside, weak March sunshine, flickering between the scudding clouds, sent shadows scurrying across the fresh green of the parkland grass. Michael sat staring at the scene as if there were nothing more fascinating in the world, while Louise stood and stared at him. It seemed to her as if he had stepped through into another place, where problems were non-existent, and he had nothing to do but watch the play of sunlight and shadows on the land.

My God, she thought, who is this man that I've married? The unwelcome answer came back loud and clear. A complete stranger, someone who you really know nothing about at all.

The next day Michael refused to talk to anyone, even Louise. He withdrew into a private world of his own and sat in his study, staring out of the window. At Louise's insistence, Lizzie Carey took some coffee and toast up to him, but when Louise entered the study an hour later the coffee was cold and the toast untouched in the toast rack.

'Are you going to London for the board meeting?'

'What?' Michael sounded as if he'd never heard of London, let alone a board meeting.

Louise longed to take him by the shoulders and shake some life into him, but restrained herself. 'Have you arranged the meeting? You were going to.'

'No,' said Michael, and settling his elbows even more firmly on the desk cupped his chin in his hands.

Louise picked up the breakfast tray and left quickly before she smashed it over his head. Rages and fearsome arguments she could deal with, but a wall of almost total silence was daunting in that there seemed to be no way she could breach it.

'Perhaps I should have smashed this over his head,' she said to Lizzie when she reached the kitchen.

'Whatever for?' Lizzie was amazed.

'Well, then he would have had to have said something,' said Louise, feeling angrier by the minute, 'even if it was only "ouch".'

'Still being quiet then, is he?'

'The understatement of the year. You'd think he'd joined a Trappist order.'

Lizzie laughed. 'At least you haven't lost your sense of humour, dear,' she said. 'As long as you can keep that, you

230

can weather anything. You're just like your mother.'

For some illogical reason that comparison cheered Louise up immensely. Yes, damn him, I will weather it, she thought, and what's more I'll do something if he won't. So she telephoned the head office at the Briam Corporation building and spoke to a director named Hugh Smith.

She chose her words carefully. 'If there is to be a board meeting,' she said, 'I think it would be best if everyone concerned could come down to Offerton Manor today. My husband is not fit to travel at the moment.' She could tell the truth, that he was refusing to do anything, even to switch on the computer and look at the share prices, normally his favourite occupation whenever he had a spare moment. 'He's rather unwell. The flu, I think,' she lied.

'There's no point in any of us meeting.' Hugh Smith's tone of voice indicated that Louise's lie hadn't fooled him. His next words confirmed it. 'So he's finally cracked,' he said. 'Well, I can't say I'm surprised. When someone has been skating on thin ice for as long as he has, it's bound to give way sooner or later.'

'No, he's . . .'

'Mrs Baruch,' Hugh Smith interrupted, his voice not unkind, 'let me give you some advice, which strictly speaking I should not. It is this: if you own any shares in any of the companies affiliated to Briam Corporation, then sell them now. Take whatever price is on offer.'

'I don't have shares. I've never been involved in Michael's company in any way.'

'Then count yourself lucky.' Hugh Smith put down the phone.

Louise had used the telephone in the library, the room so recently decorated for Christmas. But Christmas, like everything else, seemed to have receded into the dim distant past. She wandered over to the window and looked out. The view from the library window was at

231

the front of the house and looked down the sloping lawns towards the hollow by the river where they'd had the picnic the summer before Daniel was born. How uncomplicated life had seemed then. It was only later, thought Louise, that I began to realize that it was all an illusion. Little did I know that the tangled threads of a troubled future were already in place, waiting to trap us all. I was beginning to fall in love with Robert and he with me, and Michael was still seeing Veronique; his company was beginning to founder and he was already skating on thin ice, as that Hugh Smith put it. A thought occurred to her. Hugh Smith knows about Michael and Veronique; it was the resigned kindness in his voice that gave it away. Perhaps the whole board of directors knows, but what does it matter now? Everything I'd thought so secure, had, in reality, been founded on nothing more substantial than our own dreams and desires, and we were mistaken even in those.

Today the weather had changed. Gone was the blustery March wind of the day before, its place taken by balmy spring sunshine. The catkins glowed a pale yellow on the hazel bushes in the hedges, giving a warmth to the landscape which had not been there yesterday. In one of the high fields on the downland overlooking the park, a flock of sheep grazed. Louise watched them, the ewes, wearing their winter fleeces, fat, fluffy and greyish-looking, stood sedately munching at the fresh turf, while the lambs, snow white, with long legs and even longer tails, frolicked about, jumping high into the air for the sheer fun of it. Some lambs were playing King of the Castle; a huge group of them got together, then charged like little mad things, butting each other from the knoll in the centre of the field. A peaceful rural scene, a symbol of the unchanging rhythm of life. Except that my life is not like that at all, thought Louise, everything is changing all the time. She wondered if Michael really would lose everything, even Offerton Manor.

She decided to tell Michael that she'd spoken to Hugh Smith and went along to his study. When she arrived he had the computer switched on, and was watching the share prices change on the screen. The sight made her feel hopeful. He was also on the telephone.

'Michael, I phoned . . .'

'Get out,' he said.

'But, Michael, I . . .'

'Get out, damn you. I'm in the middle of something very important concerning the future. Something I must get settled as soon as possible.'

'Something concerning our future?'

For a moment his face went blank. '*Our* future?' he repeated. Then he looked at Louise, focusing properly, and all she could see in his face was complete indifference. It was as if she wasn't there, or as if he'd never seen her before, and Louise shivered. 'No,' he said, 'it's nothing to do with you. Now get out.'

Louise went, not knowing what to think. Nothing to do with her, so nothing to do with Daniel either. So what future, or whose future? Was he making sure Veronique wouldn't suffer if his empire crashed? She wouldn't put it past him. I wasted my time, she thought angrily, in coming back here. I'm no use to him, he doesn't need me or want me. She returned to the kitchen, intending to collect Daniel and go out.

'Oh, if I'd known, dear, I would have stopped her,' Lizzie Carey apologized, worried about Louise's downcast mood. 'But it's such a lovely day that Melanie wanted to take Daniel out in his pram, so Dick's given her a lift into Winchester.'

'It doesn't matter. She's probably better company for him than I am.' Louise wandered around the kitchen, picking up things at random and putting them down again.

'Why don't you go out?' Lizzie suggested. 'Go and see Beattie. She'll cheer you up. I'll keep an eye on Mr Baruch, and give him some lunch.'

'He doesn't need anyone to keep an eye on him. He doesn't need anyone, period. Not me, not Daniel, no one. Except perhaps Veronique,' said Louise bitterly.

'Now, now, dear,' said Lizzie uneasily. 'Don't start getting everything out of proportion. Of course he needs you. And you know he dotes on Daniel. He's a bit preoccupied at the moment, but that's understandable. As my Dick says, thank heavens we haven't got any money to speak of. At least if you haven't got it you've never got to worry about losing it.'

Louise turned at the kitchen doorway and gave a wan smile. 'That's one way of looking at it.'

'The best way,' said Lizzie comfortably. 'Now off you go.'

Louise left, but Lizzie's words made her worry even more. If the worst happened and Michael did lose everything, it would almost certainly mean that Dick and Lizzie would be out of work. It was obviously not something they had thought of themselves, but Louise did, and it made her feel more depressed than ever. Everyone connected with Briam would suffer if the corporation actually did go under.

Louise slumped down in Eugenia's kitchen, which was almost as untidy as her mother's. 'I had to get away from the atmosphere at Offerton,' she said. 'I hope you don't mind me plonking myself on you.'

'Of course not. What are families for, if not to turn to in times of trouble?'

'I suppose they are,' said Louise. 'It's not something I've ever thought much about before. Now I know I'm very lucky to have such a happy normal family.'

Eugenia gave a shriek of laughter. 'Happy, yes. But normal? Us? With Beattie as the matriarchal head! By some people's standards we're all raving lunatics. By the way, where is Beattie?'

'She's taken temporary refuge in her painting. I went there first, but she sent me away. Said she couldn't cope with her own financial problems today, let alone anyone else's.'

'That figures,' said Eugenia. 'She was on the phone this morning complaining about the bank manager. I gather he's sent her another rude letter.'

'When things get too much for her she just disappears in a sea of oil paint,' said Louise with a sigh. 'I envy her that artistic outlet. It must help relieve stress.'

Eugenia slid Louise a sideways glance, noting her pale face, and the dark smudges beneath her eyes. 'You're feeling stressed?' She got out a bottle of red wine from the cupboard. 'Come on, let's have a drink. Help you to relax, and so much nicer than pills.'

'But it's only half past eleven in the morning.'

'I know, and this is only Damson wine, although if you close your eyes and imagine earnestly enough it could pass for a young Beaujolais. Nouveau Gilby, Gordon calls it.'

Baby Tara, now nearly two, staggered across the kitchen towards Louise, and putting up her pudgy starfish hands, tugged at Louise's skirt. 'Louise, sad, sad,' she said in her baby voice.

'Yes,' said Louise and lifting her up, sat Tara on her lap and cradled her in her arms. She leaned her check against Tara's head. The baby down had long since disappeared and been replaced by a mass of soft blonde, corkscrew curls which gave Tara the appearance of a Botticelli angel. 'Oh, Tara,' she said, 'you have so much to answer for.'

Eugenia, pouring the wine, looked up quickly. 'What on earth do you mean? Tara has a lot to answer for?'

Louise went on rocking Tara in her arms. 'I think it was probably because she was such a beautiful baby that I wanted one of my own. As you know, Daniel was no accident, he was carefully planned before I married Michael.'

'And now you're wishing you didn't have either?' asked Eugenia. 'A husband or a baby?'

Louise shook her head. 'No, I'll never regret having Daniel.'

'And Michael, does he regret Daniel's arrival?'

'No, he loves him,' said Louise, 'that is one of the few things that I *am* certain about. As for everything else, well . . .' She shook her head, thinking of the way Michael had been acting when she left. 'Things were difficult before all these financial problems came to light, but now it seems hopeless.'

'What exactly do you mean?'

'Well, sometimes I think Michael hates me, and other times I think he doesn't even know who I am. He's behaving very strangely at the moment. Silent for hours on end, and then this morning he shouted at me. Told me to get out.' Louise sighed. 'I don't know what to think.'

'I think I do,' said Eugenia, and taking some freshly baked cheese scones from the top of her ancient cooker where she'd left them to keep warm, sat down opposite Louise and passed her a glass of wine and a scone. 'Come on,' she said. 'Tell me all about it. Everything. I've got plenty of time to listen; the kids don't come home from school until half past twelve.' The brass ship's bell, which served as a doorbell, clanged. Its echo reverberated throughout the rambling old house. 'Damn, who on earth is that? Excuse me.' Eugenia disappeared.

She came back with Robert in tow. 'I went out to Offerton as soon as I got back from Paris and heard the news,' he said. 'But those damned guards on the gate wouldn't let me in. So I looked up Beattie and she told me you were here.' He drew up a chair and sitting beside Louise stroked Tara's head. 'Tell me,' he said, 'what is there that I can do to help?'

'Oh, Robert. Everything is such a mess,' said Louise, and then to her horror, because she'd been priding herself on how well she was coping, she burst into tears.

Robert and Eugenia listened in silence as Louise poured out the story. She started with the night of the dinner party and herself listening to Michael's telephone con-

236

versation about the sale of stock, and finished with her flight from Michael, and her subsequent return. Of course, the revelations about Michael going back to Veronique were not new to Robert, but they were to Eugenia, who drew her breath in sharply.

'What a bloody cheek,' she said. Louise looked at her in surprise. She'd never heard Eugenia swear before.

'My sentiments exactly,' said Robert.

'Why on earth did you go rushing back to him?' Eugenia demanded. 'I wouldn't have done.'

Across the tumble of Tara's curls, Louise looked at Robert. 'I had to go,' she said softly. 'If I hadn't gone then I might have stayed away for ever.'

'Huh!' Eugenia sniffed. 'That might have been no bad thing. Especially in view of what's happening now.'

'You're being very hard on Michael,' said Louise. 'I went back because Daniel is his son. I thought we ought to try again.'

'I suppose you were right,' Eugenia agreed. 'But I can tell you this. I would have been so angry that he'd have probably been glad to get rid of me again.'

Robert laughed. It broke the tension a little. 'Poor Gordon. Does he know what his fate will be if he ever steps out of line?'

'Of course. I made it quite clear right from the beginning. I'm a one-man woman, and I expect him to be a one-woman man. None of this nonsense of swopping partners when life gets a little boring.'

Louise looked at her sister-in-law with a new respect. She'd never suspected that beneath Eugenia's easygoing exterior lurked a woman of steel. 'I wish I were like you,' she said.

'Nonsense,' replied Eugenia briskly, pouring more wine. 'The world would be a very dull place if we were all the same. You stay the way you are. Just get your life sorted out.'

'Amen to that,' said Robert under his breath.

'Right,' said Louise, attempting to feel positive, which by this time was not easy as she'd drunk three glasses of Damson wine. 'First of all I think I must get Michael some medical attention.'

'What's wrong with him?' Louise hadn't mentioned Michael's strange behaviour to Robert.

'Gone potty by the sound of it,' said Eugenia, not mincing her words. She turned to Robert. 'Is there someone you can recommend?'

'Yes,' he said slowly. 'There is, but only if Michael agrees to it.'

Louise rose to her feet. She passed Tara, who had fallen asleep in her arms, across to Eugenia. 'I must go. It's nearly lunchtime, and when I'm home I like to give Daniel his meals myself.' She paused, then said, 'You don't think Daniel will be . . .' Her voice trailed away into miserable silence.

'Affected by what is happening now?' asked Eugenia, balancing a sleepy Tara on one hip. Louise nodded, and Eugenia shook her head emphatically. 'Be sensible, Louise. Why should he? He's only a baby. By the time he is old enough to understand, all this business will be consigned to the dustbin of history. It will no longer be important.'

Robert walked with Louise through Gordon and Eugenia's overgrown garden to the gate which led into the lane where their cars were parked. 'I'll drive you home in your car,' he said, 'and then call a taxi to bring me back here.' Louise started to object. 'Louise,' he said firmly, 'after three glasses of Damson wine, you'd never pass a breathalyser test. Do you want to end up making headlines yourself?'

His words forced a reluctant laugh from Louise. 'No,' she said. 'I don't think I'd like that one little bit.'

'Glad to see you smiling,' said Robert. 'Try to do it more often. And remember, keep everything in perspective.'

'I'll try.'

On the drive back to Offerton Louise felt more optimistic. Robert's presence was comforting, even though she knew he'd soon be gone again. But he's right, she mused. I've been foolish letting everything get on top of me. Nothing is as black as I've been thinking. Other people have had much worse things to contend with and have survived.

Arriving at the gates of Offerton Manor, Robert tooted the horn for the gates to be opened by the security guard, then drove through the still present crowd of pressmen. Louise didn't give them a second glance; she was beginning to get used to ignoring them now.

After parking the car in front of the house, they walked slowly together up the steps of the portico. Pausing at the top they both looked back out on to the parkland. The beauty of the spring morning had blossomed into a perfect day. A soft misty green of the newly budding leaves cast a delicate haze over the landscape; the very air seemed to breathe hope. Louise felt comforted. It would be resolved, all of it. For herself and Michael. Courage was the only ingredient needed. Courage to face whatever the future held in store.

'I must telephone for that taxi,' said Robert, crossing to the phone in the hall. When he'd finished speaking he said, 'It will be here in fifteen minutes.'

'I'll wait with you,' said Louise.

He made no move to go and see Michael, and Louise didn't suggest it. I know I'm being selfish, she thought, but I want him to myself, even if it is only for fifteen minutes. They sat outside on one of the teak benches beneath the library windows. Neither spoke. Words were not necessary. The mere fact that his hand rested lightly over hers as they sat in the spring sunshine was enough. When the taxi arrived he left without a backward glance. Louise watched, a mist of fine tears blurring his outline.

When the taxi finally rounded the curve of the drive and

was out of sight, she turned and walked up the steps of the portico, and through into the manor house. But the grandeur of the black and white oval hall was not what she saw. She saw her own little house in Chesil Street, with the loving cup standing on the mantelshelf, shining like a silver star. A star she longed so much to follow, but couldn't because of other responsibilities which could not lightly be tossed aside. How many other people, Louise wondered, find that doing the right thing is so difficult? But she reminded herself of Robert's advice, and tried to keep everything in perspective.

CHAPTER 30

Veronique felt restless. Robert's visit had annoyed her. How dare he visit her in hospital, and then leave so suddenly? 'Urgent problems in England,' he had said. What was more urgent than her? And why was he free to come and go as he pleased, and yet at the same time expected her to stay put? It wasn't fair. Then she smiled. On second thoughts, perhaps it was just as well he had gone. If he'd stayed he would have seen the beautiful bouquet Michael had sent, and would have disapproved. Crossing the room she gently touched the tall-stemmed yellow irises. They reminded her of the wild irises which grew at the edge of the lake in the woods behind Michel en Greve. Everything there would be turning green now. Last year's sedge would be sinking gracefully down into the depths of the lake, to be replaced by this year's fresh, vivid spears of green. As she fingered the irises she read Michael's card again. 'Be with you soon, darling. My time here is nearly finished.'

Smiling, she gazed out of the window at the magnolia tree outside in the sheltered, walled garden. The best of its glory had passed, but there were still a few cream and pink tulip flowers to be seen amidst the bright shiny green of the fresh leaves. But the appearance of peace was an illusion. Outside the walls the sound of traffic roared, washing over into the garden, sullying the tranquillity.

'We do have lovely gardens here at this clinic, don't we, Madame Baruch?' A nurse came into Veronique's room with a glass of water and little plastic pot containing pills.

'My own gardens are better,' said Veronique. 'Much more beautiful, and peaceful.'

'Yes, I'm sure they are,' said the nurse in the soothing tone of voice one would use to a child.

Veronique darted her a bright birdlike glance, anger sparkling in her black eyes. 'Don't speak to me like that.'

'Like what?'

'As if I'm an imbecile. I may be in a clinic for idiots, but I'm not one of them.'

'This is not a clinic for idiots. This is a clinic for people who are ill.' The nurse moved towards Veronique. 'I've brought your medication.'

Veronique turned away abruptly. 'You take it. I'm not going to.'

'Now, dear, I don't think Dr Steinberg would like to hear you saying that.'

'Damn Dr Steinberg, and damn you. I'm not taking any more pills. There is nothing wrong with me. I'm going home.'

'But . . .' Veronique's words took the nurse by surprise. She'd been such a sweet and placid patient in the time she'd been at the clinic. 'You can't. It wouldn't be wise. Your brother and Dr Steinberg both agree that you need . . .'

'Damn them both.' Veronique walked across to the wardrobe, and taking out a coat put it on. 'I'm going back to my own home, and you can't stop me. I'm a voluntary patient. I know my rights.' Picking up her handbag she checked it for money. 'I must have been mad to have ever agreed to come here in the first place.' She was out of the door before the nurse had even finishing dialling Dr Steinberg's extension to tell him his patient was running away.

'Let her go,' he said when he heard. 'She'll do no harm.'

'I couldn't stop her anyway.' The nurse was indignant. 'She's gone.'

Veronique caught the train from Paris to Rennes, then took a taxi for the long drive to the coast and Chateau les Greves. As soon as she got there, and had been greeted by a startled Andrea Louedec, she went into the salon and telephoned Michael at Offerton.

It was late in the evening. Michael was alone in his study, and when no one answered the extension, he eventually picked up the phone himself.

'Michael,' said Veronique as soon as she heard his voice, 'I'm home now. Everything is ready. I can't wait any longer, I've waited long enough.'

Louise padded along the corridor towards the rooms now occupied by Daniel and Melanie. Was it really only a few days ago that she had made the decision to move Melanie and Daniel together? Then it had been for her own convenience, so that she could stay up in London when necessary. But as yet she had not stayed away, or even been into the agency; Tina was coping on her own. Apart from the hassle of trying to dodge the press, who followed anyone leaving Offerton Manor like a pack of ravening wolves, there were so many other things to do. As Michael usually refused to answer the phone, Louise had found herself spending most of the time trying to fend off questions from the press, shareholders and a million other people who it seemed were interested in Briam's fate.

And yet, Louise thought now, I have achieved nothing. All Briam's directors have resigned; only Michael is left. It had got to the point where she was merely saying 'no comment'. It was the only thing she could say. How can I tell anyone anything, when I know nothing? She fumed at the crazy situation, and tried not to think of Michael still sitting each day in his study like a stone statue, because if she did think of it, she boiled over with anger. He was being so unreasonable.

Melanie was still bathing Daniel when Louise arrived.

He could sit up on his own now, and delighted in jerking his fat little knees up and down to make the water splash. 'Just finished,' said Melanie as Louise entered the bathroom. 'Although if Daniel had his way, bathtime would last for hours.' She plucked him from the water and wrapping him in a huge fluffy towel handed him to Louise.

Louise sat on the linen box, cuddling and drying Daniel at the same time. Daniel was her little piece of heaven. Nothing would be allowed to spoil his innocence. 'Don't babies smell delicious,' she said dreamily, rubbing her cheek against his damp head.

'Only when they're clean,' said Melanie in a more practical tone.

Louise grinned. Lately the only time she could honestly say she was happy was when she was closeted away with Melanie and Daniel. 'I know, you get to do all the unpleasant jobs. Don't think I don't know how lucky I am to have a nanny. I get all the cuddles and kisses, nothing unpleasant.'

'Oh, he gives me a few kisses as well,' said Melanie, smiling. Then her face became serious. 'Can I ask you something, Mrs Baruch?'

'Of course.'

'Well, I was wondering whether I ought to look for another job, because . . .'

'Leave me?' Louise was horrified.

'Oh, not because I want to. But the papers are saying that Mr Baruch is going to be declared bankrupt. They say that Offerton Manor will be sold because there won't be any money. And I've been thinking that perhaps you won't be able to afford me. I need the money, you see, because I've bought a car on the never-never so I've got to pay back so much each month, and it's costing me quite a lot.'

'You can forget about looking for another job,' said Louise firmly. 'Whatever happens to Offerton, or indeed

244

to anything else concerning my husband's financial affairs, it will not affect you. Thank God I still have my own business and my own house. We shall not be without a roof over our heads, nor without money. I can afford to keep you, but if you would rather leave because of the scandal attached to the Baruch name, then of course I should understand. I'd be upset, but I would understand.'

'Oh, I don't take any notice of what the papers say about that,' said Melanie. 'I can't understand half of it anyway, and I certainly can't see what all the fuss is about. As far as I'm concerned there's no scandal in losing money, only inconvenience. My dad used to lose his regularly, every Friday night on the way home from work. Until my mum waited outside the betting shop and took his pay packet from him before he could go in and spend it.'

Louise smiled. 'Your mother sounds like a very sensible woman. I only wish my husband had lost his in a local betting shop, but unfortunately he placed his bets on a worldwide scale.'

'Once this is all over and done with, you'll be able to forget about it,' said Melanie, with all the comfortable optimism of youth.

'Perhaps,' said Louise. 'Oh, how nice it would be if crystal balls really did exist, and I could see into the future.'

'Oh no.' Melanie was shocked. 'I wouldn't like that at all. There'd be no surprises then.'

Louise suddenly felt about a hundred years old. 'When you get to my age, Melanie, surprises can be a little tiresome,' she said with a wry smile.

BANKS PUSH CRIPPLED BRIAM INTO RECEI-VERSHIP. The following morning's newspaper head-lines gave Louise the opportunity she needed. Now Michael would *have* to talk to her, and she'd not take no for an answer. Entering Michael's study she put the paper down in front of him. Part of her mind registered that he'd been on the phone when she'd entered, and had put the phone down quickly on hearing her, but most of her thoughts were preoccupied with the headline and what it meant to all of them at Offerton.

'What is going to happen now?' she asked, pointing to the headline.

Michael barely glanced at it. He sat, elbows on the desk, his hands together forming a steeple, and stared out of the window. 'I'm so sorry,' he said.

'If you're feeling sorry about getting your company into this mess, you've left it a little late,' said Louise, feeling a sudden surge of exasperation. 'It's no use now. Briam's gone into receivership. All you can do is co-operate with the receiver.'

Michael turned his head slowly, and Louise saw that his eyes were very dark, the pupils hugely dilated, so that they appeared like black holes in his pale face. 'You don't understand anything,' he said in a clear, deliberate voice. 'Not a thing. And what is more, you never have.'

Louise's mind clicked over rapidly, attempting to decode and decipher Michael's remark. For a moment she felt that if she put out her hand and touched him it would go straight through him because he was some kind of mirage. Then giving herself a mental shake she banished such thoughts as stupid and over-imaginative, and tried to make sense of what he'd said.

'What is it that I don't understand?'

'Nothing.' Michael turned his head away and stared out of the window once more.

'Nothing! Nothing!' Knowing instinctively that she should be calm didn't help, Louise heard her voice rising in pitch as her anger and anxiety grew. 'How can you say nothing? When are you going to face up to things as they really are?'

'I am.'

'All right then, tell me what you are going to do.'

246

'Nothing for the moment.'

'But Michael! You've got to. There are so many things to sort out. Your company has just gone into receivership. You've got to do something. What about the future? What is going to happen now?'

'What does it matter to you?'

Louise stared at him. He sounded utterly calm, happy almost. He's completely out of touch with reality, she decided. 'Michael,' she said firmly, 'as far as I can see you are refusing to face up to anything. The only thing you've done, and which you did right at the beginning, is to hire a security firm to guard the entrance to Offerton. Do you really think that by doing that you can keep the outside world at bay for ever?'

'I'm not interested in the outside world.'

'You have to be. What about Briam Corporation? Is it really finished as the paper says?'

'Yes. It could have survived, but the banks have taken an expedient course to recover their funds. The shares are now worthless, and so are all the assets. They belong to the banks, not me.'

Louise found it difficult to believe that it was Michael saying all this. He sounded so serene, unmoved by the trauma of his life's work disappearing so completely. Could this really be the same man who had been so furious only a few days ago? Saying he could run rings around any of them?

'Are you telling me that you have no money at all?'

'Virtually none.' Again that flat, calm voice.

Louise couldn't believe him; surely wealth didn't just evaporate? 'And Offerton Manor? Will that have to be sold?'

'Yes.'

'And the Careys, what about them? And the other part-time staff? What are you going to do about them?'

'They'll find out,' said Michael vaguely.

Louise looked at Michael's impassive face, and felt a

cold, tight knot grip at her throat, making speech impossible. Without a word she turned and left the room.

Louise looked from Beattie to Eugenia and back again to Beattie. 'I think Michael has lost his sanity,' she said. 'He's not living in the same world as the rest of us. And I don't know what to do.'

'Come on inside properly,' said Eugenia, pulling Louise into Beattie's kitchen. 'Don't stand there in the doorway.'

'Darling, try not to worry too much. I'm sure it's not as bad as you think. Michael must be in a state of shock. It probably won't last for long, and anyway we'll enlist Robert's help. You'll be all right.' Beattie took Daniel from Louise and laid him on the rag mat in front of the Aga where he squirmed in delight at being free, and rolled over on to his stomach. 'Look at that,' said Beattie, 'he's trying to crawl.'

'He's wonderfully advanced for his age,' said Eugenia. 'Tara couldn't sit up and crawl at six months.' Unknown to Louise, Eugenia had hurried over to the St Cross house at Beattie's request. The telephone call from Louise saying that she was on her way over with Daniel and needed help was enough to worry Beattie. She decided she ought to have moral support, and there was no one better than Eugenia to provide that, because she was down-to-earth and not a panicker.

'Yes, he is advanced,' said Louise absent-mindedly. She knew they were trying to help by talking about normal, everyday things. But for once her sole attention was not on her son, it was on Michael and his strange behaviour. 'I'm not sure that we should bother Robert about Michael. It isn't fair to ask him. Maybe we should go straight to the local doctor. Someone not involved with the family.'

'Of course we should bother Robert.' Beattie was already dialling the hospital number. 'He said he was willing to arrange some counselling for Michael, didn't he? Well, from what you've told me I think it should be sooner rather than later.' She got through to the department and asked for him. 'Damn!' she said a moment later.

'What is it?' asked Eugenia.

Beattie covered the mouthpiece with her hand. 'He's just flown out on some lecture tour of Canada and will be away for nearly two weeks. I'll try and get a contact number.'

'Are you a relative of Professor Lacroix's?' Robert's secretary was always protective of him.

'Yes,' lied Beattie firmly. 'I am his aunt, on the English side of the family,' she added hastily. 'I need to speak to him urgently about his sister.'

'Oh, I see. Just one moment.' The secretary knew that Robert's sister was receiving some kind of medical treatment in Paris; perhaps this *was* urgent after all. 'This is the telephone number of the Neurological Department in Vancouver Hospital,' she told Beattie. 'They should be able to put you in touch with Professor Lacroix.'

'Thank you for your help.' Beattie wrote down the number.

'Canada is too far away to be of any use,' said Louise, 'and anyway I've been thinking. Michael's breakdown is no sudden thing; this has been coming on for a long time. All the signs were there long before anyone knew what he was up to with Veronique, or his business empire crashed about his ears.'

'For heaven's sake!' Beattie exploded. 'Why didn't you say something before? Why keep it bottled up?'

'I have said things but no one took any real notice,' said Louise, 'and even I tried not to attach too much importance to any of it. I always found reasons for what he did or said. I suppose if I'm honest, it was less painful to shut my mind against things I didn't want to know. But ever since the episode when I left him and then returned, I've known something has been terribly wrong, and it has nothing to do with the fact that he was unfaithful. It's something else. Although I don't know what it is, or why.'

'Hardly relevant now,' said Beattie practically, 'and in view of what you've just said, I think the best course of action would be to leave Michael alone for the time being. None of us are qualified to help someone who is mentally unhinged.'

'Don't say that.' Louise put her hands over her ears. 'It sounds awful.'

'Well, it is awful. Oh my God, Louise, what a mess you got yourself into when you rushed into marriage.'

'No point in going back over old ground now,' interrupted Eugenia quickly. 'What we must do is decide what can be done for the moment, and wait for Robert to come back. In spite of what you say, Louise, I think Robert is the one person who can really help. He knows Michael better than anyone. After all, his sister was married to him for ten years.'

'That's part of the problem,' said Louise, and the other part is that I love him, she thought, although no one knows that. 'My mother is right. It is a mess.'

'Louise,' said Eugenia gently, 'Robert will not let his personal feelings for *any* of you sway his judgement. His advice will be practical, reliable and unbiased. Of that I'm sure.'

Louise heard the slight emphasis on the word *any* and looked at Eugenia. 'You know,' she said.

'Of course,' said Beattie. 'We both know. Gordon doesn't, of course, but then he's a man. His antennae are not so finely tuned as ours. But I think Eugenia and I both guessed before you and Robert knew yourselves. It's a tragedy for both of you that you married Michael. But what is done is done. Now is not the time to start unpicking anything, now is the time to try and sort out Michael's affairs as he appears to be incapable, or unwilling to do it himself.'

Louise took a deep breath. 'Yes, Michael's affairs,' she said. 'I don't know exactly where to start. But I'll find out.'

'Well, at least you'll have enough on your plate with that

250

to keep you occupied, so there won't be too much time left to worry about Michael. But in any case I'm coming out to Offerton Manor to stay. Just to keep an eye on things.' Louise opened her mouth to say it wasn't necessary, but Beattie raised her hand to silence her. 'Don't try and stop me. I'm coming.'

'Thank you.' Louise was grateful. She hadn't said so, but she couldn't clear her mind of the momentary flash of terror she'd felt when Michael had looked at her, his eyes burning black holes in his white face. She bent to pick up Daniel who had wriggled his way from the mat over to Mr Poo, and was now trying to prise the disgruntled dog out from his basket under the table.

An overwhelming desire to talk to Robert swept over her. He would know what to do, he would help. But she knew it was stupid even just thinking about him because he was not here, and this time he was much farther away than France. There was nothing else for it; she would have to cope herself, along with her mother's help and that of Eugenia. Fixing a bright smile on her face, she turned to her mother, a chuckling Daniel tucked into the crook of her arm. 'It isn't necessary,' she said, 'but your company will be welcome.'

'Where will you start with all this unravelling?' asked Eugenia.

Louise shrugged. 'With the receiver for Briam Corporation. I owe it to the Careys and the other estate workers to find out what their future is. Not that I'm very optimistic that there is one.'

In the event it turned out to be easier than any of them had foreseen. Louise made an appointment to go up to London to Briam's massive office block in Ave Maria Lane, and meet Alan Osborne, of Flint MacIntosh, an accountancy firm. He was the man the banks had appointed as receiver. Before she left for London she sought out Michael, who, as usual, was sitting in his study. He was on the telephone and as she entered he put it down quickly and wouldn't meet her gaze. His furtive movement triggered a memory. He had done just that the day before. Maybe he *was* doing something concerning his financial affairs after all, and didn't want her to know.

There was no point in guessing, so Louise asked him outright. 'Michael, are you in touch with Alan Osborne, the receiver appointed for Briam? You'd better tell me just exactly what is happening.'

He looked at her, and she saw his expression was distant, preoccupied. 'In touch with who?' he said vaguely.

Louise started to repeat the question then saw with exasperation that he wasn't really listening. 'Are you doing anything about Briam?' she asked, raising her voice so that he was forced to pay her attention.

'No,' he said, and turned away.

'I want to know. I need to know. Someone has to find out what is happening.' Louise didn't bother to elaborate about the estate staff as she had no doubt that Michael was as indifferent to them now as he had been on the earlier occasion she'd mentioned them.

'Then find out.'

Louise tried one last time to draw Michael into what was really his problem. 'But don't you *want* to? Don't you want to put up a fight? Claw back something out of your life's work?'

'No,' said Michael. He walked across the room to where an enormous antique globe of the world stood on a pedestal. Spinning it round he stood silently watching it, finally putting his finger on a spot when it came to rest. 'I don't. None of this would have happened if the banks hadn't renegued on their credit arrangements. The banks have ruined me, let *them* sort the mess out. I don't care.'

It was only after she had left the study that Louise realized that the country Michael's finger had been resting on was France.

CHAPTER 31

Alan Osborne was very nice. 'This must be very distressing for you, Mrs Baruch,' he said, 'this sudden dissolving of your wealth.'

'Not distressing so much as unbelievable,' said Louise. 'It's all happened so quickly.'

'These things do, I'm afraid,' he said. 'I hope you'll be able to manage somehow.'

Louise was having difficulty in concentrating. Her thoughts kept returning to the image of Michael standing by the globe in his study. Did Michael's finger on France mean he was going back to Veronique, or was it a mere coincidence? With an effort she concentrated on Alan Osborne's concerned face, and forced herself to listen.

'I wasn't used to a millionaire's life before I married my husband,' she said. 'I shall be able to manage on much less money, and so will Michael.'

'I'm afraid it isn't a question of less. It is none. Briam Corporation, and all the associated companies that go with it, is worthless. Your husband believed in pursuing a high-risk strategy, and worked on the basis of revolving credit facilities. If the property market had been better he might have survived the slump in Briam share prices, but as it is I doubt that the value of his assets will be enough to cover his debts.'

'When you say property, does that include our home,

253

Offerton Manor?' Louise thought of the Careys and worried. Offerton was their home as well as their livelihood, and jobs were hard to come by.

'I'm afraid it does,' Alan Osborne said gently. 'I had intended to come down to Hampshire to visit your husband, but . . .'

'I came to you first,' Louise finished the sentence for him, knowing he must be wondering why she came and not Michael. Seeing no point in pretending, she said, 'The reason I came is because I'm afraid all this has been too much for my husband. He is suffering from,' she paused, then said, 'I suppose it is a nervous breakdown. The revelations in the press have been a terrible shock to him. I think he thought that he was invincible, and could do as he liked.'

Alan Osborne smiled knowingly. 'A lot of successful business men do.'

'Well,' Louise continued, 'as a result he has closed his mind to what is really going on. I can't get any sense out of him, so I thought I'd better get on and do whatever is necessary myself.'

'This could make things very complicated. There will be papers that only he can sign.'

'He will,' said Louise firmly. 'I'll make certain of that. But I don't think it will be possible for you to get a rational conversation from him at the moment, so I'm afraid you'll have to deal with me. How soon do we have to get out of Offerton, and what about the staff who are employed there? Is there anything you can do for them?'

'Well . . .' said Alan Osborne.

'Michael ought to thank his lucky stars that Alan Osborne was dealt more than his fair share of the milk of human kindness,' said Tina earnestly. 'From what you've told me, he could have made life very unpleasant for both Michael and you.'

'I know.'

254

'And what about the threat of prosecution on criminal charges that the papers were on about at one time? Has that disappeared too?'

'Yes, thank God.' Louise heaved a sigh of relief. 'The Serious Fraud Office have apparently decided that there's insufficient evidence.'

'What does that mean exactly?'

'Alan Osborne says,' said Louise, 'that in his opinion Michael covered up his tracks better than anyone thought. He thinks that Michael probably passed a lot of money over to Veronique. Putting it in accounts in her name in Switzerland and France, years ago. The authorities know it exists, but it's hers. No one can touch it.'

'That's not fair.' Tina was angry for Louise's sake. 'What about you?'

'Tina, I don't care. I just want to get everything finished with, and then forget it.' Louise pushed her hair back from her forehead. It was the middle of May, only a few weeks since she had first seen Alan Osborne, and southern England was in the grip of a heatwave. London was hot and airless. The heat throbbing up from the pavements outside the office drained away what little air there was. Even with two fans permanently on the go, the temperature in the third floor office of the old building was sky-high. 'Michael ought to be grateful, but I don't think he realizes that to a large extent he's been let off the hook. All he's had to do is sign the papers I've put before him, and Alan Osborne has sorted everything else out, even the Careys' pension, small though it is. In fact, Tina, I can't help wondering if he even knows that the day after tomorrow we finally leave Offerton Manor for good. He just seems preoccupied with Daniel. He's started taking him for long walks in his pushchair every day.'

'Well, that's all right, isn't it? At least he's paying attention to his son. Those visits to the psychiatrist are obviously doing some good.'

'Yes, I suppose so.' Louise spoke with reluctance. 'Both

255

Robert and Dr Gilchrist say that it's good that he's relating to someone, although it is a baby who can't talk back to him. But . . .'

'But what?' Tina slid a sideways glance at Louise. Like everyone else she was worried about her. Louise had lost so much weight in the last few weeks that the expensive knitted silk suit she was wearing today hung on her. 'But what, Louise?' she repeated. 'I have the feeling that something else is worrying you apart from Michael's breakdown and money problems. Is there?'

'No.' Louise attempted a wan smile. How could she tell Tina, or anyone else for that matter, that she felt Michael was trying to take Daniel away from her? She had tried telling Dr Gilchrist, the psychiatrist, but he had laughed at her fears, saying that she should be pleased that Michael's fatherly instincts were not diminished, and that it was a sign that he was taking positive steps towards becoming reconciled with her too. Louise, however, was not convinced. She could not forget the turbulent dark forces she had glimpsed in Michael's eyes, and couldn't rid herself of a chilling sense of foreboding which permeated every bone in her body, but knew there was no point in voicing these fears aloud. No one would believe her. She shivered now, in spite of the airless heat of the day. 'No,' she repeated, 'there's nothing else.'

Tina grimaced sympathetically. 'You certainly don't need anything else. I'd say you've got quite enough to cope with already.' She went over to the tiny fridge disguised as a cupboard which Louise had in the corner of her office. 'Have a glass of ice-cold mineral water before you go out on your lunch date. That'll perk you up.'

'Damn the lunch date!' Louise had never felt less like a long business lunch in her life. 'Why can't people do business without trying to make it look civilized? Everyone knows it isn't. It's all about oozing superficial charm, convincing them that you can do the job better than anybody else, and reeling off facts and figures to prove it like some bloody cabinet minister at Commons question time.'

'The agency needs this new client,' said Tina.

'Don't remind me.' Louise drank her water and getting out her handbag proceeded to powder her nose and touch up her lipstick. 'Do you remember that day when you shouted at me, and told me that the one thing I need never worry about was money?' she asked.

'Yes.' Tina sat down opposite Louise's desk. 'I'm sorry, but I thought it was true at the time. What a good thing it is that we can't see into the future. I'd hate to know what lies around the corner.'

Louise felt the relentless cold chill of fear steal over her again. 'I wish I could,' she said sombrely. 'Then I'd know what to do.'

'You're doing all right,' said Tina gently. 'Follow your instincts like you did before. You were right and I was wrong about work. Thank God you didn't sell your house and apartment then, or the agency, and give up work completely.'

'Yes, thank God,' echoed Louise. She'd recently sold her Blackheath apartment and invested some of the money towards the Careys' pension scheme, feeling it was the least she could do as Michael hadn't provided for them. But she still had her own house in Chesil Street, Winchester, to which they would soon be moving, although she put off thinking about living there with Michael. Ever since the time Robert had declared his love for her, the house had become a very special place, and in her mind would always be linked to him. When Michael moved in she knew that she would always feel that he was an intruder. She sighed; time enough to face up to that when they actually moved.

Tina looked at her watch. 'You'd better get a move on or you'll be late. And look on the bright side, you never know, you might not have to bother with the facts and figures at all. You might get the client on the strength of your fame as Michael Baruch's wife.'

Louise smiled wryly. 'If I do, then perhaps there's something to be said for acquiring notoriety after all.'

Tina grinned and, going with Louise to the door, put her arm around her shoulders. 'That's better. Good to see you smile again. We'll get back to how it was in the old days, you'll see.'

'Yes,' said Louise, 'we will.' But as she clattered down the stairs and made her way along the shimmering hot pavement towards Cambridge Circus she knew nothing would ever be quite the same. Too much had happened. She'd been touched by the lives of too many other people, and they in their turn had changed her. How naïve I was, she thought, to think that I could arrange for a child to arrive in this world without the attendant baggage of added responsibilities. It wasn't Daniel's fault, he didn't know such responsibilities existed. But Louise did, and she could almost feel the baggage hanging like a lead weight around her neck, threatening to pull both herself and Daniel down below the surface of life. In her mind's eye she could see herself frantically swimming for her life, but she was wasting her time going round and round in circles, because she had no idea in which direction lay the shore.

CHAPTER 32

Michael got up early. He packed two suitcases, then changed his mind. 'No,' he spoke aloud, 'I'll only be able to carry one, because I'll only have one hand free.' Hurriedly he repacked his things into one suitcase, throwing discarded clothes back into the wardrobe, then he left the room, suitcase in hand.

It was only just light, and the early morning dawn chorus of the birds was deafeningly beautiful. Not that Michael noticed; he was too busy thinking. As he crept along the corridor towards his study he could see that outside it was misty. The beautiful pearly mist that foretells a hot summer's day to come. A perfect day for travelling.

In the study he dialled the number for Chateau les Greves and the phone was picked up immediately by Veronique. 'Michael,' she whispered, her voice trembling with pent-up excitement. 'You are coming?'

'Yes, today.'

'And you'll bring . . .?'

'Yes, yes, I will. But don't say too much on the phone. You can never be sure who is listening.'

Veronique let her breath out in one long, hissing sound of contentment. 'Safe journey, my darling. I can hardly wait until you are both here.'

'It won't be long now. Have a bottle of champage on ice.'

Veronique laughed. 'I'll have two. One for each of you.'

Michael laughed as well. 'We'll all get drunk.' Then he paused. 'Quiet a moment.' He waited, listening; there was a noise outside the study window, but on looking out he saw that it was only the ancient labrador from the farm on the edge of the estate. The dog, out for an early morning walk, was following an interesting scent and was scuffling amongst the bushes. 'I must say goodbye now and go. Otherwise people will be waking soon, and someone may see me.'

'Goodbye, and take care.'

'I will.' Michael put down the phone.

On leaving the study, suitcase still in hand, he made his way towards the rooms occupied by Melanie and Daniel. Cautiously he opened Melanie's bedroom door. He smiled at the sight that greeted him. Couldn't be better. Melanie was sound asleep, flat on her back with her mouth open and snoring quite loudly. Satisfied, he turned away and closed her door. She'd never hear a thing. Then he opened the door into the room which adjoined Melanie's. The soft morning light was just seeping through the blue cotton curtains patterned with pictures of Winnie the Pooh, Piglet, Eeyore and Tigger. The blankets in the cot lay rumpled and still. Silently Michael crept across and reached down into the cot. 'Hello, Daniel,' he whispered, reaching down into the cot and throwing back the blankets. Then he stopped, and beads of perspiration suddenly glistened on his forehead. Daniel was not there. In a daze he wiped the back of his hand against his head. He'd been so sure that the small hump he could see in the blankets was Daniel who had slid down a little in the cot, but now he could see that it was empty.

For a moment he panicked, holding on to the edge of the cot with shaking hands. Then reason took over. 'Of course,' he muttered to himself, 'he's teething and not been sleeping well. Louise must have taken him into her room because he was restless.'

That made things complicated. But not impossible, because, he reasoned, Louise was bound to be sleeping soundly. She'd been in London the day before, and had then been up until well past midnight the previous night arranging things for the move to her house in Chesil Street. She was bound to be exhausted.

Nevertheless it meant a delay which he could well do without, and cursing it, he made his way down the corridor towards the room he had once shared with Louise. Passing the room at the moment used by Beattie, he heard her cough, and the sound of her footsteps moving in the direction of the adjoining bathroom. Damn! Time was passing much too quickly; people were beginning to wake. He would have to hurry. Finally he reached Louise's bedroom and silently opened the door. Leaving the suitcase outside he moved across to the bed. Daniel was there, sleeping with Louise. They were lying side by side, not touching. It would be easy to pick him up. Michael reached out towards Daniel and as he did so the baby opened sleepy eyes. 'Da da,' he said, and rolling towards Louise flung a plump pink arm around her neck.

'Not time to get up yet,' Louise replied sleepily, her eyes still closed. 'Lots of time to sleep.' She wrapped her arms around her son and held him close. 'Lots more time to sleep,' she murmured.

Michael stood and stared. It was hopeless. There was no way he could pick up Daniel without waking Louise.

Daniel, aware of his father's presence, opened his eyes wider. 'Da da,' he said again, becoming excited.

Michael left the room as silently as he had entered.

Louise woke up. Was it her imagination or had she heard the door click? Daniel was wriggling and chuckling excitedly. He was ready and anxious to play. Louise sat up. The heavy curtains were moving slightly as if wafted by a soft draught, but the room was empty. She sank back amongst the pillows. 'Oh, Daniel,' she groaned, 'I am so tired, so tired. I don't want to play now.' Passing him his teddy bear and a teething ring she closed her eyes and hoped he would go back to sleep. But half an hour later she got up. Further sleep had proved impossible; she felt restless and uneasy. Looking at the door she remembered the click. Stupid how an imaginary little thing like that should wake her. My damned nerves are on edge because of today's move, she thought crossly.

Daniel smiled, and said, 'Glug, glug, glug.' Louise always fondly imagined that was the nearest he could get to mum.

'Oh, Daniel,' she said, trying to be stern, but failing utterly. 'You're a little monkey waking me up like that. But never mind, once this move is over and done with at least I know we shall be settled.' Daniel giggled, and naughtily threw his teething ring at her in reply.

'Where is Michael? He ought to be lending a hand. I know he's supposed to have had a nervous breakdown, but there's nothing wrong with him physically.' Gordon was grumpy. Willingly he'd offered to help with the move, but he had thought that Michael would be there as well. Hot and sweaty, he struggled down the front steps of Offerton Manor with a tea-chest full of books.

Equally hot and sweaty, Louise and Eugenia staggered down behind him carrying a box of Daniel's toys between them. 'I expect he's in the study,' gasped Louise. 'That's where he usually sits. But quite honestly, Gordon, I'd just as soon he stayed put and out of the way until we've finished. After all, we haven't got that much to move. Only personal bits and bobs. The removal men have taken all the large stuff.'

'If you call this lot bits and bobs, I'd like to see what you call large,' grumbled Gordon.

'You're not going to let Michael take Daniel out for one of his mile-long walks today, are you?' asked Eugenia. 'I'd hate them to be missing when the time comes to go.'

'No. Beattie has taken Daniel home to St Cross. She's

262

thrilled to bits at having him to herself all day. I shall probably pay for it tomorrow when he has an upset tummy from eating too many chocolate biscuits.'

Eugenia laughed. 'Don't worry, with a bit of luck Mr Poo will pinch half of them. He's very quick when it comes to biscuits.'

'Well, where's Melanie then? She could be helping us. I'm exhausted.' Gordon still felt there were not enough of them to load the hired van.

'She *is* helping. She's already at Chesil Street preparing her own room in the attic, and getting Daniel's room cleaned up and aired in readiness for the arrival of his cot and other things.'

'So there you are,' said Eugenia. 'Do stop moaning, Gordon. Personally,' she added quietly to Louise, 'I always think that when it comes to actually getting things done, women are better off without the family men. At least the removal men just did as you told them and didn't ask questions.'

'And with any luck should be unloading the stuff now,' said Louise, hoping they were.

'Would anyone like some home-made iced lemonade?' Lizzie Carey stood on the top step. Dressed in her best summer suit of brilliant red linen, the heels of her black patent shoes so high she could hardly totter, Louise thought she looked more like a robin than ever.

'Love some,' shouted Gordon, and heaving the tea-chest into the van, he turned and sprinted up the steps.

'Thought he said he was exhausted,' said Eugenia, watching her husband.

Louise smiled. 'Not when there's the thought of Lizzie's home-made lemonade at the end of a sprint.' She sighed. 'Oh, I shall miss her.'

Lizzie and Dick were waiting for them in the orangery. A tray was set out with tall crystal glasses, beside them an enormous jug of lemonade, the top bobbing with ice-cubes. On another tray was a large plate of delicately

263

iced biscuits. Dick had on his best suit too. 'I knocked on Mr Michael's study door,' said Dick, 'but there was no answer so I left him.'

'Just as well,' said Louise, then burst into tears. 'Oh dear, I shall miss you, but more than that I feel so guilty that it all has to end like this.'

'There, there, dear.' Lizzie was at her side in a flash. 'You mustn't feel guilty. None of this is your fault, and you've done the best you can for us. Dick and I are very pleased with our pension, and now Dick's old Aunt Mary has told us we can live in her house by the sea at Bosham, we have nothing to worry about. We're going down there this afternoon, as soon as you've finished here.'

'But will you like sharing a house?' asked Eugenia.

'Bless you, we shan't be sharing. Didn't Louise tell you?' Eugenia shook her head.

'Sorry,' said Louise, wiping her eyes, and accepting the lemonade Dick was passing to her. 'In all the rush this last week I forgot to mention it.'

'We've had a marvellous piece of luck,' said Dick. 'My Aunt Mary, who is ninety-six, has lived in a nursing home for the past six months.'

'Since she had a stroke,' interrupted Lizzie.

'We've always visited every week. She's such a nice old lady, never grumbles, and is always pleased to see us. So it's never been a chore. We were always glad to go.'

'You would have thought,' said Lizzie, 'being the nice old soul that she is, that her children would visit. But none of them, not one of the three sons or two daughters, have set foot in that nursing home since the day they put her in there.'

'Are you going to tell this story or am I?' demanded Dick, tired of being interrupted.

'You can,' said Lizzie, and busied herself with the lemonade.

'Well, when we told Aunt Mary that we might not be able to come and visit as regular as we have been doing, because of losing the job and not being sure where we would be living, she insisted that we have her house. It is by the church at Bosham in Sussex, right on the edge of the harbour. A beautiful little cottage, about three hundred years old.'

'And it's got a lovely garden. A little one at the front which runs right down to the sea wall, and an enormous one at the back,' said Lizzie, unable to resist interrupting. 'And what's more, she has said that she is leaving the house to us in her will.'

'So you see, we are very lucky,' said Dick.

'Not lucky, deserving,' said Louise. 'If my mother were here no doubt she'd say, "there you are, every cloud has a silver lining."'

'And so it has.' Lizzie looked at Louise fondly. 'You wait and see. One day you'll be able to look back on all this, and it will seem like some long-forgotten nightmare.'

'That's more or less what Robert said to me,' said Louise slowly. 'I only hope that you are both right.'

As if on cue Robert walked into the orangery. 'I thought I'd find the whole place a hive of frantic activity,' he said, 'and came to help. Instead I find a scene straight from the pages of *Homes and Gardens*. You look as if you haven't a care in the world.'

'It's an illusion I'm trying to foster.' Louise smiled wryly. 'In the hope that it may come true.'

'Now that you're here – ' Gordon drained his lemonade glass – 'there's a particularly heavy bookcase Louise wants brought downstairs. I've been waiting for another man to turn up.'

'Where's Michael?' asked Robert, frowning.

'In his study,' said Louise.

'I rang his private line before I left the hospital. But he didn't answer.'

'I think he's trying to pretend none of this is happening,' said Louise. 'We haven't seen him all day. Not answering the phone is all part of it.'

265

'Hum,' said Robert.

'Come on,' said Gordon, 'let's go and get that bookcase.'

'Where the hell can he have gone? He hasn't even packed his clothes. They're still in the wardrobes.' Robert stormed down the main staircase of Offerton Manor to the hall where Louise stood waiting.

The van had gone, driven by Gordon with Eugenia sitting beside him, hidden beneath a pile of delapidated cushions she'd found in a spare room. Being a magpie by nature, and unable to see anything go to waste, she was sure she'd find a use for them, so Louise had given them to her.

The Careys were just going, and came in to say goodbye. 'Not found him then?' Lizzie hopped from one high-heeled foot to the other, and looked awkward.

'You'd best tell them,' said Dick.

'Tell us what?' asked Louise.

'Well, it may not be important.'

'And it just might be,' said Robert, 'so for heaven's sake tell us.'

'I overheard him on the phone yesterday. It was the library phone which as you know has an extension in the kitchen. It rang and I picked it up. But so did Mr Michael and I could hear him speaking. He was talking to Mrs Baruch, I mean the ex-Mrs Baruch, and she was calling him darling. I put the phone down then because I knew I ought not to be listening.'

'Pity you didn't listen for a little bit longer,' said Robert grimly, 'then perhaps we'd know what the hell is going on.'

'He's gone to Veronique,' said Louise. 'That's the answer.'

'Oh dear,' said Lizzie. She looked at Louise anxiously. 'Do you want us to stay for a bit? We can, there's no rush. Our cottage won't move away.'

Louise shook her head. She felt utterly exhausted, drained of emotion. If Michael had gone running back to Veronique, so what, she thought wearily. She could see

266

him now, as he had been only a few weeks ago, standing in his study by the side of the globe, his finger firmly resting on France. Her subconscious had known from that day on that his plan was to return to Veronique; now she was certain, so Lizzie's remarks came as no surprise. In some ways it would solve a lot of problems, in others it could only cause more. But there was one irrefutable fact, there was nothing she could do about it.

'No, you go and get settled in your little house,' she said. 'I know Beattie is planning to visit you almost before you will have had time to unpack.'

'If you're sure.' Lizzie was uncertain; Louise looked so tired.

'I'm sure.'

'Come on, my dear.' Dick took his wife's arm. 'Robert will take care of Louise.' He passed an enormous bunch of keys to Robert. 'These are the keys to be handed to the security chap waiting in the kitchen. Once you are gone he'll lock up after you, and then the grounds will be patrolled by him and his dogs.'

'Seems a shame,' said Louise, looking back as Robert drove her away, 'to see the manor all in darkness. No life there any more. The house will feel lonely.'

'Never had much life before you arrived,' said Robert, 'so I doubt that the house will notice the difference. You and your family were just a fleeting draught of gaiety passing through.'

'Draught of gaiety,' said Louise bitterly, 'I should have thought a gale of disaster was more appropriate.'

'It's not that bad.'

'Oh, it is.' Louise turned to look at him. The last rays of the setting sun illuminated his strong, homely face. He isn't handsome, she thought, and yet he's the most marvellous man I've ever seen. 'It is for me,' she said. 'I've had to learn the hard way.'

'And what have you learned?'

'That wanting is one thing, and getting is quite another.

I never gave a thought to the little person I would be creating, or to the legacies I would pass on to him. A broken home is hardly the best start in life.'

'If you can hear me through that mass of sackcloth and ashes you're wallowing in,' said Robert, 'just remember what I told you not so long ago. Nothing is all bad, and a lot can be rectified by love. True, unselfish love.'

'I wish I could believe you,' said Louise, 'but I'm not sure of anything any more.'

When they arrived at the house in Chesil Street, and parked behind the van driven there by Gordon, Robert opened the car door for Louise. 'I'm not coming in,' he said slowly, cupping her face between his hands. 'I don't trust myself to behave like a gentleman and remember that you are still married to someone else. I might stay after Gordon and Eugenia have gone, and find myself making love to you again.'

'Oh, Robert.' Louise flung her arms around his neck. 'I need someone to hold me tight, someone to love me.'

'And I need a woman who is sure. Not one who is depressed, muddled, and uncertain of everything. Don't think I'm being noble by not coming in, because I'm not. I want to, but I want to be with you when you can think straight, when you know what you are doing. If I come in and stay tonight, you might very well regret it later.'

'Never,' cried Louise.

'You might,' said Robert, kissing her gently, 'and I'm not prepared to risk it.'

Louise watched his car go down the narrow road until it disappeared around the bend where the road turned towards the cathedral, then she went indoors to find Beattie waiting for her. She'd arrived with Daniel and was supervising Gordon and Eugenia.

'That was very sensible,' said Beattie. 'I was watching from the window, and thought you might ask him in. Time enough for that when we know whether or not that husband of yours has gone for good.'

CHAPTER 33

It was late afternoon when Michael drove off the ferry at St Malo. The early morning mist had kept its promise and dissolved into a perfect summer's day. The light, diffused with brilliant sunshine, made it difficult to see where the smooth blue of the sea ended and the blue of the sky began. As he drove past the ancient cobbled streets, and stone ramparts of the old port out of the town, the lush green countryside of Brittany opened its arms to receive him. But he was uneasy. What would Veronique say? What would she do? She was going to be so bitterly disappointed. He must make her see that it was only a temporary hiccup.

But he relaxed a little driving along the traffic-free roads of northern France. Hadn't he always given his beloved Veronique what she wanted? There'd be a way, and he'd find it. Only an hour later the headland of Michael en Greve loomed before him, and behind that stood the outline of Chateau les Greves nestling in the folding hills behind the headland.

Veronique was waiting in the salon. The moment she heard the sound of wheels upon the gravel drive she came running out. 'Darling, darling,' she cried. 'Where is he?'

Michael levered himself from the car. 'I couldn't bring him,' he said.

'But you promised,' she wailed. 'Michael, you *promised*.'

269

'I know, and I tried. Believe me I tried. But everything went wrong at the last moment and it was impossible.'

Veronique burst into a paroxysm of violent sobbing. 'You promised, you promised,' she kept repeating. 'I was so sure that I'd have my very own baby sleeping here in the chateau tonight. I've bought all the baby food, and some extra toys. Everything is ready.'

Michael put his arms around her and held her trembling body close. 'He will be here soon. You can be sure of that. But now that things are not quite the same as we originally planned, we shall have to be just that little bit extra careful.'

'Why? Why?' sobbed Veronique.

'Because if we are not, then you won't be able to keep him.'

Veronique stopped sobbing, and looked up at Michael. Her dark eyes were wild and brilliant with tears. 'Once I've got him I *must* keep him,' she said.

'Then trust me,' said Michael, and, with his arms still around her, led her into the chateau where they were greeted by Andrea Louedec.

'Daniel isn't coming tonight,' said Veronique, her voice still throaty and gruff from weeping.

'Daniel, Madame?' Andrea Louedec had no idea who she was talking about.

'My baby. But he will be coming later, won't he, Michael?'

'Of course, darling.' Michael turned to the housekeeper and smiled carefully. 'But as you can see, it will be just the two of us for dinner tonight. Not three as originally planned. That will make things easier for you, won't it?'

'Oh yes, sir. Very good, sir.' Andrea Louedec made her way back to the kitchen where her husband was sitting reading the local paper. 'Monsieur Baruch doesn't look quite as mad as Madame Veronique, but there is definitely something very strange about him,' she said.

'Strange?' queried Paul.

'Yes, strange. And they are both talking about a baby, who apparently should have come but hasn't. First I've heard of it.'

'So what? They must have made some arrangements we're not privy to. Nothing strange about that.'

'Huh!' Andrea sniffed with disbelief. 'I think it is. After all, it's not as if they're even married. They've been divorced for . . .'

'Oh, mind your own business, woman,' said Paul.

'Well, I think the whole thing is highly suspicious. There is something going on that's not right.' Andrea was adamant. 'And I think Monsieur Robert should know.'

Paul laughed and said, 'You read too many novels, but if it makes you any happier, then tell Robert Lacroix. It can't do any harm.'

Robert sat alone in his house on the other side of Winchester and thought of Louise and Michael. His daily woman, Mrs Morgan, had left his supper in the oven. It smelled good, but his mind was in such turmoil that he had no appetite. Where was Michael? Had he really gone back to Veronique as Louise thought? Did that mean that he'd left Louise for good? And if so, would she get a divorce?

His hand hovered over the telephone. Shall I ring the chateau, he wondered, remembering what Lizzie Carey had said earlier that day. He knew Louise was absolutely certain that Michael had rejoined Veronique in France, and was inclined to agree. But should he ring and find out?

His dilemma was resolved when the telephone rang and he picked it up to find Andrea Louedec on the other end of the line. 'Monsieur Robert?' she said.

'Yes,' said Robert. 'I think I know what you are going to say.'

'Oh.' Andrea hesitated. 'Perhaps I shouldn't be telling tales.'

'Tell me everything you know,' said Robert firmly. 'I have to know some time or other.'

271

'Well, it's like this. Monsieur Baruch, Madame Veronique's ex-husband, has arrived, and from what they've said I think he intends to stay.'

'I thought so.' Robert nodded his head; at least that cleared up one thing.

'They are talking about a baby. They are saying that Daniel hasn't come yet.' She hesitated, then said, 'I must tell you that they both seem rather odd and very tense to me. Something's not right, I know it. Do you know who this Daniel might be?'

Robert's heart almost stopped beating, and the warm summer night suddenly turned icy and cold. 'Daniel?' he asked faintly. 'Are you absolutely sure they said Daniel?'

'Oh, yes. Definitely it was Daniel. I've never heard him mentioned before. But apparently he is Madame Veronique's new baby. She said he will be coming to join them later. Do you know who he is?'

'Yes, I know,' said Robert slowly.

'Then I was wrong. If you know about him then it must be all right, and I was worrying about nothing. I shouldn't have rung you.'

'Not at all. I'm glad you did. Your instincts were quite correct, Madame Louedec. Things are far from right. And please, if anything else worries you, don't hesitate to let me know.'

'Of course, Monsieur.' By now Andrea was sounding very puzzled. Robert had confirmed her suspicions, but given no information. 'Is there anything in particular you want me to look out for?'

'No, just use your feminine intuition. And – ' Robert tried not to sound too worried – 'if, by any chance, a child should arrive at the chateau, then let me know immediately.'

Robert put down the phone. *Daniel*, Veronique's new baby. He could hear his own voice saying, 'Yes, I know,' so calmly to Andrea Louedec, as if he understood everything. But he didn't. What the hell was Michael playing

272

at? Going back to Veronique was one thing. But did he really think he could take Daniel from Louise and give him to another woman? If so, then he was more out of touch with reality than anyone had realized. What had happened to him to make him behave in this way? He'd always been a rational man before; except where Veronique was concerned. The niggling thought crept into his mind. He remembered thinking years before, when Michael and Veronique had first married, that their love was almost unhealthy because it went beyond the bounds of normal affection and bordered on obsession. It was the main reason he'd always found it so hard to understand their subsequent divorce. But now! His mind shied away from the conclusion gradually being forced upon him.

CHAPTER 34

'I'm not going over to France,' said Louise.

It was Sunday morning, her first free day since Michael's disappearance and the move from Offerton, and she was spending it in the garden of her Chesil Street house. She placed Daniel down on the daisy-studded turf at the edge of the river, and held on tightly to his reins. She watched him, smiling fondly as he knelt on all fours and rocked to and fro on his sturdy little arms and legs. My world is in a mess, she thought, and yet I feel quite illogically happy. I'm here in my own house, and the man I love is with me. Reaching up she tugged at Robert's hand, laying it against her cheek. It was make-believe she knew, but while they were here together she could pretend Michael didn't exist.

'Look how fascinated Daniel is by the rushing water,' she said.

Robert was torn between longing to kiss her and shaking some sense into her. 'Louise I do think that . . .'

'Robert, I am *not* going to France. I do appreciate all the trouble that you've gone to, arranging a plane and everything, really I do. But I am not going.'

Robert lowered his tall frame down on to the grass beside her and slipped his long arms loosely around her. Aching with longing, he kissed the nape of her neck. 'Darling,' he said softly, 'we could fly over from

Eastleigh airport and be back by this evening. Then we could find out what the situation really is. After all, I've only got Andrea Louedec's word for it that she thinks Michael is staying. He may intend coming back to you. Don't you want to know?'

Robert had decided not to mention the housekeeper's disturbing reference to Daniel. That could be confronted when they met Veronique and Michael face to face. That was one of the reasons that it was so essential that Louise should go, but he couldn't tell her that. Not yet, anyway.

'Oh Robert, of course I want to know. Although in a way it's unimportant now.' Louise turned so that her face was level with his, and gently touched his lips with her own. 'You see, I've made up my mind. I'm going to divorce Michael, and it's not just because of the way I feel for you, it's because of what is wrong with Michael and me. I feel cruel doing it now, when he has just lost a fortune. But there seems no point in staying married. I know he doesn't love me, but more than that I am sure that he still loves Veronique.'

Robert kissed Louise again. 'I love you,' he said.

Louise smiled. 'Knowing that makes all this mess bearable.'

Then she added, 'But tell me the truth, Robert. I'm not the only one to think that Michael and Veronique have never really separated. You think it too, don't you?'

'Yes,' said Robert slowly. 'God knows why they ever got divorced.'

'So divorcing Michael is not going to unduly upset him. Besides, there is Daniel to consider. The more I think about it, the better it seems that I should do it as soon as possible. Daniel will be too young to be affected by the split now: he won't even know it's happened.'

'He will later,' said Robert.

'I know that, and I'll cross that bridge when I come to it.' Louise peered at Robert anxiously. 'You sound almost disapproving. Do you want me to stay married to Michael?'

Robert loosened his hold on Louise so that he could look at her. 'Of course not, darling. For my own selfish reasons I want you to leave him. But . . .' He hesitated.

'But what?'

'Hasn't it occurred to you that Michael might put up a fight for Daniel? Try and claim custody.'

Louise looked at Daniel, now happily beheading every daisy he could lay his hands on. 'No, don't eat them, darling,' she said, hastily removing the remains of yellow stamens and white petals from his mouth.

There was a silence while they both looked at Daniel and Robert remembered Andrea Louedec's words with uncomfortable clarity.

Apparently he is Madam Veronique's new baby.

'You haven't answered my question,' he said.

Louise looked up, her expression very serious and determined. 'No one and nothing will separate me from Daniel,' she said in a quiet, steely voice. 'I hope I don't have to, but if necessary I will fight tooth and nail to keep him. But I won't be unreasonable. I shall let Michael have access, because after all Daniel is his son as well as mine. But a child's place is with its mother, and my child is going to stay with me.'

'You've convinced me,' said Robert with a smile that hid his unease. Would Michael make it easy, he wondered; would he even be reasonable, and agree to just having access? Scrambling to his feet Robert wished he could be certain. 'I'd better go and cancel that plane I've got standing by, and tell Beattie she'll not be needed as a baby-sitter today.'

Louise raised her eyebrows. 'You *did* have it well organized.'

'I thought I had until you put your foot down and refused to play ball.'

'I'm sorry,' said Louise, 'but I can't face him. Not yet.'

'I understand how you feel, but you can't put it off for ever.'

276

'I won't,' said Louise.

Daniel started to get restless and began to whimper. It was time for his mid-morning drink. Louise picked him up and swung him into her arms. 'I promise faithfully, Robert, I will go and see Michael soon.'

Robert smiled, and took Daniel from Louise. 'Come on, let me carry him up the steps to the house, he's getting quite heavy.' Once in the house he handed him back. 'Just remember as far as Michael is concerned, I think it should be as soon as possible. And what is more I insist that I am there with you when it happens.' He wished again that he could tell her the reason for considering it so urgent, but decided it wasn't fair to burden her with fears which he was still hoping might prove to be groundless.

'I promise I won't put it off for long. We will go to France together and see Michael and Veronique,' Louise said. 'Just let me get myself sorted out a little first.'

'I think you should do as Robert says, and the sooner the better,' Tina said. It was the end of Louise's first week back at the office. She had spent the whole week commuting in order to catch up with her overflowing in-tray.

'I will.'

'When?'

'Soon, Tina, soon.'

'What's wrong with now? After all, once you've seen him, you can go ahead with the divorce. Then all your troubles will be over.'

'Or just starting.' Louise sighed despondently, and slumping down, hunched her shoulders. 'The trouble is, I don't want to think about meeting Michael again. I'm enjoying life with Daniel, even though it is hell having to commute every single day. Although thank God I've got Melanie, she's so reliable. I couldn't possibly manage without her. She's a wonderful buffer against all the unpleasant facts of life, like washing and shopping. When I get home the evenings are still light, so I often put Daniel in his pram and walk down past the weirs and along the water meadows to my mother's house. Have a coffee and then walk back to my own house. I really enjoy that, and Daniel is fascinating now. He notices everything, and loves it when we feed the ducks.'

'Go and see Michael,' said Tina sternly.

'Oh, all right. If I'm going to have you nagging me, as well as my mother, Gordon, Eugenia and Robert, I suppose I might as well give in.'

'Exactly,' said Tina. She looked at Louise's hunched shoulders and made up her mind. 'Louise,' she said, 'we've wasted half the morning talking, why don't we waste a little more time and go and have a Chinese in Wardour Street? You haven't had much fun lately.'

'Why not,' agreed Louise, her mood lightening immediately. Ten minutes later they were tripping their way through Wardour Street, past the red and gold pagoda telephone boxes, and the supermarkets spilling their exotic wares of dried fish and strange-looking vegetables out on to the pavement.

'Let's go to the same restaurant we went to when you were pregnant,' said Tina. 'The food was delicious, remember?'

'Yes,' said Louise. But it was a mistake. Louise realized that as soon as they sat down. For the restaurant brought back all the memories of that day last year. The day she'd felt so happy until she had returned to Offerton Manor and overheard Michael on the telephone.

The hot, crowded restaurant with its shouting waiters and the overpowering smell of garlic and roasting duck disappeared, and once more she was standing outside the library, cold and shivering as she listened.

'*I had to marry Louise. It was necessary. Nothing else would do.*' At the time, she remembered, he'd denied that it was Veronique he was speaking to. He'd said it was his accountant. But now she knew differently. He had lied then, just as he must have lied right from the beginning.

278

Nothing he had said had meant anything, or had it?

Why did Michael marry me, wondered Louise. It was so obvious to her now that he had never stopped loving Veronique. So why did they divorce? Why did he re-marry? Why? Why? If only she knew the answer. Then without warning, Louise suddenly remembered her un-ease the weeks before they'd left Offerton Manor, when she had felt that Michael was trying to take Daniel away. Since his disappearance she'd forgotten about it, but now the fear came back in full flood and she felt sick.

'Louise, what do you want to eat?'

With an effort Louise dragged her thoughts back to the present, and tried telling herself she was being totally irrational. But it didn't work; the unnamed fear still churned uncomfortably in the pit of her stomach.

'Oh, I'll have this,' she said, and stabbed her finger at the first name that swam into focus on the menu.

Louise caught the early train back to Winchester and Melanie brought Daniel up in the car to the station to meet her. He crowed with delight as soon as he saw Louise, and bounced up and down so vigorously in his car seat that the whole car rocked.

'He's such a happy little soul,' said Melanie fondly. 'No trouble to look after at all.'

After cuddling and kissing Daniel, which he demanded before he would settle down again, Louise climbed into the passenger seat. 'You can drive, Melanie,' she said. 'I'm exhausted. London is so hot when the weather is fine, it drains every ounce of energy I've got.'

'Oh, I couldn't be doing with working in London,' said Melanie, who was a country girl through and through. Her round face was scrubbed and clean-looking, and had a healthy tan, as did her bare legs. She and Daniel spent as much time out of doors as possible, which accounted for the fact that he now looked like a coffee coloured cherub. 'I know they've got lovely parks with loads of flowers and

279

trees, but none of them look really fresh to my eye. Not like the trees and flowers here.' She flung her arm out towards a huge weeping willow which drooped its vivid green leaves across the road. Beneath it was a rosebed full of white bush roses. Each bloom was shining white, as if each petal had been individually scrubbed clean.

'Yes, you're right,' said Louise. 'I'm afraid the city grime spreads to everything, including the trees and flowers.' She sat up. 'Where are you going? This isn't the way to Chesil Street.'

'No, it's the way to St Cross,' said Melanie, 'where your mother has got tea ready for us. Strawberries and clotted cream. The first strawberries from her garden.'

'Darling, I hope you don't mind me asking Melanie to kidnap you and bring you here. But as soon as I knew you were catching an early train home, I decided we should eat the first strawberries of June today. I always think it seems such a terrible waste making them all into jam.'

'Especially your jam, Mother,' said Louise with a laugh. 'You've never yet mastered the art of getting the stuff to set.'

'I *shall* get some to set,' said Beattie huffily, 'even if I do it on my deathbed.'

'I can just see the headlines in the *Hampshire Chronicle*. "Woman dies while trying to get strawberry jam to set." '

'Oh, shut up,' said Beattie. 'I don't see why my jam should be the laughing stock of the family.'

Melanie's eyes were as big as organ stops. Beattie was a permanent surprise to her, used as she was to her own very practical and totally unimaginative mother. 'All you've got to do is throw in a few handfuls of red currants,' she said, 'then the jam will set.'

Beattie swung round and dramatically pointed a finger at Melanie. 'Right, you're on,' she said. 'As soon as I'm ready to start jam-making, you've got to come over and help me.'

'If you want to,' said Louise, smiling at Melanie's startled expression.

Walking through into the garden she felt relaxed and happy again. It was like stepping back into her childhood. Beattie had spread a white tablecloth on the lawn beneath an old cast-iron arch smothered with a climbing rose. The rose, one of the old-fashioned variety, was in full bloom. Delicate, pale pink petals from blown roses lay scattered on the grass and tablecloth, petals nestled amidst the brown bread and butter and wafer-thin slices of smoked salmon, golden brown scones, crusty yellow clotted cream, and strawberries. Mountains of strawberries, glistening a deep, luscious red on green Wedgwood plates. When Beattie set out food, she did it as if she were painting, making sure all the colours were shown to their best advantage so that a beautiful picture was created.

'Wow!' said Melanie, who had never experienced one of Beattie's meals.

'You've really gone to town, Mother.' Louise kissed her. 'I only hope Daniel doesn't wreck it.'

'We'll keep him in his highchair.' Melanie, ever practical, wanted to enjoy her tea. 'I'd hate to think what he could do those strawberries in one minute flat.'

'I rang Robert,' said her mother casually, 'and asked him if he might like to sample the strawberries.'

Louise felt her heart lift in happy anticipation. She hadn't seen him since the Sunday she'd refused to fly over to France. 'That will be nice,' she said. 'I haven't seen him for ages. At least a week and a half.'

'He can't come because he's on duty and has a very sick patient he needs to keep an eye on. But he did mutter something about France, and waiting to hear from you. He said to remind you.'

'Thanks,' said Louise, 'I hadn't forgotten.'

She watched Daniel struggling with his dish of strawberries. A good many of them got squashed on his face and hands, giving him the appearance of a circus clown, but a

281

good many also found their way into his mouth, and it was obvious from his blissful expression that he liked them.

'What did Robert mean? Haven't you set a date yet?'

'No, but I will. I'll ring him tonight and make arrangements.'

'Good,' said Beattie. 'I hope he is going over with you.'

'He's insisting. I think he wants to make sure that no awkward ends are left loose that might cause trouble later on. And I know he's right; I shall need someone there to make sure everything is quite clear to all concerned. I'm going to tell Michael that I am filing for a divorce, and will be asking for custody of Daniel.'

'Thank God you've come to your senses at last.' Beattie piled her plate with brown bread and butter and smoked salmon. She nodded at Melanie. 'Do take some, dear. No point in wasting it.' Then turning back to Louise she continued. 'I could never understand how you could go on pretending that your marriage could survive, when the man in question obviously preferred his former wife.'

Melanie, who'd been listening goggle-eyed, could contain herself no longer. 'Mr Michael prefers his first wife! But why did he marry you?' Then suddenly she realized that she had spoken out of turn and clapped a guilty hand over her mouth. 'Sorry,' she mumbled.

'No need to be,' said Louise with wry smile. 'It's a perfectly valid question, and one which I've asked myself many times. Why did he marry me? Sometimes I think it was because I looked a little like Veronique; not a lot, but enough to remind him.'

'But why did you marry him?' said Beattie crossly. 'I told you at the time I thought you'd regret it. Marry in hast, repent at leisure.'

'I married him,' said Louise, 'because at the time I truly thought that it was the right thing to do. I couldn't see how it could go wrong. Two sensible people, fond of each other and with a child to bind them together.' She paused a moment, then said, 'And the strange thing is that although

I know now that he always loved Veronique, I still think that he really *was* fond of me, but the ties to Veronique were too strong.'

Louise leaned back against an old tree-stump which had been cut down to make a garden seat, and kicking off her shoes spread her stockinged feet against the cool grass. The shadows were beginning to lengthen now, and the air was balmy with the scent of a clump of night-scented stocks growing nearby. All was peace and tranquillity in Beattie's sheltered green garden. Overhead, swallows and house martins wheeled and dived in graceful circles, collecting unwary insects to feed their ever hungry young. It's a shame life can't be like this moment, utter perfection, thought Louise wistfully. Then there would be no need to see Michael or Veronique. But she knew she had to. It wasn't just an ordinary breakdown of a marriage; there was something else. A mysterious puzzle which she didn't understand, and which frightened her. She didn't know what it was, but she felt that there was something which bound them together: herself, Veronique and Michael, and unless the puzzle was solved, none of them would ever be free.

'What are you thinking?' asked Beattie.

'How lovely it is here,' said Louise. She wished she could tell her mother about the puzzle, but couldn't. Trying to explain it to someone else was impossible because it was all so illogical.

'I'm glad you came,' said Beattie. 'More strawberries and cream, anyone?'

CHAPTER 35

Robert squeezed her hand as the light plane circled, ready to land at St Brieuc airport. It was windy and Louise could see the orange wind-sock on the perimeter of the airfield straining horizontally on its pole. She shivered; the closer she got to Michael the greater grew the menacing premonition that she just couldn't banish. She felt as if she were on the verge of unlocking a door to some dreadful secret, which was ridiculous. All I'm doing, she told herself firmly, is going to see my husband and his mistress and tell him that I want a divorce. Daniel, beloved baby Daniel. Oh please, God, she prayed silently, don't let Michael be difficult, don't let him try and take Daniel away.

'Don't worry,' said Robert, as if in answer to her thoughts. 'Everything will be all right.' But he too was thinking about Daniel. Perhaps he should have mentioned the strange conversation he'd had with Madame Louedec, but there had never been a right moment, and anyway there was no logical explanation. The only explanation he could think of was one he dare not put a name to.

Louise smiled. 'You always seem to be telling me everything will be all right. You're a wonderful morale booster.'

'My pleasure, ma'am,' said Robert sounding more light-hearted than he felt.

The formalities on arrival were brief, and soon they were in the hired car. The old town and harbour of St Brieuc huddled down below towering cliffs either side of the broad expanse of the river Gouet where the inland waters met the sea. The new town, of flats and office blocks, interspersed with enormous industrial estates, sprawled on the cliff-tops, and were linked by a massive viaduct across the waters of the Gouet.

'How long will it take to get there?' asked Louise.

'Not long. About an hour.'

'It's very beautiful here,' said Louise looking around. It was still windy, the cerulean-hued sky was streaked with cloud that looked like wisps of cotton wool, and two hundred feet down below the viaduct where the river and sea merged, the water was a brilliant turquoise blue.

'Of course, I'd forgotten that you've never been to Brittany. Well, perhaps later, when things are settled, we'll come back here and have a proper holiday. Then you can really appreciate its beauty.'

Louise turned and looked at Robert. 'You are still including me in your future then?'

'Of course. I can't imagine a future without you. Surely you didn't think I'd changed my mind?'

'Oh, Robert.' Louise reached out and touched his hand. 'You can't imagine how happy and secure that makes me feel,' she said, adding reflectively, 'and I never thought I'd admit that I needed someone. I always used to pride myself on being solo, on being able to manage everything on my own.'

'And you still could manage everything if you wanted to,' said Robert. 'But you are no longer solo. You've got Daniel to take care of. And, like me, you've grown a little older, and wiser, and realize that life is much richer with someone at your side. The right someone of course.'

'If only I'd been more patient,' sighed Louise, 'then perhaps I wouldn't have rushed into the doomed relationship with Michael.'

'Yes, perhaps,' said Robert slowly. 'But Michael rushed too. There was something he saw in you the first time the two of you met that made him determined that you should be the mother of his child. And I've been wondering and worrying about it ever since.'

'Perhaps, like me, he doesn't really know himself,' suggested Louise hopefully. But she shivered in spite of the warmth inside the sunlit car. Did Robert have the same uneasy premonitions as herself? If so, she wondered what conclusions he'd reached, but didn't dare ask.

'Perhaps,' replied Robert. But more and more he was beginning to think that choosing Louise had been a deliberate decision on Michael's part, and that soon they would know the reason.

They reached Chateau les Greves in just under an hour. 'What a wonderful house,' whispered Louise in awe, gazing at the grey granite building with the rounded turrets set at each corner. The steeply sloping roof covered in the traditional small grey slates of all Breton houses, glinted brightly in the sun, and the formal gardens surrounding the chateau were a blaze of colour. 'Do they know we are coming?'

'No. I thought it better to surprise them. I did telephone Andrea Louedec, the housekeeper, and asked her to try and keep them at the chateau if at all possible.' The car drew to a halt at the side of the chateau. 'We'll go and see the housekeeper first,' said Robert, 'and find out where Michael and Veronique are.'

Andrea Louedec was relieved to see them. 'Thank goodness you've come. I was beginning to think you might miss them.'

'Miss them?' Robert raised his eyebrows.

'Yes, they are packing to leave. I think they plan to go to England. They are upstairs now, finishing the packing. And they are taking baby clothes,' she added.

'Baby clothes?' Although Louise couldn't speak fluent French, she understood quite well. She stared at Robert. 'Why should they be taking baby clothes?'

'We'll find out,' said Robert grimly. 'Come on.' He waved Andrea Louedec away. 'It's all right, I know the way.'

Robert led the way and Louise followed. Through rooms with lofty ceilings and tall, glit-edged mirrors. All the rooms and corridors were furnished with priceless antiques. Although no expert, Louise could recognize quality when she saw it. 'Veronique must be very wealthy to live here; where does she get her money from?' Louise knew it couldn't be from her own family, for Robert had told her their parents had left them barely enough to live on. All he had himself was the salary he earned as a Professor of Neurology. But even as she asked, Louise knew perfectly well what the answer would be.

'It all came from Michael,' said Robert. 'When they divorced he settled millions on her, and has been giving her money ever since.'

'I thought so,' said Louise. 'In fact, to be honest, I knew.'

Robert stopped walking and turned and stared. 'You knew?'

'Yes, Alan Osborne, the receiver, found out. But don't worry for Veronique's sake. Luckily for her, it's outside the jurisdiction of the court. The receiver can't touch it because it's in her name.'

'Then Michael won't be penniless,' said Robert.

'You certainly needn't worry about Michael on that score,' answered Louise with a wry smile. 'He'll be a wealthy man if he stays with Veronique.'

They were now in a long corridor upstairs, and Robert was striding along. When he came to a half open door he gave a brief knock and flung it open. Standing immediately behind him, the first thing Louise was aware of was that it was an enormous bedroom, and that the windows looked out on to a great wide bay. She could see the shining wet expanse of smooth sand, and the sea rushing in, the tips of the waves flecked white with foam. At the side of the bay

287

was an enormous headland, dark and menacing. It seemed to loom possessively over the sea, and as she looked at it a sudden prickle of fear ran along her spine.

'What the hell . . .' Michael's words cut off in mid-sentence as he saw Louise behind Robert.

'Your wife has come to see you,' said Robert.

Out of the corner of her eye Louise was aware of Veronique, and then saw she was sidling over towards another door which led off from the bedroom. The door was open and inside she could a blue room with mobiles hanging from the ceiling. A child's room.

'Leave it open.' Louise glanced at Robert; his voice was unusually harsh.

'Why have you come?' Michael's voice was hardly more than a whisper.

With an effort Louise walked into the bedroom, and looked Michael straight in the eyes. 'I didn't want to,' she said, marvelling at how calm and self-possessed her voice sounded, 'but I thought it would be cowardly not to tell you to your face. I intend to start proceedings for a divorce, and of course I shall ask for custody of Daniel.'

'Oh no. No. NO!' Veronique gave a terrible cry like an animal in pain, and running into the blue room she flung herself at the cot. 'He's mine, he's mine. You promised,' she screamed. Her legs buckled beneath her and she slid down on to the floor. All the time wailing, a high pitched hysterical sound.

'What does she mean? He's mine?' Horrified, Louise stared at the screaming, weeping woman. The seeds of the unnamed fear, the premonition she'd been holding at bay for the last few months began to take root and germinate in her mind. She turned her head away, as if trying to escape her own thoughts. 'What does she mean, Daniel is hers?' she whispered. 'Tell me, what does she mean?' There was no answer, and Louise turned back to Michael. 'Tell me!' She had to shout to be heard above Veronique's screams. 'Tell me, damn you!'

Robert moved swiftly across to his sister, and slapped her face, hard. 'Be quiet,' he said.

Veronique stopped screaming, but stayed on the floor, sobbing quietly, still clinging to the legs of the cot. 'Mine, mine,' she whimpered.

Michael tried to step in between Veronique and Robert. 'Was it necessary to hit her?'

'Of course it was, and you know it. She was hysterical.' Robert took a deep breath. Now was the time to put into words the unthinkable. But it had to be done. 'The real reason you married Louise was to have a child for Veronique, wasn't it?'

'Yes,' said Michael.

'And you chose Louise because she looked similar to Veronique.'

'Yes,' said Michael in the same expressionless voice.

'And you waited until you'd managed to get her pregnant, and then ascertained that the baby was healthy before you married her?'

'Yes,' said Michael.

'Are you saying . . .' Louise could hardly speak. The whole idea was so preposterous, so repulsive, and yet at the same time another detached part of her mind registered no surprise. This was the unnamed fear she'd been trying to suppress for months. 'Are you saying,' she said again, 'that you cold-bloodedly selected me, and then used me as a surrogate mother?'

'Yes,' said Michael.

'And that you have been intending all the time to steal my baby from me, and give him to *her*.' She pointed with a shaking finger at the still weeping Veronique.

'Yes,' said Michael.

A great, searing rage swept over her. 'I'll see you in hell first,' she whispered. 'Lay one finger on my child and I won't be responsible for my actions.'

Somehow, she never knew how, Louise turned and reached the doorway from the bedroom into the corridor.

There her strength gave out, and she clung on to the door jamb for support. 'Please, Robert,' she said. 'Take me away. Take me away from this place. From these people. Away from this whole ghastly nightmare.'

After being fortified by a large glass of brandy in Andrea Louedec's kitchen, Louise finally, albeit very reluctantly, agreed not to leave Chateau les Greves immediately.

'You can see, can't you, darling,' said Robert urgently, 'that it's more important than ever now to get things properly settled. For Veronique's sake as much as anything else.'

Louise felt a stab of jealousy. Of course Robert was her brother; he was bound to want to help Veronique. 'But what about me,' she said resentfully, 'what about *my* sake, what about *my* baby?' All she could think about was that the woman she'd last seen screaming hysterically on the nursery floor wanted to steal Daniel. A fresh blaze of anger and affrontery set her mind on fire. 'I'm not sure I can talk to her,' she said unsteadily, unable to bring herself to even let Veronique's name pass her lips. 'Or to Michael. How dare he do this to me? How dare *they*? I still find it difficult to believe. I keep thinking this must be some terrible nightmare and that in a moment I'll wake up.'

'It is a nightmare,' said Robert soberly, 'but I'm afraid we're both very much awake.'

'But why do I need to talk to either of them? What is there to say?'

'You must.' Robert was very firm. 'Because only *you* can make Veronique understand that Daniel is *your* child, not hers. For your own sake, and the safety of Daniel, you have got to make her acknowledge that he is nothing to do with her, and never will be. Once she has accepted that, then at least Daniel will be safe.'

'Safe? What do you mean? Surely she wouldn't harm him?'

'No, but she might try and take him.'

'I hadn't thought of that.' Suddenly Louise remembered newspaper stories of desperate woman stealing babies.

'She must accept that he is your child, and then perhaps with help she'll be able to accept the fact that she can never have children of her own, and begin to get better.'

'Get better?' Still reeling from the shock of discovering how she had been manipulated, Louise was finding it difficult to think clearly.

'She's ill, of course. No one in their right mind would let the desire for a child grow to such an overwhelming obsession.'

Louise thought of the wailing, weeping woman, and slowly, and at first against her will, little trickles of understanding and sympathy began to seep into her outrage and anger.

'I suppose I can understand her a little,' she said slowly. 'But not Michael. He's a man. Don't try telling me he was obsessed with having a baby.'

'He was obsessed with Veronique,' said Robert simply. 'I'm not excusing him. I'm merely stating the truth.' He sat down at the kitchen table beside Louise and took her hands in his. Raising them to his lips he kissed them gently. 'You can spare compassion for Veronique, and Michael as well. They have wronged you, it's true, but you have Daniel, and me, and you will survive. It costs nothing to talk, and only good can come of it.'

'All right,' said Louise, and managed a faint smile. 'You are a very persuasive man. I'll talk to both of them.' Then she shuddered. 'I still find it difficult to believe that he deceived me right from the very beginning. Me, a surrogate mother. It's horrible.'

Robert opened his arms and held her close, stroking her hair. 'I know,' he whispered. 'I feel the same myself. But at least we know the worst. There are no frightening secrets left to discover now. All we have to do is set the record straight once and for all, and then we can go on from there.'

Louise raised her tear-stained face and looked up at him. 'The three of us?' she said.

'Yes, said Robert. 'You, me and Daniel.'

CHAPTER 36

'I don't know how to begin,' said Michael.

'At the beginning is usually the best place.' Robert opened a bottle of chilled white wine and poured out four glasses.

They were sitting on the terrace of the chateau, overlooking the formal rose garden. The wind had dropped now, and the scent from the roses in the afternoon sunlight was overpowering. Louise knew that the scent of the roses would always remind her of this day. Everything felt unreal, and she had the sensation that part of her was standing on one side watching the strange scene. We look like two couples enjoying a sophisticated tête-à-tête, she thought, not four people trying to unravel the emotional mess we've made of our lives. No, three people, not four, she corrected herself, glancing at Robert. He hasn't done anything except get involved by falling in love with me and having Veronique as a sister. But Veronique, Michael and I . . . Louise stopped thinking, because the more she thought the more confused everything became. Apportioning blame was not the answer. Just trying to face up to things as they were was the first step.

Accepting a glass of wine she sipped at the cool liquid, and watched a grasshopper making seemingly random jumps on the paving stones of the terrace; it had lost its way, and was trying to get back to the cover and camouflage of the grass. Poor thing, she thought; it's like us, we've all lost our way, and now we're trying to find the scattered remnants of what we once called normality. Taking pity on the grasshopper she left her chair, and carefully picking it up took it down the steps and placed it on the lawn, where it immediately merged into the colour of the grass and disappeared. It must be nice to be able to do that, she thought enviously, merge into the landscape and disappear. But as disappearing was not possible she climbed back up the steps and sat down.

'Well?' she said to Michael. 'You can begin now.'

Veronique was sitting beside Michael, hanging on to his arm. She looked very thin and frail and there were great violet smudges under her eyes where she'd been crying.

Michael looked at his ex-wife and said, 'It all started when we found out that Veronique had a heart murmur. She had a very bad bout of flu and the murmur was discovered after she'd been ill. It was after that episode that I insisted she had a thorough check-up. We were planning to start a family, and I wanted to make sure that it would be safe for Veronique to have children.'

'I didn't want a check-up, because I'd made up my mind to have a baby whether it was safe or not,' Veronique interrupted.

'Oh Veronique, darling,' said Michael sadly, and squeezed her hand. 'Don't let's think of that again.'

He's besotted with her, thought Louise. How did I ever kid myself that he loved me?

'I wasn't so keen on taking a risk,' Michael continued. 'So I booked Veronique into a London clinic and made arrangements for her to have a complete medical examination. It was discovered through a scan that Veronique's ovaries do not have properly formed Fallopian tubes and the gynaecologist told us that she could never have a baby by normal means. He suggested IVF, which of course we were more than willing to try, but when the doctor tried to take the eggs from the ovaries he found that they too were imperfectly formed and the eggs were useless. After further tests, he said that even if we used an egg from another donor he could not implant it in Veronique because the wall of her uterus was also abnormal.'

'I know all this,' interrupted Robert.

Louise touched his arm. 'But I don't, Robert. And I need to know everything if I'm ever to begin to understand.'

'Of course. I should have thought.' Reaching out he held her hand.

'It's a terrible thing to find out that you are not a proper woman,' said Veronique in a barely audible whisper. 'When I came out of the clinic I would look at other women, poor women, shabbily dressed and shopping in the cheapest shops. I wanted to rush up to them and tell them that they were richer than me because they had children, and not one, sometimes three or four. All I wanted was one, just one. But I couldn't, because I was a failure for Michael and myself. I looked the same as other women, but I wasn't. I was a sham, my female body a mere façade.'

Louise felt a throb of pity. *Not a proper woman.* Yes, she thought, I can imagine myself thinking that if I'd been told that all my reproductive organs couldn't function. The despair was easy to imagine. Then she said, 'But you could have adopted a child. Why didn't you?'

'I didn't care whether we had a baby or not,' said Michael. 'I had Veronique, she was all I wanted.'

'Adoption is not the same,' said Veronique, a fierce, almost fanatical light suddenly flashing in her dark eyes. Her voice gathered strength. 'It was Michael's child I wanted, and if I couldn't have it then I decided that another woman should have it for me.'

'Another woman should have it for you,' whispered Louise. 'You decided it, just like that. To use another woman.'

'That is when we decided to separate and divorce,' said

295

Michael, before Veronique could reply to Louise. 'So that I could be free to find a woman who looked like Veronique, and who could have a child. My child, who would bear my name, and be half of me.'

'But who would be mine eventually,' said Veronique, a faint smile curving her lips.

Louise felt a rush of almost unbearable fear. Veronique still hadn't given up the idea of possessing Daniel. She wondered if all the talking in the world was going to change anything. Instinctively she felt Veronique would never change her mind. Panic engulfed her, and she shivered so much that the hand holding the wineglass shook.

The shaking hand did not go unnoticed by Robert. He was still holding her free hand in his, and squeezed it tightly. 'But, what I don't understand,' he said to Michael, 'is why you agreed to go along with this mad idea. And it was mad, surely you must know that?'

'Because I love Veronique more than life itself. I would, and still will, do anything to make her happy.'

Louise shivered again, a numbing sense of *déja vu* gripped her in a vice-like hold, and once again she felt that Robert was mistaken; this whole afternoon was a waste of time. Michael's passion for Veronique was as fanatical as Veronique's was for Daniel.

'But Michael,' Robert said, 'surely you realize that making Veronique happy is one thing, breaking the law to do it is another. You would never have got away with stealing a child.'

'I didn't break the law,' said Michael quickly. 'That's why we didn't pay a woman to be a surrogate mother because that could have legal consequences. No, I chose Louise because she looked like Veronique as I have already told you, and because I thought she was a career woman and would soon lose interest in motherhood. Once she began to lose interest I planned to quarrel with her, and then ask for a divorce and claim custody of the child.'

'Did you really think that I'd give up my own child so easily?' Louise was shocked at Michael's assumption.

'Yes, I did at the beginning. But that was before I got to know you. And then to complicate matters I found that I began to like you, and then I loved you. I was so confused; I still loved Veronique, I never for one moment doubted my feelings for her, but I found that I loved you too, although in a completely different way. I was at my wits' end, I didn't know what to do. Whatever I did I was bound to hurt one of you. Eventually I came to the conclusion that I couldn't take Daniel from you because it would be too cruel.'

'I know you said that once, but later you said that you didn't mean it.' Veronique turned and looked at Michael, her black eyes wild and brilliant with tears. 'You let me think all the time that I . . .'

'I couldn't bear to destroy your hope,' said Michael.

'In other words, you were a coward.' Robert's voice was quiet.

'Yes.' Michael bowed his head. 'I couldn't think straight. I even tried praying. Something I had never tried it before, so I suppose it was not surprising that it didn't work. No voice from on high gave me an answer, I still didn't know what to do.'

So that's what he was doing in the cathedral. Louise remembered his face. Poor Michael, he'd got himself into even more of a mess than she had.

'Let's move on to the time you fled England, and came here to live with Veronique,' said Robert. 'I take it that by then you had decided to relinquish all claims to Daniel, leave Louise for good, and stay in France.'

'Not exactly,' said Michael. 'I knew that was what I ought to do. But – ' he stopped, then said slowly – 'seeing you here, Robert, has made me realize just how far I had strayed from the path of sanity. You may not believe this, but I had planned to take Daniel with me the day of the move from Offerton.'

'I believe you.' Robert's voice was grim.

'However, for various reasons my plans went awry, and I came here alone. Once here, we began planning again. We intended leaving for England today, and were going to kidnap Daniel and bring him here.'

Louise drew in her breath sharply. 'My God,' she whispered, 'how could you even think of it? And how did you think you would get away with it?'

'There is only one answer.' Michael looked at Louise steadily, and for the first time since she had known him she felt she was seeing the truth in his eyes. 'I didn't think, Louise. Because if I had, I should have known it was an impossible thing to even contemplate.'

'Daniel would have a wonderful life here,' said Veronique defensively. 'You saw the room I have prepared for him. He would never have wanted for anything, love or material things. Nothing would be too good for Daniel if he lived here.'

'But of course you know now that that is impossible, don't you, Veronique?' asked Robert slowly. 'Now that you have met Louise, and know that she loves her son as only a mother can. Now that you know she has no intention of ever letting him go.'

'Of course,' said Veronique, and turning a blank innocent face towards her brother she smiled. 'I know that now. It was wrong of me to think otherwise.'

She doesn't mean it. Louise was not taken in by the passionless mask. I can recognize play-acting when I see it, she thought. The latent brilliance in Veronique's dark eyes gave her away. She doesn't mean it at all. I shall never be able to let Michael have access to Daniel alone. I will always have to be there too. On his own he might be trusted to keep his word, but never when he is with her. Didn't he admit earlier in the conversation that he'd do anything to make Veronique happy? And he will; once we are gone she will wind him around her little finger again. The threat will always be there as long as she is alive, because the only thing that will really make Veronique happy is to possess Daniel.

'I want your word, Veronique,' said Louise. 'Your word that you will never try and take Daniel.'

'You have it.' Veronique turned her brilliant gaze on to Louise. For a split-second Louise had a sudden inexplicable vision of the dark forbidding headland that loomed beyond Michel en Greve and felt afraid. Then it faded and Veronique's smiling face took its place. 'You do believe me, don't you?' she asked.

'I think so,' said Louise carefully. But I'll never trust you, she thought, never in a million years.

CHAPTER 37

Four months later Louise sat looking out of the train window at the October countryside flashing past. An early frost had turned the leaves on the trees a fiery mass of red and yellow. Autumn had well and truly arrived. How long ago that summer afternoon at the chateau seemed now. Long ago, and yet at the same time, frighteningly near. Michael had been back to England only once since, to sign the necessary papers for their divorce. She'd been nervous about meeting him again, but as they had talked Louise found it difficult to believe that the pleasant man beside her had once been her husband. He seemed like a well known friend, nothing more.

'There, I told you there was nothing to worry about,' said Robert.

Louise had been fearful about Michael's rights of access to Daniel, but it was he who'd said, 'I think, for the time being, it would be better for us all if I didn't see Daniel at all.'

A brief melancholy expression flickered across his face as he spoke, and Louise felt sorry for him. 'Better for Veronique, you mean,' she said.

'Yes,' Michael agreed quietly. 'Better for Veronique. I can't risk disturbing her peace of mind.'

Now, as she made her way back to Winchester from her office in London, she had the decree nisi in her handbag, all signed and sealed. Soon she would be absolutely free. Her marriage to Michael put behind her for ever. But try as she might, she knew she would never be able to block out the memories of the scheme Michael and Veronique had hatched between them. Her memory seemed to have a will of its own; it was stubborn, refusing to let her forget.

Robert was at her house when she arrived. 'I can't stay long, darling,' he said, and began kissing her passionately. 'Decree nisi day today, isn't it?'

Louise went weak at the knees, the effect Robert's kisses always induced. 'Yes,' she said, retrieving the envelope from her handbag and waving it at him. Then wrapping her arms around him she kissed him back, looking up into his golden-flecked eyes, blazing now with love for her. 'You always make me want to go to bed,' she whispered.

'Well then, what are we waiting for?'

'We can't. Melanie and Daniel . . .'

'They've gone over to Eugenia's for the afternoon and evening.'

Robert's lips grazed her neck, and Louise pressed her body close to his. He wanted her now, just as much as she wanted him. 'Oh, Robert,' she groaned, 'you have the power to turn me into a brazen hussy. When I'm with you I'm unashamed of anything I do.' With trembling fingers she fumbled with the belt of his trousers.

'Good,' he said, laughing. 'Just the way I like my women, uninhibited.'

Unzipping her dress and disposing of her bra with one swift movement, his mouth closed over her nipples, already erect and taut, awaiting the pleasure of his tongue. No more time was wasted on words. Locked together they sank down before the open fire in the tiny living room, just as they had the night they'd first made love. Then all was silence, save for little moans and gasps of pleasure as they made love. Feverishly at first, then more slowly, tenderly and with an intensity so great that it was difficult for either of them to know where pleasure

301

ended and pain began. At last they came together, as they always did, and the whole world floated away, leaving them alone, the only two people in the universe.

Later, lying with her head pillowed comfortably in the hollow of Robert's naked shoulder, Louise said, 'Only six weeks to the decree absolute.'

Robert sighed contentedly, gently caressing the smooth skin of her back with a slow, circling movement. 'Then you'll soon be able to make an honest man of me,' he said.

'You mean, get married?'

Raising himself on to one elbow Robert gazed down at Louise. 'Nothing else will do,' he said seriously. 'Being lovers is wonderful, but for me it's not enough. I want the permanency of "till death us do part." Nothing less.'

'Oh, Robert.' Suddenly, Louise was afraid. 'I've made a mistake before. Do you think . . .?'

'Yes,' said Robert firmly. 'I do.' He kissed her. 'Second-time lucky, darling.'

'Isn't the saying third-time lucky?'

'Not where you are concerned, my darling. I shall be your second, and definitely your last husband.'

'Sounds good to me.' Louise turned over and rolled on top of him. 'Do you think there's time . . .?'

'Definitely.' Robert's voice was gruff, his body suddenly grown urgent, his hands pulling her down closer, closer.

Louise sighed and slid down over him, luxuriating in the exquisite sensation of the feel of him rising up inside her. Making love with Robert is like music, she thought dreamily, letting her body follow the dictates of its own needs. One note follows another, and it's all so natural and beautiful. Then she stopped thinking, and let the desire wash over her again and again, until she cried his name out loud.

The next day, on returning from London, Louise popped in to see her mother before returning to Chesil Street, wanting to show her the decree nisi.

'Is that it?' asked Beattie looking at the paper. 'It looks terribly ordinary. Just a piece of paper. I feel it ought to be edged in gold as it represents freedom.'

'Not quite freedom,' said Louise. 'In six weeks time I'll get the decree absolute and then I'll be free of Michael. Or as free as I'll ever be,' she added sombrely. 'I wish, though, I could stop thinking of Veronique.' And as always whenever she thought of her, a chilling vision of the bleak headland swam into view. With an effort Louise closed her mind up tight, shutting out the unwanted vision.

'Try not to get paranoid, dear.' Beattie leaned over the cake she was icing, smoothing it carefully with a hot knife. Mr Poo was sitting on a chair beside her, watching with interest. He had a very sweet tooth, and every now and then she gave him a blob of icing.

'No wonder that dog is fat,' said Louise. 'He's no use for anything.'

'He barks loudly,' said Beattie, 'he's my burglar alarm. Oh damn!' She sat down. 'Louise, do you think Daniel will mind having a snow scene on his birthday cake, even though it is only October? I cannot get the bloody icing to stay smooth.'

'Of course he won't,' said Louise absent-mindedly; she was still thinking of Michael and Veronique. In spite of her resolve not to worry, the granting of the decree nisi had given fresh impetus to the very thoughts she was trying to put behind her. She'd thought of telling Robert, then decided that he would think her ridiculous. Besides, he might misunderstand and think she didn't trust him. And I do trust him, thought Louise, with my life. It's his sister that I don't trust. The kitchen clock showed that it was late. 'I'd better be going,' she said. 'I said Melanie could go out tonight. She's got a boyfriend now.'

'Mmmn, I know.' Beattie had another go at the cake. 'A nice young chap, works as a chef at the College Arms. Wonderful cook, I hear. Perhaps I should have asked him to do this cake.'

303

Louise laughed. 'Mother, Daniel won't notice what it looks like. As long as it has a candle on the top which he can blow out, and tastes good, he'll be pleased.'

Beattle put the knife down again. 'A whole year,' she said. 'It hardly seems possible that on Friday Daniel is a year old. What a lot has happened in a year.'

'It doesn't feel like a year, it feels like a lifetime,' said Louise, and picking up her handbag went towards the door. 'By the way, will you tell Eugenia that I'll take up her offer of making the sandwiches and jellies for Daniel's birthday tea? I've got a very heavy day on Friday, four prospective new clients to see, and then I must catch the half-past-three train back to Winchester if I'm not to miss my own son's birthday party. Tell her I'll pay her whatever it costs when I see her.'

'I'll tell her.' Beattie followed Louise to the door, her mind moving on to the future. 'In six weeks time you'll be free to marry Robert,' she said, smiling.

'Do you think I ought?'

'My God, surely you're not having doubts about that!' Beattie exploded. 'If it's the one thing you ought to do, it is that. The man loves you, and you love him.' Louise didn't reply. 'Well, you do, don't you? If you don't, what are you doing sharing his bed so frequently?'

'Yes I do love him, but . . .' Louise stopped.

'But what?' her mother demanded.

'If I marry him that will make Veronique my sister-in-law.'

Beattie threw up her icing-covered hands in exasperation. 'For God's sake, stop being so neurotic. You've got a divorce. You've got Michael's legal undertaking that he will make no claim on Daniel whatsoever, not even for visits. And you know Veronique has been having treatment and she and Michael intend to remarry as soon as possible. She's probably quite all right now. Robert seems to think so. I know he's her brother, but he is a doctor as well, and he knows about these things.'

Louise was not convinced. 'Robert is a man, and all her doctors are men. I don't think they can see into her innermost psyche.'

'And you think you can?'

'Mother, if you'd been there on that day in June when the truth finally came out, I think you'd agree with me. Perhaps it takes a woman to know a woman. I recognized things in Veronique that I know lie deep within me.'

'There but for the Grace of God, you mean,' said Beattie.

'In a way. I do feel terribly sorry for her, but I shall never be able to trust her. I'm not sure that any treatment will work, and I don't think she will ever stop wanting Daniel.'

Beattie put her hands on her hips and planted her feet firmly apart, always a sign that she was about to make a pronouncement. 'Louise,' she said severely, 'I'm sorry to say this about my own daughter but I really do think you are being paranoid. Veronique is with Michael in France, not even in this country. He will look after her and make certain she is no threat to you or Daniel. And once you are married to Robert there will be three of you. You'll feel safer. You can't let the failed plottings, *failed*, remember that, of a half-crazed woman cast a blight over the rest of your life.'

Louise grinned at her mother's fierce expression. 'All right, I'll marry Robert. You're right, of course. You always are.'

'Takes a woman to know a woman,' said Beattie, echoing her daughter's own words of a moment before.

'But when I marry I'll have to move,' said Louise, thinking of the small house in Chesil Street. 'It's fine for occasional visits from Robert, but it's not large enough for family life, and of course I'll still need Melanie because I'm not giving up the agency. The trouble is, I love Chesil Street, and I've always had this dream of Daniel fishing in the River Itchen when he's old enough.'

'There's an enormous house for sale at the lower end of Chesil Street. The big white one with the lovely lawns which slope down to the river near the water-mill,' said Beattie. 'I've told Robert about it, and he's made arrangements to view it.'

'Mother! Are you organizing my life for me?'

'Yes,' said Beattie firmly. 'I am. I've worked it out. There is time for you to buy that house, and get married before Christmas. Then Robert can be a real part of the family for the Christmas celebrations.'

'You certainly like to have all the ends neatly tied,' said Louise, laughing.

'Maybe it is because I was always so hopeless at tying my own ends neatly,' said Beattie, 'and maybe it is because I want to see my one and only daughter really happy.'

'And I will be,' said Louise. 'Who'd have thought that when I first met Robert I'd end up marrying him.' She sighed happily. 'I know life with him is going to be one long rose-coloured dream.'

'Good God!' said Beattie, 'that sounds like a recipe for disaster. You can't sleep your way through life in a dream; it needs to be punctuated every now and then with a bit of excitement.'

'Mother, I've had enough excitement over the past year to last me a lifetime,' said Louise. 'From now on I'm opting for a peaceful existence.'

CHAPTER 38

Michael put down the phone and smiled fondly at Veronique. 'That was Robert,' he said. 'He and Louise are getting married the week after next. Exactly one week after us.'

He put his arms around her and pulled her towards him. She was really well now, and had put on some weight which made her more beautiful than ever. And best of all, he thought, pushing aside her long dark hair and kissing the nape of her neck, she has forgotten all about Daniel. Now, when Michael looked back to his brief time with Louise it seemed like some far-off dream. Even Briam Corporation and all his ambitions of becoming an Establishment figure in Britain seemed unrealistic, and he wondered now why he had ever thought that was what he had wanted.

The occasional journalist managed to track him down to the chateau and wanted an interview but he always refused, and merely issued the same formal press statement. *Michael Baruch is living in quiet retirement and has no intention of re-entering the world of commerce.* The journalists usually hung around for a day or so, questioning the Louedecs if they got the chance, or some of the Michel en Greve villagers, but all confirmed that Michael and Veronique Baruch were living quietly, and apart from long invigorating walks on the headland, they hardly ever left the environs of the chateau. None of it was news-worthy so the journalists always left.

'It will be good to be the proper Madame Baruch again next week,' said Veronique. 'Proper proper, not ex and make-believe like I am now.'

Michael laughed. 'I've never thought of you as anything else but the proper Madame Baruch,' he said. 'The only thing the ceremony next week will do is put it down officially on a piece of paper.' He kissed her slowly, and felt Veronique move her body sensuously against his. Nothing could diminish her sexuality; even when she had been ill she had wanted him, and he knew from her gently rotating hips that she wanted him now.

'Let's go to the headland.'

For once Michael demurred. 'Darling, it's cold, it's blowing a gale, and it's raining. Let's go to bed.'

'No, that's too dull and respectable.' Veronique laughed, and pulling away ran out of the salon. 'You'll have to catch me,' she called over her shoulder.

Andrea Louedec saw them from her kitchen window, and watched Veronique run into the stables with Michael in hot pursuit. 'Honestly, those two!' she said disapprov-ingly. 'Sex mad. They do it all the time and in all sorts of places. They think people don't know what they get up to on that headland, but there's hardly a body in Michel en Greve who doesn't.'

'Pity *you* don't like sex a bit more often,' muttered Paul, looking up from the television.

'There's a time and place for everything,' said Andrea primly. Through the open stable door she could see Michael pinning Veronique against the wooden half-door of one of the loose boxes. She averted her eyes; the way her mistress was rubbing herself up and down it was quite . . . She chopped up the onions she was preparing for soup with unexpected viciousness. She didn't want to think about it. It wasn't decent.

'Huh! I always seem to miss the time *and* the place,' said

her husband and went back to the television, and the comfort of a rugby match.

In the stable Veronique escaped Michael once more and scrambling up the ladder climbed into the hayloft. Once there she made no attempt to escape from him when he joined her. He was as aroused as she was and neither wasted time on preliminaries.

'Lovely, lovely,' she whispered, holding the velvet-soft but rock-hard rod that reared out through Michael's unzipped trousers. With one deft movement she slid it between her thighs, pausing only to push aside the flimsy crotch of her panties. Neither of them could wait, and they rocked together so violently in a climax that wisps of hay drifted down on to the startled horse standing below.

Later they undressed each other and made love again, this time more slowly. Veronique's mouth is made for love, thought Michael, as her sensual lips moved over his body. Nothing was taboo, nowhere was too intimate for her probing tongue. When it came to making love Veronique was perfection itself.

For her part Veronique was arousing Michael almost without thinking; making love was like breathing to her. While her mouth and hands were busy her mind wandered, and she thought of Robert and Louise. And of Daniel. When Robert married Louise she would be Daniel's aunt. One step closer. Let Michael think she had forgotten, let them all think that. Only she knew the truth. One day the right time would come; until then she could wait. With an adeptness grown easy with practice she switched her mind from Daniel and concentrated on Michael. 'Darling,' she said softly.

Michael felt the familiar warm glow stealing over him as his body began to rise towards yet another climax, and it suddenly occurred to him that since that day when they had been confronted by Robert and Louise and the truth had come out, Veronique had gone out of her way to please him as well as demanding satisfaction for herself. It was almost as if she had replaced the obsession for a child with an obsession for sex. Michael smiled; that was good. She really was forgetting about Daniel, and as for himself, he knew that he didn't want to share her with anybody, not even a child. 'Aaah!' he groaned. 'Oh God, Veronique, you are wonderful.'

It was late afternoon and beginning to get dark before they were both exhausted and lay, still panting, side by side in the hay. Michael wrapped them both in a clean horse blanket.

'You haven't told me what you think about your brother marrying Louise,' he said. 'You don't mind, do you?'

Veronique pulled Michael's head down into the hollow between her breasts. 'Of course not,' she said. The eyes in the pale face staring over Michael's shoulder suddenly burned feverishly. The terrible, gut-wrenching pain she experienced whenever anything or anyone close to Daniel was mentioned was something she knew she could never share with him. So she kept it to herself, tightly buttoned up inside the core of her being. But in spite of knowing the answer she couldn't help asking, 'Do you think that Louise will let me see Daniel?'

'We've all agreed that it is wiser if you don't.' Michael raised his head and stared down at her. 'You don't still hanker after him, do you?'

'Of course not, silly.' She pulled his head down and silenced him with a kiss. 'I don't want to share you with anybody,' she said when she released him.

Michael relaxed. 'And I don't want to share you,' he said. She felt the same as him. That was good. Their time of madness and longing for the unattainable had passed. Now they were together again, and that was all that mattered.

At dinner that night Veronique said, 'I think we should send Robert and Louise a present. Do you know the time and place of the wedding, or where they are having the reception? We could send a present there.'

'That would be a nice gesture,' agreed Michael. 'I'll get something.'

'No, I'll do it. Men are so hopeless at choosing presents. You give me all the details of their wedding, and I'll arrange for a present to be sent so that they can open it at the reception. A piece of crystal I think; I'll ring Harrods and discuss it. They have the best selection in Europe.'

She smiled at Michael, surprising him with the sudden brilliance of her smile.

CHAPTER 39

The move to the four storey White House in Chesil Street, Winchester, was accomplished one week before Robert and Louise were to be married.

'I still can't believe we did all this so quickly.' Louise stood in the second-floor room which they had decided to use as the main living room. It stretched almost the entire width and depth of the house, and had two enormous sashed windows reaching from floor to ceiling. The windows looked out over the sloping lawns, shaded by an ancient magnolia tree, down to the river, and caught all the afternoon sunlight. Louise had chosen ivory and cream for the decor, enhancing the natural light, and had exaggerated the space by having furniture on different scales; a huge milky beige settee dwarfed a low rectangular rustic wooden table. Enormous swathes of buttermilk muslin hung at the windows to be pulled across if the sun became too fierce, and the same milky beige of the settee was picked up in the heavy slub silk curtains hanging either side of the windows. In pride of place, and reflected by an oval mirror, stood the silver loving cup on the mantelshelf of the wide ivory coloured alabaster fireplace.

Robert looked around in delight. Louise hadn't let him see the room until it had been finished. 'What a change from my bachelor pad,' he said. 'The only prominent thing in my living room is my computer.'

'I had noticed,' said Louise, pulling a face at the thought of Robert's Spartanly furnished house. 'In this house your computer is banished to the study where you can work in complete peace and quiet.'

Robert put his arms around her. 'I have the feeling I'll be spending much more time in this room with you than with my computer,' he said.

'I thought we could have the reception for the wedding in here,' said Louise. 'We don't have an enormous number of people coming, so there is plenty of space. And I shall be able to relax and enjoy myself knowing that Daniel will be safely asleep upstairs.'

'Not still worried about anyone stealing him surely?' Robert frowned, sensing something of Louise's anxiety.

'Of course not,' Louise lied. My mother said I was paranoid, and I know I am, she thought, wishing she could confide in Robert about the worry which refused to go away. 'That is all behind us now,' she said firmly, as much to convince herself as Robert, 'and I hope that Michael and Veronique are happy.'

'They are,' said Robert. 'And now that Veronique is so much better, Michael tells me that he's off to Paris next week to oversee the reinvestment of some of the money he gave Veronique. He intends to make up a good portfolio, so that they can live comfortably off the income. That way he needn't work away in an office, and never need leave Veronique alone too often. He feels that is best for her, and I agree.'

'You mean you don't think she's entirely stable?' asked Louise, and before she could hold the vision back she could see the sea rolling in over the wet shining sand, and by the side of it the black mass of the headland jutting out into the deeper water of the ocean.

'She'll never be entirely stable,' said Robert. 'But with Michael by her side she should be all right.'

If I told Robert of my premonition, of my frequent visions of that damned headland in France, would he think I was unstable, wondered Louise. The answer was probably yes, she decided, so she remained silent.

The guest-list for the wedding was in her handbag, and Louise got it out and showed it to Robert. Anything to take her mind away from Veronique and France. 'You'd better check it,' she said, 'to see whether or not I've left off anyone important.'

'I'm sure you haven't.' Robert took the list. 'Seems OK to me. Now, show me the rest of the house. But you'll have to be quick, I've got a postgraduate teaching meeting at seven-thirty this evening.'

After Robert had gone Louise felt lonely. She went up to the attic rooms which had been converted into a tiny self-contained flat for Melanie, so that she had somewhere to entertain her friends when she was off duty. There she found Melanie cooking herself supper. Louise thought it looked terribly complicated, borlotti beans, garlic, peppers, two kinds of cheese and home-made pasta which Melanie was in the process of cutting into strips to make tagliatelle.

'You don't have to cook for yourself all the time,' she said, 'you know you're welcome to eat in the kitchen downstairs.'

'Oh I know that, but – ' Melanie pursed her lips in concentration – 'I want to teach myself to cook. Mum would never let me into the kitchen, and anyway all she ever cooks is plain English food. I'm starting with Italian.'

'I can see that. I think you are very ambitious.' Louise prowled around the little flat. Melanie had made it very homely with the bits and pieces Louise had given her, and with other things she had bought herself. 'You can hear Daniel all right when you are up here?' The thought suddenly worried Louise.

'Oh yes, don't you worry about that. When he howls, he

314

howls loudly. And anyway I keep popping up and down to make sure he's fast asleep. I won't neglect him.'

'I know you won't. All the same, I'll be happier when that intercom system is fitted. The electrician has promised to do it by next week, before the wedding.'

'You worry too much, Mrs Baruch.'

'You'll soon have to call me Mrs Lacroix,' said Louise, smiling, before leaving Melanie to her borlotti beans and tagliatelle. 'I'll keep an eye on Daniel for the rest of the evening, so that you can get on with your cooking in peace.'

On her way downstairs she went into Daniel's room. That too looked out on to the lawns and river and was decorated in primrose yellow and ivory. The toadstool lamp at the side of the bed cast a warm glow over Daniel's face. Louise stood for a moment gazing down at him. What perfect features he had, a beautifully rounded head, now growing a soft down of very dark hair. His eyelashes were very dark too, and fanned out over his cheeks, curling up slightly at the ends. His pink mouth was slightly open so that his four teeth showed gleaming white in the night light. After a moment she went across to the window and pulled aside the curtain. In the darkness she could see the river glistening in the light of the street lamps which illuminated the pathway leading between Winchester's two water-mills. The path was on the far side of the river, away from the garden. It was almost like living in a house with a moat. Louise relaxed, feeling secure and happy. Nothing could possibly happen to Daniel, and she was stupid to think that it could.

Drawing the curtains back across the window she went downstairs to the tranquillity of the living room and telephoned her mother. There was nothing Beattie liked more than talking about the forthcoming wedding.

'And I still haven't decided what to wear,' she said.

'What about something quiet and sedate?' suggested

Louise hopefully. 'Something in keeping with being a mother and grandmother.'

'If you had your way,' grumbled Beattie, 'you'd have me looking like the Queen Mother. All feathers and pearls, and those awful Minnie Mouse shoes.'

On the Friday morning of Robert and Louise's wedding, Michael had his appointment with a broker in Paris. 'Are you sure you don't want to come?' he asked Veronique. 'We could make it a little holiday.'

'I'm sure,' said Veronique. 'I hate Paris. It reminds me of the time Robert put me in that clinic. No, I'll stay here and wait for you to come home. Who knows, I might even get you a special present to welcome you back.'

Michael laughed and kissed her affectionately. 'I shall only be gone for two days, that hardly warrants a welcome home present.'

'We'll see,' said Veronique, giving him one of her brilliant smiles.

It was only on the drive to Paris that Michael had a fleeting moment of doubt. Veronique's smile had been a little too brilliant, a little too purposeful, as if she had placed it there to mask a reality she wanted kept hidden. He pulled off the autoroute and phoned the chateau. Veronique herself answered.

'It's Michael here. Are you all right?'

'Darling, of course I'm all right. Why do you ask? It's only an hour since you left me.'

Michael breathed a sigh of relief. She sounded well enough, not agitated or excited, the usual danger signals when she was about to do something reckless. 'Promise me that you won't go climbing on the headland while I'm away,' he said. 'It's December and you know how dangerous the winds can be.'

'I promise,' said Veronique. 'Is that why you rang me?'

'Yes,' said Michael quickly, glad that she had unwittingly provided him with a much needed excuse for the phone call. 'I worry about you.'

'Well don't. I promise I won't go near the headland. Now you'd better get going or you will be late for your first appointment.'

Andrea Louedec tapped impatiently at the recall button but nothing happened. 'The phone is dead,' she told Paul who'd just come in for the midday meal.

'I'm not surprised.' Paul sat down and poured himself a generous glass of red wine from the earthenware pitcher on the table. 'The wind out there is building up to hurricane force. I dare say some of the lines are down.'

'Oh dear.' Andrea took the steaming pot of cassoulet from the top of the stove and began dishing out the chunks of pork, garlic sausage and the rich mixture of haricot beans, tomatoes and white wine. 'I promised Monsieur Robert I would let him know if anything happened.'

'And what has happened?'

'Madame Veronique has gone. She took a small overnight bag with her and said she might be back tonight, if not definitely tomorrow morning. Now I know Monsieur Michael wasn't expecting her to go away, because he took me aside and asked me to keep an eye on her while he was away in Paris.'

'For God's sake, she's not a child,' said Paul irritably. 'She's free to come and go as she pleases. You take your duties far too seriously. Now, sit down and eat, because if the phone is dead there is nothing you can do anyway.'

Andrea sat down and sipped a small glass of wine anxiously. 'I suppose you're right,' she said. 'There is nothing I can do.'

'Exactly,' said Paul. 'So eat, woman, eat, and stop fretting.'

'There are problems with the telephone lines to the area you dialled,' said the recorded voice. 'This is due to

317

adverse weather conditions.' Michael put the phone down and worried. He hated being cut off from Veronique.

At St Brieuc airport Veronique was engaged in a furious argument with the pilot, an Englishman named Jeff Stevens, who was due to fly the small four-seater plane she had chartered. 'I'm sorry, Madame Baruch,' the pilot said, 'but the weather conditions are worsening all the time. You can't fly to England this morning. Not in a plane this size.'

'Do you have a jumbo jet available then?'

'Of course I don't.'

'And has the control tower officially closed down the airfield?'

'No, but in my opinion . . .'

'In my opinion you are a coward, Mr Stevens,' said Veronique icily. 'It is imperative that I get to England this morning.' She turned away and began to walk towards the small terminal building. 'I shall find a pilot who is not afraid of a little wind. A man who is experienced.'

'I am f . . .' he bit the expletive back, 'well experienced. I flew in the Falkands War, I've flown through snow blizzards, hurricane winds, fire and dense smoke.'

Veronique turned and flashed him one of her brilliant smiles. 'Then the weather today shouldn't bother you. Anyway you know what meteorologists are, they always err on the worst side just to be safe.' She smiled again. 'Besides, I am not afraid. If it is meant to be, then we shall arrive in England safely, if not . . .' She shrugged expressively.

'All right, I'll take you. But we'd better go right now if we *are* going, and I warn you, be prepared for a very rough ride.'

'I don't care,' said Veronique, and throwing the overnight bag in before her, she climbed into the cramped interior of the tiny plane.

The plane accelerated down the runway, and the hea-

318

vens opened. Rain lashed across the windscreen, and as they became airborne a great gust of wind lifted the plane and practically threw it forward on to its nose. The pilot glanced over his shoulder at Veronique. 'Rough enough for you?' he said.

'Wonderful.' Her face was transfigured. It shone with a wild and reckless excitement. Her black eyes blazed with an eerie luminosity. 'I love the wind.'

Jeff Stevens brought the plane down safely at Eastleigh airport. The very strong winds had not yet reached southern England; it was merely gusty, and gave the plane a slight buffeting as it taxied along the runway before coming to a halt outside the terminal building. 'We've arrived,' he said unnecessarily.

Veronique climbed out. 'Don't forget I expect you to fly me back tonight. Just wait here until I arrive. And no excuses about the weather. We shall fly whatever the conditions. Is that understood?'

Jeff Stevens shrugged. She was paying him well. Very well, in fact. 'Understood,' he said, and watched her slim figure hurry towards the 'Arrivals' door of the terminal. He looked at his watch; it was eleven-thirty a.m. Time for one scotch before lunch. After all, he wasn't due to fly again until tonight, and he certainly deserved something stronger than coffee.

At precisely eleven-thirty a.m. Robert kissed his new wife in the registrar's office at Winchester. After that the small party hurried outside for the photographs. Besides Robert and Louise there were only six people, Gordon and Eugenia, Dick and Lizzie Carey, Beattie and Richard Meacher, Robert's colleague from the Department of Neurology, and best man. Arrangements had been made for all the other guests, including Gordon's children, to meet at the White House where Melanie and Daniel were waiting to receive them. Louise wanted everything to be very informal.

319

The photographer, a small, rather nervous little man, fussed about with his tripod.

'You'd better get a move on,' shrieked Beattie, desperately hanging on to the enormous cartwheel of purple which was her hat. 'The wind is getting stronger by the minute.' The purple silk trousers of her trouser suit flapped about her legs and the wind got under the loose jacket and it billowed up, giving her the appearance of a hot air balloon about to take off at any moment.

'I thought you said she'd be wearing a Queen Mother outfit,' said Robert, trying not to laugh.

'Even the Queen Mother must have her off-days.' Louise began to giggle. Her mother did look funny.

'Smile please,' the photographer said.

'How can I smile when my teeth are chattering,' said Beattie crossly, and stood next to Lizzie Carey, who as usual was wearing brilliant red.

'I think perhaps one of you should move,' said the photographer looking at the clashing colours. He put out a hand to move Beattie, saw her fierce expression, and changed his mind, and moved Dick and Lizzie to the other side of the group instead.

Eugenia took a bag of confetti out of her handbag and tossed the contents over Robert and Louise.

'No throwing of confetti on the premises,' shouted the registrar from the doorway.

'What did he say?' Beattie, who had heard perfectly well, also took out a bag.

The registrar rushed out, waving his arms. 'No throwing of . . .' He choked as the wind took Beattie's handful of confetti and blew most of it into his mouth.

'Have your photograph taken with us,' she said, and clutched him to her purple side.

'Now if everyone would just move round.' The photographer tried to push Beattie and the registrar out of the way. 'Just the brother and sister-in-law with the bride and groom.'

320

'I want one on my own with my daughter and her husband. Do that first.' Beattie planted herself firmly at Robert's side, and the registrar took the opportunity to scurry back to the safety of his office.

'That purple woman is a menace,' he told his clerk, still spluttering and spitting out pieces of confetti. 'People like that bring down the whole tone of the place. This is Winchester, after all, the county town of Hampshire.'

The clerk giggled. 'I think she looks rather fun. Certainly makes a change from the tweeds and pearls we usually get.'

The photographer, terrified of Beattie, took a photo of the trio as she wanted.

'I really do think that because of the weather it would be better if we went home now,' said Louise to the photographer. 'You are coming back to the house, aren't you? I'd like a photograph with my son, my nephews and nieces, and all the other guests.'

'Well, I was.' He eyed Beattie fearfully; perhaps going back to the house wasn't such a good idea.

Louise noticed his apprehensive expression. 'Please don't worry about my mother. Her bark is much worse than her bite.'

'Truly. She's an angel really,' said Robert.

The photographer looked doubtfully at Beattie and began folding up his tripod. 'Well, I suppose it is possible to have a purple angel,' he said.

CHAPTER 40

Outside the wind gathered in strength and the meagre light of the December afternoon dwindled into darkness even earlier than usual. Louise glanced out of the window; the bare branches of the magnolia tree silhouetted against the street lamps of the path on the other side of the river waved as if in greeting. On any other day, she thought, I'd probably think a wet, windy and dark afternoon depressing, but not today. Today even the bleakness outside seemed to have a special cheer of its own.

Tina, swaying slightly, came across to Louise with husband Alistair in tow. 'I think I've had one too many champagne cocktails,' she said.

Louise laughed. 'I think everybody has.'

'Just as well we booked into a hotel for the night,' said Alistair. 'I'd hate to be breathalysed.'

'What about your boys?' Robert knew Tina had two teenage sons because Louise had told him. 'You should have brought them.'

'My sister is staying with them. Although they are quite old enough now to look after themselves.'

'One day I'll be saying that about Daniel,' mused Louise, watching her mother proudly showing him off to anyone who showed the slightest sign of interest.

'Yes, and when he's a teenager you'll understand why we didn't bring them to the wedding. Teenage boys hate having to get clean and dress up, and they hate having to

322

be on their best behaviour for more than ten minutes.'

'In other words, kids are absolute pests,' said Alistair, 'but we love them. Although I must say Gordon's kids are angels, all of them.'

Robert laughed. 'I wouldn't normally agree, but today, they are.' He looked across at the settee where Natasha, Rupert and Milton were sitting quietly side by side, looking sleepy.

Eugenia, carrying Tara, interrupted. 'The only reason they're quiet is because they're sloshed,' she said. 'The little devils told me they were drinking lemonade, when all the time it was champagne.'

'At least they've enjoyed themselves,' said Louise.

'This time tomorrow, I doubt that they will remember a thing.' Eugenia was cross. 'Gordon really should have kept a closer eye on them.'

Beattie came across with a slightly grumpy Daniel. 'He's getting tired,' she said. As if to prove her point Daniel reached up, and more by luck than judgement, managed to grasp her hat and throw it across the room. The purple cartwheel disappeared between the assembled guests' legs.

'I'll get it.' Melanie went off to retrieve it.

'I think you ought to cut the cake now,' said Beattie, 'so that you can have a photograph done of yourselves, and then one with Daniel between you. After that, Melanie says she will take him upstairs and put him to bed.'

Outside in the rain and darkness a woman stood on the path by the side of the river. The lights from the big room in the White House cut a swathe through the night and sparkled on the swiftly flowing river. They were cutting the cake, she could see it clearly, and could see too the small boy in blue standing between the bride and groom; he was jumping up and down on his sturdy little legs. A young girl came forward and took the baby out of the room, and a few moments later the lights in the top two storeys of the house came on. It was time to make a move.

Veronique stepped out of the shadows and walked quickly down towards the weir by the mill. A wooden pathway led across the top of the weir through to Chesil Street on the other side of the river. Veronique took the narrow wooden path and was soon in the street outside the White House. Suddenly the door opened and light from the hall flooded down the stone steps which led into the street, causing Veronique to shrink back into the shadows. Richard Meacher, Robert's best man, paused, looking for his car keys in the light. His radio pager started bleeping. Irritably he answered it. 'All right, all right, I'm on my way. I'll be with you in less than five minutes.' Pulling the door to behind him, he sprinted down the steps to where his car was parked on double yellow lines with a DOCTOR ON CALL notice stuck on the windscreen. A second later he had disappeared in a cloud of exhaust fumes.

Veronique climbed the steps and pushed at the huge white wooden door. It swung open easily; in his haste Richard had not closed it securely. Stepping inside the brightly lit hall Veronique carefully closed the door behind her. It made only the slightest click, far too small to be heard by any of the raucous guests upstairs who were all laughing and talking at once.

Up in the living room, Mr Poo, who'd been stuffing himself on smoked salmon, chicken pieces and latterly wedding cake crumbs, heard the click. As Beattie was always telling Louise, he might be fat, but he had very sharp ears and was a good guard dog. Now he knew that there was someone in the house who shouldn't be there. With a high pitched yap of rage he hurled himself at the door and demanded to be let out.

'Whatever is the matter?' Beattie rushed over and opened the door, and Mr Poo hurtled down the stairs as fast as his bulk and short legs would allow. 'He must have heard something,' she cried, following the dog down the stairs.

'Daniel,' gasped Louise.

'Nonsense.' Robert's voice was very firm and quiet. 'Melanie is with him now; she's bathing him, remember? And we've got the intercom switched on. Listen, you can hear Melanie and Daniel talking bath-time talk.'

It was true. Louise could hear Melanie crooning, and Daniel laughing and splashing in the water. She relaxed and clung on to Robert. 'I think I'm a little neurotic,' she said.

'A little,' Robert agreed, 'but I still love you. Now, let's go and see what that dog is making all the fuss about.'

Downstairs in the hall Veronique heard the dog's initial bark, and the thumping on the living room door before it was opened. It gave her enough time to dive into the tall cupboard beneath the stairs. With an almighty effort she hauled herself up on to the top shelf and lay flat behind piles of Robert's old waterproofs and fishing tackle which he had piled in there out of the way.

'He's barking at the cupboard door,' said Louise.

Robert opened the door and Mr Poo rushed in. He scurried round the cupboard, knocking over wellington boots and a pile of fishing rods which were stacked in the corner, then he ran out again and barked excitedly, bouncing up and down like a furry ping-pong ball. His little flat-iron face appeared almost human in its excitement, and he snorted and snuffled until Beattie was forced to wipe his nose with a handkerchief. 'Of course he's not bred for trailing a scent,' she said. 'He just gets excited by noises.'

'I can see that,' said Robert, coming out of the cupboard. 'There is absolutely nothing there. Are you sure that dog hasn't been drinking champagne?'

'I'll take him away and calm him down,' said Beattie, picking up a furiously squeaking Mr Poo and carrying him off upstairs.

An hour later when all the guests had finally departed, Robert and Louise cleared a space on the settee and sank down exhausted amidst the clutter of empty champagne bottles, glasses, half-eaten *vol au vents*, shrivelled chicken legs and curled up sandwiches. 'I can't bear to look at it,' said Louise.

'Then don't,' said Robert, pulling her head into the hollow of his shoulder. 'We'll close our eyes and pretend it is the way it was when you first showed the room to me.'

A knock on the door heralded the entrance of Melanie. 'Daniel is sound asleep,' she announced. 'The party tired him out. He didn't even want to play with his teddy tonight, just laid straight down, closed his eyes and was out like a light.' She looked around the litter-strewn room. 'Do you want me to start clearing this up?'

'No. We are pretending it isn't there,' said Louise sleepily. 'And I've got a cleaning firm coming in tomorrow to clear up. They ought to be good, they're called Whistlestop Cleaning Services.' She yawned. 'Let's hope they do a whistlestop job and are in and out before we know it.'

'It's all right if I go up to my flat then?'

'Of course. The intercom is still on, isn't it?'

'Yes,' said Melanie, 'I wouldn't switch that off.'

'Goodnight then, and thank you for all you've done.'

'Yes, thank you, Melanie,' said Robert, unable to stop yawning himself. He lay sprawled back, his eyes closed.

'A pleasure,' said Melanie and closed the door quietly behind her.

Outside, Eddy Parker, her new boyfriend, stood waiting. 'Can I come up to your flat then?'

'Yes, but be quiet.' Melanie put a finger to her lips and led the way upstairs.

'What's that?' Eddy pointed to the switch and the wire running up along the wall from Daniel's bedroom up the stairs towards the attic rooms.

'That's the intercom. If Daniel even so much as whimpers I can hear him.'

'And?'

'And I have to go down to him of course,' said Melanie, surprised at his ignorance.

'Oh, I see,' said Eddy, and as he went up the stairs behind her he flicked the switch into the 'off' position.

CHAPTER 41

'Oh, Robert, do you think we ought?' Louise protested feebly as Robert came back up from the kitchen with yet another chilled bottle of champage in an ice bucket.

'Definitely,' said Robert. 'You and I drank hardly anything at the reception. We were far too busy being the perfect host and hostess, making certain everyone else enjoyed themselves.'

'That's true.' Louise sighed and stretched out on the settee. 'I feel absolutely exhausted.'

'Besides,' continued Robert, waving the bottle towards her, 'this is something I bought especially for us. A particular vintage of Krug that I like. I thought we could get gently sloshed together.'

Downstairs in the hall cupboard Veronique waited until Robert's footsteps on the stairs had ceased and she heard the door into the second-floor room close. Then she carefully climbed down from her hiding place, stretched her cramped limbs, and silently opening the cupboard door crept out and started up the stairs. A sharp blade of light from beneath the door cut across the passage outside the living room, and Veronique could hear Louise laughing.

'Oh, Robert, you may be a very clever doctor, but opening champagne is definitely not one of your strong points.'

'It was not part of my university training,' said Robert, frowning in concentration, 'and the wire around the top of this bottle is strong enough to use on a damned suspension bridge. Aah!' He loosened the wire at last, and the cork flew off with a satisfactorily loud explosion, shooting over the back of the settee and hitting the door. 'Done it,' he said.

The ear-splitting report and the sudden thump on the door startled Veronique, who happened to be immediately outside the door at that moment. In the darkness she stumbled, and her foot scuffed loudly against the wooden wainscot running the length of the passage.

'Goodness, this old house is noisy. Hark at that bump, sounds as if there is an elephant outside in the passage,' said Louise, watching Robert pour the golden sparkling liquid into two clean champagne glasses. 'The wind gets in through all the window frames, making everything rattle and bump.'

Robert joined her on the settee. 'Maybe we should invest in some double glazing just as soon as we can afford it. That would cut out most of the draughts and rattles.'

Outside, holding her breath, Veronique could hear them talking but not the actual words. Then she heard the champagne glasses clink as they toasted each other, and she relaxed. They'd heard nothing then, thank God for that. She continued on her way along the passage, but not before she had taken out a pencil slim torch from her pocket and switched it on. She needed to see where she was going; the last thing she wanted was another noisy accident.

Upstairs on the next floor Daniel's room was easy to find because the door was half open, and the warm glow from his toadstool lamp lay like a welcoming blanket across the floor outside. From the rooms above she could hear the murmur of more voices, a young man's and a girl's. The nanny must be entertaining a friend. Good, couldn't be better.

Pushing open the door, Veronique crept noiselessly across the room and looked down at the sleeping form of Daniel. Her heart pounded as she looked at the sleeping baby. How beautiful he was. Dark just like herself and Michael. Tears began to trickle down her cheeks. He was hers, *hers* and no one else's. In that moment as she looked at him, she felt that she knew exactly what it was like to have expelled him from her own body. Truly, he was part of her, and always would be. 'Darling,' she whispered, her voice ragged with pent-up emotion, 'it's been such a long, long time. But now I've come at last.'

Upstairs in Melanie's flat Eddy had already opened a bottle of wine. 'A Magdelaine 1982 red Bordeaux,' he said. 'A premier grand cru classé, St Emilion.'

'1982, isn't that a bit old?' asked Melanie, who knew nothing about wines, and had not the slightest idea what a 'grand cru' was.

'It's a classic as wines go,' said Eddy, 'and not easy to get hold of now.'

'Is it expensive then?' asked Melanie in awe.

'Yes, but not to me. It's one of the perks of being a chef. Being able to take the occasional good bottle of wine from the cellar. It's the right temperature, but we really ought to let it breathe a little more, but as we haven't got all night . . .' He poured Melanie a glass. 'Go on, taste it.'

Melanie sipped. 'It's not very sweet,' was her verdict.

'My God, of course it's not sweet.' Eddy regarded her in exasperation. 'Drink some more. Get used to the feel of it on your palate. The more you drink the better you will like it.'

'Are you trying to get me drunk?' Melanie was suspicious.

Eddy laughed. 'I could use cheap cider if that's all I wanted to do.' He shifted closer to her on the sofa, and putting his arm around her, slid one hand inside the top of her dress and caressed a plump breast. 'But it's not a bad idea,' he added.

'Ooh, Eddy, I don't think you ought to do that,' said

330

Melanie, and taking another gulp of wine belied her words by turning invitingly in towards him.

'But you like it though, don't you?' said Eddy, rubbing the tip of her nipple and feeling it grow pleasantly hard. 'Leave your wine, it will taste better later.'

Melanie obediently let Eddy take the glass from her. When he unbuttoned the top of her dress and after pushing aside her bra began to suck at her nipples, she shivered and whispered, 'That's lovely.'

'Not half as lovely as it's going to be,' whispered Eddy, and slid his hands up beneath her skirt.

'I mustn't forget to listen out for Daniel,' said Melanie as Eddy began to climb on top of her.

'Don't you worry about him. He'll be all right.' With one deft movement he slid her pants off and felt for her tender spot.

'Ooh, what are you doing?' Involuntarily Melanie felt her hips begin to rise as a pleasant hot prickling sensation spread throughout her body from where Eddy's finger was gently rotating.

'Getting you ready,' said Eddy, 'for this.' And with that he slid into her. The legs of the old sofa creaked and Melanie gasped. Daniel was forgotten, and so was everything else as she squeaked in ecstasy at her first orgasm.

Veronique heard the rythmic squeaking of the sofa legs on the attic floor above, and gave a smile. The nanny, Melanie, was not likely to come down for a little while yet then. Things could not have worked out better.

'Come on, darling,' she said to Daniel, and lifting the sleeping child out of the cot she wrapped him in the cot blanket. So exhausted was he that he didn't wake at all; his sleeping head lolled against her shoulder as she held him close to her body and started on her way downstairs.

She reached the hall without incident and silently opened the front door and stepped out into the street. Outside it had stopped raining, but the chill wind woke Daniel. He wailed suddenly, a frightened, high pitched sound. Veronique began to hurry down Chesil Street, away from the White House and towards the rented car she'd parked down by the water-mill. Once there she knew Daniel would be quiet, for she had a carrycot she'd bought that morning, extra blankets and some rusks for him to chew on.

In the living room Robert had turned the light off, and he and Louise were sitting in the darkness, drinking champagne and watching the storm-tossed branches of the ancient magnolia tree in the garden making weird and wonderful patterns of shadows in the light cast by the street lamps.

Louise heard the wail. 'I wonder what that is,' she said sleepily.

'Cats fighting,' said Robert, 'although you'd think they'd have more sense, and stay indoors in the warm on a night like this.'

At Eastleigh airport Jeff Stevens looked at his watch and yawned. Nearly half past seven; it was getting late.

There was one other pilot waiting, drinking coffee and feeling bored. 'What time is your passenger due? French, isn't she?' he asked.

'Yes, she's French, and she didn't give me an exact time.' Perhaps his strange passenger wasn't going to turn up after all. Just as well, because now he was on terra firma he was not so keen to fly back to France tonight. True, the wind was not as bad as it had been, but the weather forecast was of sudden unexpected gusts coming in from the Atlantic later that night. He looked at his watch again and decided. 'I'll give Madame Baruch another ten minutes, then I'll park the plane and go home.'

The other pilot got up. 'Here are my two. Well tanked up by the look of them. No wonder British industry is in such a mess, most of the business negotiations seem to be done in an alcoholic haze!' He raised his eyebrows and grinned at Jeff. 'Ah well, Birmingham here we come.'

After they had gone the terminal was silent. Only one office which doubled up as customs and immigration was in operation, and that was in the front of the building. Otherwise the place was deserted apart from the control tower.

Shrugging his shoulders into the leather flying jacket he always wore, Jeff walked out of the single storey airport building into the darkness outside. It was cold, and he shivered. The December wind had the bitter edge of winter to it. Out of the corner of his eye he became aware of a figure emerging from around the corner of the building. It was a woman, struggling with a heavy box, and she was coming towards him.

'Good, I can see you are ready. Let's go.' Startled, the pilot realized that it was his passenger Madame Baruch, and that the box was a carrycot containing a baby.

'You didn't tell me there would be two of you.' He was suspicious.

'Daniel hardly counts as a passenger, he is so small.'

'Did you check in properly? Has he got a passport?'

'Of course,' lied Veronique. 'I have checked in through the proper channels and he has got a passport.'

'Whose baby is he?'

'He's my nephew, Daniel,' said Veronique, 'and his mother's ill. That's why I had to get to England today in order to collect him.'

'Well . . .' Jeff Stevens fidgeted, shifting his weight from one foot to another. Bloody strange this, a woman turning up in the dark with a baby she'd never mentioned before. 'Why can't you stay in England and look after him?' he asked.

'For family reasons I'm afraid that is impossible. I only wish it were not so.' Seeing that he was not convinced, Veronique used all her feminine wiles and smiled confidentially. 'The father has gone off with another woman and is not interested in the welfare of the baby, and the mother, my sister, has had a nervous breakdown and been taken into a secure psychiatric hospital. The doctors are afraid she might harm the child.'

'Sounds a bit of a mess,' said Jeff.

'It is, and the sooner I get him home where he can be cared for properly, the better.' Veronique started towards the tarmac where the planes were lined up. 'Which one is yours? I can't let him stay outside in this chill wind, he'll catch cold.'

'That one over there.' Jeff took the carrycot from her. The baby looked contented enough, and was chewing sleepily on a rusk. Yes, they were both dark haired and dark eyed. He decided Veronique probably was his aunt. He'd fly them to France now; the wind had dropped to practically nothing more than a freezing breeze, no danger from the weather yet. The wind which had been forecast was obviously still well out in the Atlantic. He looked at the sleepy baby, and then back at Veronique. It was a little odd though, just turning up with a baby she had never mentioned before. He carefully stowed the carrycot containing Daniel into the plane. I will make certain she clears properly with immigration in St Brieuc, he thought, even though it's not really necessary.

Once airborne, he could hear Veronique crooning lovingly to the baby behind him. She seemed very fond of him. He settled down and concentrated on the flight.

'No Eddy, you can't stay all night. What would Mrs Baruch, oh, I mean Mrs Lacroix, say if she found you here in the morning?'

'She's a woman of the world, she probably wouldn't say anything.'

'That's not the point. I don't want you to stay. I'd be embarrassed.'

Eddy chuckled. 'You weren't embarrassed a while ago.' He kissed Melanie.

Melanie kissed him back enthusiastically, but was still firm about him leaving. 'You're not going to get round me like that,' she said. 'Now come on, I'm going to let you out before anyone knows you've been here.'

'Can I come again?' whispered Eddy, creeping down the stairs behind her.

'Of course.'

'Next time I'll take precautions. We don't want you getting pregnant.'

Melanie stopped, and turned back towards Eddy in the darkness. 'For all you know I could be pregnant already,' she said.

'Crumbs, I hope not.'

A faint light filtered down the stairs from the open door of her attic flat and Eddy saw a big grin spread across her face. 'Don't worry,' she said, 'I'm on the pill. Have been ever since I met you. Knew it was bound to happen sooner or later.'

'Why you scheming little . . .' Eddy ran out of words.

'Minx is what they always say in novels,' said Melanie with a giggle, and carried on down the stairs.

They crept past Daniel's door, illuminated briefly by the light from the lamp in his room, and Eddy reached out a hand and switched the intercom back on as he passed. Minx, he thought, as he followed Melanie downstairs, that was the right word for her!

On the second floor the light from the living room still slid out into the dark passage, and they could hear the low voices of Louise and Robert talking. On reaching downstairs and the front door, Melanie allowed Eddy one last, long passionate kiss.

'I'll definitely be back for more,' he whispered as she let him out into the bitter December night.

'Only when I invite you,' said Melanie. 'Now, off you go.'

'What are you going to do?' Eddy was reluctant to leave.

'I'm going back upstairs to check on Daniel. I've left him alone for far too long. He usually wakes for a drink at about this time.'

'Goodnight then.' Eddy turned and left, and Melanie closed the front door then climbed back up the stairs towards Daniel's room.

Louise and Robert, arms wrapped around each other, still sat on the settee. The champagne had been drunk long ago but they both felt too lazy to make the effort to get up and go to bed. A sudden sharp rap on the door startled them both.

'Yes, come in,' called Louise.

The door burst open and a wild-eyed Melanie stood in the doorway. 'Have you got Daniel?' she asked.

'Of course not. He's in bed,' said Robert, standing up.

Louise stood up as well. Her heart turned to stone, she could feel it, a cold dead thing struggling to beat. She couldn't breathe, and suddenly the light and airy room was filled with darkness and the sound of the sea was pounding in her ears. She could hear her own voice, and yet it wasn't her voice. It was someone else's, high pitched and hysterical. 'Tell me he's in bed,' it was saying, 'tell me he's in bed.'

Melanie began to sob and scream at the same time. 'He's gone, he's gone. The cot is empty. I've looked all over the house. Daniel isn't here.'

It was then that the darkness overwhelmed her and Louise felt herself falling. She knew where she was. She was on the headland which jutted out into the sea at the side of the great flat bay. And she was falling down, down, down towards the jagged rocks where the dark sea foamed and boiled. She could see the blackness rushing up to meet her. With a gasp she choked, as the dark waters closed over her head.

CHAPTER 42

Halfway across the channel the wind increased, gusting spasmodically. It was then that plane's radio began to crackle, and reception became intermittent. 'Dear, God! Please don't let the damned thing fail now,' Jeff prayed out loud.

'What did you say?'

Startled, Jeff turned his head away from the lighted instrument panel, and stared at Veronique, crouched in the back by the side of the carrycot. 'What?'

'I said what did you say?'

Suddenly the anxious pilot realized he had spoken his thoughts out loud. 'I was radioing ahead to St Brieuc airport, to give them our ETA,' he said hastily, praying that he would be able to do just that within the next few minutes.

He could see his passenger's face in the dim light from the dials on the instrument panel. She was smiling, a radiant, triumphant smile. 'Then we are nearly there.'

'Yes.' Jeff turned back and looked out of the windscreen into a blackness which stretched as far as the eye could see. 'Not long now.'

He flicked the transmitting key down and spoke into the mouthpiece, then turned the switch back up and waited for a reply. Nothing came. A cold sweat broke out across his forehead. Now was not the time to lose contact. Not now when he was breaking all the rules. No flight plan had been submitted. St Brieuc were not expecting them. He'd counted on getting in touch by radio halfway across the channel. If anything happened . . . no, he wouldn't think of that. The radio crackled again and his hopes rose, but then it went completely dead. Not even a faint hiss. Shit! Why hadn't he had it overhauled last month when it was due? The answer was, of course, because he couldn't afford it. If only he had known in advance that this rich French woman would pay him a small fortune to take her back and forth across the channel he would have had it done and told the bank manager to go to hell.

'What time should we land?'

'In about fifteen minutes.' Jeff forced himself to relax. What was he getting in a stew about? The radio might be out of order but everything else was perfect. He always made certain of that. He could land without assistance from the control tower, his instrumentation was in perfect working order. St Brieuc was a small regional airport, no one else was likely to be arriving tonight. Once he could see the landing lights he'd be all right.

And there they were. Far away in the distance, and straight ahead of them he could see the tiny spots of the orange landing lights, strung out like a welcoming string of pearls.

Veronique, looking over his shoulder, saw them too. 'Is that St Brieuc?' she asked.

Jeff relaxed even more. 'Yes,' he said.

Then it happened. A sudden gust of wind hit the plane, slapping it like a huge hand from heaven, and tipping it on its side. Veronique screamed, and so did Daniel as he was thrown out of his carrycot and hit the roof of the tiny cockpit. The lights of St Brieuc disappeared. But Jeff Stevens had not flown in hazardous conditions before for nothing: with grim determination he righted the plane and gritted his teeth. Jesus! They'd dropped nearly a thousand feet! He prayed they wouldn't hit another air pocket like that again, and thanked his lucky stars that he'd been flying high enough to withstand it. Suppose his altitude had already been low in preparation for landing. No, he wouldn't think about that either. With a sigh of relief he saw the orange lights strung out once more before them. Larger this time. Less than ten minutes, and they'd be down.

'What was that? What hit us?' Veronique had Daniel in her arms, and was wiping blood from his head.

'Wind, Madame Baruch, that was what hit us.'

'Is the weather getting worse then?'

'Seems to be.' He dare not tell her that he didn't know. Had that been a freak gust? Or were there more to come? If only the sodding radio was working.

His anxiety communicated itself to Veronique. Suddenly she felt afraid, and hugged Daniel into her body tightly. 'Darling,' she whispered, 'I couldn't bear it if anything happened to you. Not now. Not now when at last you are mine.'

In the control tower at St Brieuc everything was quiet. Only one man would soon be left on duty, for to all intents and purposes the airport was closed. No more flights were expected that night because of the appalling weather conditions rolling in from the Atlantic.

'You might as well go on home, Jean-Pierre,' the older man said. 'I know it's ten minutes before you should go, but nothing will happen now.'

'Something is happening.' Jean-Pierre stared out of the control tower windows.

'What do you mean, something is happening?' Gaston, the elder of the two, looked up from his newspaper.

'A plane is coming in. It's going to land.'

Gaston was on the radio immediately. 'St Brieuc tower here.' There was no reply. The tiny plane continued to fly in towards the landing lights.

'A smuggler?' suggested Jean-Pierre.

'Smugglers land in fields, not airports. No, that is a mad man,' said Gaston, 'flying a small plane like that when we're about to be hit by hurricane-force winds any minute.'

In spite of repeatedly trying, there was no reply on the radio, and there was nothing the two men in the control tower could do but watch. They alerted the emergency services, which at this time of night consisted of one small and rather ancient fire appliance. Then they waited.

'Decreasing speed and descending for landing,' said Jeff, trying to sound confident. He was fighting with the plane now. God knows what the wind speed is, he thought, desperately trying to compensate the drift of the aircraft.

The ground came rushing up to meet them. Veronique, sitting behind the pilot and holding on to Daniel, could see the blaze of orange lights, one moment below them, the next moment level with the cockpit.

'We've landed,' she said to Daniel, 'you're safely home now.'

'Not quite,' said Jeff, as a gust of wind picked the plane up and hurled it forward. 'Bloody wheels won't stay down,' he said as the plane bounced along the runway.

The next moment the lights and ground were where the night sky should have been. This is it, thought Jeff. We are all going to meet our maker, all three of us. Then, miraculously the plane turned back the right way up. He could see that they were sliding out of control towards the virtually deserted car park. Thank God it's not the middle of the day, and the car park is not full of people and cars. That was his last conscious thought as the nose of the plane hit a parked lorry, and crumpled like tissue paper.

CHAPTER 43

Robert put down the phone. 'Still no connection,' he said. 'I've spoken to the international operator, apparently there are some problems in northern France with the phones; they've had high winds and flooding. That must be the reason I can't get Chateau les Greves.'

'Do you think she will harm him?' Once Louise recovered consciousness, had drunk some strong black coffee and collected her scattered wits, she knew without a shadow of doubt who had taken Daniel. It was Veronique. She tugged anxiously at Robert's arm, and asked again, 'Do you think she will harm him?'

Robert shook his head. 'No, she wants him for herself. I'm sure she won't hurt him.'

'You're sure?' Beattie was as doubtful as Louise. 'If Veronique is emotionally unstable, then surely that's dangerous?'

'Unstable yes,' said Robert wearily; he was racking his brains, trying to think where Veronique might have gone on a cold December night in Winchester. 'But dangerous, definitely not.'

Gordon was trying to comfort a still sobbing Melanie in the corner of the room. 'And you didn't hear anything?' he asked. 'Nothing at all?'

Melanie shook her head. She wished she could stop crying, but she couldn't, she felt so guilty. If only she

341

hadn't let Eddy upstairs. If she'd been alone she might have heard something.

By this time, as well as Beattie and Gordon, the local GP had also arrived. He'd been called in by a panic-stricken Melanie when Louise first collapsed. The police were represented by an elderly sergeant, Sergeant Hodges, whose pronounced Hampshire accent made him appear rather slow and deliberate, and a young policewoman, WPC Millett, who was the complete opposite. She was small, blonde and very intense.

'Hold on, hold on. We don't know yet as to whether this, Veronique Baruch,' he wrote the name out very slowly, asking twice how to spell Veronique, so that Louise wanted to shake him, 'has taken the baby. You can't accuse someone without proof. And you say she weren't at the wedding.'

'No, she lives in France,' said Louise.

'Lives in France.' The sergeant wrote that down. 'Long way to come,' he said thoughtfully, 'to steal a baby. Women who steal babies usually take the nearest one, on impulse, like. They don't usually travel to another country, break into a house and then kidnap a baby in the middle of the night.'

'It wasn't the middle of the night,' Louise shouted, 'it was during the evening. And Veronique didn't want *any* baby, she wanted mine. Only mine would do. There was nothing impulsive about it. She's been planning it for months.' She collapsed sobbing into Robert's arms. 'Oh, I'm sorry I shouted,' she said to the policeman a few moments later, 'but if only you knew how worried I am.'

'I think I do, ma'am,' said the sergeant quietly. 'Tell me, why are you so certain that it was this, this, Veronique Baruch,' he stumbled over the name again, 'who took him?'

'Because it is much more complicated than you think,' said Robert. 'Veronique Baruch is my sister, and is married, for the second time, to Michael Baruch. Michael

342

Baruch is the father of the baby. His wife at that time, in between my sister's marriages to him, and the mother of Daniel is Louise, who is now my wife.'

'I see,' said Sergeant Hodges, who didn't, and had got completely lost with all the different relationships, so much so that he had given up trying to write it down.

'I've got all that, Sarg,' said the policewoman, hastily scribbling.

'Well done, don't know what I do without you,' he said with relief. Sergeant Hodges looked at Robert through narrowed eyes. 'I know I'm a lot older than you, sir, and because of that perhaps I'm a might old-fashioned. But I can't for the life of me see what all this husband and wife swopping has got to do with a baby being stolen. Or why you're so certain that it is your sister who has done it.'

'It's because Veronique can't have children of her own,' began Robert, and went on to explain the plot Michael and Veronique had hatched between them in order to get a child.

WPC Millet's eyes grew larger and larger as Robert told the story. She looked at Louise when he'd finished. 'How awful,' she whispered, 'an unwitting surrogate mother!'

Beattie and Gordon had also been listening open-mouthed. 'Is all this really true?' Beattie asked Louise.

'I'm afraid so,' said Louise. 'Sordid, isn't it.'

'Not sordid, terribly sad,' replied Beattie. 'Why haven't you told us before?'

'We only found out ourselves fairly recently,' Robert explained. 'And since then Veronique has been receiving psychiatric treatment, and Michael assured me she had got over it. He said that she was finally facing reality.'

'Perhaps,' said Beattie quietly. 'But what kind of reality? Hers or yours?'

'Oh God. Something terrible is going to happen to Daniel, I just know it,' said Louise, and burst into tears again.

'I think perhaps a mild sedative would be a good idea,' said Dr Turnbull, who until now had remained silent.

'It's not a good idea, it's a ridiculous idea,' said Louise angrily. 'Don't you dare sedate me. I want to stay awake and find my son.'

'I know. But, darling, you've got to try and keep calm,' said Robert, 'no matter how difficult that might be.'

'That's why I thought a mild sedative . . .'

'Oh do shut up, Ian,' snapped Beattie who had known the doctor for years; they had both gone to the same village school as five-year-olds. 'Would you want a sedative if your son had been kidnapped?'

'Well . . .'

'Of course you wouldn't . . .' Beattie answered for him. 'You'd be out searching for the child. Which is what we ought to be doing.'

'No point in rushing out into the night at this moment,' said Sergeant Hodges calmly, putting away his notebook. 'But what we will do is alert all the ports and airports to look out for Veronique Baruch accompanied by a baby boy. Have you got a recent photograph of your sister, sir?' he asked Robert, 'and one of young baby Daniel?'

'Yes, I'll go and get them immediately.'

'Sergeant.' Melanie decided she had better tell the whole truth; so far she'd only told the police about going into Daniel's room and finding that he was missing.

'Yes, my girl.' Sergeant Hodges thought that Melanie had something else to say. 'What is it?'

'I didn't lie when I said I was upstairs in my flat all the time and that I didn't hear anything. But,' Melanie sniffed, gulped and then went on, 'I wasn't on my own. I was with my boyfriend, Eddy Parker. After the wedding party was over I let him come up to my flat, and we opened a bottle of wine and had a drink. I didn't go down and look at Daniel until he'd gone, at about ten thirty. It was then that I found Daniel had been taken.' Tears started to stream afresh down her face. 'Oh, I'm so sorry. If I'd been on my own, I might have heard something.' She looked at Louise. 'How can you ever forgive me?'

344

Louise forced herself to be calm. 'Melanie,' she said, 'we gave you the flat so that you could have friends in. Robert and I were here too, and the intercom was on all the time. None of us heard anything. It's not your fault.'

'And the intercom was still switched on when you eventually did go in to look for Daniel?' WPC Millett asked.

'Oh yes, that was the first thing I looked at when I saw he wasn't there. It was on. Normally Daniel wakes for a drink of water at about nine o'clock, but tonight he didn't. He was so tired when I put him to bed that he immediately fell into a deep sleep. He had stayed up late for the wedding party, you see.'

'That explains it then.' WPC Millett's sister had a baby, and she knew about such things. 'Daniel probably never even woke up when he was taken. It wouldn't have made any difference whether the intercom was on or off, he wouldn't have made a sound anyway.'

Gordon put his arm around Melanie's shaking shoulders. 'So you see, you have nothing to blame yourself for.'

Later when Melanie recounted the conversation to Eddy he shivered but said nothing, although he resolved never again to tamper with other people's belongings. Alarms or anything else. Like Melanie, he too felt guilty. If they hadn't been so intent on their own pleasure they might have heard something.

Robert came back with the two photographs. 'The most recent I could find,' he said, handing them over to Sergeant Hodges.

'Right, sir. We'll get these faxed to all the south coast ports and airfields straight away. Although in my opinion if your sister has taken the baby, she's probably gone into a hotel somewhere near here, and is tucked up snugly with the baby. We'll get out a bulletin on the early morning radio and television news, with a description of them both.'

345

When the police had gone Robert tried once more to telephone Chateau les Greves but the line was still out of order.

'I don't care what the police say or do, I'm going over there first thing tomorrow morning,' said Louise.

'I can't believe that she is there.' Robert shook his head.

'I agree with Robert,' said Beattie. 'There hasn't been enough time for her to take Daniel this evening and get to France tonight.'

Louise paced the room restlessly, then suddenly spun round. 'I know when she got in,' she said. 'It was when Richard Meacher left. Do you remember Mr Poo going mad, barking like crazy and rushing into that downstairs cupboard. He was barking because Veronique had got in; she was hiding down there.'

'But I looked everywhere,' said Robert. 'No one was . . .' his voice tailed off. 'I didn't look on that wide top shelf, though,' he said slowly. 'She could have been up there.'

'And that's why Mr Poo was so agitated,' said Beattie. 'Not that it does any good knowing that now.'

'If she came in then – ' Louise continued her pacing as she thought things through – 'then she probably took him almost as soon as Melanie went up to her own flat, while Robert and I were sitting in here drinking. That was quite early on in the evening. She would have had plenty of time to get one of the ferries from Portsmouth or Southampton.'

'Or even a private flight, if she'd already booked it, from Eastleigh airport,' said Robert. 'I'll check.' He picked up the phone and made enquiries, then put the phone down. He looked worried and puzzled. 'A light plane did take off for France tonight, according to the control tower. It left Eastleigh at twenty hundred hours. But passport control say no one came through to board it, as far as they know it was just the pilot flying solo back to France. Apparently his passenger never arrived.'

'She's in France,' Louise was positive. 'I know it. And tomorrow I'm going there.'

'We'll both go,' said Robert, 'but now I think you ought to get a couple of hours' sleep.'

'I'll never sleep,' said Louise. But she did. Although it was a dark and fearful sleep, punctuated with the sound of crashing waves, and the high pitched sound of the cold winter wind humming over the stunted trees and streaming marram grass of the dark headland jutting out into the sea on the northern coast of France.

CHAPTER 44

Gaston and Jean-Pierre reached the crumpled wreckage of the plane before the fire engine, which had much farther to come. As they scrambled towards the nose section both heard the noise at the same time. The sound of a car starting. It was about eighty metres from where they were, but in the darkness it was impossible to see what type of car it was, or who was in it.

'Someone in a bloody great hurry,' said Gaston. The car swung round in a huge semi-circle, the tyres screaming in anguish at the angle, then it made for the exit, and zig-zagged between the half-pole barriers. 'I've always told the authorities those damned barriers are no good. Anyone can get in and out if they want to. No security at all,' he grumbled.

'Perhaps I was right about smugglers,' said Jean-Pierre. 'Those were the accomplices waiting to pick up the goods, and once they saw the accident they decided to scarper.'

'Maybe. But smuggler or not, we've got to get the pilot out if he's still alive.'

The fire crew arrived with their resuscitation equipment, but it was a waste of time. The pilot was dead. His brain punctured by a thin strip of metal beading ripped from the mangled cockpit. Apart from that he was hardly bruised.

'What bloody bad luck,' said one of the firemen. 'That

piece of metal could have gone anywhere, but it had to go straight through his head.'

'Tonight had his number marked on it.' Gaston was fatalistic. 'Every hour of every day and night has someone's number marked on it. It's just a question of waiting for your turn to come up.'

'Is he always as cheerful as this?' the fireman asked Jean-Pierre.

But Jean-Pierre didn't answer; he couldn't bear to look at the dead man. He turned away towards the rear end of the aircraft, and it was then that he saw the carrycot. 'There's a baby's cot here,' he said, reaching over and pulling the cot towards him. 'It's empty. Oh, Jesus! You don't think that?'

'He had a baby as a passenger?' The fireman said. 'Bloody hell, I hope not. If he did, where is it?' They all searched frantically, in the wreckage, around the wreckage, finally working their way out to the far perimeter of the car park, but there was no a sign of a baby. Dead or alive.

'It must have been empty,' said Gaston at last. 'Maybe he was bringing it in for someone, they're probably cheaper in England than in France. You can see it's brand new.'

The ambulance arrived to take the body of the pilot away, and Gaston and Jean-Pierre as well as the two firemen spent the rest of the night with the *gendarmes*, filling in forms in triplicate.

'Bloody bureaucracy,' grumbled Jean-Pierre. 'I should have been at home sound asleep by now.'

'Thank God for small mercies,' said Gaston. 'It could be you being carted off to the mortuary with a lump of steel through your head.' He looked at the paperwork spread out before him. 'I wonder if that Englishman had any family. If so, they've got bad news waiting for them in the morning.'

'Hey!' Jean-Pierre showed one of the *gendarmes* the plane's flight plans and booking forms. 'This plane was

349

chartered by a French woman. Madame Baruch from Chateau les Greves, Michel en Greve, Cote D'Amor. The pilot took her over to England this morning and was supposed to bring her back tonight.' He checked one set of papers against some others. 'He radioed in OK when he flew out, waited for clearance in the regular way. According to this it was all above board, he flew in here from Eastleigh airport in southern England, which was where he dropped her off this morning. So why didn't he radio us on the way back? And why wasn't he carrying her as a passenger?'

'Maybe she stayed on in England, and as for the radio, perhaps it wasn't working,' suggested the *gendarme*. 'Anyway it will be checked along with everything else by the accident investigators. We'll know more then.'

'Not that a radio would have made any difference tonight,' said Gaston. 'He made a perfect landing; it was that final gust of wind that did for him.'

'Well, that's about it.' The *gendarme* gathered together the mound of papers. 'We'll check on Madame Baruch's movements first thing in the morning. I'm going back to the office to put my feet up and try and get some shut-eye. My colleague can answer the phone.'

'Thanks,' said the other *gendarme*, longing for the day when he too could pull rank and put his feet up on a long night's duty.

Left alone in the control tower the two flight controllers looked at each other. 'Gaston,' said Jean-Pierre, 'I've been thinking.'

'So have I. We forgot to tell the *gendarmes* about that bloody car that drove off just after the crash.'

'Yes. But there's more to it than that.' Jean-Pierre was thoughtful. 'Supposing, just supposing that it was Madame Baruch driving that car. Why would she be in such a hurry to get away from the scene of the accident?'

'Why indeed,' said Gaston.

* * *

350

Veronique drove through the night, crouched over the wheel of the car, staring ahead at the narrow beams of the headlights illuminating the darkness ahead. She could have taken the dual carriageway from the airport, but chose instead to take the narrow country lanes which wound their way through hamlets and villages, past sleeping granite cottages all in darkness like the night.

Blood trickled down the side of her mouth where she'd bit her lip in the crash, and a huge lump was beginning to rise on her forehead. Her mind was blank, but she drove towards Michel en Greve with the blind instinct of a homing pigeon.

In the back of the car, wedged in as safely as she could manage, was Daniel. He was crying now, loudly, and his face was covered in blood from a cut on his scalp. 'Please God, let him be all right,' Veronique prayed. 'Don't let him die.' She remembered reading somewhere that if babies cried loudly then it was a sign that they were well and strong. It was when they stopped crying that it was necessary to worry. The thought was comforting; he would be all right. God wouldn't have let her get him only to take him away again. No one, not even God, could be that cruel. Besides, she thought, once we are on the headland, we will be safe. The rocks will rise up and fold themselves around us, and hold us both in their strong safe arms. Once we are there we shall have no need of anything or anyone. We shall be together, my son and I. And that is all we need, each other.

An unnamed worry prompted Michael to leave Paris that night. Still unable to get through on the phone he felt an urgent need to make sure for himself that Veronique was safe. He drove through the night towards Brittany and Chateau les Greves, and as his car was buffeted by the ever-increasing wind, so he felt an immense feeling of worry grow inside him, and at the same time he felt a strange sense of purpose. It's almost as if I've reached the end of something, he thought. I'm being pulled along towards something I have to do. Yet I don't know what it is.

Driving along the dual carriageway past St Brieuc airport he saw the headlights of a plane eerily shining down through the pitch blackness of the night. He saw the lights wavering as the wind hit the plane, and slowed down a little to watch, pitying the occupants of the storm-tossed airplane. He saw it land, and found he'd been holding his breath, for now it came out in a long hissing sigh, glad that whoever they were had landed safely. Then to his horror he saw the plane bounce up from the tarmac like a rubber ball and saw it hurtle forward, overshooting the end of the runway, skidding crazily, and eventually careering to an abrupt halt as it wrapped itself into the side of a huge lorry.

Standing on his brakes, he was prepared to try and turn around and go into the airport and help. But then he saw figures, silhouetted against the runway lights, running from the control tower, and heard the wail of the airport fire engine and saw the flashing blue light as the fire and resuscitation appliance sped towards the crash. No point in trying to help, Michael thought, I'd be a liability. They are experts, I am not, I'd be of no use at all. So he drove on towards Chateau les Greves.

On hearing the sound of the car wheels crunching in the gravel of the drive, the door to the Louedecs' kitchen opened, and Andrea Louedec came rushing out. 'Oh,' she said, staring at Michael. 'I wasn't expecting you, I was hoping that it would be Madame.'

'What do you mean?' The fear, some of which had dissipated during the long drive from Paris, returned anew. 'You hoped it would be Madame? Isn't she here?'

'She left not long after you had gone to Paris. She took a small bag, not much, and said she might be back tonight. If not, then she would definitely be back in the morning.'

'I see,' said Michael, wishing he did. Where could she have gone? Surely she couldn't have . . .? No, that was not possible. She had been so normal lately. So happy. They'd both been happy together, just the two of them. Thoughts chased through his mind, dark moths of the night, battering against his brain. 'How did she seem in herself?' he asked at last.

'She seemed perfectly all right. But . . .' Andrea Louedec's voice tapered off.

'But what?'

'It's not right for me to say, sir.'

'For goodness' sake, say it, woman,' said Michael. 'I need to know everything.'

'It's just that, well, I have this feeling that she was too happy. Abnormally happy you might say. Paul says that I am imagining things, but I can't help it. I *feel* that something is wrong. I tried to telephone Monsieur Robert in England, but the phone is out of order.'

'I know it's out of order, that's why I came back,' said Michael. Then he looked sharply at his housekeeper. 'But why Robert? Why didn't you try and telephone me?'

'Because I think she might have been going to England. I don't know why. I'm only guessing about England.'

'Best not to guess at anything,' growled Paul Louedec, coming to the kitchen doorway. 'Best to wait until we know for certain.'

An ominous prescience that an unknown tragedy was unfolding, threatened to swamp Michael, making coherent thought impossible. With an effort he shook himself free of it.

'You're right,' he said. 'It is best to wait until we know something for certain. There's nothing we can do now, so the best thing is go to bed. As soon as it's light I'll get the telephone fixed and we'll start trying to find Veronique.'

'Yes, sir.' Reluctantly Andrea rejoined her husband who'd gone back to the open fire in their kitchen. 'He thinks that something awful has happened,' she said.

'He didn't say so,' said Paul.

'He didn't have to say anything. Couldn't you see it? It was written all over his face.'

353

Alone in their bedroom, his and Veronique's, Michael was unable to sleep. Instead he leaned on the wide window-sill and stared out at the sea. Even in the darkness of the moonless night, he could see that the tide was in and that the sea was a mass of foam-flecked waves. Like wild, white horses galloping in across the enormous width of the bay, the sea thundered in, pounding everything in its path to pieces. Then his eyes were drawn reluctantly to the dark shape of the headland jutting out to where, tonight, the sea boiled even more violently around its base. He felt it pulling him, and sat watching the vast dark hump until it was translated into rocks, and cliffs, and trees and grass by the grey light of the dawn.

The tide began to change, and the white horses slipped silently out of the bay to meet their companions in the cold Atlantic Ocean, leaving behind a great, grey, shining expanse of flat wet sand. A shaft of light stretched a faint, silvery thread across the bay from the east. Michael thought of himself and Veronique, and suddenly it was as if he could see their life together represented by that silvery grey thread. But it was a fragile thread and he knew that if it ruptured they would not survive. It was then that he knew that death was stalking someone on the headland, and that soon he would know who, and why, and what the inevitable outcome would be. Shivering he turned away from the cold grey scene, instinctively rubbing his chest where he felt a pain. Indigestion, he decided, remembering he had eaten nothing since lunchtime the previous day.

CHAPTER 45

Robert held Louise's hand tightly. 'Have courage,' he whispered. 'I know Veronique will take care of Daniel.'

'I know that,' said Louise in a low voice. 'I know Veronique would never intend to harm Daniel, but I can't help thinking that if she's been hurt herself, then perhaps she will be unable to care for him.'

'She can't be hurt that much, not if what we've been told is true.'

Thanks to Sergeant Hodges and the *gendarmerie* at St Brieuc they now knew that Veronique had been on Jeff Steven's plane which had crashed on landing at St Brieuc. A storekeeper at the Eastleigh airport, moving some freight in readiness for an early morning flight, had seen Veronique with the carrycot getting into Jeff Stevens's plane. What he hadn't realized at the time was that she had evaded passport control, which was why officials at the airport thought the plane had taken off with just the pilot on board.

What had really happened at St Brieuc, however, was less clear. No one could say with absolute certainty that it had been Veronique with Daniel who had driven off at speed a few minutes after the crash, because no one had seen anything clearly. Not the car nor the driver. But everything pointed to the fact that it almost certainly was Veronique. The empty carrycot in the plane, her distinctive yellow Citroën which had been seen in the car park that morning, but which was now no longer there.

Robert wished yet again that they had been able to get in touch with the chateau, but the phone was still out of order. He felt it ominous that the phone at Chateau les Greves was, as far as the telephone engineers knew, the only phone in the district which was still not working. He was sure that it had a significance, but had kept his anxieties to himself. There was no point in worrying Louise even more.

Louise shivered. They arrived in France just as dawn was breaking, flying into St Brieuc on the first flight Robert had been able to arrange. On landing, Louise had averted her eyes from the crashed plane still embedded in the side of the lorry, unable to bear the thought of Daniel's tiny body being involved in such a violent impact.

Now they were driving through the cold grey of a December morning towards Michel en Greve. Towards the chateau, towards Michael, and hopefully towards Veronique and Daniel. But also, Louise shivered again at the thought, they were driving towards the place where the headland jutted out into the sea, the place of her nightmares. The place that both fascinated and repelled her, but which, with each passing day, she knew held the secret of her destiny. Such a dark forbidding place filling her with an insubstantial fear which she had never been able to confess to anyone, not even to Robert, because there was no name she could put to it.

'I hope if that was Veronique who drove out of that car park last night, that she didn't drive as fast as that all the way,' Louise said, trying to keep her mind on the reality, and not let the fear and fantasy overwhelm her.

'She must have been very frightened at the time; that's why she drove fast.' Robert's calm voice was comforting. 'But once she got away from the crashed plane she is bound to have composed herself. Don't forget that.whatever happens, Daniel will be her priority. She'll be thinking of his welfare all the time. I *know* my sister. Believe me.'

'Yesterday,' said Louise slowly, 'was our wedding day, and then I foolishly thought I could see golden, sunlit years stretching ahead. Now it is etched on my mind like some far-off piece of history. It's difficult to believe it even happened.'

Robert reached out and grasped her hand. It was icy cold. 'It *was* real, and so were your dreams,' he said softly. 'We'll get the sunshine back. It's just that we're on the dark side of the sun at the moment.'

The chill grey of the morning seemed to penetrate the car. 'Dark side of the sun,' Louise said shakily, 'I wonder how far we shall have to travel to get back to the bright side.'

'Not far,' said Robert, forcing his voice to have a warmth that in reality didn't exist within him. 'All we have to do is follow the light.' He gave her hand another squeeze before removing his own hand to change gear. 'Now put some gloves on, for goodness' sake; it's like having a block of ice sitting beside me.'

Louise smiled and fishing in her coat pocket found her gloves. Robert is a good man, she thought, I am lucky to have found him. As if on cue, a pale thread of light, the first rays of the sun rising over the eastern rim of their little part of the world, speared its way through the gloomy morning mist. 'Look,' she said, 'there is the light. Maybe everything is going to be all right.' She felt more cheerful, more positive, more determined. Together, they would *make* it all right. Tonight Daniel would be back in England in his own bed in the White House. That pale thread gave her hope.

It was the same thread of light Michael was looking at from his window at Chateau les Greves. The one which filled him with a prophetic feeling of doom.

'Do you want to stop and try telephoning the chateau again?' Robert asked.

357

Louise thought a moment, then said, 'No. Perhaps it is better that we don't. If the *gendarmes* haven't yet told him about Veronique's flight to England, then Michael will know nothing about that or any of the subsequent events. It will be bad enough for him when he does know, without us trying to explain it over the telephone.'

'I'd forgotten that he might not know yet, and of course,' Robert added, 'I realize now why Veronique came over to England yesterday. It wasn't just because of our wedding and knowing that we'd all be distracted by the celebrations, it was because Michael was in Paris. She chose the one and only day that he was going to be away. So until he returned to the chateau, presumably last night, he wouldn't have known of her disappearance.'

'Do you think he would have stopped her if he had been there?' asked Louise doubtfully. 'After all, the initial plan was made by them both.'

'I'm sure of it. Michael's months of madness came to an abrupt end when we confronted them both in the nursery.'

'Yes.' Louise remembered Michael's eyes when they had talked later that afternoon. 'Yes, I think you are right.'

'In my opinion, Michael knew then that the rest of his life would be spent caring for Veronique,' continued Robert. 'And he accepted it because he loves her. To him, I think she's half child, and half woman. It's a strange relationship, and one which I find difficult to understand.' Robert looked towards Louise. 'I prefer my relationship with you, a partnership. One man and one woman.'

'So do I,' said Louise.

'And I'll tell you another thing, if Veronique turns up on the doorstep this morning with Daniel, Michael is going to be very surprised.'

For the first time since Daniel had been kidnapped, Louise managed a wan laugh. 'Robert, you've just made the understatement of the year,' she said.

* * *

358

'There's your fault, sir.' The telephone engineer pointed to a wire amongst the wisteria branches at the back of the chateau. 'Nothing wrong with the telephone service of France. Someone has purposely cut the wire.'

'I don't understand it,' said Michael, but he was beginning to think that he did. Veronique had not wanted him to know that she had gone.

'Probably someone planning a burglary,' said the engineer busily repairing the wire. 'I hope you've got a separate alarm system for this place.'

'Yes,' said Michael vaguely. He was thinking of Veronique. Where had she gone? And why hadn't she come back last night? Had she really gone to England as Andrea Louedec suspected? As soon as the phone was repaired, there were phone calls to make.

Robert and Louise passed the distinctive yellow telephone van in the drive of the chateau. It was leaving as they entered.

'The phone must be repaired,' observed Robert.

Louise sat up and looked about her. A weak, watery sunlight cast long shadows over the formal gardens of the chateau, and a strong wind blew the clipped topiary bushes so that the exotic yew tree birds appeared to be almost about to fly off. She felt nervous, afraid, and yet at the same time excited and sure. Daniel would be here, Veronique would have put him in the blue nursery she had so lovingly prepared. Soon the ordeal would be over for all of them; except for poor, demented Veronique. With a sudden rush of sadness Louise realized that perhaps for Veronique it would never be over. There would always be that hopeless longing for a child of her own. Pathetic Veronique, she was destined to remain for ever on the dark side of the sun, and nothing and no one could ever really help her.

The wheels of the car had barely stopped turning before Michael had appeared at the door and was running across the gravel to meet them. As soon as he saw it was just the two of them he stopped dead in his tracks. And as he skidded to a halt, all the certainty, the anticipation of a joyful reunion with Daniel vanished. Louise knew from Michael's expression that Veronique and Daniel were not at the chateau, and that he did not know their whereabouts.

'I . . . I thought . . .' He stopped.

'You thought we might have Veronique with us,' said Robert quietly. 'Michael, my friend, I only wish to God that we did.'

'She's gone,' said Michael helplessly, 'and I've no idea where. I was just about to phone you, the line has only just been repaired. I've been frantic with worry, I've seen no one, heard nothing.'

'Oh God, then the *gendarmes* haven't told you yet,' said Louise.

'Told me! Told me what?' The pain of indigestion began again, and Michael rubbed irritably at his chest.

'Are you all right?' Robert's trained medical eyes noticed the rubbing, and Michael's grimace of pain.

'Bloody indigestion, something I could do without right now. Too much stress, and one too many of Andrea's buttered croissants eaten too quickly.' Michael brushed the question aside. 'But tell me about Veronique. Where is she?'

'Let's go inside. It's far too cold to talk out here.' Louise shivered violently. She was bitterly disappointed. She'd been so sure that they would find Veronique and Daniel here.

In the chateau Michael led the way to the Louedecs' kitchen. 'I can't bear the rest of the rooms,' he said. 'The whole place seems so cold and empty.' He shuddered. 'More coffee please, Andrea,' he said as they entered the kitchen.

'Perhaps not the best thing for you,' said Robert, thinking that Michael looked most unwell.

'Maybe not, but I was in Paris all day yesterday, and didn't sleep at all last night. I need Andrea's strong black coffee to keep me going.'

'And he's not eaten properly either.' Madame Louedec shushed her husband out of the kitchen, and put out the enormous coffee bowls always used for breakfast, and took a tray of croissants from the oven and piled them on the table. 'Monsieur Michael should have had an omelette or some ham last night, but he had nothing, and this morning he's only eaten croissants.'

'No wonder you look so awful,' said Robert and insisted Michael have milky coffee.

Andrea Louedec was about to leave the kitchen once all the breakfast things were on the table, but Michael was adamant that she stay. 'You were here when Veronique left,' he said. 'What is more, you probably know her state of mind as well as the rest of us. So stay and tell us all you know.'

Louise thought she'd never be able to eat a thing, but found she was hungry, as was Robert. As they crunched their way through the warm croissants and drank steaming cups of coffee, the story was told. All of it, from the time Veronique had left the chateau and Andrea Louedec had first discovered the telephone was out of order, until the last time Veronique was seen climbing into the plane at Eastleigh airport. From then on it was a question of guessing.

'Assuming that it was Veronique who drove out of the airport car park after the plane crash,' said Michael slowly, 'and I'm certain now that it must have been, why isn't she here?'

'Yes, that is a puzzle,' agreed Robert.

'Supposing she has crashed the car,' said Louise, voicing her worst fears.

'We'll check.' Robert went into the salon and made a call. When he returned he shook his head. 'I've spoken to the accident control centre for this area,' he said. 'There have been no serious accidents at all this morning, and even the minor ones have not involved a yellow Citroën or a woman and child.'

'I was so certain that she'd bring Daniel here,' said Louise. 'Bring him to her home, to the nursery she had prepared.'

'Not if she wasn't thinking straight,' said Madame Louedec, speaking for the first time since she had told them her part of the story.

'What do you mean?' Robert looked at her. Andrea Louedec was voicing an anxiety he'd been feeling for some time at the back of his own mind. 'Not thinking straight?'

'Well,' Andrea hesitated then decided it was necessary to speak out. 'In the past, I've often noticed that it only took a small thing, a minor disagreement with me perhaps, or a phone call from Monsieur Michael when they were divorced, to upset her. And when I say upset, I don't mean that she was necessarily unhappy, I mean she was not normal. Wild, I would call it. Yes, that's it, she was wild. And when she became like that she always ran away from the chateau and went to the headland.'

'To the headland?' At last Louise thought she began to understand, as her nightmares and fantasy began to merge into a frightening reality. Suddenly she knew, without any shadow of doubt, that there, on that desolate wasteland of the dark headland, her own fate and that of Daniel's would finally be resolved.

'The headland?' repeated Michael. Louise looked at him and saw her own nightmare mirrored in his expression. But there was something else; his nightmare was worse. For a second as his dark eyes looked into hers, Louise saw that he was battling with a sense of futile helplessness, and that he was thinking of death. And she knew that he was terribly afraid, more afraid even than she was herself.

'Michael,' she said softly, feeling an impulsive need to

362

comfort him. To try and erase his sense of futility, and the appalling desolation she instinctively knew was eating into his soul.

'We will find them, both of them,' Robert said firmly. 'Stop worrying, that's an order to both of you.'

Michael smiled suddenly. 'You're right,' he said. 'Of course we will.' Then he turned to Louise and said, 'Daniel is safe and alive, I know it.'

'But will he live?' asked Louise, her voice shaking. 'Will he *stay* alive?'

Michael didn't answer. An unknown hand had plucked him away from the group at the table and placed him alone. Now he could see the figure more clearly, it had the familiar shape of someone he knew. The chilling shadow was moving purposefully over the headland, stalking through the marram grass, past the stunted sloe bushes, and across the rocks with slow, deliberate steps. Moving towards an appointment made in time long, long ago.

Then he was back at the table with the rest of them. 'Yes,' he said slowly. 'Daniel will live.' But even as he spoke Michael wondered why he had said it when he could see that fearful figure so clearly.

Andrea Louedec's sensible Breton voice cut across their fears. 'That's where she'll be now,' she said firmly. 'She'll have taken that baby up on to the headland because it is there that she feels safe. And you'd best be getting up there yourselves as soon as possible.'

'We must take some blankets,' said Robert, standing up.

'I'll get them,' said Michael, 'and some waterproof jackets for the three of us.' He looked at their shoes. 'Yes, your shoes are OK for clambering over the headland.' He left the room to find the coats and blankets.

Louise began to feel more and more afraid, but held her head high, determined not to show it. They were going to get Daniel. Now was not the time to go to pieces. Daniel needed her.

'Madame Louedec,' Robert continued, 'can you make

363

up a flask of warm milk, please. Not hot, just warm enough for the baby.'

'Don't you think she's fed Daniel?' It was something Louise hadn't thought of.

'It's a possibility.' Robert looked serious. 'We must be prepared for every eventuality,' he said, knowing he was adding yet another fear to Louise's already heavy burden of fears, but knowing also that he must prepare her.

Michael came back into the kitchen and distributed the waterproof jackets. 'These will keep out the wind as well as any rain,' he said. 'It will be very, very cold up there.' As he spoke he desperately tried to ignore his own personal chill which seemed to settle over him, wrapping icy fingers around his heart.

Robert sensed rather than saw Michael shudder. 'Are you all right?' he asked again.

'As well as can be expected.' Michael's face looked grey with worry, his lips blue and pinched, and his dark eyes enormous in his face.

Robert picked up the blankets Michael had brought in, and rolled each one separately then tied it with the string which Andrea Louedec passed to him.

'What are these for?' asked Louise when he passed her one.

'To wrap Daniel and Veronique in when we find them,' said Michael.

'If they've been up on the headland since early this morning, they are both going to be suffering from hypothermia. They'll need all the warmth we can give them.' Robert's voice was calm and matter-of-fact.

But that didn't stop Louise thinking, people die of hypothermia, *especially* babies, because they are so small. She kept her fears to herself however, merely saying, 'Then the sooner we get going the better.'

Andrea opened the kitchen door for them, watching them cross the kitchen courtyard, and walk across the gravel towards the parked car. Her lips moved in silent prayer. Above the kitchen door was a small statue of the Virgin Mary, tarnished with age. It had been passed down through the Louedec family for generations. Genuflecting before the statue, she crossed herself and whispered, 'Holy Mary, Mother of God, let the Lord look mercifully on them.' Then turning, she went back into the warmth of the kitchen.

'Just one thing,' said Michael as they hurried across the gravel, shivering in the biting north-easterly wind, towards Robert's car. 'When we do find them, whatever you do, be careful not to startle Veronique. Leave the talking to me. The last thing we want is for her to stumble, and either of them to fall.'

'You're very late.' Andrea's voice was filled with scorn. There were two local *gendarmes* who looked after crime, such as it was, in Michel en Greve. They were both fat, both near to retiring, and in Andrea's opinion, both lazy. Now they had just ambled into her kitchen. 'You should have been here first thing this morning.'

'There didn't seem any point. The people here at the chateau can take care of themselves. Anyway, there's nothing we can do about a runaway wife. Where is Monsieur Baruch?'

'He's gone up on to the headland, with Monsieur Lacroix and Madame Lacroix.'

'The headland? What, on a morning like this?'

'They are looking for Madame Baruch and the baby she has stolen,' explained Andrea Louedec in some exasperation, 'and I think you ought to get up there as well.'

After much grumbling about the cold, the strong wind, and how many other things they had to do, and the fact that they were not as young as they used to be, and too much was expected of them, the two *gendarmes* eventually drove off in the direction of the lane leading up on to the point of the headland.

Paul watched them go. 'Do you think that was wise?' he asked.

'What do you mean? Wise! They had to be told what was going on.'

'I suppose so.' Paul had an even lower opinion of the two *gendarmes* than his wife. 'But do they understand that Madame Veronique is highly neurotic? If they start shouting at her, goodness knows what she might do.'

'Oh my God!' Andrea clapped her hands to her mouth. 'I hadn't thought of that.'

'Too late now. We'll just have to pray that they use what little sense God has seen fit to endow them with, and keep their mouths shut.' Then seeing Andrea's panic-stricken face, Paul felt guilty. 'Don't worry,' he said, 'they are so unfit that they'll probably be too out of breath to speak, let alone shout.'

CHAPTER 46

Louise sat in the back of the car, behind Robert and Michael, twisting her hands nervously with unspoken apprehension. As she watched the dark hump of the headland gradually grow into distinct little hills, hollows, and rocky outcrops, she felt even more nervous. Now, at last, she was about to set foot in the land of her nightmares, in the place that she'd only seen from a distance, and which had existed largely in her imagination. Now it would be real.

'We'll drive up as far as we can,' said Robert, looking over his shoulder at Louise. He saw her expression. 'Don't look so worried. I know it looks enormous from the village but once you actually get there it's not nearly as high as one imagines.'

'If you are afraid,' said Michael, 'you can stay here in the car. Robert and I will go together and get Veronique and Daniel.'

'I'm not afraid,' lied Louise. 'I shall come with you. I've got to go.' She didn't want to, but was powerless to stay behind. Unknown forces beyond her comprehension were driving her on. It was not a question of freedom of choice. Whatever was going to happen, she was part of it whether she wished it or not.

'*You'll* be taken care of,' said Michael gently. 'There is no need for you to worry.' He turned to Robert and smiled. 'Or you,' he said. 'You will be all right as well.'

Robert glanced at Michael, and saw with relief that he was looking better. The greyish tinge had disappeared from his skin and his lips were a normal colour. He looked relaxed, resigned almost. But then, reasoned Robert, he knows where Veronique will go, he knows all her favourite and secret places. If Louise and I were here alone we'd be stumbling around and spending hours searching in the wrong places. All the same, Michael did seem strangely sure, as if he already knew the outcome of their search.

'That's an odd thing to say,' he said. 'How can you be so certain that Louise and I will not come to any harm?'

'I'm not certain, not in the normal sense one would usually mean it,' said Michael slowly. 'But I feel as if a curtain has been lifted in my mind and I can see into the future. The annoying thing is that I can't see everything, only a part. But the part I can see is good for you.'

'And Daniel as well?' asked Louise anxiously.

'And Daniel as well.'

'I don't believe in such things as second sight, clairvoyance, or whatever you like to call it,' said Robert abruptly. He had no wish for Louise's hopes to be raised, only to be dashed by reality. 'I think it is better not to talk about such things, but to wait until we are all safe and sound.'

'Yes, you are probably right,' said Michael, and lapsed into silence.

'I am right,' said Robert firmly, wishing to nail any speculation on the head there and then. 'There are no certainties in this life until the final curtain comes down.'

'Yes, the final curtain,' murmured Michael.

It only took a few moments to drive past the bay. The tide had partially receded now, and the pale flatness of the wet sand picked up what little light there was of the December morning and reflected it back. They drove through the square of the tiny village of Michel en Greve, past the church with its ornate twelfth-century

368

tower, and the cemetery filled with granite headstones perched on the edge of the sands, and took a road which narrowed sharply and began to climb steeply at the same time.

They came to a narrow fork in the road, and both roads narrowed even more into lanes which led up higher. 'Which way?' asked Robert.

'Follow the signs for Beg a Forn,' said Michael. 'That's as far as you can take the car, and it's quicker than walking the cliff paths to the Pointe de Sehar, which is where we are aiming for.'

Once on the actual headland Louise was both relieved and surprised to find that it seemed quite normal. The lane was deep, sunk low between granite banks which sprouted ferns and luxuriant plants she had never seen before. 'It isn't cold and windswept,' she exclaimed. 'Not at all like I imagined. It's almost cosy here.'

'Here it is,' said Michael briefly. 'Once we get away from the shelter of these ancient cuttings it won't be.'

Almost as soon as he had spoken the car shot out of the shelter of the lane and was on the exposed headland. Louise looked about her. This was the place she'd seen before. This was the alien land where every living thing adapted to the sea and the ever-constant winds, or perished. The sloe bushes, bereft of leaves in December, bent low, their prickly branches reaching down to the ground in submission. The bracken, dead and brown now, had long ago given up the unequal struggle with the wind and lay flat and lifeless. But the marram grass and the tamarisk bushes were strong and thin, and bent and waved in the wind like seaweed.

Then they saw Veronique's distinctive yellow car. It was parked by a clump of pine trees. Robert parked the car, and Louise looked fearfully about her. So Veronique was here. She looked up at the trees, hoping to gain some strength from their solidness. But their spirit too had been changed by the salty wind; they were not tall and proud, but gnarled and humped, their evergreen needled arms seeming to reach pathetically inwards towards the mainland, as if longing to join their brethren in a more tranquil forest. And all around was the sea, seething and churning on the jagged granite rocks far below, every now and then reaching up hissing white fingers, ready to catch any unwary creature who ventured too near.

Louise hated it, and only the thought of Daniel, somewhere in this bleakness, forced her to take her nerves under control and get out of the car.

Once out in the open, the full force of the wind hit them, and it was difficult to stand up. 'Don't forget this.' Robert handed Louise a rolled blanket to carry. Michael took another and Robert carried a blanket slung on his back with the flask of milk wrapped safely inside the blanket roll.

There were two tracks leading from the clump of pine trees, one to the left and one to the right of the headland. Michael stood for a moment and thought, then said, 'This way,' and started leading them along the track leading to the right. 'Veronique has a place she always calls her secret place along here. It quite a way down, but it's sheltered by granite rocks. We'll try there first.'

The wind snatched at his voice, and although they couldn't hear everything, Louise and Robert caught the gist of his words. They nodded assent, and began to follow.

The track was very narrow, as if made by animals, which it probably is, thought Louise. She found that she had to concentrate on the ground because of the sharp lumps of granite which protruded up through the earth every few yards. Because she was watching where to place her feet she wasn't aware, until Michael stopped for a moment, of how far down they had actually climbed. Looking back, she could see raw lumps of granite towering out above them, but on looking down, the sea seemed to be as far away as ever, although logic told her it could not possibly be so.

'Why have we stopped?' Robert asked.

Michael held up a hand. He came back so that he did not have to shout. 'From now on, we must go more slowly. If I am right, she will be around the corner of that rock.' He pointed towards an enormous perpendicular slab of granite leaning in from the cliff-edge at an angle towards the land. 'Whatever you do, be careful. We must not frighten her.'

The two *gendarmes*, once they had decided that perhaps Andrea Louedec was right and they ought to go to the headland to assist, actually moved with remarkable speed. They didn't take the road to Beg a Forn, but took the *gendarmerie*'s inflatable dinghy with an outboard motor, and sped across the waters of the bay to a tiny cove known only to the locals, and which was navigable at most states of the tide. From the sea none of the coastline looked safe for a boat, but for those in the know it was possible to skim behind a seemingly impenetrable wall of granite and find the tiny half-moon cove of Baie de la Lune.

'Old mother Louedec thinks we are incapable,' grunted Jean-Yves once they had landed and were changing into climbing boots. 'We'll show her.'

'Too true,' said Guy. 'Come on, I know a really good shortcut through the rocks so that we end up below Beg a Forn, with a good view either side of the point of the headland. It's actually on Pointe de Sehar.'

The two men made rapid progress, much more rapid than the party of three clambering along the cliff-top path. But then, they had the advantage. They had scrambled over the rocky headland since they had both been in short trousers. Every generation of children in the village knew all the secret nooks and crannies, and the quickest way to get from point A to point B. It was a knowledge passed on to them by their grandfathers, all of whom had been smugglers of one sort or another in their day. And although now smuggling no longer existed, and the villagers were law abiding citizens, the old paths were not forgotten.

They reached the point Guy had been aiming for, and stopped, Jean-Yves gasping a little as he was more unfit that Guy. Together they started scanning the rocky outcrops of the cliff face. 'Look,' said Guy, 'there she is. That must be Madame Baruch, and she's got the child with her.'

Jean-Yves followed Guy's pointing finger. 'Yes,' he said slowly, 'that must be her.' The slender figure of a woman in black, holding a baby wrapped in a white blanket was quite clear. She was standing, leaning back against the granite, and rocking the baby in her arms.

'If we climb up this way,' said Guy, 'we can surprise her from her right-hand side.'

'Right.' Jean-Yves tightened his boot laces. 'You lead the way.'

Louise thought she now knew the true meaning of the expression 'to have your heart in your mouth'. Hardly able to breathe from fear, she struggled along behind the two men. 'Please God let Daniel be all right. Don't let her have harmed him. Please let him be safe.' It didn't matter that she prayed out loud; no one could hear her, because the wind took her mumbled words and tossed them to the elements. She only prayed for Daniel, not for Veronique; unable to bring herself to even think much about the woman who had stolen her precious child.

They came to the granite rock. Vaguely Louise realized that it was a menhir, one of the ancient standing stones of Brittany. Leading the way Michael gradually moved around the edge of the menhir until they could see into the sheltered hollow.

'Look,' he whispered.

'Thank God,' said Robert.

Veronique was there. She was standing and leaning back against the rock for support, clad only in a thin black suit,

372

no coat, and she was holding Daniel wrapped in a thick white blanket, in her arms. Daniel was crying lustily. That means he is all right, thought Louise, her knees nearly buckling under her with relief. No sick child could possibly be crying so loudly. Then her eyes were drawn to Veronique's face, and all the confused feelings of fear, anger, and dislike for the woman who had stolen her child, vanished. In that first moment Louise felt she was looking into the soul of the woman before her. For Veronique's face was transparent with a love so beautiful, so intense, so painful to behold that Louise felt like crying. 'It isn't fair,' she found herself whispering, 'that she should be denied a child.'

'Sometimes life isn't fair,' said Robert. He was by Louise's side and slowly reaching out he took her hand, and turning his head slightly he smiled sadly. 'But I'm glad that you understand and don't hate her.'

'I can't hate her for longing to love a child,' said Louise, her eyes bright with tears. 'I only wish I could help.'

'We will help her. All of us,' said Robert. 'We'll find a way. Once we've got them away from this place.'

Michael moved forward gently. 'Veronique,' he said, making his voice just loud enough to carry across the whining of the wind, but not so loud as to frighten her.

'Michael!' For a moment Veronique's face lit up with a radiant smile, then she saw Robert and Louise behind him, and held Daniel in closer to her body in a defiant gesture. 'He's mine,' she whimpered. 'Mine.'

'Veronique, you must . . .'

Louise stepped forward and putting out her hand interrupted Michael. 'You love him,' she said gently.

Veronique nodded her head. 'Oh, yes, yes, I love him.' Her dark eyes scanned Louise's face, half trusting, half suspicious. 'Do you understand how I feel?'

'Yes,' said Louise simply. 'I do understand.'

Daniel must have heard Louise's voice for he began to struggle in his blanket, and howled louder than ever. As

Veronique bent her head to shush him, her hair blew back and Louise saw the enormous lump on her forehead which by now had turned almost black with bruising. Realizing that Veronique must have had an almighty blow on the head when the plane crashed, Louise's immediate worry was that she might collapse, faint, or fall, and if she did then Daniel might . . . With a great effort Louise stopped herself thinking anything of the sort, and did not allow herself a single glance down to the jagged rocks below, set in the boiling cauldron of the sea. Cross one bridge at a time, she told herself, and then we will all get out of this in one piece.

Veronique's face crumpled with worry. 'He's hungry,' she said. 'And I haven't any milk.'

'I have,' said Robert. 'Shall I give him some?'

'Yes.' She stopped abruptly. 'No no, if I let you, you'll take him.' Veronique held on to Daniel even more tightly.

'You give him the milk.' Louise held out her hand to Robert and he placed the flask in it. She held it out towards Veronique. 'Take it. You'll have to be careful, but he should be able to drink a little from the cup on the top of the flask.' Crouching down she slowly slid the flask towards Veronique. 'I'm not going to snatch him from you, I promise,' she said. 'Trust me.'

Veronique took the flask, and managed to unscrew it while still holding Daniel. Then crouching down along-side Louise, she held the cup to the baby's lips. Daniel guzzled thirstily, and Veronique looked up, smiling. 'He loves it,' she said to Louise. 'Look.'

Louise moved nearer and could see Daniel. She could see that he too had an injury, but that it was a small graze on his face which had left a smear of dried blood. 'When he's finished drinking,' she said quietly, 'why don't you take him back to the chateau and put him in his lovely nursery.'

Veronique kissed the top of the baby's head, then rubbed her cheek against his face. Her eyes were misty with love, and Louise knew that Veronique was in a world of her own, a world which only contained Daniel and herself. Instinct told her that if only Veronique could stay in that world, then everything would work out well.

'Yes,' said Veronique dreamily. 'It is getting a little chilly. I think Daniel ought to be getting back to bed now.'

'Can I come with you?' Louise hardly dare ask, but it was important to know. She'd already made up her mind that if Veronique said no, then she was going to entrust Daniel to Veronique's maternal instincts and pray that she would get him back to the nursery safely.

Behind her, both Michael and Robert had realized what was happening, and had slowly retreated a little, leaving a space between themselves and the two women.

Veronique gave Daniel some more milk. It nearly broke Louise's heart to see his little starfish hands come out of the shawl, wildly grabbing at the cup. How she longed to take him in her arms herself. But she held back. Not only was Veronique's need to hold him for just a little longer much greater than hers, Daniel's safety depended upon it.

'His nursery is beautiful,' said Veronique, wiping a dribble of milk from Daniel's chin with the edge of the shawl. 'Quite beautiful. All blue, you know. Blue for a boy.' She looked at Louise. 'Some people say blue is a sad colour. But I don't think it is. For me it is a happy colour because to me blue means Daniel.'

'I can see why it makes you happy, because Daniel is a happy baby, isn't he?' said Louise carefully. 'I'd love to see him snuggled down in his own little blue cot.'

Veronique made up her mind and stood up straight. 'We'll go straight back now,' she said, her eyes shining. 'And I'll bath Daniel and put him to bed, and you can watch.'

Relieved, Louise stood up too. 'I'd love that.'

Veronique had just started to move out towards the path that led around the edge of the menhir as the heads of

375

Jean-Yves and Guy appeared above the rocks on the edge of the cliff before the two women.

'Well, well, Madame Baruch,' shouted Jean-Yves loudly. 'What have we here? Been stealing other women's children, eh?' He scrambled over the top and came towards her, holding out his arms. 'You'd best hand him over to me, Madame.'

'Oh my God,' Robert clutched his head in his hands. 'I thought they taught policemen psychology nowadays.'

'This bloody man hasn't learned any, that's obvious.' Michael swore.

They all looked towards Veronique, waiting for her reaction. Louise waved at the *gendarmes* to be quiet, and for a moment thought that Veronique, still in her own little world, hadn't heard him. For she smiled vaguely, and didn't seem at all startled. 'Pardon?' she said politely.

Guy hadn't seen Louise's signal and, still panting a little from the climb, pushed past Jean-Yves. 'Hand over the baby, Madame. We've wasted enough time. You can't keep him. That baby is not yours.'

That baby is not yours. Those were the words that broke the spell. The words which shattered Veronique's dream world, and dragged her back to the frightening confusion of the world around her. For a moment she looked wildly around, and Louise felt she could almost see the panic-stricken thoughts tumbling one over the over in Veronique's poor, bewildered head. Then she let out a terrible cry. A wail of such utter desperate grief that Louise felt the hairs on the back of her neck stand on end. A moment later Veronique began to run.

'Veronique!' called Michael. He pushed past the two stupified *gendarmes*, who were standing bemused. They had not expected such a dramatic reaction to their demand. 'Veronique!'

Running after her Michael could see that her usual sure-footedness had deserted her. Now she was stumbling, and slipping, Daniel's blanket trailing behind her, every now and then causing her to trip even more. And all the while she was making her way towards the most dangerous part of the cliff-face.

'You fools! Look what you've done.' Robert turned angrily on the *gendarmes*.

'Stupid, stupid men,' screamed Louise, unable to contain her anger, or the tears which were now trickling down her cheeks. 'Couldn't you see that the woman was distressed?'

Unable to grasp the complex subtleties of the situation the two *gendarmes* stared at each other. 'We were only trying to help,' said Guy, 'I'd have thought you would be . . .' He stopped. No one was listening to him apart from Jean-Yves; they were all following Veronique. Jean-Yves shrugged, and the two men followed, but at a slower pace. They were not so keen to end up being dashed to pieces on the rocks below; this part of the cliff-face was known to be unstable.

Veronique ran, tears streaming down her face. 'They say you're not mine, not mine,' she sobbed, clutching Daniel. 'But I can't let them take you away, I can't.' Blinded by tears she ran into a cul-de-sac in the rocks. There was no way forward, only down or up. Gasping now with strain of running and carrying Daniel, Veronique paused for a moment and looked up and down. Then started down. Here the granite was interleaved with a softer rock, and as she started on the descent her feet sheered off slices of granite which thundered down into the seething whiteness of the sea below.

'Veronique!' shouted Michael again. Regardless of his own safety he clambered down too, sending more slabs of rock tumbling down the cliff-face. 'Darling, darling, please wait for me. Veronique, Veronique, let me help you. Let me help you and Daniel.'

She slipped.

Robert and Louise could only watched horrified as the

piece of rock beneath Veronique's feet fell away, leaving her clinging on to Daniel with one hand, and the rock-face with the other. Guy and Jean-Yves following behind saw too, and both stopped and automatically crossed themselves.

Louise clenched her hands together; looking down she could see her own bone shining white through the skin. 'Please God,' she prayed as she had never prayed in her life, 'if you are listening, please help Veronique and Daniel.' As she prayed, she suddenly realized that she was praying for them both, because now Veronique mattered too. All hate was gone. All she wanted was their safety, both of them.

Michael inched his way down to where Veronique was clinging, and put his arm around her. At the same time Robert and Louise crept forward cautiously. 'Stay behind me,' Robert ordered Louise.

Louise prayed silently, watching Michael's every move through terror-stricken eyes. Michael's breath was coming in shorter and shorter gasps. Veronique was gasping too. She was a deathly white, and the bruise on her forehead stood out a sharp, almost navy blue colour. 'Darling,' he said, 'we're going to be all right. Just do as I say. Pass Daniel up to Robert.'

'No,' panted Veronique. 'No, I can't do that.'

'All right, I'll help you both up.' Michael wedged his feet into two cracks in the cliff-face. Slowly he let go of his own handholds and put his arms around Veronique and Daniel. 'If I lift her up can you take her?' he called to Robert who was leaning down from above.

'Yes. I'm ready.'

Louise held her breath. Veronique looked as if she was about to die any moment. Her lips now were almost as blue as the bruise on her head, and her eyes were glazed over with fear. But against all odds she still held on to Daniel, who was not helping by wriggling violently, and kicking.

Michael started to lift Veronique, inch by slow inch,

towards Robert's waiting hands. Louise prayed as she had never prayed before. 'Our Father, who art in heaven . . .' The familiar words helped. Surely if there was a Father in heaven he wouldn't let them fall. Not Daniel, an innocent baby. And not Veronique, who was not responsible for her actions. 'Please, please, God. Save them.'

Robert's hands grasped Veronique's shoulders. Slowly but surely the woman and child were hauled to safety.

Chest heaving with the superhuman effort he'd just made, Michael clung exhausted to the rock face. Looking up he could see Louise tenderly wrapping a blanket around Daniel and then Veronique. He smiled. They are safe, he thought. All of them. Suddenly, for no reason at all, his mind sped back more than forty years, and he remembered being in church with his mother. He remembered the strange feeling of goodness he'd felt when the priest had put his hand upon his head. He felt like that now. By saving Veronique and Daniel he was receiving a benediction, a form of grace, which he had thought he'd lost so many years ago. I could pray now, he thought, and I know I'd get an answer.

'Michael.' It was Robert's voice. 'Can you manage to come up now? Give me your hand.'

He reached up, and felt the warm strength of Robert's hand. His body felt as light as air as he scrambled up the cliff-face on to the safety of the rocky ledge.

'Michael.'

Louise was speaking. She was looking at him, smiling through her tears. She had forgiven him the wrong he'd done her. She had forgiven Veronique. There was nothing else to do. With surprise he felt the pain in his chest grow and grow, felt his muscles convulse as a burning shaft turned and twisted into a spiralling agony. With a blinding flash of panic he knew that he had saved Veronique and Daniel only to lose them again. The benediction is all I have. Nothing more. I must be content with that. The pain exploded and he fell.

Louise was beside him. 'Robert,' she was calling. 'Robert, come here. Michael is ill.'

'No, not ill,' Michael said, but was uncertain whether she heard him or not. Then he remembered, there was something he had to say. With a strength summoned by urgency, he whispered, 'Take care of Veronique.'

'We will,' said Louise, and he knew she meant it. 'Don't worry about Veronique.'

'Where is the pain?' That was Robert's voice.

But there was no more pain. To Michael it seemed that the grey December sky was suddenly filled with the bright sunshine of a summer's day. The sky arched clear and blue above him. He felt so tired, there was nothing to do but let go. He closed his eyes and lay back. He could see it all now, the final curtain gradually closing, not dark or frightening, but shining, blue and gold. The familiar figure was there, the one he'd seen before on the headland. Michael waited, knowing that this time the figure would turn. It did, and he found he was looking himself in the face. At last he knew why the figure had seemed so familiar.

EPILOGUE

Beattie poured herself a generous measure of gin, and a Spartan amount of tonic. 'One should never drown gin,' she said defensively, seeing Robert watching her.

He laughed. 'I was just thinking of your liver, woman.'

'I've just had my sixty-ninth birthday,' said Beattie, 'and my liver has lasted me all these years. If it conks out now, well, so what! I'm not sure that I want to get to seventy.'

Robert frowned and getting up moved away from the fire where he'd been sitting with Beattie, and pulled the curtains across the wide windows of living room. 'Why not?' he said.

'Because seventy sounds so bloody old.'

'Pardon?' Louise, with Daniel following closely behind, entered the room. 'What did you say?'

'Your mother has decided to drink herself to death because she doesn't want to reach the age of seventy,' said Robert.

'Sounds typical of you, Mother,' Louise grinned. 'And I can't think of a better way to go. But I think we'd all prefer it if you could stick around for a bit. We need you.'

'You don't. Daniel will be going to school soon. Natasha, Rupert, Milton and Tara are all grown up.'

'I don't call being fourteen, twelve, nine or six grown up,' said Robert. 'Not by a long way.'

'Nobody needs me,' said Beattie, determined to be miserable.

Louise drew up a stool by her mother. 'You're missing Mr Poo, aren't you?' she said.

Beattle sighed. 'Yes, I am. How could he be so inconsiderate, turning up his toes and snuffing it like that? He was the last one left I had to spoil. And now Robert has just told me that you're all going away this Christmas with Gordon and his tribe.' She poured herself some more gin and added gloomily, 'Now I know what it's like to be old and unwanted.'

'You're not old and unwanted, Grandma,' shrieked Daniel. 'And Mummy says that you are bloody well coming with us, even if we have to prize you out of your house with a shoehorn.'

'I didn't put it *quite* like that, Daniel,' said Louise severely. 'And how many times have I told you not to say bloody?'

'Lots,' said Daniel, totally unrepentant.

'I expect I shall be one of those old ladies you read about in the newspapers,' Beattie grumbled on. 'Found dead and alone at Christmas by the cold ashes of her fire, nothing in the house . . .'

'Except a dozen bottles of gin,' said Robert and laughed. 'Did you hear what Daniel said?'

'Yes, he said, you're bloody well coming . . .' Beattie suddenly stood up and put down her glass. 'Am I invited as well?' she said.

Louise threw up her hands in exasperation. 'Of course you are. If only you'd listen, instead of reading Robert the riot act and telling him that you've never left your house at Christmas for the last forty years, etcetera, etcetera, you would have heard the first time. You didn't really think we'd all go off and leave you at Christmas, did you?'

'But everyone has always spent Christmas at my house,' said Beattie.

'Then you are definitely due for a change,' said Robert

firmly. 'But before we tell you where we are going, there are two things we want to do. The first is, Daniel wants to give you your Christmas present early.'

'I'm not sure I want it early.' Beattie was unwilling to be prised out of her grumpy mood entirely. 'What's wrong with Christmas Day?'

'We'll come to that later,' said Robert and nodded at Daniel who shot out of the room like a cannon ball out of a cannon.

He re-entered two or three minutes later, carefully carrying something very small and squeaky. 'I think you'd better sit down, Grandma,' he said. Beattie sat, and Daniel crossed over to her, carefully depositing a small furry mink coloured bundle in her lap. 'It's a Poolet,' he whispered, 'and he's only half awake.'

Beattie burst into tears, and held the furry bundle up to her face. 'Another Mr Poo,' she said, between sniffs.

'No,' Daniel was very serious. 'He isn't a Mr Poo, because he's only a baby. He's a Poolet.'

'Daniel's name for a baby pug dog,' explained Robert.

Beattie kissed him and the puppy sneezed so hard that his tiny little furry ears practically flew off his head. 'Why can't I keep him, now I've got him?' she said. 'Oh, he's adorable. The best present you could have ever given me.'

'There are two reasons,' said Robert. 'First, he's a little too young to leave his mother, we're taking him back this evening, and second, you can't take him with you where we're going for Christmas.'

Beattie settled the puppy in her lap, where he turned round half a dozen times before finally curling up in a ball, watched by a fascinated Daniel. 'Why not?' she asked.

Robert switched on the television. 'Because this is where we are all going,' he said.

'This isn't it,' said Daniel.

Louise settled herself on the settee and Robert sat beside her. 'No, darling. This is the end of the news. It's the next programme we want to watch.'

The news finished. 'Always depressing,' said Beattie. 'Why on earth they can't talk about jolly things I don't know. Who wants to know who has blown up who, or why?'

'The next programme will be jolly,' said Daniel, 'and nobody gets blown up.'

'How do you know?' Beattle was suspicious.

The credits started to roll and the narrator's voice spoke as the camera panned across a wide bay, with the tide half in. It was summer; the sea, a pale turquoise colour, lapped across silver white sand.

'How different it looks now,' said Louise softly.

'How different it *is*.' Robert reached out and clasped her hand in his.

'We are about to tell a remarkable story of a remarkable woman,' the narrator said. The camera panned across the beach and up into the countryside behind, and zoomed in on to a stone chateau, its grey slate roofs shining brightly in the summer sun. The gardens were a riot of colour, and full of children.

'Isn't that Chateau les Greves?' asked Beattie.

'Yes,' said Louise.

Then a plump, dark haired woman came into view. 'There's Auntie Veronique,' shrieked Daniel excitedly. 'And there's Andrea and Paul Louedec behind her.' He crawled towards the television to get a better view.

'Sit back,' said Robert, 'you'll damage your eyes.'

Obediently Daniel crawled back to Beattie's side, and putting out a hand fondled the puppy.

'I'm going to call him Poolet,' whispered Beattie. 'What do you think of that?'

'Lovely,' whispered back Daniel. 'He'll never be like Mr Poo.'

'Of course not,' said Beattie. 'He'll be himself. Poolet.'

'Are you two going to watch or not?' demanded Louise.

'Yes,' said Beattie meekly.

'This is the story of a woman who triumphed in the face

of adversity, and in doing so has brought happiness to many. This is the story of the newly-formed Baruch Foundation, which tries never to turn away any child in need. Not so many years ago Veronique Baruch was a childless widow, unable to come to terms with the fate life had dealt her. Although wealthy, she was bitter and unhappy and sought frequent counselling from psychiatrists. But all that changed the day she met Mathilde, a ten-year-old child living rough on the streets of Paris. Moved to pity by her plight, she invited her to come and live with her at her chateau in Brittany. In three short years the first Mathilde has been joined by many others. All have one need, a place to stay, where they know they are safe and need never leave, and a place where they are surrounded by people who care for them. A place where all can be children once again.'

And so the story went on. When it finished there was silence. 'I knew Veronique was running an orphanage,' said Beattie.

'They're not all orphans,' interrupted Louise. 'The one thing they all have in common is that they are all unwanted, for one reason or another.'

'Except that Auntie Veronique wants them,' said Daniel.

'I hardly recognized her,' said Beattie. 'She looks so different. Not glamorous any more, much more, well, sort of homely, I suppose is the word.'

'She is different,' said Robert. 'There's no time to be glamorous now. She's not interested in how she looks, she's too busy organizing funds, and helping look after the children at Chateau les Greves. Even the village has got involved. The local school has had to expand and engage another three teachers to cope with all the extra children. Michel en Greve is livelier now than it has ever been.'

'And that's where we are all going for Christmas,' said Louise. 'Because we want to help her celebrate this new charitable foundation, the Baruch Foundation. There is another big house being opened up soon in Hungary,

385

where some of the orphans from the Bosnian war will be able to live in peace.'

'Because we're going to France, Poolet will have to stay here,' said Daniel. He looked up at Beattie. 'But you don't mind, do you?'

'Of course not. He does need another couple of weeks with his mother. I can see that. Then when I come back and he comes to live with me permanently, he will be weaned.'

'What's weaned?'

'It means he won't need his mother's milk any more. He'll be able to eat ordinary food and drink ordinary milk.'

'And have chocolates?'

'How about trying to keep him a slimline Poolet,' said Louise, looking severely at her mother.

'Of course,' said Beattie, then smiled at Daniel. 'But just the occasional choccy drop won't hurt.'

Robert stood up. 'Come on,' he said to Daniel, 'you'd better take Poolet now, and if you're very good, I'll let you ride with me in the car and take him back to his mother.'

Beattie kissed Poolet goodbye and handed him over to Daniel. When Robert and Daniel had gone, she looked quizzically at her daughter. 'You haven't actually met Veronique since . . .'

'That terrible day on the headland.' Louise finished the sentence for her. 'No I haven't. Cowardly of me, I know. It's not Veronique herself I'm afraid of, you know that. Why, I've even let Robert take Daniel over to see her. He likes her, and the Louedecs who still work there. I'm always hearing about Andrea Louedec's wonderful crêpes and how she pours the batter on to a big black hotplate, and flips the whole crêpe over with one flick of a wooden knife, and why can't I do that! No, it's not the people. It's that place, the headland.' She shivered. 'I'm afraid to go back.'

'I see. So you are taking the whole family with you as moral support.'

Louise smiled sheepishly. 'Something like that. Robert says I've got to conquer such an irrational fear, and I know he's right.' She went across to her mother's side and crouched beside her on the stool by the fire. 'You will come, won't you? I don't want to go without you.'

Beattie reached out a hand and fondled Louise's head. Like a small child, Louise laid her head in her mother's lap. 'Of course, my dear,' she said softly. 'I'll help you lay your ghosts.'

A noisy crowd streamed out of the little church by the sea at Michel en Greve after Midnight Mass. Eighteen children from the chateau, plus Veronique, her helpers and Robert and Louise and her family. The parish priest was pleased to see that the number of villagers attending the Christmas service had increased since the opening of the chateau as a children's home. No one wanted to be left out. Two of the younger men of the village volunteered as bell ringers, and tonight, for the first time in ten years, the sleepy little village of Michel en Greve echoed to the sound of Christmas bells.

The Bar Tabac in the square was open, its door open, and the warm yellow light from inside was spilling out on to the cobbles. The men from the congregation with one accord put on their blue berets and flat caps and made their way in. No need to order anything. Trays of kir were laid out ready for the first drink of Christmas day. The wives hung back, gossiping a little, before going in and dragging their menfolk away from the bar and back to their beds.

Louise and Robert stood back a little on their own, watching the party from the chateau as the chattering mass of children, which now included not only Daniel, but Natasha, Rupert, Milton and Tara, made their way back up the slight incline towards the chateau. Gordon and Eugenia were helping shepherd the excited children in the right direction, and collecting up the odd stray who'd got distracted by something exciting on the way.

Beattie came and stood with Robert and Louise. 'All right now?' she asked.

Louise nodded; she knew what her mother meant. 'I was wrong,' she said. 'There are no ghosts, there's nothing to be afraid of.'

Beattie smiled. 'Of course there's nothing to be afraid of. But you're wrong about the ghosts. They are all around us, they always are. Couldn't you feel them in that old church, pushing and jostling for position. They wanted to be part of that happy service, as they once were many years ago. But unlike us earthbound creatures they are free to go as they please, to float in the smoke of the incense throughout the church, and now they are flying high in the sky, riding the chimes of the bells.'

'The trouble with you, Beattie,' said Robert, 'is that you've got an over-active imagination.'

Beattie laughed. 'If you lose your imagination,' she said, 'you lose your youth.'

Louise flung her arms around her mother and kissed her. 'You'll never be old,' she said. 'Never.'

As she finished speaking two figures emerged from the church. One was the priest, the other Veronique. The priest raised his hand in salutation and turned to walk the short distance to his small house on the other side of the cemetery. Veronique came towards them.

'I'll catch up with the others,' said Beattie and started off up the incline.

Veronique joined Robert and Louise, coming to stand at the side of Louise. 'I'm glad you came,' she said quietly. 'I've been wanting you to come. But I knew I had to wait.'

'I should have come before,' said Louise.

Veronique shook her head. 'No, the time to come was when you were ready.'

'I'm glad I came.'

'And you are no longer afraid of me, or – ' she hesitated – 'this place?'

'I know now that there was nothing to be afraid of. But I had to come to find that out.'

The light from the Bar Tabac shone on Veronique's face, and Louise found herself thinking that in a strange way she was more beautiful than before. Now her face was round and without make-up, and in her sweatshirt and anorak, jeans and sturdy boots, she looked a very ordinary woman. But she had an inner light of contentment, something she'd never had before, and it was that which gave her beauty.

'I regret many things,' she said, and Louise knew without her needing to say, that she was thinking of Michael, 'but I cannot regret what I have now.' She turned towards the chateau. 'Come up as soon as you're ready. I know Andrea Louedec is making cinnamon waffles for all the children. I doubt that anyone will get to bed for another hour and a half.'

'We'll be with you in five minutes,' said Robert, and taking Louise's arm, turned her round towards the bay. Together they walked towards the shore and stood silently on the edge of the bay. The headland stretched out into the sea, black and silent.

'It looks like some great sleeping creature,' said Louise.

'And so it is. It's been sleeping there, with the sea washing its toes for the last several million years, and will continue to sleep for the next several million. I suppose one day it might wake up and move, but I doubt that we shall be here to see it.'

'And you accused my mother of having an over-active imagination,' said Louise.

'That's not imagination, it's a scientific fact. Sooner or later it is bound to move. The geological formation of these rocks is . . .'

'I don't care about geological formations. I want a cinnamon waffle.' Louise turned to walk back towards the chateau. 'Doesn't it look wonderful at night with all those windows lit up? Like a fairytale castle.'

'Huh! Glad I'm not paying the electricity bill,' said Robert.

'Good heavens, you sound just like Gordon.' Louise laughed and began to hurry. 'I can actually smell the cinnamon,' she said. 'It makes me hungry.'

'How can you be hungry? We had an enormous meal this evening.'

Louise paused and waited for Robert to catch her up. 'Ah,' she said, 'but *I am* eating for two.'

'You mean! . . . we . . .'

'Yes,' said Louise. 'We are. We're going to have a baby.'

Robert picked her up and swung her round in an exultant circle. 'Now you know that we really *have* got to the bright side of the sun,' he said.

Louise linked her arms around his neck, and laid her head in the hollow of his shoulder. 'Our secret,' she whispered. 'Just for the two of us. Let's keep it that way for a little while.'

'Our secret,' Robert agreed. 'Our own special Christmas secret.'

THE EXCITING NEW NAME
IN WOMEN'S FICTION!

PLEASE HELP ME TO HELP YOU!

Dear *Scarlet* Reader,

As Editor of *Scarlet* Books I want to make sure that the books I offer you every month are up to the high standards *Scarlet* readers expect. And to do that I need to know a little more about you and your reading likes and dislikes. So please spare a few minutes to fill in the short questionnaire on the following pages and send it to me. I'll send *you* a surprise gift as a thank you!

Looking forward to hearing from you,

Sally Cooper

Editor-in-Chief, *Scarlet*

P.S. Only one offer per household

QUESTIONNAIRE

Please tick the appropriate boxes to indicate your answers

1 Where did you get this Scarlet title?
Bought in Supermarket ☐
Bought at W H Smith ☐
Bought at book exchange or second-hand shop ☐
Borrowed from a friend ☐
Other _____

2 Did you enjoy reading it?
A lot ☐   A little ☐   Not at all ☐

3 What did you particularly like about this book?
Believable characters ☐   Easy to read ☐
Good value for money ☐   Enjoyable locations ☐
Interesting story ☐   Modern setting ☐
Other _____

4 What did you particularly dislike about this book?
_____

5 Would you buy another Scarlet book?
Yes ☐   No ☐

6 What other kinds of book do you enjoy reading?
Horror ☐   Puzzle books ☐   Historical fiction ☐
General fiction ☐   Crime/Detective ☐   Cookery ☐
Other _____

7 Which magazines do you enjoy most?
Bella ☐   Best ☐   Woman's Weekly ☐
Woman and Home ☐   Hello ☐   Cosmopolitan ☐
Good Housekeeping ☐
Other _____

cont.

And now a little about you –

8 How old are you?

Under 25 ☐   25–34 ☐   35–44 ☐
45–54 ☐   55–64 ☐   over 65 ☐

9 What is your marital status?

Single ☐   Married/living with partner ☐
Widowed ☐   Separated/divorced ☐

10 What is your current occupation?

Employed full-time ☐   Employed part-time ☐
Student ☐   Housewife full-time ☐
Unemployed ☐   Retired ☐

11 Do you have children? If so, how many and how old are they?

_____

_____

12 What is your annual household income?

under £10,000 ☐   £10–20,000 ☐   £20–30,000 ☐
£30–40,000 ☐   over £40,000 ☐

Miss/Mrs/Ms _____

Address _____

_____

_____

Thank you for completing this questionnaire. Now tear it out – put it in an envelope and send it before 31 May, 1997, to:

Sally Cooper, Editor-in-Chief

SCARLET
FREEPOST LON 3335
LONDON W8 4BR
Please use block capitals for address.
No stamp is required!

Scarlet **titles coming next month:**

WICKED IN SILK Andrea Young
Claudia is promised a large sum of money for her favourite charity if she will act as a kissagram at Guy Hamilton's birthday lunch. What she doesn't know is that his headstrong daughter, Anoushka, has arranged the whole thing. So when Claudia finds herself in Greece with Guy and Anoushka, anything might happen . . . and it does!

COME HOME FOR EVER Jan McDaniel
Matt and Sierra were lovers ten years ago . . . then she betrayed him by marrying another man. Matt hadn't married Sierra because he didn't want to bring a child into the world. What he doesn't know is that the child Sierra brings home for Christmas is *his*!

WOMAN OF DREAMS Angela Drake
Zoe has a secret which she finds difficult to accept . . . and when she falls in love with François, the gift seems to become a curse. To avert disaster, Zoe decides never to see François again . . . but *can* she survive a marriage without love?

NEVER SAY NEVER Tina Leonard
Dustin Reed needs a housekeeper . . . Jill McCall needs a job. What Dustin doesn't need is a single mother with a baby to care for, though that seems to be exactly what Jill is! Oh, of course, she denies the baby is hers . . . telling Dustin that the little girl was left on his doorstep! Whether he believes Jill or not, this is clearly going to be one Christmas Dustin will never forget.